SCREENPLAY

What I Really Want to Do is Direct

WRITTEN BY
YVONNE COLLINS & SANDY RIDEOUT

RED
DRESS
INK
™

WHAT I REALLY WANT TO DO IS DIRECT

A Red Dress Ink novel

ISBN 0-373-89541-0

© 2005 by Yvonne Collins and Sandy Rideout.

www.RedDressInk.com

Printed in U.S.A.

We are grateful for our friends and family, who continue to promote us shamelessly. Special thanks to Dave, for his endless patience, and to Kathryn Lye and Jenny Bent.

For the film technicians who toil in the trenches. *Cinema is the most beautiful fraud in the world.*
—Jean-Luc Godard

Prologue

"*Gross Me Out* is brilliant! The rare film that charms and disgusts all at once! A remarkable debut for director Roxanne Hastings! We'll see her at the Oscars one day!"

—*Pine Ridge Book Club Newsletter*

A hand-painted Bristol board sign reading "THE END" fills the screen and the applause begins.

"Bravo Roxanne!" my mother calls. "Absolutely first rate!" She turns to the crowd. "Can you believe she's only thirteen?"

Mom thinks I'm a genius. That's why she invited everyone we know, from her book club to my piano teacher, to see my first film. She transformed our living room into a mini-theatre, complete with popcorn, and every seat in the house is full, including half a dozen lawn chairs.

"Speech! Speech!" our mailman yells.

I stand at the front of the room and begin nervously. "I would like to thank my mother for being so encouraging, and for giving me the idea to make the film, and for suggesting that I ask my best friend Libby to star in it and—"

"—for buying you the camera?"

"Mom! Do you think Spielberg's mother interrupts? But yeah, that too. And I would like thank Libby for being a great leading lady and for hardly complaining that she was so much taller than the leading man."

"Roxanne!"

"It's my speech, Lib, and I get to say whatever I want. So thanks to everyone else who helped out. Please come to our post-screening reception in the backyard. Mom made her seven-layer salsa dip."

Escorting me along a red carpet made of crepe paper, Mom says, "Your father will be so proud, Roxanne. He's sorry he couldn't make it."

Dad's at the office, like he is every weekend. He said he'd watch the movie when he gets home, but I know he'll forget. Still, it's pretty much the best day of my life so far.

Gross Me Out is a romantic comedy-horror-drama inspired by my crush on Mark Steed, although he hasn't actually noticed me in real life. Maybe he will if he hears about the movie.

The only way Libby would agree to costar was if I also cast Greg Gilman, the guy she likes from school. He's no Mark Steed, but it all worked out, because Greg's parents let us use their basement for the Pacman scene.

When I notice that Libby has Greg cornered at the refreshment table, I grab my video camera and head over.

"Back off, Rox," she says, leaning in so close that her lip gloss practically sticks to the lens. "This is real life now."

"You're going to thank me for this footage when I'm an Academy Award winner. Stand a little closer. And….action!"

Sighing, Libby and Greg wrap their arms around each

other. He hasn't had his growth spurt yet and his head practically fits into her armpit.

"Cut! Libby, your legwarmers are crooked. Fix them and we'll go again."

She snatches the camera out of my hands. "Show's over."

Chapter 1

Libby is starstruck. I know this because she is standing on tiptoe to get a better view. At 6'5" in heels, Libby hasn't actually needed to stand on tiptoe since junior high.

"There's Oliver O'Brien!" she says. "He's getting out of the limo…he's on the red carpet…he's posing for pictures…*he's gorgeous!*"

"Didn't you say he isn't your type?" I ask.

"So he's six inches shorter than I am…I can stoop."

Both Libby and my father professed complete indifference to the celebrity factor when I invited them to this Toronto International Film Festival Gala for *Seattle*, but Libby was trilling with excitement even before we took our seats at the screening. I had to shush her three times during the show and she cheered as my credit rolled at the end. It was mortifying, but at least it roused my father, who snored through the movie.

Now we're outside the Drake, the hotel hosting the post-screening party, and Dad is shielding his eyes from the popping flashbulbs. "Let's go inside," he says. "This is a circus."

Libby trails after us. "There's Meredith Connor. Wow, she looks like a bobble head doll."

"The bigger the cranium, the bigger the star," I agree. "It's an unwritten rule."

At the door, a young guy wearing a "TIFF Volunteer" T-shirt stops us with a raised hand. "Private party," he says in the monotone reserved for the plebes.

Maybe I wore the same snotty expression when I was in film school, but my struggles to get ahead in this business have taught me some hard lessons in humility. "Busy night?" I ask, offering a sympathetic smile.

He nods almost imperceptibly. "A lot of wannabes trying to crash the party."

"No worries here. I'm Roxanne Hastings. I'm on the list."

The kid flicks his eyes over his clipboard. "I don't see your name."

"But I was on the *Seattle* crew."

"Step aside, please." He lifts the velvet rope to allow a stream of industry shakers and beautiful people to pass.

"Maybe we'd better go," Dad says.

I stand firm. "Could you check your list again?"

A bouncer the size of a Winnebago appears out of nowhere and clamps onto my arm. "Let's not cause a scene," he says. "This is a big night for the people who made the film."

Well, some of them anyway. But I haven't survived this long in the business by being easily discouraged. There's always another route to the free champagne if you're thirsty enough to keep looking.

My father and Libby shift anxiously beside the Dumpster as I pry open the alley door. I curse quietly after one of my nails snaps.

"Roxanne, really," Dad says. "This is unseemly."

I shush him and step into the hotel's kitchen, where a group of line cooks gapes at us. "Spot check by the Health Inspector," I explain, nodding toward my father, who is, as always, wearing a pinstriped suit and carrying a briefcase. Before anyone can ask for identification, I propel Libby and Dad across the kitchen and through the swinging doors into the party.

Libby shakes a carrot peeling from her heel and resumes her animated commentary. I'm happy she's enjoying herself but for me, the real buzz came at the theatre. *Seattle* is a good movie—possibly the best on my résumé, which features more big-budget trash than I'd like. Finally, I have a credit worth bragging about, even if it's buried in a long list that speeds by at the end of the movie. One day, it will appear over an opening sequence: *A Film by Roxanne Hastings.* I just hope that day arrives before I qualify for the senior's discount at the ticket booth.

I decided at age thirteen that directing was my calling. According to my plan, I was to win my first Oscar by age 28 and find the perfect man shortly thereafter, who would give up his career to raise our family. Now 34, I am years behind my modest goal of taking Hollywood by storm. As for my personal life, well, happy endings are overrated anyway.

While I ponder my squandered potential, my father is concerned about more immediate challenges. The poor man can't get a drink, and as a high profile lawyer he isn't used to being ignored. His suit may have worked wonders in the kitchen but here it's a liability. Casually dressed film execs will see the best service tonight, because most of the waiters are aspiring actors, writers, or directors. I recognize some faces from my own days of carrying a tray.

"It's Sunday night, what's with the briefcase?" I ask my father.

He sets it between his buffed shoes. "I have briefs to review on the way home." Scanning the room, he frowns again. There's too much flesh on display for his comfort and the breeze from all the air kissing is fluttering his comb-over. Still, I know he's thrilled I invited him. He's always complaining that he doesn't see enough of me.

I gasp as a hand slides down my back and settles on my derriere. It belongs to Hank Sanford, the director of *Seattle*, who gives me a snaggle-toothed leer.

"Darling, you look wonderful," he says, his English accent suggesting better breeding than he actually has. "You've lost weight."

I offer my cheek for the obligatory kiss and he dives for my lips. Thanks to an Oscar and a host of successful films, Hank is used to taking liberties.

"*Seattle*'s fantastic," I say, discretely wiping my mouth. "You must be proud."

He continues to eye me appreciatively. "You've been hiding some dangerous curves under your scruffy work clothes and there's absolutely no excuse for it. Time to consider a career *in front* of the camera."

"Ah, but then I'd have to indulge flirtatious directors." Smiling sweetly, I take two quick steps sideways and wave at a passing waiter. The move has worked on Hank before, but tonight his hand travels with me.

"It's a tough business," he says. "But anyone who wants to get ahead knows it's wise to keep me happy. Even that cranky boss of yours."

True, but Damon Laporte, *Seattle*'s cinematographer and my cranky boss, probably hasn't felt Hank's spidery hand on his butt. "I know enough to stay on your good side, Hank." I glance guiltily at my father. "Dad, this is Hank Sanford. He's directing *Illegal Alien*, the film I start work on tomorrow."

Withdrawing his hand from my butt, Hank nonchalantly offers it to my father, who deliberately pauses for a moment before taking it.

"Your daughter is the best camera assistant I've worked with," Hank says. Either he's drunk, or he's trying to placate Dad because Hank is not the sort of director who throws praise around. "I used to be a cinematographer myself, so I know how hard it is to keep a film in focus."

I'm so thrilled by Hank's comment that Dad's skeptical expression barely irritates me. I've worked with Hank on three films, but the only indication he's given that he likes my work is that he hasn't fired me.

My hopes that he will say more are dashed by the arrival of Oliver O'Brien and Meredith Connor. Despite the graying hair, Oliver's face is boyishly young and his smile contagious. He shakes Hank's hand before leaning over to kiss my cheek. Meredith, a real-life Snow White, merely stares at me blankly as she takes out a cigarette. Hank stops pawing her bare shoulder long enough to give her a light. Although smoking is prohibited, no one says a word.

Hank snaps his fingers and a waitress instantaneously appears with a tray of champagne flutes. "Please keep our glasses full all night," he says.

Shoving his briefcase aside with one foot, my father steps forward to shake Meredith's hand.

Oliver looks up at Libby with eyes as blue as Mexican glass and says, "Hey Stretch, do you like ice cream?"

Libby, who hates being called Stretch, titters and nods so hard her curls bounce. We follow Oliver to the ice cream station and I marvel over his transformation. On *Seattle,* he frequently held up shooting with his desperate need for reassurance; tonight he's oozing confidence and charm, having flipped the magic switch that turns an actor into a star.

Poor Libby gazes at him speechless, her ice cream untouched.

"Do you still think he looks smaller in person, Lib?" I ask, winking at Oliver.

Libby's flush starts at her collarbone and surges north.

"Think I'm too short for you, Stretch?"

"No," she protests, now red to the hairline. "I said I could stoop." She claps her hand over her mouth in horror.

Laughing, Oliver chases a brandied cherry around his sundae and presents it to Libby on a long spoon.

"You're inspiring a whole chapter in her memoirs, Oliver," I say, as he captures another cherry and offers it to me. I cup my hand under it and open my mouth.

"Roxanne!" The cherry flies off the spoon and rolls toward Damon's feet. "Are you crazy? There are photographers everywhere."

"Any publicity is good publicity, Damon," Oliver says. "How about a cherry?"

Damon drapes a protective arm around his wan girlfriend, Genevieve. "I'm allergic."

"That's Damon?" Libby whispers. She's heard his name often but never seen him. "He's way cuter than I imagined. You made him sound so uptight."

"It's possible to be cute and uptight," I answer.

Reluctantly releasing Genevieve into Oliver's orbit, Damon pulls me aside. "What were you and Hank talking about?"

"In a nutshell? His brilliant directing and the benefits of sucking up to get ahead."

"Hang on to that last thought," he says. "Did he mention Fledgling?"

Fledgling Films is the production company Hank recently formed with two other industry kingpins. Their goal is to make modest films with artistic value.

"Is it finally off the ground?" I try to sound casual, but excitement is stirring. A new production company like Fledgling will be scouting for good scripts and raw talent to direct them—two things I just happen to possess.

"Their first feature is shooting in Morocco when *Illegal Alien* wraps," Damon confirms. "Since Hank's moving on to executive produce, I want him to let me direct."

Damon and I share the same career goal, but he's far closer to achieving it. At 37, he's one of the most respected cinematographers in the country. Not only has he lit over a dozen feature films, he's also directed a handful of low-budget independents, some of which had critical success at festivals. It's only a matter of time before he gets a real break.

"This is great news," I say.

Misconstruing my enthusiasm, Damon raises a cautionary hand. "I can't promise anything, Roxanne. First I have to land the job. Then I'll see what I can do about making you cinematographer."

It's not surprising that Damon would think my goal is to become a cinematographer. I sometimes forget myself that the camera department was supposed to be a short-term layover. Years ago, I did a brief stint as a camera trainee as part of my effort to gain an overview of the entire business before making the push to direct. I ended up enjoying the job far more than I expected and when Damon offered me a promotion to film loader, I accepted the challenge. He promoted me to focus puller three years later and again I accepted, telling myself that the directors I admire most have a firm grasp of camera.

Damon and Hank have proven it's possible to make the

leap from cinematography to directing, but there is a faster route: owning a script so good that it creates its own break. Two years ago, I stumbled over a short story called *The Lobby* at a garage sale and paid someone to adapt it for film. Pitching it is daunting, but in a business where the cheeky wheel gets the champagne, I keep trying. I've had enough nibbles to sustain my faith.

Sometimes I toy with the idea of borrowing money and making a scaled down version of *The Lobby*. Without studio backing, however, the chances of getting the film distributed are very slim. I'm too much my father's daughter to go into debt for a film that no one will ever see. Besides, *The Lobby* deserves to be a full-length feature and Fledgling has the budget to do it properly. Moreover, Fledgling has ties to studios that could get me a "name" actor and publicity, which would in turn lead to distribution, box office sales and ideally, a flourishing career as one of Hollywood's hot new directors.

Time to warm up my pitching arm.

"Hank is alone at the bar," I tell Damon. "Let me talk to him about Morocco for you."

"I suppose you'd get more information out of him than I would," he concedes. "Hank's a sucker for a pretty face. So go work your wiles—and grab me a drink on your way back, will you?"

My father clears his throat conspicuously. "Hank just went into the men's room. I hope you aren't sending my daughter in there to 'work her wiles'?"

Damon has the decency to blush. "You must be Roxanne's father," he says, backing away. He snatches Genevieve from Oliver's clutches and retreats.

"I don't like the way he speaks to you," my father says.

"Oh, Dad, it's just Damon. We spend so much time together that we skip the niceties. He's a genius behind the camera."

"Then he shouldn't have to chase anyone to the urinal." Dad points to Genevieve, now lurking outside the men's room. "You're no one's maid and he should treat you with respect."

"The notion of respect probably varies by industry."

"What's happened to your standards?"

"I'm just following the rules of the game. Remember, you're the one who gave me the video camera."

"The camera was your mother's idea. Mine was to give you a summer job in my law office. Why didn't that stick?"

"I'd suffocate in an office job. I need more variety."

"Well, we can't all play for a living."

Fury rises in my throat. "I work my ass off, Dad. You have no idea what it takes to bring a vision to life. And you never supported me the way Mom did."

Dad's eyes widen in surprise. "I just want you to earn a steady living. Is that so wrong?"

"I do earn a steady living." I've been supporting myself nicely for a decade, yet my father doesn't see this as real work.

Libby's arrival breaks up the fight. Holding out her forearm, she says, "Oh my God! Oliver did a body shot with me."

"A what?" My father sounds alarmed.

"A body shot. He licked my arm and sprinkled salt on it, then swallowed a shot of tequila and licked the salt off my arm."

"Libby, that's disgusting."

"That's the tame version, Mr. Hastings. Sometimes you pour liqueur into someone's navel and—"

"I don't want to hear this."

"Oh, Dad, you'd jump right on the bar if Meredith invited you to do a body shot."

"I most certainly would not." He permits himself a small smile. "It would wrinkle my suit."

Drunk and bedazzled, Libby says, "I am never washing my arm again."

"Tim might complain," I say.

She cranes around to locate Oliver. "Who?"

"Tim? Your boyfriend?"

"He can't expect me to sit home and pine while he travels the world."

The body shot must be kicking in. Libby adores Tim, who's in Europe with the youth orchestra he conducts. "He's only been gone two weeks."

Lib doesn't hear this. She is already heading for the dance floor, where Oliver beckons.

Libby is alone at the bar when I return from seeing my father off. "The film business is so much fun," she says, "that I'm thinking of writing a script."

"You wouldn't even consider adapting *The Lobby* when I asked," I point out. As a political speechwriter and an author, Libby could have saved me a bundle if she'd fallen for Hollywood earlier.

"You and your ever-present video camera put me off moviemaking, but Oliver has changed all that."

"This business isn't all champagne and body shots, Libby. Tonight you're seeing the shining tip of a dirty iceberg."

"Well, Hank does seem like a sleazeball."

"Yes, but a talented, powerful sleazeball."

"I didn't see you putting up much of a fight. I'd bite his arm off."

"That probably wouldn't further your new screenwriting ambitions. Notice even Meredith didn't bite his arm off."

"Ah," she says, immediately grasping the dilemma. "No biting a valuable contact."

"Groping, on the other hand, is absolutely encouraged."

Hank turns his back on Martin Speir, the celebrated Canadian director, and pulls me closer. "Do you know, darling, I've always had a weakness for strawberry blondes with big—" his eyes flick from my chest to my face "—teeth. You have such a beguiling smile."

"Why thank you," I say, ignoring Libby's smirk. "I hear your new company has finally 'fledged'."

"Damon already approached me about the Morocco project."

"He'd do a good job."

"He always does, but he has a chip on his shoulder."

"Since when has that been a barrier to directing?"

"Let me introduce you to my good side, darling, so that you'll recognize it in future. Now, tell me why you're so interested in promoting Damon."

I shake my head. "We're not a couple, if that's what you're implying. Damon is seeing Genevieve, the makeup artist."

Hank leans in, his breath heavy with smoke and scotch. "And you?"

"I try not to mix business and pleasure, myself. Besides, who has time?"

He turns abruptly to Libby and slides a hand down her back. "How about it, Stretch?"

"Sorry, pal, I've lost my heart to Oliver." I notice that Hank's arm is still attached to his body. How soon we compromise.

"You and half the women on the planet," he replies. "All right, Roxanne, what's really on your mind?"

I take a deep breath and say, "*Five lives are changed forever when a sexy con artist is hired to redecorate the lobby of an exclusive Miami hotel."*

Hank stares at me silently through pale blue eyes and Libby transfers her champagne glass from one hand to the other and back. Around us, conversation splinters into audible fragments.

"If we were in an elevator," Hank says at last, "I'd swear that was a pitch."

"First floor—champagne, caviar, scripts." I grin at Libby, who is stunned by my nerve. I used to wait for the perfect opportunity to deliver the pitch, but eventually realized that the perfect opportunity only looks that way in retrospect. Now, whenever there's an open window, I dive through it. "Think *Short Cuts* meets *The Crying Game*—appearances deceive, passing acquaintances are forced into intimate situations, longtime commitments are shattered."

"Do you own this script?" he asks, sounding mildly intrigued.

"I do. It's called *The Lobby.*"

"And you want to option it?"

"I want to direct it."

A smile spreads across Hank's face in slow motion. I can't tell if he's impressed or amused. Setting his glass on the bar, he runs both hands through his thick, gray hair. Finally he says, "I'll read your script, Roxanne, but only because I admire a woman with balls."

He admires a woman with vital signs. "And I'd get to direct?"

He puts his hand on my butt again and this time I barely flinch.

Libby is still gushing about my courage as we climb into the cab. "I'm so impressed by the way you laid it on the line, Rox."

I snort. "Were you listening? He told me I'd have to work like a dog for the next ten months before he'd even think about letting me direct."

"But he agreed to look at your script. That's huge."

"He could be stringing me along, Lib. Happens all the time."

Her grin blazes on. "Your mom would have been so proud."

I turn to stare out the window. It's been nearly three years since my mother died, but my breath still catches when she's mentioned in the past tense.

Lib senses this and shifts gears. "What did Damon say?"

"I didn't tell him. He'd kill me if he knew I'd struck a deal with Hank." I explain that Damon doesn't know about my desire to direct. He's grooming me to be his own cinematographer and he considers the climb up the camera ranks a rite of passage. It's not as if I've misled him. I love the camera department and becoming a cinematographer has always been my back-up plan.

Libby tells the cab driver to take us to the after-hours club Oliver mentioned.

"Oh, no you don't," I say. "I've got an early call time and you're not going alone. Tim would never forgive me."

Libby leans back in her seat and sulks. "Well, don't think any of this impressed me." She's holding a large gilt trout, the centerpiece from the sushi table. A suspicious clinking emanates from her purse whenever we hit a bump. "And don't think it makes up for neglecting me for the next three months while you're filming."

"I promise to stay in touch this time."

She opens her purse, selects a champagne flute and hands it to me. "Then you can have mine—but I'm keeping Oliver's."

Chapter 2

ILLEGAL ALIEN
Exterior, Countryside, Fall Day: Detective Penny and Sergeant Trowbridge are on horseback, pursuing the alien through a field and into the woods.

"We got damn lucky with this storm, chaps," Hank yells above the howling wind. "Get the stunt doubles on the horses and roll the camera!"

Charging forward into the muddy field, the Range Rover picks up speed as it approaches the two chestnut horses. I am harnessed to its hood beside the cranelike contraption that secures the camera. The cold rain drives into my face and down the collar of my raincoat as I struggle to keep the shot in focus. Each time the truck hits a pothole at high speed my organs rearrange themselves in new and interesting ways.

"Cut!" Hank says. "We've got it, people."

The Range Rover slows to a standstill and Damon

emerges from the cab, where he's been operating the camera remotely. He watches as the grips unhook me and hold me upright. When they let go, I collapse into the mud. After that three-hour joy ride, I've lost all muscle control.

Damon laughs so hard that he has to lean on the Range Rover for support. Even our female leads, Shawna Glass and Zara Duncan, who have just arrived for their close-ups, crack a smile.

From the ground, I see the paramedic's sturdy boots running toward me. At least someone is showing concern for my welfare. "Ms. Duncan!" he calls, leaping over my prostrate form. "I'm your biggest fan. Would you sign my DVD copy of *Jackie the Ripper*?"

Hank offers me his hand. "On your feet, darling. Remember, what I said at the party last night—prove you're the best damn focus puller on the planet and I'll let you direct. You can't do it lying on the ground."

My brain may be jarred from the ride, but I know his offer wasn't that simple. What he actually said was that if I impress him as focus puller, he'll upgrade me to cinematographer in Morocco and only if I continue to prove myself at that level will he consider letting me direct. And that's assuming he loves the script for *The Lobby*. It's a tenuous offer at best, but it's all I have at the moment.

After Hank helps me to my feet, I trudge over to the actors' tent to thaw my frozen hands beside the heater. This is star territory, but I'm too cold to worry about formalities.

Zara squints at me from her director's chair. "Excuse me," she says, "since you're already filthy, would you mind taking Chiquita out to do his business?" She proffers a leash, at the end of which is a long-haired chihuahua, and a plastic bag.

Damon does a doubletake as I parade by with the dog. "Rox, you can audition as personal assistant to the stars later.

I need this camera re-rigged and I want you to grab another camera from the truck and set it up for the close-up. I'm trying to get two shots in one so that the actors don't have to be out in this rain for too long."

I return Chiquita to Zara, who is waiting at the entrance of the tent. She accepts the leash without a word and as she turns, a strong gust blows her hair back from her face. That's when I realize the rumors are true: Zara really does have her skin taped close to the hairline every morning in a cheap, convenient face-lift. When her fluffy platinum hair is artfully arranged, no one is any the wiser.

But even the biggest stars can't control the wind.

The mysterious trail of slime leads into the studio and ends at the craft table, where someone in an elaborate green costume dripping with strings of mucuslike resin is surveying the pastries.

As a confirmed method actor, Burk Ryan believes that wearing the sixty-pound alien costume at all times will help him feel more like an alien.

"Hank says we're to call him 'Creature' when he's in costume to help him stay in character," Damon says. "Unless he takes his head off, that is."

The Creature does indeed remove its rubber head, signaling the transformation into Burk Ryan, has-been action hero. Now seriously overweight, Burk is winded from the effort of reaching for a croissant. The angular face that graced so many magazine covers over the years has lost its definition.

Though the flesh may be weak, the ego is still willing. "Hey Focus Girl," he says, lumbering over to me. "I hope you're good at following the action because I don't like to be restricted by marks."

I shake the crumb-laden tentacle he extends. "I'll try to keep up."

Burk turns to my assistant, Christian, who is marking an actor's position on the floor. "You keep laying down that tape if it makes you happy, Marks Guy, but I won't be paying any attention to it."

Then he corners Props Guy to tell him that the Creature fancies $80 Cuban cigars.

I wonder what Producer Guy will have to say about that.

My job is listed in the *Guinness Book of World Records* as one of the top ten conversation-killers of all time:

"So, what do you do?"

"I'm a focus puller for feature film productions."

"What does that actually mean?"

"Uh, it means I keep the shot in focus."

"How interesting… Have you tried the artichoke dip?"

"Really [sounding desperate], it's an important job."

In the film world, it is an important job. Keeping a movie in focus may sound straightforward, but it means knowing precisely how far the actors are from the camera at any given moment and adjusting constantly as they move around the set. Even when they stand in one spot, I have to compensate for the slightest movement because an inch can make the difference between sharp and soft. What's more, I do all this while standing beside the camera, because it's the cinematographer who actually watches the image through the lens when we roll.

To my mind, the key to doing the job well is respecting the camera. It's a complicated piece of machinery. For starters, it's as sensitive to temperature changes as a mood ring. Batteries die without warning, circuit boards blow for no reason, and many of its component parts are so precisely integrated that loosening one microscopic screw can have a disastrous effect on the image. One must be part technical genius, part psychic to keep it happy.

I have a natural aptitude for camera work but I would never have become as skilled as I am had Mom lived. When she was diagnosed with cancer, I put my directorial ambitions on hold and threw myself into focus pulling as a distraction. For years, I practically lived on a camera truck. I was the first one there in the morning, the last to lock up at night, and if a film fell behind schedule and needed crew to work weekends, I'd volunteer. Ironically, my efforts to distract myself from personal pain were seen as selfless dedication to the craft and I became known as one of the best focus pullers in town.

I've earned the right to coast, but there's no such thing in this business. Maintaining a good rep is a full-time job in a culture where only the toughest survive. To stand out, one must be organized, efficient, unobtrusive and, most important, fast. I can set up five cameras in under an hour, build a Steadicam in nine minutes, and currently hold the industry record for changing a magazine and threading the film into the camera.

I also have some pretty impressive war stories. For example, I once kept the camera rolling on an aggravated skunk long after the cinematographer had fled. Another time, when a train didn't stop on its mark, I kept the camera running until it was almost on top of us. At the last possible second, I rolled off the tracks with the camera and down the embankment to safety. The camera was fine, but the shot cost me fifteen stitches.

Hanging off skyscrapers and out of helicopters won't keep me ahead of the pack forever. Younger, keener focus pullers are already nipping at my heels. I just hope I can find the energy to give 110 percent, 24-7, to impress Hank and move on.

All signs indicate that *Illegal Alien* will be a demanding shoot. It's a comic-book style thriller about superhero Detective Penny, played by Shawna Glass, who takes her special crime-fighting powers from bewitched lingerie. Zara plays Sergeant Trowbridge, her partner and boss. Rounding out the three-diva marquee is Burk, who plays an evil alien that regularly morphs into an FBI agent. With this line-up and a hundred-million-dollar budget, it's a big movie, but it certainly isn't Hank's usual fare.

Shawna is one of Hollywood's current "it" girls whose popularity is increasing faster than her bra size, despite the fact that she's a director's worst nightmare. We're hours behind schedule because she "came down with something" during transport via limo from the field to the climate-controlled soundstage for the afternoon's scenes. According to the grapevine, the poor woman has a terrible case of double vodka martini.

With her long résumé, Zara Duncan is technically the star of this movie, but Shawna will be the bigger box office draw. Everyone accepts this reality except Zara herself, who hasn't adjusted to her unspoken demotion. Therefore, when Hank moves up her scene and pulls her out of makeup early, she's livid.

Gizmo, the production's key grip, nudges me as Zara walks onto set. "Crack out the vanity filters, Rox. This one's been ridden hard and put away wet."

I smile. No matter how crude the guys are, I try to smile. Otherwise, the "fembo" comments start flying. In a trade where women are a rarity, being seen as humorless is the kiss of death. Besides, I realize that the coarse humor is a coping strategy in this artificial world where beauty and status are so prized.

Damon steps forward to help Zara onto her mark so that

he can take a light reading. The chihuahua struggles in her arms as she tries to read her script. "Damon, be a doll and hold Chiquita, will you?"

Damon obligingly takes the dog before turning to me with a stricken expression.

"Wow, she learned your name first," I say, choking back laughter. "Aren't you special? Here's *your* chance to audition as personal assistant to the stars."

"Quiet," he says, thrusting the dog into my arms. "By the way, you've got something on your chest."

I look down to see a coffee stain from my last cappuccino run. Casually covering it with Chiquita's little body, I ask, "What were you doing looking?"

"I take inventory every day," he says, "just to make sure everything's where it should be."

I love being the only girl on an all-boy team.

Fourteen hours into the day, I give Gilda a good cleaning while waiting for the electricians to finish lighting the last set. Gilda is a millennium special edition, 35mm motion picture camera, serial number 133. I was the first to use her when she came off the production line three years ago and she's been with me ever since. I named her after Rita Hayworth's character in the movie of the same name. Gilda rolls with me from show to show and when I'm be-tween films, the guys at the rental house (whom I bribe with expensive French pastries) tuck her safely away on a shelf. I take far better care of Gilda than I do of my own health, keeping her purring with the right combination of oil and silicone, and sending her into the shop for frequent tune-ups. In return, she never lets me down. It's a perfect relationship.

Burk and Shawna are arguing about character motivation

while I polish Gilda's pressure plate. Looking tired and discouraged, Hank joins me.

"*Seattle* this ain't," he says, sighing as he leans against Gilda. I clear my throat and look pointedly at Hank's butt. "Oh, come now darling, it's just a camera."

I pat Gilda protectively. "In the same way that Alfred Hitchcock was just a filmmaker." Everyone on set knows that Hitchcock is Hank's hero.

He rolls his eyes, but moves away. "Hitchcock would have been smart enough to turn this movie down."

"It's only day one. And you have a huge budget."

"Big stunts and big effects cost big bucks. So do Shawna and Zara, for that matter. I'm not deluding myself, Roxanne. This movie isn't about the story, it's about the action. I knew that when I agreed to direct, but I couldn't say no. World Studios nearly doubled my usual rate after seeing the cut of *Seattle*. It meant I could launch Fledgling six months ahead of schedule."

At the mere mention of Fledgling, my heart beats faster. I'm dying to ask Hank if he's looked at *The Lobby*, but I only gave him the script this morning. There's no way he could have read it yet.

Unless he flipped through it at lunch.

But no, I can't ask. If I seem too desperate, Hank will use that against me. I know that. I won't ask. I won't ask.

"Hank, have you looked at my script?"

"Patience, Roxanne." He smiles and rests a nicotine-stained hand on my shoulder. "As I was about to say, we all have to make compromises to get what we want."

The old teabag had better not be thinking of warming the pot with me. This girl will only go so far to get a break.

Damon's arrival saves me from telling Hank so. "Am I interrupting something?" he asks.

Hank purposely keeps his hand on my shoulder a second longer. "I was just giving Roxanne some tips on how to get ahead in this business."

"I don't imagine your tips included socializing when there's work to be done," Damon says, before turning to me. "I've been lit for five minutes and I don't have a lens to look through. If you're not too busy, how about doing your job, Focus Girl?"

Hank calls a cut from the other side of the set wall, where he's sitting at a bank of monitors with all seven of the show's producers. The majority will soon migrate back to the California sunshine, but they always show up in force on day one.

"Roxanne," Hank shouts, "either there's a problem with my monitor, or you buzzed Burk on that close-up."

I turn to Damon. "Did Burk look soft in the viewfinder?"

Damon shakes his head. "It's probably the monitor, but we'd better go again if Hank's worried."

I walk over to Hank, who now comprises the stuffing in a producer sandwich. Although Burk refused to use marks, I'm pretty sure I kept him sharp. Still, there is no way to know for certain until the film is processed overnight. Not knowing the result of my work until the following day is one of the biggest challenges of focus pulling. "Maybe you should do another take to be safe," I suggest.

"We're already two hours into overtime," a producer snaps.

A few minutes of overtime is a hell of a lot cheaper than reshooting tomorrow, and fortunately Hank sees the sense of this.

Burk is another matter. It took him eight takes to get his lines right and he isn't anxious to tempt fate with take nine.

While the special effects guys help him with his costume head, I take advantage of his distraction to run a measuring tape from the camera to his position. He swats at it. "Jesus Christ, Focus Girl, I'm exactly where I was during the last take."

"Just checking," I say, although my tape indicates that he's eighteen inches closer to the camera now.

"I'm warning you, I'm not in the habit of doing extra takes for a hack who can't do her job." Burk turns to the special effects guys. "Whoever heard of a chick pulling focus anyway?" And here it comes, the stupid joke I hear on every set: "They can't judge distance properly," he says. "They all think this—" he holds his tentacles a good foot apart "—is only six inches!"

The effects guys laugh as if it's the first time they've heard it.

Pulling into the driveway of the rundown Victorian I call home, I find a motorcycle in my parking spot, surrounded by spare parts.

Again.

Cursing, I back into the street and leave the Jeep halfway up the block, risking the twenty-dollar ticket.

It's 3:00 a.m., but the lights are still on in the basement. I consider stopping to give Crusher a piece of my mind but decide against it and proceed up the stairs to my apartment. Better to leave it 'til morning when I can rouse him out of a deep slumber. I kick off my shoes and walk into the kitchen, gasping as my feet hit the cold puddle stretching out from the refrigerator.

The Doobie Brothers are Rockin' down the Highway when I bang on the basement door. A massive form blocks the light as my landlord, a biker in his late forties, greets me. It's a cool night, but he's wearing a leather vest over a bare chest. All the better to showcase the tattoos, one of which stretches across his big belly, reading *Ars longa, vita brevis.*

"What's up?" he asks.

"I had to park on the street again."

"Sorry, I got distracted." He strokes his long, grizzled beard absently. "I didn't expect you home so soon."

"It's 3:00 a.m. And there's water all over my kitchen floor. You promised you'd get me a new fridge weeks ago. And I don't mean another crappy used one, either."

"So what you're saying is, you're here as a tenant."

"Of course I am here as a tenant. What do you expect at this time of night?"

"Jesus, you're cranky. Why don't we take Elvira out for a run to calm you down?"

I'm quite certain that I will not find a ride behind Crusher on his big Harley at all calming, especially not at this hour. "What I want is a cold beer."

"Why didn't you say so? Tough first day?"

Nodding, I duck under his hairy armpit and fling myself onto his couch. Crusher retrieves a six-pack of Budweiser from his fridge, opens a can and hands it to me without offering me a glass. "I'm so tired I almost drove off the road."

"That's what you get for working for the man." He cracks open another beer and downs it in a few gulps before crushing the can and tossing it across the room and into the recycling box.

"The film business is hardly the establishment."

Crusher is proud of the fact that he has never held down a "real" job, preferring to live humbly on his own terms. "What do you think?" He points toward an easel whereupon his latest project resides: a half-finished painting of a motorcycle on black velvet. Crusher's portraiture has quite a following at biker clubs throughout the city.

"A Yamaha FZ1," I say. I've seen a lot of bikes come and go in the years I've lived here and I've learned a thing or two. "I believe I just saw her in my parking spot."

"Had to fluff my model," Crusher replies. "Gave her a polish and a few minor enhancements and she's good to go."

Painting portraits for besotted motorcycle owners might be how Crusher keeps himself in Budweiser, but he's actually a talented, self-taught artist who works in many media. There's a beautiful charcoal drawing of someone's hands on the wall that always rivets me. That's partly because he refuses to tell me about the model. Whenever I bring it up, he changes the subject. Seeing me glancing at it now, he walks into the kitchen.

"Speaking of fluffing, how's the cast?" He opens a can of soup and heats it in the microwave.

"Zara's a bitch, Shawna's a lush, and Burk's an incompetent chauvinist pig who refuses to use marks. I'm doomed."

"You told me Oliver O'Brien couldn't hit a mark to save his life and *Seattle*'s as sharp as a tack."

"Yeah, but I'm under more pressure on this movie. Hank is sort of auditioning me."

"Auditioning you? For what?"

"He said he'd consider me as cinematographer for a movie he's doing in Morocco. But more importantly, if I show him I have the chops, his new production company might take on *The Lobby*."

Crusher pours the soup into two chipped bowls and lays a piece of Wonderbread beside each one. "Huh."

"What's that supposed to mean?"

"It means did he put it in writing?"

"Not yet."

"So he's got you busting your hump for nothing."

"Not for nothing. If I impress him, he'll promote me."

"But you still don't know if he'll buy your script."

"It's a great script. He's going to love it."

"It's been rejected before."

I throw my spoon on the table. "Could you be a little more negative?"

"I'm just being realistic. Hank's not offering guarantees. And from what you've told me over the years, being promoted to cinematographer by a director you barely know is a pretty major break. Didn't Damon light a ton of rock videos before he got to shoot a film?"

"Hank knows my work. It's our fourth movie together. And FYI, lots of people land their first cinematography job on a feature film." I've heard of one, anyway. "I'm ready for it. In fact, my new motto is: Start Big and Stay Big." That's the beer talking. There was nothing about today's shoot to encourage such bravado.

"If you're so ready, why hasn't Damon promoted you yet?"

"He's waiting for the right opportunity."

"But Hank's just going to hand it to you? What's in it for him?"

"An original screenplay that's going to make his company a lot of money. Plus the satisfaction of giving an up-and-comer a break."

Crusher smirks. "So few successful directors spend time mentoring. Hank's my hero."

"I can handle Hank."

"He's counting on it."

"Shut up. He knows I did a great job on *Seattle*. I just have to show him that I'm ready to take it to the next level."

"Or take it to the bedroom."

I rise, Wonderbread uneaten, and stalk indignantly to the door. "This is about my untapped talent. You'll see, big guy."

"It's about Hank's unbridled libido, and you'll see, little girl."

"I've been in this business ten years and I'm not naive. Hank wants me to prove myself before he puts his company's money into something I direct. It's simple."

"If you say so." Crusher reaches for my Wonderbread and crams the whole slice into his mouth. "We still on for the Richard Avedon show on Saturday?"

At least I think that's what he says. "I'll wake you at noon. And take care of the fridge, will you?"

Chapter 3

6:51 a.m.

The day's off to a bad start. I am supposed to have the camera built and on set in precisely nine minutes, and since I'm just pulling into the crew parking lot that obviously isn't going to happen.

Gizmo is pacing outside the camera truck when I arrive. He tells me that Christian is also late and I'm not surprised. Although it's only the end of week one, a stretch of eighteen-hour days has worn us all down. Christian and I have put in extra hours on top of that to haul camera gear to and from inaccessible locations. But Damon has already set up the first shot and excuses aren't going to cut it.

I unlock the truck, build the camera in record time and check the film magazines. "Damn! There's no daylight film loaded."

ZOOM IN on Gizmo's expression of dread. "Is there anything in particular you'd like on your headstone?"

"Relax, Giz, I'm still capable of loading film." At least I

think so. It will take time to rediscover my technique and Damon is growing crankier by the day. Like me, he's auditioning for Hank, hoping to land the director's job in Morocco.

I'm groping around in the darkroom when Damon arrives and thumps on the door to let me know he's frustrated. "Hurry up, Roxanne. Hank wants to get some sunrise shots before the actors arrive. Don't make me look bad. I can't make you my cinematographer if I don't get to direct."

I drop the film into the can and seal it before unlocking the door and popping out of the darkroom to retrieve new stock. "You practically said you wouldn't make me cinematographer in Morocco anyhow."

"I said 'no guarantees.' You want to be able to walk before you run, right? If the Morocco job looks too challenging for a new shooter, I won't put your name forward—for both our sakes." He turns to hop off the truck. "And you can kiss any recommendation goodbye if you don't have that camera on set in five minutes."

Gizmo and I watch him walk away before Gizmo says, "He's making *you* a cinematographer? Well, don't ask me to be your grip. The only chick I ever worked for got the job because she was banging the producer. Didn't know how to light a match, let alone an entire set."

I head back into the darkroom without bothering to answer. In an industry where female cinematographers are as rare as real boobs, it's a shame to hear about one doing a poor job. A woman can light a set as well as any man. Maybe I'll prove that by becoming the first female cinematographer ever to receive an Oscar...

My gown of blush chiffon is sequined and strapless—wait, I'm hitching it up as I cross the stage—*it's sequined with spaghetti straps. I'm gliding gracefully toward the microphone in my four-inch heels*—wait, I step on my train and trip—*make that three-inch heels and no train. My hair is swept into a smooth French roll and my makeup is flawless, with a trace of glitter*—wait, hold the glitter, it's for dewy twenty-somethings. *I reach out to accept the Oscar, surprised by its weight. The presenter Russell Crowe*—no, make that Richard Gere—*kisses my cheek and congratulates me. He slips a finger under one of my spaghetti straps and slides it back onto my shoulder before turning me to face the microphone. I look out into the sea of faces.*

"My mother and I had a pact," I tell the audience. "She agreed to finance my video cameras until I graduated from university as long as I promised to take her to the Academy Awards one day. While the small print in our contract specified that my nomination would be for directing, *I think she would have agreed to overlook this clause, providing I gave her credit for launching my film career. Mom, I wish you'd been here to see this."*

"Hey, Rox, you okay in there?" Gizmo is pounding on the door of the darkroom.

"Uh, fine," I say, startled. If my eyes weren't damp, I'd almost think I'd dozed off for a second. I bend down quickly to grope for the scissors and hit my forehead on the shelf above the bench. "Jesus!"

"Are you *sure* you're okay?" Gizmo sounds panicky and I'm getting that way myself. Damon could come back anytime and throw an aneurysm-inducing tantrum.

"Stay calm," I tell myself, "and think of the glory when you arrive on set bleeding, but with a loaded mag. You'll be a hero."

7:12 a.m.

Damon is kicking back with a coffee when Gizmo and I rush onto set. Eyeing the gash on my temple, he quips, "Another catfight?"

So much for glory.

"Where's Hank?" I ask. "You said we needed sunrise shots."

"Too much cloud cover. We'll have to come in ahead of call one day next week."

Terrific.

7:32 a.m.

I'm in the craft truck fetching a round of cappuccinos when I hear the news. Shawna, now known amongst the crew simply as *Martini,* stepped out of the makeup chair and into Lake Ontario this morning while reportedly admiring the Toronto skyline. It will take two hours to make her camera-ready again.

8:05 a.m.

Waiting.

8:45 a.m.

Waiting.

9:30 a.m.

Still waiting.

It never fails to amaze me how much time it takes to process a beautiful woman through hair and makeup. It can add hours to the already considerable time we spend waiting for equipment to be moved and set up, for repairs to be made, for a break in the clouds.

10:00 a.m.

Martini is on set at last, but Burk is still in his trailer. A production assistant says he's on the phone with his agent.

10:30 a.m.

Burk is off the phone and on the set, but Martini has returned to her trailer. The production assistant says she's making the point that no one keeps her waiting.

11:15 a.m.

Waiting some more.

Generally, there's plenty of banter during our downtime, but thanks to a difficult cast, complicated stunts and problems with the Creature's costume, this has been an unusually stressful week. When a movie falls behind schedule so quickly, the studio puts pressure on the producers, the producers put pressure on the director and they join forces to put pressure on the crew. Fingers point and people lose their jobs. Burk's dresser has already been fired, as has Zara's stunt double.

So we sit in silence, wondering where the ax will fall next. Those who smoke, smoke continuously. The rest of us patrol craft services at intervals for snacks. Waiting and worrying are behind a lot of paunches in this business, including my own.

As I work my way through a stack of cookies, my mind wanders to F. C. Kugelman, esteemed writer of *Illegal Alien*. Having gained prominence with his art-house films of the early nineties, he embraced commercial success with the gore-fest *The Mauling,* followed by *Death Detective.* I have credits on the latter two, both shot here in Hollywood North. Huge box-office profits prompted World Studios to give Mr. Kugelman carte blanche for future projects and freedom has had its usual effect: the man has lost all sense of proportion. *Illegal Alien* is crammed with so many stunts and action sequences, it doesn't even need a story.

The violence and inanity of his scripts notwithstanding, Mr. Kugelman apparently fancies himself something of a Noel Coward. I haven't had the pleasure of meeting him, but I'm curious about his enviable life.

CLOSE ON a screaming kettle being lifted from a burner.

WIDEN OUT to reveal F. C. Kugelman standing by a designer range, dressed in a smoking jacket and cravat. He pours boiling water into a china pot and adds loose leaf tea. While it steeps, he sections a grapefruit and places it, with a scone, on a stylish leather tray. Popping a single carnation into a bud vase, he sets a cup and saucer and a sterling tea strainer on the tray beside the teapot and climbs the stairs to the second-floor loft. Sunlight spills across his mahogany desk as he pours his tea and waits for the computer to boot up. Then, using only his manicured index fingers, he picks out the words:

```
Detective Penny is sitting at her
desk in the precinct when the call
comes.
```

11:45 a.m.

"Rox, let's go!" calls Damon. "Shawna will be sitting at the desk. I want a high-and-wide shot. Mount the camera on a twelve-foot ladder."

Mr. Kugelman shakes his head, holds down the backspace key and starts over.

Detective Penny slams the phone down and races down the hall toward the stairwell.

"Roxanne!" Damon yells. "Script revisions! This is going to be a Steadicam shot instead. You'll be running backward down the hall beside the camera as Shawna comes toward you. The stairs are going to be a bitch."

Later, Hank steps over Roxanne at the bottom of the stairs. "I hope you got that shot before you tripped, darling."

3:15 p.m.

Waiting again.

Damon says, "So, Hank has the hots for you."

"Nah, he has a girlfriend in London."

"Genevieve says the girlfriend is history and he's after fresh blood."

Unfortunately, Genevieve's intelligence is usually reliable. She gets the juiciest gossip straight from celebrity mouths during makeup.

"Not to worry," I say. "Hank likes 'em young and I'm past my prime. If I have to, I'll tell him about my rule against dating guys in the film business."

Damon raises an eyebrow and glances away. "A rule of convenience, as I recall."

My face flushes. He has reason to know: a few years back, we took the title of *The Mauling* too literally and groped our way back to Damon's place after the raucous wrap party. I had recently broken up with a long-term boyfriend and was trying to purge him from my system. Damon was the perfect antidote. I've always been a sucker for that boy-next-door type. When he's smiling, Damon resembles James Denton from *Desperate Housewives.*

The fling served its purpose but it couldn't become more. Damon was my boss, after all, and it would have been dreadfully awkward. The morning after, I blurted, "Let's forget it ever happened, okay?" He seemed equally eager to put it behind us and never mentioned it again until today.

Most of the time, I do forget it ever happened, which is great, because I'm fond of Damon despite the fierce temper. He's smart, talented and decent. In fact, he deserves far better than the lanky, lovely and lethal Genevieve, whom the grips call the Praying Mantis.

After examining my cracked and dirty nails, I finally tell Damon, "It's a good rule, not dating colleagues."

"Especially directors," he agrees. "Most of them are assholes."

12:20 a.m.

It's our second meal break and Damon's eyes suddenly widen at the sight of a camera colleague, Alana Speir, in a low-cut, blush-colored evening gown with spaghetti straps. Her golden hair is in a perfect French roll and even from across the room I can see the glitter on her face. She leaves her father, the director Martin Speir, and glides toward us on four-inch stilettos.

I pull the brim of my baseball cap lower, hoping she'll mistake me for a grip.

"Roxanne! Damon!" She leans down to kiss my cheek, thereby offering Damon an unobstructed view of her décolletage.

"Hey, Alana." I try to inject a little warmth into my voice. After all, she was my trainee on *The Mauling* and my film loader on *Death Detective*.

"We've just come from a fund-raiser and Daddy wanted to stop and say hi to Hank. Rox, sweetie, I've been meaning to call you. I'm shooting some television promos next month and I wondered if you'd pull focus for me?"

My heart sinks into my scuffed running shoes. Alana is six years my junior and spent all of five minutes as a focus puller. She's not very good, but thanks to her father's influence, she's catapulted up the camera ranks and is already getting cinematography gigs. That she has achieved this success with a great rack incenses me. The belief that my bustline stands between me and my big break has always sustained me.

"Thanks, but I'm already booked," I say.

"I haven't told you when it's shooting. Come on, it would be *amazing* to have an all-girl team." She raises pink-lacquered nails to throw invisible quotation marks around the word *amazing*. "And you could upgrade on days when we run two cameras. You're shooting, too, right?"

Damon puts his fork down to gape at Alana without fear of stabbing himself. "I keep Roxanne busy, Alana," he says. "She doesn't have time for independent projects."

"Oh, too bad. I really could have used an old pro on my set. Well, I must run. Hank is leaving for set."

She's gone as fast as her Manolos will carry her. Damon watches, nostrils flaring to catch a last whiff of her cologne.

"Can you believe her, parading in here in that dress?"

"I didn't notice any dress. Must be those eyedrops Genevieve gives me."

"And offering me a job as her assistant? The nerve of her!" I'm working myself into a righteous rage now.

"What do you mean? She was just being nice."

"Nice!"

He looks flummoxed at my fury. "Well, yeah. She thinks you'll make a great team."

"She thinks I'll do all the work while she keeps her nails nice. Have you ever seen a cameraperson with nice nails?"

"I've never noticed."

"Well, ask Genevieve."

"You're taking this the wrong way. She wants to work with you, it's a compliment. Wait a second... Are you jealous?"

"Not at all." I walk with dignity to the dessert table and select a brownie for my green-eyed monster.

Since I can still hear Damon laughing, I retreat to the camera truck to ponder the mystery of why straight men are constitutionally unable to recognize a wolf in a blush-colored designer gown.

4:44 a.m.

Burk is refusing to play the last scene of the day as written. "Give me one good reason why the Creature would kill these two innocent citizens or I will not shoot this scene," he says to Hank, before pulling the rubber alien head over his own. He crosses his upper tentacles and throws himself into his director's chair.

"You want to know what your motivation is for killing people?" Hank asks. The Creature nods. "Because you're the *bad guy!*" Hank explodes. "You're the deranged fucking alien! It's not that big a stretch!"

The Creature attempts to rise but his long webbed feet are stuck in the bottom rung of the director's chair.

"Or how about because it's five o'clock in the fucking morning and we all want to go home?"

Freeing itself, the Creature lumbers down the hall leaving a slime trail. Hank leaps from his chair to give chase.

"How about because you signed a fucking contract?" His voice reaches a maniacal pitch as the Creature enters the stairwell. Hank leans through the doorway and bellows, "HOW ABOUT BECAUSE NO ONE ELSE HAS HIRED YOU SINCE 1998?"

5:15 a.m.

The Creature is standing in front of the camera. Hank, now eerily calm, declares that it will be more terrifyingly convincing if the Creature walks on all fours.

Burk used to do all his own stunts, but these days he'd have trouble bending over even without a costume. Gizmo and two other grips lower him to the floor, where he scrabbles around muttering unintelligibly behind the mask. The effect is far from terrifying.

I concentrate on getting my focus marks, knowing that if I start laughing, I won't be able to stop. When the take is over I look at the director's monitor and find Hank grinning at me. Obviously, he intended to make Burk look like a fool.

Burk knows it, too. After the guys help him upright, he accosts the wardrobe mistress. "I demand to take this costume home," he insists.

"That's impossible, Mr. Ryan," she says.

"I am the Alien! The star of this movie!" shouts Burk, getting hot under the rubber collar. "I must spend the weekend—my own time, you realize—perfecting my prowl."

"There's only one suit, sir. We can't risk anything happening to it."

Burk screeches, "DO YOU KNOW WHO I AM?"

For the first time, he is kind of scary.

6:51 a.m.

I'm driving into a sunrise as glorious as the one that started my workday. "Hi, Libby, it's me."

"Out here in the real world, calling this early on a Saturday is socially unacceptable."

"Sorry. We just wrapped a twenty-four-hour day and I lost track of the time. Bet you wouldn't complain if it were Oliver O'Brien on the line."

"Oliver is a very busy man. I'd have to make some allowances."

"Well, make an allowance for an old friend, because I just picked up a voice mail from Miguel. He's in town to meet a producer and wants to have dinner."

Libby sighs and I can hear her punching her pillow. "Roxanne, you don't need me to tell you that you don't want to see him anymore."

"Right. Why was that?"

"Something about his being a sexist pig, I believe."

"That's it. Last time he ordered my dinner without even asking me what I'd like."

"And you went back to his hotel anyway." Libby yawns. It's not the first time we've had this conversation.

"He has a hypnotic effect on me, I couldn't help myself."

"Well, you've always loved a man with an accent."

"This accent is more trouble than it's worth. I have to carry a Spanish-English dictionary with me."

"Toss it. Miguel's not the man for you, but while he's conveniently in the picture, you'll never move on. You need to make way for the right guy."

"That's what I really needed to hear."

"I know. I should make a recording."

"Well, you can go back to sleep now. I'm in control."

"Don't call him back."

"I won't. Good night."

I hang up and run my finger along my enormous DVD collection to find something relaxing. *The Godfather*...too long. *Deliverance*...too scary. *Talk to Her*...too Spanish; it will remind me of Miguel. I abandon the DVDs and pick up the remote to channel surf.

7:31 a.m.

"Okay, what did you buy this time?" Libby asks. "And don't lie to me, I hear the Jumbotron in the background."

That's Libby's nickname for my forty-two-inch plasma-screen TV. She can't understand how I could spend more on a television than she did for her car, especially when the rest of my furniture could use updating. *Early Thrift Shop* is how my mother used to describe it.

I'd probably have an apartment full of new furniture if I could buy it from the shopping channel. After a long day of filming, I fall prey to the product demos and testimonies more often than I care to admit. The more stressed I am, the less resistance I have to the host's wiles, particularly if the product involves food or weight loss. Indeed, my closets are overflowing with many versions of "the only exercise machine" I'll ever need.

Knowing she won't drop the subject, I confess. "An ice-cream maker."

"Oh, come on, Rox, you never cook."

"But I do eat ice cream."

"Cancel your order. You will never use it and you need the money in your filmmaking fund. And on that note, I've been thinking more about writing a script."

Uh, oh. Libby's obviously taken the idea of making a short film to heart and it's only going to cause trouble. She'll expect me to read it, or worse, actually make the movie. I don't have the time or the inclination for it, nor do I want to blow my savings on a short when I might need the cash for *The Lobby* if things don't work out with Hank.

Besides, Libby and I have never seen eye to eye on the arts. She loves rock and roll, reads constantly and hates art galleries. I listen to European DJ compilations, visit art galleries often and collect coffee-table books on art and architecture. She abhors "art" films; I live for them. She adores romantic comedies; I detest them. We're a cultural Odd Couple.

"Yeah?" I head into the bathroom and start brushing my teeth as I listen.

"Here it is. I'm going to write a script about weddings."

I choke on toothpaste. "Weddings!"

"More like a send-up of traditional weddings, actually. Think *Spinal Tap* or *Best in Show*. It's the story of a single woman who's so fed up with spending money on wedding gifts for friends and family that she plans a big, traditional wedding for herself."

Not this old chestnut again. Libby's obsession has eased somewhat since Tim arrived on the scene, but she still knows more than any normal woman does about the history and traditions of weddings. She's attended at least twenty, played bridesmaid in nearly half and written a book on Canadian weddings with her friend Lola.

"I'm thinking 'mockumentary,'" she rattles on. "We'll follow the bride around as she orders flowers, tries on dresses, books the caterers or etcetera—all for a wedding without a groom. The final scene will of course be the ceremony. I'm calling it *The Counterfeit Wedding.*"

I caught the "we" she buried in there. "Sounds fun, Lib, but you know I hate weddings."

"You're not still sore about Shelley's?"

"Actually, I am. She begs me to shoot her wedding video—for free, I might add—and freaks out when I try to do my job."

"Rox, you yelled 'cut' during the vows."

"Wouldn't you want to get your lines right on the biggest day of your life?"

She sighs. "Then think of *The Counterfeit Wedding* as the ultimate revenge on bridezillas like Shelley."

"Tempting, but there's a lot on my plate right now, with Hank's offer and all. Besides, it's hard enough to be taken seriously by men in my business. If I made a film about weddings, they'd think I'm a bitter spinster."

"More like clever and satirical."

"Let's talk about this later. I'm exhausted and I've got to meet Crusher in a few hours."

I hang up, mentally kicking myself for taking her to the *Seattle* party. That's where she got bitten by the glitter bug. At this very moment, she is sitting down at her computer to work on her opus.

And I'll bet there's a cameo in it for Oliver O'Brien.

Chapter 4

I always enjoy walking into an art gallery with Crusher. The expressions of barely concealed horror on the faces of other patrons are worth the price of admission alone. Mind you, he always shows respect for the artist by wearing a T-shirt, even if it's one with the sleeves torn off and the words Please Don't Make Me Kill You printed across the front of it. Today he's also wearing his studded leathers and biker boots. I assume this is for additional shock value, since I drove.

To Crusher's disappointment, I consistently refuse his offers to squire me about town on Elvira. That's largely because a bad experience long ago put me off two-wheel transportation forever. After film class one night, another student invited me for a drink. I hiked up my long, flowing skirt and climbed onto his bike behind him. Revving his engine, he took off like a rocket down Spadina and turned right onto Queen. At least, I assume that's the route he took. I didn't actually notice the scenery because my skirt billowed over my visor. I was too terrified to let go of the guy and push it back down, so I simply endured the stiff breeze, not to mention the jeering and honking. Thank God for the anonymity of the helmet.

Crusher walks ahead of me to cut a swath through the masses, his graying hair streaming down his back. The Avedon exhibit is at the Art Gallery of Ontario for the first time and it's drawing a big crowd.

"How come Libby didn't join us?" he asks.

"I invited her, but she said something about preferring to drive a stake into her eye. Libby's not exactly an art lover, you know."

"Too bad. Maybe loving an art lover will open her eyes."

I laugh. "She has a boyfriend, Crusher."

"So? Until there's a ring on her finger, she's a free agent."

"Even if you could charm her away from Tim, you don't have much in common."

"What do you know?"

"I know that she wants to write a script for me about a wedding. How lame is that?"

"What a great friend!" He says this without a trace of irony.

"Excuse me, Mr. Anti-Establishment, I said she's writing about *weddings*."

"I heard you, Princess of Fear. You'd shoot down any idea that threatened to get your ass in gear to direct something on your own."

"This from a guy who doesn't even have a social security number."

"It's your ambitions we're talking about. Besides, I'm sure Libby's script is about more than just a wedding."

"It's a mock documentary about a spinster who stages a big traditional wedding to cash in on the gifts even though there's no groom."

"It's clever and satirical. Think *Spinal Tap* or *Best in Show*."

"Did she call you?"

"I wish. It sounds like it could showcase your directing skills."

"When would I find the time or energy to put a film together, Crusher? You know how hard I'm working."

"Chasing a dream is exhausting," he agrees.

"I thought you liked *The Lobby*. Why are you so down on it lately?"

"I like the script, but I've been watching you try to sell it for years. Maybe it's time for a backup plan."

"Working my way up to cinematographer is my backup plan."

"It wouldn't hurt to get a little directing experience in the meantime. It's a small project and you've already got the coin. Plan it on weekends and shoot as soon as *Illegal Alien* ends."

"Making an independent film is one thing, getting it distributed is quite another."

"You could get lucky."

"It's a long shot."

"Whereas Fledgling Films is a sure thing?"

"Remember my new motto—Start Big And Stay Big. For a so-called free spirit, you're sounding like a boring old fart."

"It's unhealthy to hold in your wind."

"Could we please just enjoy the show? I didn't get up early to be nagged."

As we approach the crowd around the first photograph, Crusher offers a genial "Howya doing?" to the other viewers, who step back hastily to give us breathing room. Then he turns to me and asks, "You're seeing that Spanish fop tonight, aren't you?"

It's not the first time he's pulled off this feat. Maybe he

can hear my telephone conversations through the heating ducts. "No, why?"

"You look awfully animated after a ninety-hour work week—like someone who expects to see some action."

"Well, what if I am? We're both consenting adults." He looks meditatively at the portrait as an excuse not to respond. "Miguel and I have a long-term, yet casual relationship. I think it's very mature."

"The man wears a beret, how mature can it be?"

"Many directors wear berets," I offer, my mouth twitching. "Look at Danny DeVito."

"I rest my case. All I'm saying is, you're not really the type for a 'long-term casual relationship.'"

"What do you know? You haven't had a serious relationship since I met you."

"By choice, whereas you're a romance novel waiting to happen. And the Spanish fop is holding you back."

"Jesus, you sound like Libby."

"And you said we have nothing in common."

"Miguel's a great guy. He's taught me—"

Raising a beefy hand, he interrupts. "Can you shut up? I'm trying to enjoy the show." For the benefit of our fellow patrons, he adds, "Maybe you'd learn something if you stopped talking about your sex life for a minute."

I walk to the other end of the exhibit to work my way back alone.

Miguel takes a generous mouthful of red wine and sloshes it around in his mouth. He purses his lips, tilts his head backward and makes gargling noises. The couple at the next table pause, forks in the air, to stare.

"He's an oenophile," I explain to them in a faux-confidential whisper.

"A what?" the man asks.

"An oenophile—a wine lover. I had to look it up myself. Apparently the sloshing unleashes the secrets of the vine."

"Roxanne." Miguel is not amused and the tone translates perfectly.

"Sorry, I'm just killing time until you make sure the wine is acceptable."

"It's fine, so stop talking and have some."

"I thought you asked me out to enjoy my sparkling conversation."

"As a beginning, yes. *Usted es hermosa.*"

I have no idea what he means, but it must be good, because he leans toward me and takes my hand. There's something about the way his dark eyes focus so intently on me that gets me every time. I flatter myself that it's insatiable desire, but he's probably just trying to keep up with what I'm saying.

Miguel and I have been seeing each other on and off for three years. His home base is New York City, but when he's in Toronto, he takes me for nice dinners. He'd take me for *really nice* dinners if I were willing to go to restaurants where we might encounter someone from the business. Today, when I proposed a steak house in the suburbs, he accused me of being the only woman in the city who's ashamed to be seen with him. That's when I suggested 92 Harbord, a restaurant unusual enough to intrigue him, yet obscure enough to be private.

I'm not ashamed to be seen with him, despite the beret. On him, it actually looks cool in a Che Guevara sort of way. He's a slim, handsome man with a dramatic streak of gray running from his widow's peak through his dark hair and a trim salt-and-pepper beard. At the same time, he has a compelling air of authority about him, as most directors do. Mind you, he also has a less compelling tendency toward arrogance, particularly when he's talking about film, wine, food, music, travel or art. Okay, most subjects. It's annoying, but after all, neither of us is in this for the long-term. Which is exactly why I don't want my colleagues knowing about our relationship.

"So, you're in town to see a producer," I say. "What does he want you to direct?"

An expression of disgust crosses his face and he releases my hand. "I don't want to talk about it." Breaking a fundamental rule of wine appreciation, he chugs his rioja. "Big-budget trash. They insult me. *¡Cabrones!*"

"Action? Horror?"

"High school—what do you call it?—gross-out humor."

Miguel did a series of small, critically acclaimed films in his native Spain, but after moving to New York, he really struggled to make a living in the business. In recent years, he's taken on increasingly commercial projects, culminating with a romantic comedy two years ago that really galled him.

"Well, we all make compromises, right? That's what Hank says."

Frowning, he turns to the waiter who's just arrived to take our order. "The lady will have the *codornices.*"

The waiter writes busily; obviously I am the only one in Toronto who doesn't speak Spanish. "Excellent choice, madam," he says.

When the waiter leaves, I say, "I hate it when you do that."

"Why do you American women have such trouble being treated like ladies?"

"*Canadian* women have this weird independent streak that makes them want to choose their own meals."

"Seriously, Roxanne, you are afraid of your femininity. If you capitalized on it, you could succeed in other areas of the film business, say in public relations. Or you could become an agent."

"You know I want to direct. And I want to capitalize on my skills, not my estrogen. Is that so hard to understand?"

"It is hard for me to understand why you're wasting your time as a camera assistant. Pulling focus is one of the most stressful jobs on set. If you want to direct, start directing."

"Have you forgotten how hard it was to break in?" Miguel mortgaged his house to make his first film and it took him years to get out of debt—for a film that only a handful of people ever saw. Then he drove a cab for ages before getting another directing job. "Anyway, Damon is starting to get some directing work and he might upgrade me soon. You've said yourself that becoming a cinematographer would be a good way to work up to directing and earn a decent living in the meantime."

Miguel sighs dramatically. "Must we talk about that hack?"

"I mentioned him to illustrate a point. But Damon is not a hack and you know it."

Miguel and Damon worked together years ago on a couple of films and never got along. The irony is that despite their clashing egos, both movies won awards for directing and cinematography.

"I don't like hearing about the other men in your life."

"Damon is just my boss."

"Some might wonder if Damon is the reason you're still in the camera department."

"That's ridiculous. I'm not interested in Damon and besides, I may not be working for him much longer. Hank's finally got Fledgling off the ground."

"So I've heard. What does that have to do with you?" His eyebrows shoot up as I smile knowingly. "Fledging has bought *The Lobby*?"

"Well, not exactly. Not yet." I explain Hank's offer, trying to put the best possible spin on it.

"That's a lot of *ifs*," Miguel says. "Has he read the script?"

"He's in the process."

"So you might be breaking your chops for nothing."

"*Busting* my chops." This conversation is beginning to sound very familiar. "Look, a minute ago, you were telling me to start directing, and now you're saying I shouldn't go for it with Hank. What have I got to lose?"

"Hank isn't known for giving people breaks. He does what's good for Hank."

"So maybe Hank thinks *The Lobby* will be good for Fledging."

"Or maybe he thinks making empty promises to you will be good for his sex life."

"First you've got a problem with Damon and now Hank. There's a pattern here."

He waves my protests away. "You know I believe in your script, but a small production company is the right place for *The Lobby*."

"Fledgling *is* a small company."

"Fledgling is owned by three of the biggest names in Hollywood. If they make *The Lobby* and it doesn't sell, you'll be blacklisted."

"Thanks for the vote of confidence."

"It's a heartless business."

The food arrives and I discover he's ordered tiny birds for me. Quail, perhaps. Or squab. Surely he realizes no woman wants to pick at little bones on a date.

"There's no meat on these sparrows," I say, eyeing his steak.

"Good, then you'll have energy later. I've got plans for you."

Angry at his lack of support, I say, "Your hotel had better not figure into these plans."

"You always come back to my hotel."

"Well, don't assume I will this time."

"Roxanne, I just don't want you to be disappointed if it doesn't work out with Hank. Directors are unpredictable." He slices off a generous piece of his steak, slides it onto my plate and smiles.

"You can't buy my affections with a piece of beef," I say, tucking into it eagerly.

"I know that," he says, running a finger lightly up my bare arm until every hair stands on end. "But I'm hoping that booking your favorite hotel suite might make a good impression."

I pause with my fork in the air. "The one with the Philippe Starck tub for two?"

He nods. "I also picked up the milk-and-honey bubble bath you love."

"You remembered my favorite bubble bath?"

"Of course. I make it my business to remember all of your favorite things."

My resolve melts like butter in a hot pan and we're both flirting shamelessly when the restaurant's manager comes over. A tall, ethereal-looking blonde, she falls promptly under Miguel's spell. It happens all the time, but few women are as well-informed about the La Rioja region as this one. It is some minutes before they remember my presence.

Miguel shrugs at me as the manager retreats. "Don't be jealous, Roxanne. I came with you and I'm leaving with you."

"Invite the blonde back to your hotel instead," I say, standing to leave. "She looks like she could survive on sparrows."

★ ★ ★

"Querida," Miguel pleads, "is there nothing I can say to make you change your mind?"

"Not this time, Miguel." Disentangling myself from his arms, I reach for the phone beside the bed. "Room service? A bottle of your best Canadian chardonnay, please."

Chapter 5

It's a beautiful morning and red and yellow leaves are blowing in the street as I drive toward the lakeshore. I won't have much opportunity to enjoy it, however, because we're shooting in and around a sewage plant today. Besides, it's colder than it looks; I stuffed most of my winter gear into the trunk, including a parka.

Pulling into the crew parking lot, I turn the stereo down. I've been blasting it to drown out the voice in my head. Miguel's comments about Hank have been playing on a continuous loop since I saw him and I have an uneasy feeling that I've made a deal with the devil. The truth is, Start Big And Stay Big doesn't really reflect who I am. I'm more of a "keep a low profile and hope that they recognize my talent" sort of girl, but that approach doesn't go far in an industry that embraces publicity and self-promotion.

Since I can't afford to pass up even the smallest chance to move ahead, I must prove to myself and everyone else that I've got what it takes to be a cinematographer. Hank may be slimy, but surely he wouldn't upgrade me on the first movie he produces if he thought I wasn't up to the job? For the next ten weeks, I'll work hard and study Damon's expert lighting. I can pick up some pointers on how he adapts his techniques to suit Hank's unique style, which would give me a real edge.

If I'm going to impress Hank, though, I'll have to improve my attitude about *Illegal Alien*. Sure, it's a stupid movie and the first week of shooting was grim, but this week can be different. No more coasting when Hank's not looking. No daydreaming on set, no slacking off, no distracting idle chitchat. I will be on time; all shots will be sharp; I will anticipate every filming need. What's more, I'll make it all look effortless. I am *Super Focus Puller*, always the consummate professional. When my big break arrives, no one will question my merit.

The Creature steps out of his trailer on time and approaches set briskly on all fours. Sensing all eyes upon him, he capers into the parking lot, hits an ice patch and splays himself out with a rubbery thud.

I join the stampede to his side. At the count of three, we hoist him upright and follow him, arms outstretched, to the director's chair that reads Creature/Burk.

Hank catches my eye to make sure I'm appreciating the scene before walking over to the disgruntled alien.

"Look, we'll get some treads for the costume," he says soothingly, offering Burk a coffee.

Burk rejects it. "Clearly you don't share my vision for this character. I see him—*it*—as bipedal."

"Believe me, Burk, the Alien will be fearsome on all fours. Besides, how many roles let you explore your feral side?"

While Hank sweet-talks Burk, I double check Gilda. Attention To Detail is my other new motto.

Damon appears at my side and hands me a coffee. Still miffed that he sided with Alana last week, I consider refusing it. After all, if he were truly contrite, he'd have made me a cappuccino. Still, there's no sense in wasting good caffeine, I decide. Caffeine will make me alert and an alert focus puller is a super focus puller.

"Thanks," I say, frostily.

"I was hoping for a thaw by now."

"If it's sunshine you're after, call your new friend Alana."

"Oh, lighten up, Rox. You're twice the cameraperson Alana is, and you know it. She just has the connections. It's an accident of birth."

"You fell for her whole 'nice girl' routine."

"I'm not the first guy to get sidetracked by a low-cut dress," he says, grinning. "But I brought you a little gift."

"I don't want it."

"Then you'll be sorry…I feel a midnight exterior scene coming on."

I see the sense in accepting the set of hand warmers he offers. One can't take a snit too far on a cold day.

Keisha heads toward us with a tray of scones. "Move or bleed!" she yells, causing the gaffer and his electricians to scatter. Keisha's cheerful yet forthright nature has made her my best—and only female—pal on set.

"What's the news from the rumor mill?" I ask. As the person who keeps people nourished between meals, Keisha has access to every crew member, equipment trailer and cast Winnebago. She gets even more dirt than Genevieve.

"Slow news day so far, but things could get interesting." She lifts her chin to indicate something behind me.

I turn to see a group of fourteenth-century monks on unicycles riding around in the parking lot, one of whom has a lemur on his shoulder. The "monks" are actually stuntmen brought on for today's nightmare sequence. If there's a given in showbiz, it's that stuntmen goof around. Now they surround Creature, cycling around him in increasingly tight circles. Removing his head, Burk asks for a ride. Much to my disappointment, the stunt monks decline. I guess Burk's megastar insurance doesn't cover unicycles.

As Burk walks past us to the hair-and-makeup trailer, I notice that the sweat trickling down the back of his neck is brown.

"Did you see that?" I ask Keisha. "The man doesn't wash."

"It's not dirt," she says. "It's runoff from the spray-on hair product he uses to hide his bald spot. I noticed the can in his trailer."

Ah, Good Looking Hair—GLH, for short. The late-night infomercials never mention it's not waterproof.

The first nightmare sequence is set in a dark tunnel in the plant's basement. The monks are wearing fright masks and the set is lit only by torches. A couple of live boa constrictors hang from the rafters and the lemur is perched on a monk's shoulder.

Noticing a bulky alien crouching in the shadows, I ask Gizmo, "Why is Burk on set so early?"

"He's studying the lemur, obviously." The *duh* is silent.

After a few takes, Damon asks me to move the camera to the spot where Burk happens to be standing, rubber head tucked under one tentacle.

"Excuse me, Mr. Ryan," I say. He doesn't respond or make the slightest effort to move, so I haul the heavy equipment around him and set up the camera close by.

Sensing his eyes on me, I turn to find him giving me a tight-lipped smile. Considering he's barely acknowledged me before, I take this as a positive sign. Maybe watching me struggle with Gilda has enlightened him about how hard I work for this production. Or maybe he's seen the dailies and realizes that even without marks I've been keeping him in focus. A lot of actors need proof that you're competent before deciding you're okay.

Returning his smile, I ask, "How's it going?"

"It would be going a helluva lot better if you'd get your fat foot off my tail, Focus Girl."

I look down to see that I am indeed standing on the slimy green tip of his tail. "I'm so sorry, I thought it was an electrical cable."

Ignoring my apology, he shuffles over to the animal trainer to interrogate her about typical lemur behavior.

Hank notices that Burk is holding a stick he took from the lemur earlier. "Put the stick down, Creature," he says.

"I need it to help me stay in character." Burk's voice is barely audible through the mask.

"You can't walk on all fours with a stick in one claw. Give it up."

"No." It's muffled, but he sounds annoyed.

"Roxanne, get the stick," Hank directs me. He and Damon exchange smiles.

I look at him incredulously. How is it that I—the only woman on set at the moment—must engage in a tug-of-war with a 270-pound alien? It's certainly not a job for Super Focus Puller. But as one must look obliging at all times, I approach the Creature.

He turns to face me and it sounds like he's snarling behind the mask. The costume doesn't feature opposable thumbs, however, and I'm able to retrieve the stick after a brief tussle.

"I'll give it back to you after the scene," I promise him.

"Fuck you, Focus Girl," the Creature says.

That sort of talk penetrates rubber quite well.

Shawna arrives on set with a pronounced limp. "I sprained my ankle during the blocking this morning," she says. "But don't worry—I'm a pro and the show must go on."

Shawna definitely wasn't limping when she left set earlier. In fact, she jumped on Burk's back for a piggyback ride, nearly causing his second collapse of the day.

I take a moment to consider my professionalism, then shrug. "Ten bucks says Martini tripped over a vodka bottle in her trailer," I challenge Damon, who can never resist a bet.

"You're on. I say she fell down the stairs after makeup."

Within minutes, there's a crew-wide *What Really Happened to Martini* pool. When we uncover the real story—and the truth always comes out—the person whose explanation is closest wins the pool.

"Remember when I won $300 on that rock video for figuring out which extra was clocking overtime in the lead singer's trailer?"

"Yeah, I remember," Damon says, "you wasted it on a stupid spa day."

"That pool is mine," I boast. "I'm booking a facial and manicure now."

A consummate professional must always look her best.

"Someone get me a viewfinder!" Hank yells.

I abandon the camera and rush over to him. Normally I'd send Christian, but I have an ulterior motive: Hank will know how Shawna sprained her ankle and I want to collect on the bet. "Poor Shawna," I say, oozing sincerity. "How terrible about her accident."

"I already know about the pool, Roxanne."

"Did you throw in your ten bucks?"

"Of course not. It wouldn't be appropriate for the director," he says. Eyes twinkling, he adds, "I used a proxy."

"So, what really happened?"

"You didn't hear it from me, but she tripped over an empty bottle in her trailer."

"*Yes!* The pot's up to $220. I can get a facial, a manicure *and* a pedicure."

"Someone will have to buy you a nice dinner afterward. It would be a shame to let a manicure go to waste."

Oh-oh, walked right into that one. "What's really a shame is that I never have any energy to go out after a long week of shooting," I babble while backing away.

He turns businesslike immediately. "Tell Damon I've changed my mind about the next scene. Let's shoot it outside."

"Uh, sure. It will take close to an hour to move the equipment."

"You've got ten minutes. Just enough time for me to have a cup of tea."

From now on, I'll stick to impressing Hank from afar.

CLOSE ON two monogrammed slippers on an ottoman before a fire.

WIDEN OUT to reveal F. C. Kugelman in his sunny office, laptop resting on the lap of his maroon silk smoking jacket. Frost sparkles on the windows, but F.C. is comfortable in a leather club chair, his golden retriever at his feet. He cracks his knuckles before typing,

It was a warm summer afternoon.

And poof, Roxanne is standing beside the camera in shorts, a T-shirt and sunglasses.

"No," says F.C., back in the toasty den. "Too predictable."

    It was a gray, breezy summer after-
    noon.

Roxanne runs to the camera truck to grab a sweater.

"Hmm…" grumbles F.C., "summer isn't right for this story. Late autumn would work. It's so much bleaker. Yeah, bleak is arty. They give away Oscars for bleak."

    It was a bleak afternoon in late
    November.

Roxanne turns back and fetches a Gore-Tex coat.

"Nighttime would be moodier," F.C. decides.

    It was a cold, bleak night in No-
    vember.

Roxanne shivers in the darkness and pulls on mittens and a headband.

"It still needs some atmosphere," F.C. says, sipping a steam-ing cup of tea.

    It was a bleak, foggy night in late
    November.

Scowling, Roxanne grabs a flashlight and roots through her weather bag to find a towel to throw over the camera.

"Okay, F.C., now you're rolling. Onwards…"

A light drizzle fell.

Roxanne replaces the towel with a clear plastic cover.

"Not harsh enough," says F.C., lighting a cigar. "It's gotta be grim. Critics love grim—it turns a movie into a film."

The bitter winds approached gale force as the hurricane slammed into the shore.

Roxanne waddles off the camera truck wearing three layers of long underwear under her yellow rain gear and a balaclava on her head. She wraps the camera in saran and attaches a spray deflector to the lens before covering everything with two plastic rain covers. The temperature is hovering at the freezing mark as the director announces a full rehearsal with wind and rain. The rain towers spew great gushes of water in every direction while huge fans with airplane engines bend every tree within a thirty-foot radius. The special-effects coordinator cranks up a hose, sending a stream of ice-cold water over Roxanne's head. When she turns to protest, the spray hits her square in the face. Her cursing is drowned out by the wind machines.

Rain teems down as we follow Detective Penny's point of view chasing the Alien into the parking lot.

★ ★ ★

Converting the camera into handheld mode, Roxanne slides hand warmers into her dripping mittens to bring sensation back to her frozen fingers. "Hey, it could be worse," she says to Christian, her assistant. "We don't have to haul the equipment too far!"

But F.C. is unsatisfied. "Boring, boring, boring! It needs something more...rural."

```
Rain teems down as we follow Detec-
tive Penny's point of view chasing
the Alien into the marsh.
```

Roxanne staggers through mud while hauling the camera equipment into the swamp.

F.C. nods at the screen. "Shaping up nicely, but just one more thing..."

```
Sleet slashes down as we follow De-
tective Penny's point of view chas-
ing the Alien into the marsh.
```

Christian hands Roxanne a screwdriver and she begins to chip away at the ice that is building up on the camera cover. "One day," she tells him through chattering teeth, "I'm gonna meet the guy who writes this crap and tell him what I think about his work."

Through a great act of will, she forces herself to stop shivering long enough to peel the rigid covers off the camera, dry her hands, reload the camera with stiff fingers and cover it again for another take. Hank is complaining about how long this "simple reload" is taking, but his words are muffled by the walls of the heated tent, where he and the actors reside in comfort.

Damon yells for his light meters. Finishing the reload, Roxanne grabs the meters and spins away from the camera. She trips over a slippery root and crashes to her knees.

Stubbing out his cigar, F.C. sits back and smiles. "F.C., you're a genius! Make room on your mantelpiece."

Chapter 6

EXTREME CLOSE-UP on a pair of dirty hands winding a tensor bandage around a bruised knee.

WIDEN OUT TO REVEAL ROXANNE, pant leg over her knee, securing tiny metal clasps.

"Stop fidgeting," says Damon, who is sitting beside me on the dolly. "I'm trying to show Hank a steady frame here." He's looking through the camera with his right eye, but manages to glare at me with the left.

I roll down my pant leg and stick my tongue out at the side of his head. "Don't thank me for saving your light meters instead of bracing my fall yesterday," I say. "It was my pleasure, and the swelling will go down eventually." He hops off the dolly and crosses the warehouse floor to speak to Hank. I turn to Gizmo. "I guess he's jealous because I won the *What Really Happened to Martini* kitty. That's three pools in a row."

"Quit bragging," Gizmo says.

"I'm not bragging. My intuition isn't a skill, it's a God-given gift."

Keisha, Seductress of the Craft Truck, arrives with a tray of steaming breakfast burritos. My hand hesitates over the tray. I ate a perfectly healthy bowl of bran flakes not two hours ago. I do not need a burrito. This is how my weight creeps up over the course of a film. As the hours get longer, sleep deprivation begins to trump willpower.

"Just say no, Rox," Gizmo says, helping himself to a couple of burritos. "You really packed it on when we shot *Seattle.*"

I look pointedly at the beach ball he's seemingly swallowed. "Whereas you've kept your boyish figure."

He tosses one burrito back, scowling.

Keisha tactfully intervenes. "How's the knee?"

"Chances of survival are high, *thanks* for asking." The emphasis is for Gizmo.

Shawna makes a dramatic entrance on crutches. She raises one in a theatrical flourish and knocks over half a dozen director's chairs. "Lez shoot, everybody!" she bellows. "It doezunt matter that I'm sufferin, I'm a profeshnal. Rrrrrrroll it!"

Keisha whispers, "Dr. Bradshaw came by to check Shawna's ankle."

Dr. Bradshaw, better known as Dr. Feelgood, is on the speed dial of every Toronto production office. Rest and recovery aren't an option in this business, so when a director, producer or actor takes ill, Dr. Feelgood races to set with his magic pillbox. The perk doesn't extend to focus puller level.

Shawna's miracle cure has left her irritable. "Whataya mean, they're not ready for me?" she bawls into the production assistant's face. "I'm the *star* of thiz film. I decide when I'm ready and I'm ready now!"

Flinging her crutches aside, she stands and shrugs off a fleece robe to reveal massive breasts, restrained only by the lacy, mauve brassiere of her "superhero" costume. It's an impressive sight, but unlike my intuition, not a God-given gift. I don't even need to see how she performs on the three-part *Reality Chest* test to know that Shawna paid for those.

Test 1: Is there normal cleavage?

Shawna slaps away the production assistant's hands and adjusts her bra to display her assets to maximum effect. Despite recent advances in lingerie technology, there's a chasm between them the size of the Grand Canyon.

Status: Failed.

Test 2: Do they move?

Shawna shoves the production assistant into the director's chair and runs toward the camera equipment. Her breasts are nearly inert.

Status: Failed.

Test 3: Are they squeezable?

Damon sprints across the warehouse on an intercept course, cutting Shawna off just a foot from the camera. She throws an arm around his shoulder and a mauve torpedo drops into his flailing hand. Damon jerks away, muttering, "Sorry, sorry."

Shawna doesn't seem to notice. "I'm ready fer my cloze up, Mr. Cameraman."

Having already zoomed in far closer than he meant to, Damon turns an even deeper shade of plum.

Status: Undetermined.

As someone who is naturally well-endowed, I can't understand why women would want to augment their bustlines. I was the first girl in grade five to need a bra and I've been self-conscious about my chest ever since. In high school, I was desperately jealous of the sporty A-cup girls who could wear the best sundresses, bathing suits and camisole tops. Running around the track became a torment because the guys lined up along the bleachers to watch. Thus began a long search for a bra that would minimize and restrain without rendering me totally shapeless. My current discovery is a sturdy, ugly sports bra that prevents full expansion of the lungs. I wear it to work every day. It may be a coincidence, but I find I'm asked to do more running on set than anyone else on the crew.

Not that anyone is thinking of my bustline today. All eyes are on Shawna's, and no one is complaining about authenticity. In my experience, guys don't have a problem with breast implants. As Gizmo the Pig so aptly puts it, "Any boob is a good boob, especially if it's a *big* boob." Even Damon, who maintains that he disapproves of surgery-happy "Frankenstars," has an expression of goofy appreciation.

Steadying Shawna with an arm around her bare shoulders, he calls, "Rox, get Ms. Glass a chair. The poor woman is in pain."

It's Zara's first sex scene with an alien and she simply isn't in the mood. Again.

Scene 81 has become the crew's favorite joke. In it, Sergeant Trowbridge makes love to the Alien while he's in his FBI agent form. He morphs into the Creature mid-act and she is so caught up in the moment that she doesn't even notice.

Hank tried to shoot the scene on the first day, but it keeps getting bumped. Each day the carpenters build the set wherever we're shooting. Each day, Damon lights it. And each day, Zara comes up with another excuse to refuse. First she said the bed wasn't right and demanded an upgrade to the $10,000 custom-made, stainless-steel sleigh bed. Then she said the sheets were too scratchy and requested 500 thread count, Italian cotton sheets. Next the nightstand had to be replaced because it was too low; this week, it was too high. And still Goldilocks has a headache.

It doesn't help that Burk is creepily enthusiastic.

While Damon is lighting the set, I indulge in an on-set ritual: checking voice mail. Working on a film set is so isolating that most of us are voice mail addicts. We can't receive calls on set, because one ill-timed ring would be disastrous, but the moment a director yells cut, all hands are groping for that outside lifeline.

My secret belief is that I am one voice mail away from greatness. Each time I punch in the numbers, I get the same fizz of excitement, hoping that there will be a message about *The Lobby.* Instead, I hear a computerized voice telling me over and over that I have no new messages.

Today, I don't even get that: my cell phone battery is dead. Hank is in the same boat and has commandeered the production phone. Since he's standing between me and the message that will change my life, I dare to approach.

"Of course you can borrow the phone, darling," he says, placing it in my hand and folding his around mine.

I pry my fingers out of his sweaty palm, one by one. "I'll need those to dial."

Giving me the phone, he steps behind me and starts rubbing my shoulders. The massage is another set ritual. It's a bonding exercise that reassures us that we have support in this odd, artificial world. After all, for the next ten weeks, these people will seem closer to me even than Libby because we're sharing the same strange adventure.

Movie people are a lot like circus people: we put up our tents, build our own community, develop close friendships and when our work is done, move on. Many of my friends are film technicians whom I see every day for three-month intervals. During this time, we often socialize on our downtime as well. Who else is available at 4:00 a.m.? When the show wraps, we go our separate ways and the phone calls become fewer as we get caught up in the next film and next crew. Down the road, another film will reunite us and our friendship will simply pick up where it left off. This onagain, off-again approach doesn't fly with friends outside of the film "tent."

Massaging one's colleagues probably doesn't fly in the real world either, but it's a ritual I particularly enjoy. Still, I know better than to court this sort of favor from Hank. Keeping the phone, I jump quickly out of reach.

"Roxanne, tell me where you'd set the camera for this master." Hank's voice is deceptively casual, as if this were a normal request of a focus puller.

It isn't. Setting the master is something that the director and cinematographer decide and I would be overstepping to make that call. The master shot is like the blueprint for the scene. It establishes the geography of the set and the position of the actors. Every shot in the scene corresponds to the master.

"Let me get Damon," I say. At the moment, he's across the set with Zara.

"I make the ultimate decisions around here," Hank says, "and I'm asking for your opinion."

I catch Damon's eye and beckon, but he shakes his head and continues to adjust a light over Zara. The Creature waltzes by in full costume, flops onto the bed and arranges his tail suggestively between his legs. Then he lifts the head off the costume to suck on a fat cigar. Zara flounces off the bedroom set in disgust.

Hank is missing all this because he is staring at me, silently pressuring me to respond.

Finally I say, "Damon would want to shoot over top of the action to see it all."

"I didn't ask for Damon's opinion, I asked for yours. You're the one who wants to be my cinematographer in Morocco."

Though reluctant to step on Damon's toes, I want Hank to know I'm capable of setting up a master shot. "If it were really up to me, I'd set a semicircular piece of dolly track around the bed and move the camera back and forth very slowly, allowing the actors to block each other from time to time. It would give the scene a voyeuristic feel."

Hank raises his eyebrows, seemingly impressed, and turns to call Damon, who is now towing Zara back to the bedroom set.

"You'd better have a chat with Burk or we're not going to get this scene," Damon tells Hank. "Zara is ready to walk out."

Hank dismisses this. "She isn't getting any younger and she's nervous about the nudity. All she needs is some reassurance from her director."

"It's more than that."

"When I want a woman to take her clothes off, I never have to ask twice," Hank says, winking blatantly at me. "Roxanne, tell Gizmo to set up the circular track. I like your idea for the master shot."

Throwing me a savage look over his shoulder, Damon follows Hank to the bedroom set. Zara appears to be immune to Hank's powers of persuasion, because she gathers her negligee close to her throat and storms off the set. Hank watches her go with an expression of comical surprise on his face.

Seizing the opportunity, I switch on the production phone and call my home voice mail. Nothing. Not even from Miguel, who is back in L.A.

Damon snatches the phone out of my hands. "I'm ready for the camera."

"It's built and standing by," I say. Then I jokingly add, "I'm allowed to check my messages, you know. I negotiated a special clause in my contract."

"You mean the contract that says 'focus puller' at the top?"

"What do you mean?" But I know what he means.

"I mean it doesn't say 'cinematographer.' In case you've forgotten, I set up the shots. You just keep them sharp."

Before I can defend myself, the first assistant director yells, "We're dropping Scene 81 for today, people."

Damon fires a parting shot. "Next time, don't distract Hank with idle chitchat when there's a crisis with the actors."

Shawna's liver is still earning danger pay, but having lost Scene 81 again, Hank is determined to nail the fight sequence.

In superhero guise, Shawna is to shoot down three stories from the catwalk on a guide wire. We filmed the wide shots with a stunt double, but we need a close-up of Shawna dropping the final ten feet. It's straightforward: the stuntmen will lower her gently to the floor, she'll find her balance, release herself from the harness and step out of the shot.

They strap her into the harness and hoist her into the air.
We roll sound.

We roll cameras.

"And...ACTION!"

The stunt guys pull on the guide wire and lower Shawna
into frame. Her feet touch the ground, but she doesn't make
any attempt to stand.

The mike picks up a muffled snore.

Several of us hurry over to help the stunt coordinator
but I reach them first. He unhooks Shawna and tries to support her, but she's so limp that she slides out of his hands.
Her arm catches my tool belt and knocks me off balance.

When we hit the mat together, Shawna's bra pops open.
She awakens with a snort. "What the—?"

I scramble to my feet and bolt away, taking no comfort
whatsoever from the fact that I've just contributed to some
interesting fantasies among the crew.

It's the kind of story that would usually have me on the
phone to Libby, but today I am too disheartened. The wheels
of my career are spinning wildly and shooting a drunk on
a wire isn't going to give me the traction I need to make it
to the Oscars.

In the camera truck at wrap, I use Christian's phone to
check my voice mail.

BEEP— "Hi, Roxanne, Andy Holmes from Video
Link. I'm directing an infomercial next weekend. It's
just a couple of days' work and the pay is grim, but I
thought you might do it for the experience as a cinematographer. I'm calling a few people, but you're first
on my list. If you're interested, call me."

★ ★ ★

My spirits soar. I'd love to get some real cinematography experience under my belt. This is where the rubber hits the road!

Pressing Five for the time stamp, I discover that Andy called nine hours ago. With Damon in a snit, I didn't dare check again before now.

> BEEP— "Andy Holmes again. I didn't hear from you so I called the next person on my list. She dropped by this afternoon and the producers loved her. Maybe you've worked with her—Alana Speir. Anyway, maybe next time."

Chapter 7

The camera truck is still locked up tight when I arrive the following day. Christian is leaning nearby.

"If you want coffee, you'll have to hit The Donut Hole drive-through," he says, looking up from his newspaper. "Transport isn't even close to having the unit parked." He summarizes the problem with an eloquent roll of the eyes: the Winnebago Wars are raging again.

For celebrities, the Winnebago is the six-wheel equivalent to a penis: the bigger the better. The star with highest billing on the production has the Winnie of consequence. On *Illegal Alien,* that means Zara gets the biggest trailer and it's parked closest to the set. Shawna gets a slightly smaller, slightly older Winnebago and that is parked a little farther away. Burk's is smaller and older still. And so it goes down the line to day players, a notch above extras, who get a cubbyhole on the honey wagon (the truck with the bathrooms on it).

Because of her ankle injury, Shawna has usurped the primo parking spot for the past couple of days. Zara initially let it slide because the transport guys managed to park the

Winnies an equal distance from set. This morning, Christian explains, they parked Shawna's closer to set because Zara's new trailer is too wide for the main street.

I'm incredulous. "Another new trailer?"

"Why so surprised?" he asks. "Anyone could see the first two defied the rules of feng shui."

"I have the same complaint about the camera truck," I say. "The darkroom is in the romance sector."

Christian snorts. "You're probably onto something there. Damon and Genevieve just broke up."

"They did?" How could I have missed this news? Keisha is slipping.

"I heard it was mutual, but it's gonna be rough for the boss, giving up regular sex with a babe and becoming reacquainted with Mr. Hand."

There are plenty of smart remarks I could make, but all of them would sound humorless to the male ear.

Christian is burbling with excitement when I return to set with trays of coffee. "Guess what? I just got asked to shoot a rock video for the Rushing Muses. Their bass player is one of the daily grips."

"Shoot?" I try not to look as shocked as I feel. "I didn't know you were already getting jobs as a cinematographer."

"Just freebies and it's only my third video. I'm starting small to see how it goes."

Christian is twenty-five and passes for fifteen. Hell, there's a Game Boy sticking out of his coat pocket. How could he possibly have more experience than I have?

Echoing Miguel, I say, "You want to learn to walk before you run."

"Exactly. I'm sure you did the same thing when you were starting out."

"It's the safest approach," I agree, beating a hasty retreat before he can inquire further. I'm not eager to share the details of my early efforts, namely short videos for the amusement of friends and family. It's a stretch to call it cinematography, but there are dozens of them lined up on my bookshelves at home. I gave this up when my mother died. With my first and best audience gone, what was the point? The creative spirit eventually started to stir again, but by then my career in the camera department was flourishing and I didn't have time to play with my camcorder.

Anxiety wraps its clammy arms around me. I haven't looked through a viewfinder of my own in years, yet I'm angling to shoot Hank's film in Morocco. Even Christian is taking the cautious approach to climbing the camera ranks. How many times do I have to hear the same message before it actually sinks in?

The camera-truck driver calls after me, "I'll have you parked in 10, Rox."

That gives me about nine minutes to become more legitimate. I reach for my cell and call Andy Holmes to apologize for not getting back to him about the job Alana stole, er, sort of. He offers to recommend me to a colleague who's recruiting for a music video. Since the Video Link offices aren't far from where we're shooting, I agree to come for an interview during my lunch hour today.

I study my interview outfit regretfully. As usual, I'm wearing a "set sweater." I have half a dozen of them, all in shades of dark. Not only do they hide the dirt, they prevent Super Focus Puller from causing reflections when shooting into glass or other shiny surfaces. Each sweater has a hole in exactly the same spot on my midriff where Gilda's hooks continuously catch. The knee of my faded jeans has worn through from kneeling and my work boots are scuffed. I have nicer clothes, but I don't wear them to set for fear of ruining them. Instead, I wait until I'm tired of them before relegating them to work wear. This means I spend eighty percent of my life in clothes I dislike.

Still, I'm having a good-hair day. I may not exert myself often, but I am well aware of the power of a good blowout. Mine is nearly perfect, with just enough bounce and a fetching flip.

I'll walk into the interview, toss my head around long enough to distract the director from the fact that I don't have a reel and walk out with the job.

Nothing to it.

I cross my arms in front of my chest. "I'm not wearing it."

Barring my path, Gizmo crosses his arms in a mirror image. "You're wearing it."

"I'm not, and you can't make me."

"I *can* make you, actually," he says. "I won't give the go-ahead to shoot until you put it on."

We're filming a shoot-out in a run-down building in an old distillery. Detective Penny will jump out, guns ablazing, as she corners the Alien in a dirty basement. Blazing guns mean special effects and special effects mean protective gear.

"I've got earplugs and I'll be behind the plywood shield."

Gizmo is having none of it. "You need the helmet and full ear protection. Crap will be flying all over once the explosions go off."

"Look, it's just that—"

"—you want to keep your hair nice. I get it."

I muster righteous indignation. "This is not about my hair, it's about claustrophobia. I have panic attacks when I pull down the visor."

"Claustrophobia? I'm just hearing about it now?"

"I'm in therapy and finally able to admit it."

"Look, you can either tell Hank all about your break-through, or you can put the damn helmet on so we can stay on schedule for a change."

Sulking, I pull the helmet over my head and add the enor-mous, hair-crushing earmuffs. Generally I'm all for wearing protective gear, but I was counting on my hair to support me in the interview this afternoon. Now I'll have nothing to fall back on but my sparkling personality.

Gizmo gives the first assistant director the thumbs-up and the latter raises the megaphone: "Clear out if you don't need to be on the set, people. We're going hot on special effects. Let's have more atmosphere smoke!" Just as we're about to roll the camera, the AD yells, "Hold it! Who the hell is that?"

A hundred pairs of eyes follow his gaze across the smoky set to the intruder silhouetted in the bright daylight of the doorway. Something about the way the man holds himself seems familiar. I raise my visor to get a better look.

The AD speaks into his megaphone again, "Sir, could you close the door? You're letting out the smoke."

The man turns and closes the door with his left hand. In his right, he is carrying a briefcase. He says, "I'm looking for Roxanne Hastings."

Obviously, Dad's eyes haven't adjusted to the light, because I'm standing directly in his line of vision.

A hundred pairs of eyes shift to me as I remove the safety helmet and run to my father's side. "What are you doing here? Is something wrong?"

I lower my voice, knowing that a hundred pairs of ears are tuning in to the discussion. It's not every day that film-ing is derailed by a family reunion. People will assume it's an emergency and that's on my mind, too.

"Nothing's wrong, dear," Dad says, patting my arm reas-suringly. "I was leaving some contracts with a client when I saw the trucks. Can't a father drop by his daughter's work-place to say hello?"

I study his face for clues. "You've never visited a set in my ten years in the business."

"Sure I have. Remember the time you were shooting on our street in Rosedale?"

I do remember, actually. He dropped my mother off and kept on driving. That was usually the way it worked. Mom loved movies and she never missed a visit to one of my shoots. In fact, there's a signed photo of her with Burt Reynolds on my coffee table at home and she never looked happier. Dad's only interest was work. He holed up in his den while Mom ran off to the theater, art openings or literary readings with her girlfriends, who called themselves the "Cul-ture Widows."

Despite my parents' lack of common interests, they were fond of each other. My father brought my mother a single long-stemmed red rose each week of their married lives. You couldn't count on him to remember dentist appointments or dinner party commitments, but he never forgot that. After Mom was diagnosed, he delivered a fresh rose every day so that she'd never see one wilt.

A few days after Mom died, a widowed neighbor arrived on Dad's doorstep with a casserole. Then it was muffins. Zucchini bread. A fruit pie. When she turned up with an elaborate chocolate layer cake, he cracked. In an impossibly short time, he was dating again.

It's taken me longer to get over a one-night stand.

The Casserole Queen didn't last, but the relationship ig-nited something in my father. For the first time in years, he started going out and there were plenty of women who were eager to go with him. He visited all the places he'd never been with my mother. He bought new clothes, grew a mustache and bought a shiny new sports coupe. As if this weren't distressing enough, his conquests got progressively younger until I recognized a woman from one of my university art classes.

Whether he was "getting on with his life," as he said, or "in freefall," as I said, it was too hard to watch. So now I mostly avoid him until he puts pressure on me. Then I invite him to tag along to something like the *Seattle* premiere where there are lots of people around to distract us from each other. It's relatively pain free and it gets me off the hook for a while.

I take Dad's arm and start pulling him to the sidelines.

The first assistant director says, "Feel free to stay, sir, but you'll have to stand over by the monitors where it's safe."

"What do you mean *where* it's safe? Isn't it safe here, where my daughter is working?"

I squeeze his arm. "Dad."

"Your daughter will be fine. She has protection for the explosion."

"Explosion! What kind of explosion? Do you people have personal injury insurance?"

"*Dad*. It's okay, really. Please go stand by the monitors."

To my surprise, Damon leaves the monitors and comes over to shake my father's hand. He pries my fingers off Dad's arm and leads him to a director's chair.

Sighing with relief, I put my safety helmet and earmuffs back on and turn my attention to the camera. Just before we roll, I glance over at the monitors and notice that Hank is sharing his private supply of organic almonds with my father.

"ROLL CAMERA!"

"CAMERA SPEED!" I yell over the noise of the high-speed camera. I duck behind the shield and hit the dirt. Literally. The floors in the old distillery have never been finished. An hour ago, I had a sound blanket to kneel on, but when Shawna started shivering in her skimpy costume, Damon gallantly draped my blanket around her shoulders.

"Fire in my hole!" Shawna hollers, flinging my blanket to the ground and racing through the cellar in her lacy mauve underwear. Since I have to keep my eyes on the action, I'm obliged to settle for imagining my father's expression. As Shawna runs, she fires her .45-caliber semiautomatic gun at the "bad guys." I can feel each shot vibrating in my chest, and even with the ear protection, the sound seems deafening. Fireball explosions ignite behind Shawna and stuntmen wired with squib hits start falling to the ground. My boots, which protrude from the protective plastic shield, are spattered in movie blood.

By the time Hank calls lunch, the sticky red gel is seeping up the cuffs of my jeans. I fight my way through the stampeding crew to the monitors, where Damon is waiting to tell me that my father had to get back to work.

I'm relieved, because I only have twenty minutes to make myself presentable and drive to Video Link. I give Damon the slip at the honey wagon and start resuscitating my lifeless hair. Despite much back combing and hairspray, I am soon forced to accept that it's a lost cause.

In my next career, I am going to start a mobile spa business, racing around town in a fully equipped van, ministering to grimy wenches in need.

DAY EXTERIOR, TWILIGHT: Video Link's red neon sign is reflected in the glass *of mirrored Oakley sunglasses. We widen out to reveal ROXANNE behind the wheel of her rusty Jeep. A light rain begins to fall as she circles the block in search of a parking space. Her face is bathed in an eerie green light and a squeaky wiper blade sweeps across her face obscuring an expression of panic before we cut to—*

CLOSE-UP OF THE DASHBOARD CLOCK: We see that the glowing digital numbers are casting the green hue and stay on the clock as the number changes. Then we tilt up to Roxanne's face. Her eyes flick to the time. In exactly two minutes, she will be officially late for her job interview. Muttering profanities under her breath, she slips the Jeep into a loading zone half a block from Video Link. The rain is coming down in torrents. She gropes in vain under the seat for an umbrella before leaping out and making a mad dash for the door.

EXTREME WIDE SHOT OF LOBBY: Roxanne catches a glimpse of her reflection in the floor-to-ceiling mirrors and gasps. Water is dripping down her cheeks and off the ends of her limp, stringy hair. Her mascara has pooled in raccoonish circles. We tilt down to capture the dirt and blood at the bottom of her jeans that has congealed into a reddish brown muck. There is camera tape stuck to one thigh. Roxanne plucks off the tape and attempts unsuccessfully to fluff her sodden tresses.

CLOSE-UP ON RECEPTIONIST: A look of disgust spreads across her face as her eyes travel from Roxanne's disheveled hair, past her ratty sweater, down her muddy jeans to the reddish tracks her scuffed running shoes have left on the ivory carpet.

RECEPTIONIST
[curtly]

Couriers report to Security.

ROXANNE

Actually, I have an interview with Steve Eustace. I've come straight from set. A gunfight. With an alien. You know how it is.

RECEPTIONIST

Not really. Have a seat. Er, better yet, would you mind standing on the mat by the door instead?

ROXANNE

Sure, no problem. I'll just lean against the—

RECEPTIONIST

Please don't. Steve will be out shortly. He's running late with his current interview.

EXTREME CLOSE-UP OF GLEAMING BRASS NAME-PLATE: STEVE EUSTACE, DIRECTOR. We hear the muffled sounds of a male and a female voice behind the closed door. Steve laughs.

ZOOM OUT TO REVEAL Roxanne, now perched on the edge of a sofa outside of Steve's office. It looks like she's been there for a while. She has removed her coat and is discretely scraping the dirt out from under jagged nails with a tissue. In the background, the receptionist purses her lips in disapproval.

SWISH PAN TO OFFICE DOOR: Alana Speir steps out with Steve Eustace close on her high heels. Alana's blond hair cascades down her back in the lustrous waves of a 1940s starlet. Her makeup is impeccable, and she is wearing a trendy, yet elegant, winter-white pantsuit with matching leather boots. Her manicured hands clutch a businesslike Coach bag. Racing ahead of Alana to reach her shearling coat, Steve trips over Roxanne's foot and glares at her.

STEVE

Thanks so much for bringing in your reel, Alana. Is 1:00 okay for lunch Friday? I'll book my regular table at North 44.

ALANA

Sure. Looking forward to it.

Alana walks toward the exit and Roxanne stands to introduce herself to Steve. Ignoring her, he steps back into his office, closing the door behind him.

MEDIUM TWO SHOT: Alana turns and notices our heroine for the first time.

ALANA

Roxanne! I didn't see you there, sweetie. Are you here for an interview, too? You'll love Steve. He's so nice. By the way, you have lipstick on your teeth.

CUT TO CLOSE-UP OF ROXANNE'S UPPER LIP SLAMMING DOWN OVER HER TEETH as she watches Alana's retreat in silence. When the elevator doors close behind her, Rox desperately slides a finger into her mouth to wipe her teeth.

IN A WIDE SHOT: We see the look of distaste on Steve's face as he opens his door and notices Roxanne pulling her finger out of her mouth.

STEVE

May I help you?

ROXANNE

I'm Roxanne Hastings. I'm here for an interview.

Tilt to capture Rox trying to discretely wipe her finger on the leg of her jeans before extending her hand to Steve. Steve merely stares at it. Rox lets her hand drop to her side.

STEVE

I guess you'd better come in. Did you bring your reel?

THE CAMERA STAYS IN THE WAITING AREA as the door closes on us. We lock off on the empty room. In less than a minute, the door swings open again and Roxanne exits. Through the open door, we see Steve prop his feet on his desk and reach for the phone.

CLOSE-UP ON Roxanne's disappointed expression as she struggles into her sodden jacket. In the background, we hear Steve's voice asking the receptionist to arrange lunch at North 44. We stay on Roxanne's receding form as she trudges down the hall toward the exit until she is almost invisible.

CRANE THROUGH NEARBY WINDOW AND TILT DOWN TO STREET: Roxanne steps out of the building in a steady downpour and runs over to the empty spot where her Jeep was parked. Her head swivels to the left, the right and back. She sees the flashing lights in the distance. The camera zooms in on the lights and we see a tow truck hauling Roxanne's Jeep away. A second later, Roxanne enters the bottom of our shot, waving her arms and shouting after the tow truck. It continues its journey, Roxanne in full pursuit. As Rox becomes a speck traveling across the screen, we—

FADE OUT.

★ ★ ★

By the time we wrap, I'm too drained to head down to the car pound, so I hail a cab instead. Slumped in the backseat, I check my voice mail. I know full well that Alana has the Video Link job sewn up, but I remain desperately hopeful until I hear it from the horse's mouth.

The first of my three messages is from the horse.

BEEP— "Steve Eustace here. Thanks for coming in today, Roxette, but we've gone with someone else."

The second is from Libby.

BEEP— "Hey, Rox, remember me? That sometime-friend you often call in the middle of the night? Check your e-mail when you get home. I've sent you an outline for *The Counterfeit Wedding* and a couple of sample scenes. Let me know what you think."

BEEP— "Rox, me again. I just noticed the picture in today's paper of you and Miguel at Bistro 990. It's just the back of your head, but your hair looks incredible. Did you get a perm?"

My stomach lurches as if the cab has plunged over a cliff. I lean forward and ask the driver to pull over at a newspaper box.

There, on the entertainment page, is a photo of Miguel staring raptly at a blond woman. Their wineglasses are touching in a toast.

Only a very good friend would see my limp locks in those lustrous waves. On the other hand, Libby quite kindly overlooked what appears to be the start of a bat wing under the blonde's raised arm.

Now, if Alana worked half as hard as she schmoozes, she'd have no reason to be ashamed of those triceps.

Chapter 8

"Hello?"

"*Hola, mi querida.*"

"Who's speaking?"

"Don't be cute, Roxanne."

"Sorry, *número incorrecto. Adiós.*"

"*¡Maldígalo!* Don't hang up, it's Miguel!"

"I knew a Miguel once, but we haven't spoken in ages. I believe he's in L.A., or maybe New York. Or maybe he's moved back to España."

"I saw you just last month. You know I've been up to my eye sockets casting for my next picture."

"I noticed who you cast for your dinner date at Bistro 990," I say. "There was a time when you called me first when you were in Toronto."

"You are the first person I called. Martin Speir called *me* in New York and arranged dinner for Thursday night. I had no idea his daughter would be joining us."

"Eye*balls.*"

"What?"

"The expression is 'up to your eyeballs,' not eye *sockets.*"

"So you forgive me."

"Says who?"

"If you are making the effort to correct me, you must be over it."

"That's a big assumption."

"*Querida,* this hotel is lonely without you. Get into your Jeep and come over."

"I can't, it got towed. How about you climb into your up-scale rental car and drive me to the impound lot so I can spring it?"

"Roxanne, how does this always happen?" he asks, his tone changing swiftly from pleading to exasperation. He's never recovered from my getting his Porsche towed after I (accidentally) parked it in a handicap spot overnight. "You need to pay attention. This means more points against your license."

He knows about the speeding tickets, too. How can I help it? With my hours, I often sleep through my alarm and I have to make up time somewhere.

"Look, if I wanted a lecture, I'd ask my father to take me to the impound lot. Then I wouldn't have to put out afterward."

"Okay, okay, no more lectures. And don't make it sound like such a chore to visit me. You always leave satiated, as I recall."

I consider correcting that to "satisfied," but either way, it's quite true.

Miguel signals the waiter to bring us another bottle of 1994 Ribera del Duero. For the past hour, I have been complaining incessantly about my exorbitant parking ticket, my humiliating interview, my stalled career, my sorry life. The tirade has slowed only long enough to drink most of the wine. Usually I'm fighting Miguel for every mouthful, but tonight he's giving me free rein.

Actually, he's being uncharacteristically sympathetic and supportive. This probably has much to do with the fact that we weren't able to squeeze in a stop at his hotel room between running my errands and dinner. So that's what it takes to earn eight straight hours of his undivided—even cheerful—attention. I've never held out that long before.

Over dinner, Miguel presents a number of convincing arguments about why I'm better off without the Video Link job.

"It's a hack outfit. I've heard that they don't always pay their crew."

As for the director: "Steve Eustace? Never heard of him. Why would you want to work with a nobody?"

And the state of my person during the interview: "Who cares if you had mud on your jeans? It proves you're a hard worker. Fuck him if he can't see that."

And the towing of my car: "I can't imagine why you would park in a loading zone, Roxanne, it's so careless."

Okay, so I was pushing it with that one. Still, I'm more than ready to seduce the man. He's been just the tonic I needed and I can't wait to wrap my arms around his naked body. I'm about to tell him so when he continues, "I really don't understand what you've got against Alana Speir. The way you go on about her, I was expecting a monster. She was perfectly likable."

The warm feelings I had toward him vanish faster than the wine. "Perfectly beautiful, you mean."

"She is beautiful, but also good company and smart."

"Oh, please. Dazzling you with a fresh take on Einstein's theory of relativity, was she?"

"Now, Roxanne, I know she is a thorn in your ass…"

"Thorn in my *side. Pain* in my ass."

"I get your point. She had only flattering things to say about you."

I find that hard to believe. "Really."

"She said that you are one of the best focus pullers in the city and that she learned so much from you it made her climb very short. In fact, she said she had to move quickly because she's too vain to be a focus puller. She's unwilling to sacrifice looking good to do the job."

Miguel chuckles, pleased with himself for remembering all these details.

Since the waiter has arrived with the new bottle of wine, I make an effort to sound genial. "You consider her comments flattering to me?"

"Of course."

"Run that whole conversation back through your reality filter and see if you come to the same conclusion."

The waiter pours a mouthful of wine in each glass. Miguel buries his nose in his, inhaling deeply before sucking the wine through his front teeth and sloshing vigorously. Then he nods approval to the waiter, who tops up our glasses and leaves.

After twirling the wine a while longer, Miguel finally concedes, "Maybe she isn't quite as nice as I thought. But you can't let her bother you so much. It's no secret that she's getting a leg over from Martin. Why won't you let me help you? If you are so convinced that cinematography is your road to directing, I could hook you up with someone who directs at least one commercial a month. He's looking for a regular cinematographer and unlike your Steve What'shis-name, he's respected."

"I appreciate the offer, but I can't sever my relationship

with Damon to work with a stranger a couple of days a month. Besides, I'd be far more comfortable getting a 'leg over' from Damon or Hank. At least they know my worth."

"I don't want those two getting anywhere near your legs."

Again with the jealousy. "You don't call for a month, yet it matters who I'm shooting with?"

"Unless something has changed, Roxanne, you like our relationship this way. 'Mature,' is what you said, and I respected that. If I started calling every day, you'd complain about that, too."

Maybe I'm tipsy, but something about the way he's watching me suggests that if I asked, he might very well start calling every day.

I rearrange my cutlery for a moment before muttering, "I suppose you're right."

Miguel's expression is inscrutable. I can't tell whether he's disappointed, relieved or simply pondering the merits of the wine. Finally he smiles. "Then it is what it is, *querida*. So why don't we finish this bottle and blow up this ice-cream stand?"

"Or we could blow the Popsicle stand."

"That sounds kinky, but I'm willing to try anything tonight."

NIGHT INTERIOR, A SMALL APARTMENT: The couple is naked in the antique bed, an illustrated copy of the Kama Sutra lying open on the floor beside it. The woman curls up beside the man, a pale ghost against his olive skin. The tension of a stressful week has been flushed from her body and she dreams peacefully, comforted by his presence.

CLOSE-UP ON: The slight smile playing across the woman's face. Perhaps in sleep, she is reliving the evening's lovemaking exploits. Suddenly, the bed begins shaking and the woman's eyes pop open.

Miguel tosses restlessly, bouncing from side to side until he is completely tied up in the bedclothes. I clutch the tiny triangle of sheet he has left and try to chase my dream back into my subconscious, but it's no use. I know it was a good dream, so why do I have this vague feeling of unease?

Glancing down, I notice the *Kama Sutra* and the memory comes flooding back.

It started promisingly, with more wine, some dirty talk, the suggestion of adventure. I got brave and pulled out the book. To my surprise, Miguel became uncomfortable. He demanded to know who gave it to me and refused to believe it was Libby. Using my best feminine wiles, I got things moving in the right direction again.

Everything progressed nicely until I tested my Pilates training by attempting the Mallaka position, otherwise known as the Wrestler. At first, Miguel was intrigued, but then he got a cramp in his quadriceps and started bellowing like a wounded buffalo. I massaged it until the knot finally melted away.

That wasn't the only thing that had melted away. Nothing I tried could revive the mood and Miguel rolled away from me, mortified. "This has never happened to me before," he said, before falling asleep.

Bounce, bounce, bounce. Miguel is getting perilously close to the edge of the bed. I could just reach out and... Oops!

I crawl to the side of the bed and peer over to find Miguel looking up at me. "Did you just push me?" he asks incredulously.

"Of course not, you were dreaming." I withdraw quickly

before he sees my lips twitch. While he climbs back into bed, I gather the blankets, clutch them to my chest and roll onto my side with my back to him. Finally, I drift back to sleep.

NIGHT INTERIOR, A SMALL APARTMENT: The couple lies naked in the antique bed. The sound of light snoring fills the room. Despite the proximity of their bodies, there's a gulf between them. The woman has her back to the man. He tosses fitfully, perhaps disturbed even in unconsciousness by his impotence. Rolling onto his side, he takes all of the bedclothes with him.

TIME CUT—A HIGH, WIDE SHOT: The couple asleep. A gust of frosty air wafts the curtains aside. The man sleeps on, swaddled in the down duvet. The woman awakens to find her naked body exposed to the elements.

I yank on the duvet but Miguel's unconscious weight pins it down. He always insists on sleeping with a window open, but he's usually more generous with his body heat. Sliding off the bed, I close the window and grope in the darkness for flannel pajamas and socks. Then I crank the thermostat and jump back into bed with a blanket.

As the morning light filters into the room, the woman thoughtfully examines the man's muscular shoulders, wondering if there's a possibility of resolving some unfinished business. He opens his eyes and stares at her.

"*¡Jesús Cristo,* Roxanne! Are you trying to grow orchids in here?"

"I was getting frostbite from that open window."

"You know I need a cold room to sleep."

"Well, it was as cold as a meat locker in here last night."

Miguel's face flushes with anger. "Is that a crack about my performance?"

"It's a crack about your stealing the blankets."

He throws back the duvet, leaps off the bed and strides down the hall. "I know I was a disappointment," he calls from the bathroom as he turns on the shower, "but if you wore something sexier than those pajamas, a man might be more inspired."

I follow him down the hall and lean on the bathroom counter as he pulls the shower curtain across. "Oh, so it's all my fault?"

"All I'm saying is, this has never happened to me before. You know, you could learn a thing or two from Alana about dressing seductively."

Ouch! "Since I was naked at the time this happened, what you're really saying is that you wish I had Alana's figure."

"I'm talking about sex appeal, not body types, Roxanne. But Alana probably doesn't snore."

I try counting to ten, but when I reach four the compulsion becomes too strong: I lean over and flush the toilet.

"AUGH! *¡Mujer loca!*" A satisfying cloud of steam floats over my *Finding Nemo* shower curtain. "What the hell did you do that for?"

"I read that abrupt changes in temperature open the lymph glands. It should flush out your toxic personality."

I surf out of the bathroom on a wave of Spanish expletives. Back in the bedroom, I slip into yoga pants and a sweatshirt. Then, as the shower curtain scrapes aside, I hastily grab Miguel's briefs and one sock and shove them between the mattress and box spring.

Leaving a trail of wet footprints on the hardwood, he comes into the room with a towel wrapped around his waist.

"Listen to the teapot calling the stove black," he continues, as if there's been no time break. "I may be toxic, but you are vindictive."

He searches through my cluttered bedroom for his clothes, pulling things on as he finds them. There is something gratifying about watching this elegant man stump around dressed only in one black sock and a turtleneck. Eventually, he gives up the search for his underwear and steps into his pants without them. He follows me downstairs and into the kitchen, one bare foot slapping on the tile.

Helping himself to a glass of orange juice from the refrigerator, he asks, "Are you going to make coffee?"

"Why would I make coffee when you're about to leave?"

"My meeting isn't until late this afternoon."

"But you're still leaving."

Miguel puts down his juice and reaches for me. "*Querida*, don't be like this. So we had a little fight. Where I come from, fights are just a good excuse to get the blood pumping before you make up."

I untangle myself from his clutches. "You just told me that you'd find me more attractive if I had a body like a chopstick and clear nasal passages. I don't know when the 'make-up' mood will strike, but it sure as hell won't be this morning."

"Let me take you out for breakfast and tell you how much I love your body. It's so—what's the word?—*Rubenesque*."

Why not kick me in my five-squares-a-day gut and be done with it? I cross over to the front door and hold it open.

He leans against my rickety old bookcase, looking bewildered. How can he be so oblivious to his insults? "I am not leaving until we work this out," he says.

I snatch my purse from the bench beside the door. "Fine. Stay if you want, but you can kiss my Rubensque ass goodbye."

"Don't be silly, you know I love a woman with curves."

I slam the door as hard as I can and run down the stairs. I hear the video cases topple off the bookcase and crash to the floor. Judging by the yelp, a sharp corner connected with his head, or perhaps a bare foot.

Still, I am punished in kind as I bang on Crusher's door. In my effort to make a dramatic exit, I didn't take time to put on a coat or shoes and there is a fine layer of frost on the ground. My plan, if one could call it that, was to hide out here until that Spanish worm slithered back to charm school. But Crusher, oddly enough, doesn't appear to be home.

Well, I'll be damned if I hop back upstairs, licked by my own lack of foresight. Instead, I dig the keys to the Jeep out of my purse and run down the driveway, my bare feet sticking to the pavement. I back away with a screech of tires and careen around the corner. Then I pull over to consider my options. Miguel hasn't emerged, so he's obviously planning to wait me out. I'll need to kill a few hours. Croissants and a caffe latte at Patachou would be perfect, except for the matter of footwear. Libby would welcome me, but I'd get a lecture about Miguel and besides, her feet are size twelve. Which leaves my usual last resort.

"Barry's Bagels," Dad answers his cell, yelling above the din of clattering dishes.

"Dad? Where are you?"

"Hi, honey. We're having breakfast down at the farmers' market."

"Who's 'we'?" Dad never went to the farmers' market when Mom was alive.

"I'm with Gayle, my lovely lady friend." There's a giggle in the background. "Why don't you come down and join us? I really want you two to meet."

"Maybe I already know her. I used to babysit a Gayle." I regret the jab almost immediately, but who could blame me? I've just thrown myself out of my own apartment, yet my father's love life flourishes.

Dad asks Gayle to get him a coffee before responding. "Roxanne, that isn't funny." He sounds disappointed. "And for the record, I have never dated anyone younger than you."

"Exactly my age, though." I just can't stop myself.

"Whether you like it or not, this relationship is getting serious. That's what I stopped by your set to tell you the other day."

"Hah! I knew it wasn't just to see me."

"It's been three years since your mother died and you know she would have wanted me to be happy with someone."

My feet may be losing all feeling, but my brain is still functional and I can't deny that he's right. That is exactly what she would have wanted—for both of us—and moreover, that we be happy for each other.

He senses his advantage and presses it. "Why don't you come down here and meet her right now?"

"I can't, Dad, I forgot my shoes."

"There's no need for silly excuses." Now he sounds nettled.

"It's silly, but it's no excuse. I locked myself out of my apartment and Crusher isn't home. I'm calling because I wanted to wait at your place."

"When your mother was alive, you would have just dropped by."

"When Mom was alive, there was no risk of surprising you in your satin boxers as you served breakfast in bed to a stranger." That memory will haunt me for years.

"Look at the bright side, hon, at least I had my shorts on."

★ ★ ★

As I soak in my father's tub, I ponder the situation with Miguel. We've never had a fight like that before, and I can't help wondering if it stems from the exchange at dinner. It never occurred to me that he might want to take our relationship to a more serious level, especially after so long. If he's wanted this to be less casual, he's never said so. In fact, I thought his odd moments of unwarranted jealousy were simply Spanish machismo. I don't expect him to remain celibate between our encounters and he knows that. I just don't want him dating Alana.

I like Miguel very much and I'm attracted to him, but he isn't "the one." The fact that I've never wanted to introduce him to my father, or Libby for that matter, says it all. After a failed long-term relationship and my mother's death, all I wanted was a no-strings-attached affair.

Last year, I decided that I was ready to pursue a serious relationship and set my sights not on Miguel, but Gavin, a carpenter I met at a set auction. Bending my ever-flexible "never date a guy in the business" rule, I put Miguel on hold and launched into a whirlwind romance. I was quite certain that Gavin would become the love of my life. Unfortunately, he had already found the love of his: a beagle named Daisy. I tried to rise above my jealousy, but after months of playing second fiddle to a hound, Gavin's charms began to fade. When Miguel started shooting in Toronto again, I sent Gavin back to the country, where, I trust, he is living happily ever after with Daisy.

I've always believed that I was little more than a convenience for Miguel. I see him when he's in town, or occasionally visit him in New York or L.A. He's said many times that the no-commitment relationship is a man's dream come true. I doubt that he'd be capable of a normal relationship, given that he puts his work above anything or anyone else. On my last birthday, he flew in, took me up north to a luxurious spa resort and promptly returned to the city when an influential producer called.

As usual, I was infuriated—for about a week. Then we settled back into our old groove. I know that if I had to endure his behavior full-time, it would drive me crazy. Someday I will find a man who considers me more important than his career, which will never be the case with Miguel, no matter what he says. I'd have to follow him wherever he worked and my career would always take a back seat to his. It would be a life of luxury, loneliness and boredom.

Climbing out of the tub, I tell myself that there can be more to a relationship than that. I have only to look around this bathroom to see proof of it. There, tucked on a shelf between my father's shaving gear and what I sincerely hope is Gayle's cellulite cream, I see a half-empty bottle of my mother's perfume. Beside it lies an unopened tube of her favorite lipstick. My mother was one of those perfectly turned-out women who would never be caught dead without her lipstick on. And she wasn't, as a matter of fact.

I wipe a spot clear on the mirror and examine my reflection. I look more and more like her every year. I have her bone structure, her features, her skin tone—and sadly, Dad's fine, strawberry-blond hair. I reach for her perfume but think better of it. Smell evokes too many memories and I'm in no mood for flashbacks. Instead, I slide the plastic off the lipstick and try it on. It's the perfect shade, as if my lips had been stained by my favorite cheap merlot. Knowing that Dad will understand, I slip the tube into my pocket as my new talisman. Then I pad into their bedroom and search the back of their closet for some of Mom's things. I dig out an old pair of golf shoes, now somewhat yellowed, and put them on. Another perfect fit.

It may be either the shoes or the lipstick, but something prods me as I am about to lock the front door behind me. I slip back into the house and write a note.

Dad,
I haven't forgotten your birthday.
I'll cook dinner for you and Gayle.
Cocktails at 7:30.
Love, Rox

Crusher can join us. Maybe he'll scare Gayle off.

A small, stubborn part of me hopes that Miguel will still be waiting in my apartment when I get back. As I unlock the door, I tell myself that it will be for the best if he is gone. It's time to make a clean break and if I don't see him, it will be far easier. Patting the lipstick in my pocket, I chant my new rules out loud: *no caving in; no inviting him back here; no racing to his hotel the next time he calls.* I will resist his groveling and I will tell him it's over.

This may prove to be easier than I thought, because there is no sign of him. No note on the counter. No voice mail message.

No more Miguel.

Chapter 9

The Thighmaster is exactly where I left it: in the hall closet under the ice cream maker I haven't yet opened. At my computer, I start squeezing as I check my e-mail. Miguel may like curves but me, not so much.

Libby's outline for *The Counterfeit Wedding* mock-doc has arrived and it makes me laugh out loud—against my will, I might add. I don't want to like it, because I don't want to shoot it.

The phone rings and I launch myself across the room to grab it, dropping the Thighmaster on my foot. Normally, I'd let Miguel plead his case to voice mail, but I'd only have to call him back and speak to him directly. Any etiquette book would insist that a three-year relationship, no matter how casual, requires a voice-to-voice dump.

Crusher's voice makes me irritable instantly. "Where the hell were you this morning?" I ask.

"Whoa, did we get hitched when I was too stoned to notice?"

I can't help laughing. "Okay, that came out the wrong way. I locked myself out and you weren't home."

"You're not the only one who has needs, Roxanne. And speaking of the Spanish fop, I suppose you two have been dueling again?"

"What makes you say that?"

"You're out of breath."

"I'm exercising, not fighting."

"If you're exercising, you've definitely been fighting. You only dust off your crazy contraptions when some guy is on his way into or out of your life."

"Madam Crusher, palmist to the stars."

"If you buy me breakfast, I'll wear my spangled caftan and predict your future with him—again."

Crusher and I have been sitting in Voula's section at the Metropolitan Diner nearly every Sunday for the past six years. We call it breakfast although we rarely arrive before two.

Crusher pulls off his leather jacket to reveal his *Ride With Pride* Cycle Demons T-shirt.

"What, no caftan?" I ask, as Voula hurries over with a pot of coffee and two cups.

"I've got an image to maintain, Hastings. Nice footwear, by the way."

I look down to see that I'm still wearing Mom's tasseled golf shoes.

Crusher grabs a copy of the *National Inquisitor* from the magazine rack and reads aloud, *"Desperate and dumpy has-been action hero gets diet advice that's out of this world."* He holds up the paper to show me the full-page photo of Burk Ryan shaking hands with a so-called alien. Talk about life imitating art.

Voula points her pen at Crusher. "Home fries or beans?"

"Home fries, thanks." Crusher always has the lumberjack breakfast: three eggs over easy, sausages, buttered white toast and two buckwheat pancakes (with corn syrup, not maple). Once in a while, he substitutes beans for the potatoes.

Voula nods and heads back to the grill.

"Wait," I call after her, "I haven't ordered."

She comes back. "French toast, right?"

"How did you know?"

"You always have French toast when your face looks like that." She turns to Crusher. "You gonna find out why she's so miserable?"

Crusher wraps himself in his paper, bored. "Just the usual, Voula."

"That Portuguese actor?"

I say, "He's a Spanish director."

"Same difference," she says. "He's no good. You know what you need?"

"A nice, reliable Greek boy?"

"Exactly. My nephew is full of modern ideas. He might not even care that you're past childbearing."

"I've still got eggs!"

Crusher says, "They're pretty much cooked, Rox. Does your nephew earn a decent living, Voula?"

I hit Crusher's arm. "You're worse than my father."

Once Voula has gone to place our order, I tell Crusher about my week. He half listens to my Alana-bashing as he reads the *Inquisitor,* but when I start dissing Damon, he offers his full attention. Crusher has been my "date" at a few film parties and the two bonded over Damon's longing for a motorcycle and Crusher's interest in art. Today, Crusher defends Damon's recent moodiness as the normal fallout of any breakup, pointing to my current "bitchiness" as proof. He gives

me a knowing glance before raising the newspaper barrier
again.

"Okay, so I'm a little crabby," I admit to the newspaper,
"but it's not about Miguel. I'm worried about my deal with
Hank. What if he promotes me and I don't have what it
takes? I could blow my entire career."

Crusher puts the paper down. "You're exaggerating."

"Not according to Miguel. Since Fledgling is run by
major power brokers, he thinks I could hurt my reputation
by failing in Morocco."

Voula slides our plates in front of us and Crusher gives
his a liberal dusting of salt before squirting a river of catsup
across his eggs.

"Why would you fail?" he asks. "You know you're ready
to move up."

"How could I know? I haven't actually shot anything
before."

"Before Damon hired you, you hadn't pulled focus, either.
You've got to start sometime."

To nourish my angst, I drown my French toast in maple
syrup. "Maybe I should start smaller."

"What happened to Start Big And Stay Big?"

"When I made the pitch to Hank, I didn't realize that
there'd be so much at stake. I suppose I'd feel more confident if I'd landed that Video Link job."

Crusher loads three different food groups onto his fork
and lifts it to his mouth. "People learn more when they teach
themselves to play the game."

"You're talking in fortune cookie, Madam Crusher.
Translation?"

He chews the huge mouthful and swallows. "Make your
own movie."

"I told you, I don't want to blow my entire life's savings

on *The Lobby* if no one will ever see it. How will that advance my career?"

"Make a different film, just for the experience. Something smaller. Something that wouldn't cost a fortune. Something by a local screenwriter."

"You're working for Libby."

"I'm working for me. I don't want breakfast every Sunday ruined by your whining. If you really want experience, make the short film. People like Hank and Damon will respect your chutzpah, if nothing else. Tell Libby to finish the script and then shoot it when *Illegal Alien* wraps."

I almost choke. "Are you crazy? It wraps in eight weeks. I'd need to organize equipment, locations, crew, supplies, film stock. No, it's too much."

Crusher mops his plate clean with a slice of toast. "You told me once that the equipment rental house would lend you gear for free if you needed it."

That's true. If I shot something as soon as *Illegal Alien* wrapped, I could probably roll the gear I need straight onto *The Counterfeit Wedding*. I might be able to talk some of the crew into volunteering their time for me. But even if I got the crew and gear free of charge, I'd still need costumes, props and set decorating, not to mention locations.

Reading my mind, Crusher continues, "Your apartment looks like a perpetual garage sale. I'm sure you can find whatever else you need in your own closets."

I look at him skeptically. "I don't have a wedding dress, for starters."

"Try a secondhand shop."

"What about film?"

"How about that short-end guy?"

Damn him, he actually listens to me. There is indeed a local producer who stores short-ends of film and provides them to small filmmakers free of charge. A short-end refers to the unexposed film left on a roll after a scene is shot. It often amounts to thousands of dollars' worth of film, but most cinematographers won't touch it because it's only good for a minute or two of filming and they'd have to reload after every take.

"I can't do *The Counterfeit Wedding,* Crusher. *Illegal Alien* is all I can handle."

"But you really want to do it, I can tell."

"Think so? You haven't even looked at my palm."

"I'm reading your plate instead." He points a beefy finger at the two intact slices of French toast sitting before me. "You're already planning the movie."

He's right. While he's been shoveling down his breakfast, I've been imagining some of the scenes and the lighting. Making this short would give me experience in both directing and cinematography. If it turns out well, it will silence any critics who might not see me as director material.

Like me, for example.

Further, I'd have a reel to demonstrate my skills to other investors if things fall through with Hank on *The Lobby* front.

It wouldn't cost a bomb to shoot. Although postproduction can be expensive, I might be able to find some shortcuts later. In the meantime, I'm just looking at the cost of a few specialty props, equipment trucks and feeding the crew.

Finally I pick up my fork. "You know, Crusher, if I could somehow get the locations for free, I could probably make *The Counterfeit Wedding* for about five or six grand."

"What kind of locations are we talking about?"

"Wedding planning locations."

"I know a florist in the Distillery district and a caterer in Cabbagetown. I could probably also get Vera Wang in Yorkville. Would that help?"

"Are you kidding? How did you get to be so connected?"

"There's an underground network of motorcycle afi-cionados in this city."

"Don't tell me Vera Wang rides with the Cycle Demons."

"No, but the manager of the Toronto store commis-sioned me to paint a bike last year. Naturally we stay in touch."

"Know anyone who owns a rental truck company? I need two cube vans and a couple of Winnebagos."

"Consider it done."

By the time Voula comes to clear the table, we have a strategy.

"Look at that smile," she says, squeezing my cheek. "Crusher's done it again." She tips her head at him sugges-tively. "Maybe you don't need my nephew after all."

Crusher and I look at each other and burst out laughing. "We'd spontaneously combust on contact," he says.

"Better as friends," I concur, raising my coffee cup to him. "And business partners?"

He clinks his cup against mine. "Right on."

Libby eyes me suspiciously from the passenger seat. "You just passed the Paramount."

"The Paramount isn't the only theater in town, Lib."

"No, but it is the theater showing the Drew Barrymore flick I wanted to see."

Libby is a die-hard blockbuster fan whereas I favor smaller, independent films. Choosing a movie is always a compro-mise, which explains why we usually meet for dinner or drinks instead. Since we're going to be making our very own movie, however, it seems fitting that we should see one to-gether. That way I can point out some of the goals I have for *The Counterfeit Wedding*.

I didn't protest when Libby suggested the romantic comedy. I learn something from every movie I see and I like to stay current. But after I hung up I noticed that *Day for Night,* one of my all-time favorite movies, is playing at the Art Gallery theater. Knowing that Libby would resist, I simply offered to drive—and took her hostage. It's for her own good and she will come to thank me for it.

I learned to appreciate good films from my mother, who took me to see *His Girl Friday* at a drafty old second-run movie house downtown when I was only ten. The moment I saw Cary Grant's face on a thirty-foot screen, I understood. It became a passion we shared.

Libby hasn't had the benefit of this early exposure and groans when I turn onto Dundas Street. "Please tell me we're not going to the Cinematheque."

"You said I could choose, remember?"

"No, you said *I* could choose, and I picked the Drew Barrymore flick."

"I can understand why you're confused. You're still stunned by my buying your screenplay."

"Oh, is there actual money involved? Maybe I should get an agent."

"It's enough to cover tonight's admission, anyway. And I guarantee you'll find this movie interesting. It's classic cinema."

"Like that 'classic' carpet movie you dragged me to last year?"

"*Gabbeh* is such a moving film."

"For the rug-loving crowd, maybe. I can't even pronounce the director's name."

"Mohsen Makhmalbaf is one of Iran's most influential filmmakers. And *Gabbeh* isn't about a rug, but a fable about a woman named after the rug."

Libby fakes a snore. "Tell me tonight's epic is about a man whose spirit has possessed a vacuum cleaner. That might actually be interesting."

"You'd better find this interesting. It's about making a movie."

As we line up for our tickets, I explain to Libby that the term "day for night" refers to shooting in daylight using filters that will make the scene look as if it were shot at night. It's a good way to cheat if you don't have the money for a lot of big lights, but today's sophisticated audiences tend to know when you've been cutting corners. In any case, the title actually refers to the illusion of filmmaking. It focuses on the behind-the-scenes lives of the actors and technicians and it might help Libby understand my own passion. She knows I love film, but that I often find the business of making it infuriating. Maybe François Truffaut can explain the allure better than I can.

"Watch how the camera is always moving," I whisper as the lights in the theater dim. "Truffaut likes to follow his actors, but you have to look for it, because he follows the action so tightly it's almost imperceptible. And watch how he doesn't cut into every scene. I love that."

Libby pulls a crackling bag of Licorice Allsorts from her purse. "Uh-huh."

"You'll see that the camera pans from one character to another or from one room to another, all in one seamless shot."

"Got it." Libby tears open the candy bag. "Licorice?"

Another thought occurs to me. "There's a fantastic black-and-white dream sequence."

Libby shoves a handful of candy in her mouth and mumbles, "If I'm not having a dream sequence of my own, I'll definitely watch out for it."

"It's not boring, I promise. Open your mind."

"Open your wallet. Dinner is on you tonight."

★ ★ ★

We grab the last two seats at Rouge's scarlet acrylic bar.

"I had a manicure with a nail polish about this color once," I say, running my ragged nails across the sleek surface of the bar. "I think it was called Whore Red." Crimson lights flood down on us and I notice my reflection in the mirror behind liquor-lined shelves. "Jesus, whose great idea was that? Being lit from above with a red light is flattering to no one."

"Can we please have one hour tonight where we don't discuss lighting or camera angles?" Libby asks, reaching for the bourbon the bartender brings.

"Sure." I sip my Crimson Tide martini. "Did you like the movie?"

"See, you couldn't even go thirty seconds. But at the risk of leaving myself open to more of these so-called classics, yeah, I liked it. I didn't understand why the characters were making such a stupid movie, though. *Meet Pamela* is a waste of celluloid."

"The point is that the quality of the product didn't matter. They just love the process of filmmaking. They live for it."

"Sounds like someone I know."

"I guess. But the quality of the product does matter to me."

"Then it's a good thing you've finally decided to use your own vision." Libby clinks her glass against mine. "I promise that *The Counterfeit Wedding* will be better than *Meet Pamela*."

"Just keep in mind that it's a twenty-minute short and we don't have a big budget. You'd be surprised how expensive the simplest things are."

She sips her bourbon. "You mean no car chases? Infernos?"

"No explosions of any sort. And promise me you'll keep it edgy."

"I promise."

"And satirical."

"Check."

"Nothing too mainstream. Make it a bit quirky."

"Got it."

"And of course, you'll dump the bridesmaid scene."

Libby's eyes settle on her drink. "Who said anything about a bridesmaid scene?"

Libby has lots of reasons to want to mock traditional weddings. After all, she's had the freakish luck of catching thirteen wedding bouquets—without trying. She's attended around twenty weddings and even more showers, which adds up to a lot of gift giving. What she hates most of all is playing bridesmaid, where her otherwise sane friends are taken over by Bridezilla. I've seen the dresses; she has reason to be upset.

"Lib, I know you. There's a bridesmaid scene."

"Okay, there is."

"There was."

"I think if you just take a look—"

"Dump it."

"But it's funny—"

"Hit Delete."

Libby pouts. "I see that someone is already trying on the tyrannical director role."

"We have to keep this simple. We don't need a bridesmaid scene to tell the story, and I would have to find more actors to play them. With my limited budget, we can't afford to embellish."

"I must have a maid of honor."

"One maid. But no fru-fru bridal arches or ice sculptures." I note Libby's sheepish grin. "There's an ice sculpture, isn't there? Get rid of it—unless you're planning to carve it your-self."

Libby offers me a clipped salute and summons the bar-tender. "We're celebrating a business deal, here. I'll have a mini-bottle of the Veuve Clicquot and your most expen-sive vegetarian entrée, please." She points to me. "Charge it to the director."

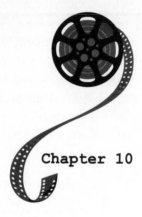

Chapter 10

Shawna, back on set after a two-week liver makeover, calls a meeting of the higher-ups, thereby giving the crew an unexpected break.

The willpower I displayed when we started this film has long since disappeared, so I lead the charge to the craft table. Later it may bother me that my jeans are tight—even the $200 designer pair that I purchased before shooting began as insurance against gaining weight—but not now. Now I am more concerned about tackling the last bagel before the electrics clear-cut the table.

"Does anyone know what's going on?" I ask Christian, layering my trophy with peanut butter, honey and banana slices.

He shakes his head. "Everyone's been kicked off set. Keisha tried the ol' 'cappuccino delivery' ploy but they shut her down, too. If they're turning away caffeine, it must be serious."

Keisha walks into the studio and places a fruit tray on the craft table. "Can't you give us anything, Keish?"

She shakes her head. "Not much. There were raised voices and I think it has something to do with a bra."

Why doesn't that surprise me?

★ ★ ★

I move the camera to a deserted corner of the studio where the grips are scrambling to assemble a gray backdrop.

"Roxanne, get over here!" Hank hollers from the monitors.

How can I refuse such a gracious invitation? I secure Gilda and walk over to his director's chair.

"The studio heads have decided that Shawna's enchanted bra ensemble is too feminine," he says.

"Aren't bras inherently feminine?"

Hank reaches for my hand. "I'm sure yours are, darling, and any time you want to prove it, just let me know."

A glimpse of my current minimizer would likely disappoint. "You do know there's a sexual harassment clause in my contract?"

"Sure, and if you keep asking, I'll deliver. At the moment, however, I'm harassing you with an opportunity."

"I'm not sure I want an opportunity that involves bras."

"They've sent up a costume from L.A. and they want a wardrobe test," he says. "I want you to shoot it while we light the next scene."

"Uh, let me check in with Damon first."

"It was his idea. And don't worry, luv, I'll be behind you every step of the way."

That's exactly what I'm worried about.

I ask the electrics to bring the lights I've seen Damon use a hundred times for wardrobe tests before it occurs to me that I have the freedom to try something different. A wardrobe test may not be a big deal to anyone else, but for me it's a chance to prove myself.

LOW ANGLE DOLLY: The camera creeps along the floor past Roxanne's battered, steel-toed safety boots and Hank's spotless Timberlands. We pause as one of the Timberlands slides toward a safety boot and rubs up against it suggestively. The safety boot briskly kicks the Timberland away.

Hank limps to the dolly with a pained expression. I wink at Gizmo before saying, "Oh, Hank, was that your foot? I thought it was Gizmo goofing around." I take my place at the viewfinder in front of Hank.

The camera crawls farther down the track until it comes to rest on a dark, bare section of concrete floor. A needle-thin beam of light appears and widens into a spotlight. A pair of shiny, black patent leather boots steps into the center of the spotlight. We start at the four-inch spike heels and track around. At the front of the boots, the camera begins to tilt up. Slowly we travel up, up, up the gleaming leather. Where the leather ends, a shapely thigh encased in a fine, red fishnet stocking begins. We pan around it to reveal the seam in the back. Continuing our upward tilt, we follow the seam to the lace band at the end of the stocking and up to the red satin garter belt. Here, the camera widens out slightly to reveal toned buttocks clad in chain-mail panties. We pan around and tilt up once again to take in the expanse of toned midriff. The camera tips up to investigate two interesting triangular shadows. There's a loud scraping of metal against metal.

"Watch what you're doing, you morons," Shawna says, resting a hand on one of the steel cones of her new bra. "That's my livelihood you're battering." She swats at the camera with her free hand.

I roll quickly out of the way. "Sorry."

Shawna ignores me. "Enough detail shots for the studio, Hank. I want you to get a couple of wide shots now. And make sure you're rolling sound."

"We don't need sound, sweetie," he explains patiently. "This is only a wardrobe test."

"Don't condescend to me, Hank," she replies, sounding surprisingly clear-headed. "I know what we're shooting and why. And I'm saying, no sound, no test."

She beckons her keeper, who promptly enfolds her in a fleece robe.

Christian snaps the slate. "Wardrobe screen test, take one."

The pointy toe of a black patent boot nearly clips him in the ear as he dodges out of the frame. Shawna performs a series of wobbly kung fu moves for the camera, and then strikes a pose.

"Okay, Howard," she says, staring straight into the lens and addressing the studio head who will watch this later in L.A. "You may be aiming for 'kick-ass' with this outfit but what you've got is 'absurd.' First, there is no way I can chase aliens in these heels. I've already injured my foot once making this film and you probably don't want a lawsuit on your hands."

She executes a few more lame moves, stopping abruptly when the chain-mail panties get snagged on her stockings. "Whose bright idea was this?" she asks, indicating the panties. "Do you have any idea how heavy this getup is? My fans expect me to *shake* my booty, Howard, and I can barely move it." To underscore her point, she bends over and presents her behind to the camera, waggling feebly.

Straightening and facing the camera, Shawna knocks on the side of a bra cup. "I did not pay eight grand for these to squeeze them into metal cones, Howie. Don't think I won't sue you twice if they stay pointy. It's fucking uncomfortable, too." Her eyes wander to the left of camera. "Hey—you, behind the camera. You've got a great rack."

As I am the only one on set with any rack at all, I have to assume she's addressing me. Still, I keep my right eye pressed to the eyepiece, feigning ignorance.

"Would *you* want to run around saving Dodge City wearing this boob trap?" she demands.

I don't answer.

"Hank, is she deaf?"

Hank taps me on the shoulder. "I believe she's speaking to you, darling." His voice sounds strained, as if he's choking back laughter.

Shawna asks, "Would you want to carry an extra ten pounds on your chest during hand-to-hand combat?"

Too embarrassed to look up from the eyepiece, I pan the camera back and forth as a negative response.

"I rest my case," she says triumphantly. "By the way, are yours real?"

I move the camera up and down.

There's an odd snuffling behind me that suggests Gizmo is about to lose it, but Shawna is satisfied. Staring directly into the lens again, she says, "See, Howie, even the camera girl wouldn't want to wear this thing."

Wow, Camera Girl. My upgrade from Focus Girl is official.

"Besides," Boozy Girl continues, a hand on each cone, "why the hell would you hide my best assets under metal? Your audience will be full of teenage boys and you know they're paying to see these."

Shawna steps out of frame abruptly. "Cut the camera. I've made my point."

When she's out of hearing, Hank says, "Hey, Camera Girl, when you're finished blushing, get your rack over to the next set."

Gizmo drops to the floor, unable to control his mirth any longer.

★ ★ ★

Hank walks with me as I carry the camera to the bedroom set for our sixth attempt at Scene 81.

I still can't look at him, but I say, "I'm surprised you haven't dropped this scene altogether."

"I wish I could, but it's an important story point."

"Have you convinced Zara of that?"

"No, but I've convinced her agent that she'll be in breach of contract if she doesn't do the damn thing. We're crossing that scene off our schedule today, mark my words."

"Bring the 5K around a little more." Damon motions to his lighting gaffer with one arm, while Chiquita squirms under the other.

From my vantage point at the craft table, I see that he's wearing the strained smile he puts on for the talent when he's actually ready to blow. I decide to stay out of his sightline. In my experience, shit travels downhill faster than water and it will only be a matter of time before he tests the gravitational pull.

Damon takes pride in being one of the fastest cinematographers in the country, so it is particularly stressful for him that the entire crew is waiting while he relights according to Zara's ever-changing specifications. Each time he tries a new lighting setup or camera position, she simply pronounces it "unacceptable."

Finally she enlightens us. "As Hank can tell you, I'm entitled to refuse to be photographed if I feel that the lighting is unacceptable. He recently made his familiarity with my contract abundantly clear to my agent."

Zara's temper is simmering today. According to Keisha, there was a four-hour standoff earlier between our star and the wardrobe designer. Months ago, the designer helped

Zara choose pink satin fabric for the negligee and ordered it from Paris. At the fitting, Zara professed to be thrilled with it, but when she saw it again today, she claimed that the color had faded and now washed out her complexion. Although the designer presented a dozen other options, nothing would do. The designer ransacked every high-end lingerie shop in Yorkville until Zara agreed to a fuchsia lace number.

Far from satisfying our star, however, this spat merely served as an appetizer to the main event.

"Damon," she says, "could you put a hand under Chiquita's bottom? He looks uncomfortable."

"Roxanne!" Damon shouts, scaring the dog who starts growling and pulling on the buttons of his shirt. I stroll to the dolly, knowing what's coming. "Give me a hand with this thing."

The moment I take him, the little dog settles. Zara lifts her head from the pillow and snaps her fingers at me, indicating her permission to approach. "What's your name?" she asks.

"Roxanne Hastings." With six weeks of constant contact, you'd think she'd have picked that up. She has the capacity to memorize pages of dialogue, after all.

Zara scratches Chiquita's head with a single fuchsia talon. "Well, Roxanne, Chiquiy seems to trust you, so I will, too. You can tell Damon that this lighting will do. And while you're at it, let Hank know that I'm ready to shoot."

All these years of struggle and it's a dog that points the way to my true calling as set interpreter.

The Alien suit has been rigged with four additional tentacles for this scene, making it so cumbersome that Burk needs the help of three wranglers to lie down on the bed and assume his position. The prosthetics department is on hand to slime him up every few minutes and two animatronics guys are hiding behind the headboard to control the tongue and penile protrusions.

As they test his equipment, Burk whistles "Tonight's the Night."

Shuddering, Zara crawls under the sheets beside him. As I arrive bedside to get focus marks, she says, "No rehearsal, Roxanne. If I am going to lie next to a hunk of phlegm, we damned well better be burning film. Tell that to Hank."

Hank is standing within earshot, but I say, "I'll let him know."

I take her marks, but Burk is a bigger challenge. He bounces around in the bed, adjusting the sheets, pulling his script out from under his pillow—anything to prevent me from getting a sense of what he'll be doing during the scene. I let my measuring tape fall to my side, hoping he'll tire of his defense so that I can attack with my tape.

Zara isn't in a mood for delays. "What the hell are we waiting for?"

"I just need a few more focus marks," I offer, soothingly. "Mr. Creature, sir? Do you think you could stay still for a moment?"

Burk continues to thrash on the bed.

Zara says, "Burk, I want to finish this scene before Chiquita ends up in an urn on my mantel. Show her where you're going to be."

Burk pauses for a nanosecond so that I can get one measurement, not the four I really need. I utter a silent prayer that Damon will be able to compensate if Burk decides to improvise. After all the trouble we've had with this scene, it will be a career ender if the footage is out of focus. Hank will never get Zara back into bed to reshoot, contract or no contract.

Hank yells action and Burk winds a tentacle around Zara, who continues to lie absolutely motionless.

"Cut!" Hank springs out of his director's chair and walks over to the bed. "Zara, show some passion for Christ's sake. It's a love scene."

Zara examines her talons and yawns.

Hank's color rises. "Are you listening to me?"

Zara glances around for a moment in mock confusion before turning toward me. "Excuse me, Roxanne," she says in a stage whisper, "do you hear someone speaking?"

I look helplessly at Hank. "Uh, yes, Ms. Duncan, Hank had a question."

"Call me Zara, dear, but I think you must be mistaken—Hank speaks to me only through my agent. So tell him if he needs to relay information, he'd best give her a call. Either that, or he can convey it through you. Incidentally, you could tell him that I'd like some privacy for this scene."

I pick up Hank's microphone, feeling like an idiot. "This will be a closed set everybody! All nonessential crew have to go." I lower the mic and raise it again. "And keep the monitors clear, too, you guys." This causes a ripple of laughter. A favorite crew trick during a closed set is to gather around the monitors and spy from a distance.

"Camera speed," I say.

Damon calls, "Frame," signaling to Hank that we are ready to go.

For several seconds, nothing happens. Then Hank pokes me in the ribs.

"Oh, right," I say. *"Action."*

The animatronics guys once again maneuver the Alien's tentacle around Zara's scantily clad body.

THE SCREEN FILLS WITH AN EXTREME CLOSE-UP OF A SCALEY TENTACLE. WE WIDEN OUT as it snakes around Sergeant Trowbridge's tanned leg. As the tentacle moves slowly upward, a globular substance glistens in its wake. WE TRACK IN ON THE TENTACLE as it disappears beneath the scalloped hem of the negligee. The flimsy material attaches itself to the slime and the nightgown travels upward until we reveal the thick, unsightly gusset of Zara's control-top panty hose.

"CUT!" Hank shouts in my ear.

"CUT!" I echo, warming to my new role as directorial mouthpiece.

Hank strides onto the set and leans over the headboard to accost the special-effects guys. "Did you two have to fail a test to get this job? The tentacle is supposed to take a slow and steady course up Zara's leg *under* the negligee. It is not supposed to haul the negligee along with it."

"It's the slime," one of them replies. "It's catching the negligee."

"No shit. Why the hell didn't you test for this before instead of wasting our time on set?"

"We tested the satin negligee we were given, but Ms. Duncan is wearing a lace negligee today."

ZOOM IN ON DIRECTOR'S EXPRESSION OF OUTRAGE.

The crew breaks early for lunch while the special-effects and wardrobe departments figure out how to work with the lace number.

Later, Hank covers the scene from eight different angles

and shoots no fewer than ten takes on every setup. In fact, we cover Scene 81 for nearly nine hours straight, until the tape holding up the right side of Zara's face gives up the fight. She looks as if she's had a mild stroke. Hank calls cut and when Zara catches sight of her reflection in the camera filter, she bursts into tears and flees.

Hank's driver pulls the Navigator alongside of the camera truck. "Hank wants me to tell you they're screening the wardrobe test tomorrow," the guy says.

I lean down to peer into the car to find Hank grinning back at me. "No one speaks directly to anyone anymore. It's the latest Hollywood trend. Be at the lab an hour before call if you want to see the rushes."

"I'll be there. Thanks again for the opportunity, Hank."

"Fledgling only considers the best, darling, so I need to see what you're capable of doing."

Since he's opening the discussion, I blurt out the question I've wanted to ask for weeks. "What did you think of the script?"

"What script?"

I can't tell from his expression whether he's joking. "*The Lobby.* I gave it to you the day we started shooting, remember?"

"Oh, right, the political thriller. It was gripping, lovie, gripping."

I have a sudden sinking feeling that Miguel is right: Hank is merely stringing me along. "It's a black comedy, Hank."

"Of course it is, darling. Don't look so worried, I'm just teasing. I loved the script and I've passed it on to my associates."

"Really? What did you like best about it?"

"That you gave it to me, of course."

"Seriously, Hank."

"All shall be revealed in due course. Unless you'd like to hop in and we'll discuss it on the way to my hotel...?"

Ignoring this, I persist, "When do you think you'll have a decision?"

"Let's start with the wardrobe test, shall we? One thing at a time."

I tentatively raise the other issue that's been on my mind lately, "Are you worried about considering someone with limited experience to shoot your next film?"

"We all have to start somewhere, Roxanne, and it doesn't always have to be at the bottom. Some waders out there will tell you to ease in cautiously. But then there are people like you and me—people who have the guts to jump straight into the deep end. The first picture I ever shot was for World Studios and the first picture I directed had a $30 million budget. Someone took a chance on me and it worked out."

"So you like to give people breaks."

"Of course. Fledgling needs fresh blood and fresh ideas. Mind you, if I hire you and the dailies are crap, I won't hesitate to fire you." He lets out a hearty guffaw.

My confidence whistles out as I open my mouth again. "Did you really read the script, Hank?"

He starts rolling up the window. "Last chance to discuss it as we drive, darling."

"Hey, Rox!" I turn and see Damon and Gizmo standing at the door of the camera truck, beers in hand. "Want us to put Glenda to bed for you?" Gizmo calls.

"It's *Gilda,*" I say, "and don't you dare touch her if you're drinking."

I turn back and Hank's car is already pulling away.

On the truck, Damon hops onto the counter as I break Gilda down.

I say, "Thanks for letting me shoot the wardrobe test. Hank told me it was your idea."

"I keep telling you I'll give you opportunities when I can and this was the perfect start. You just need to be patient, Rox."

"That's easy for you to say, you're nearly where you want to be. By the way, has Hank mentioned letting you direct in Morocco?"

"No, but even if he hires someone else to direct, I'll probably offer to shoot it for him."

I splutter, "Why would you do that? You haven't touched anything with a budget under $40 million in years. This is a $5 million indie film."

"I know, but it would be a foot in the door with Fledgling."

This is awful. I can't compete directly with Damon for the job. I must dissuade him. "Hank says he's looking for less experienced shooters willing to work for scale."

"I'd do it for half of my usual rate if they promise to let me direct their next film."

"But you can't!"

"Why is this throwing you, Rox? I'll take you along as focus puller, you know that. And hopefully we can both upgrade on the following film."

I can't bring myself to explain that I already have big plans for Fledgling's next film and they involve *The Lobby*. Instead, I force a smile and continue breaking Gilda down for the night.

Chapter 11

The projectionist is taking his sweet time about threading up the wardrobe test. At the rate he's going, my teeth will be stumps by the time it finally screens, because I'm grinding them so hard. I deserve better, considering I've already endured an hour of footage of the love scene; mercifully, it was in focus.

Although I felt calm enough yesterday while shooting the wardrobe test, my heart is pounding now that I'm about to see my work on screen in front of Hank, two producers and a handful of my peers. Damon's presence in the next seat particularly unnerves me. What if Hank lets it slip that he considered this an audition for shooting his Morocco picture? Worse, what if I screwed up and Hank laughs my ambitions out of the screening room?

The projector finally starts and the screen comes to life. Ten…nine…I watch the rack leader flicker past. Eight…seven…six…I'm vaguely aware that I'm clenching my teeth harder and harder as the countdown continues. Five…four…I should never have strayed from Damon's method of lighting.… Three…two…If I'd shot it the same way he does, I wouldn't be sitting here risking a root canal. One… Too late!

I watch as the pinhole of light grows on the screen and Shawna's fishnet-clad leg appears. The footage looks fine. Better than fine. After what feels like an eternity, but is actually no more than five minutes, the test is over and the lights come up. The wardrobe team bustles out of the theater with the producers close behind. Damon turns to speak, but Hank, already walking up the aisle toward us, beats him to it.

"Bravo, gorgeous! Jolly good job!" He rubs two nicotine-stained fingers against my cheek.

I am too thrilled to push his hand away. "Really?"

"Really. Well done."

"Did you like the light effect at the beginning?" I ask, proving the rule that you can always spot a rookie by her desperate attempts to pump for compliments.

"Very theatrical." He moves his hand from my face to my wrist. "You'd like a copy for your reel, I presume?"

A reel! I have a reel!

"I'd love one!" The rookie is also prone to gushing.

"Why don't we speak to the editors about transferring this onto a DVD for you?"

He tugs at my arm and I follow him to the projection booth. Damon passes us en route and walks out of the screening room without so much as looking my way. My heart sinks. The rookie is inevitably shattered by her mentor's indifference.

"Hank," I ask, "have you thought any more about hiring Damon to direct your picture in Morocco?"

He watches me shrewdly. "Hoping to cover all bases by plugging your boss?"

"Not at all. I have a better shot at that cinematographer's

job if I continue to impress you. Damon certainly isn't making any promises."

"Well, I'm not making any to him."

"Why not? He'd be great! Did you see *The Only Girl*? He won best direction at two festivals for that one."

Hank becomes bored instantly. "It showed promise, yes."

"So, what more do you need?"

"As I've said before, Damon can be a hothead. I'm waiting to see how he does on *Illegal Alien* before making a decision."

"Damon isn't a hothead. He's just passionate about filmmaking."

He rolls his eyes. "Enough about him. This is your day in the sun."

Indulging the rookie, he offers compliments and bits of cinematic wisdom all the way to the parking lot.

If it weren't Hank, I'd be downright weak in the knees.

Damon is extra passionate about filmmaking this afternoon.

"The sun's coming out, Gizmo," he calls. "I want six reflector boards lined up along the beach. I'll let you know exact positions—if the camera ever gets here."

"You just asked me to move it," I protest.

We're at the Beaver Rowing Club and this is the third position he's chosen in the last ten minutes. First, he wanted the camera a quarter of a mile down the road from the camera truck. Next, he asked me to move it onto the roof of the clubhouse and now he's demanding the camera be on the beach. Damon is either distracted or he's punishing me. I can think of a couple of reasons why it might be the latter.

I haul all seventy pounds of Gilda down a ladder and

across a hundred yards of deep sand. My muscles are shaking with fatigue when I reach him. So much for the seventy-five dollars I dropped last weekend on the Noni juice, the latest purchase in my ongoing quest for a natural elixir. The physical demands of this job, combined with long and irregular hours, are aging me at twice the normal rate for humans. Over the past few years, I've choked down liquid vitamins, greens powders, fish oil and sea algae all to no avail. My cupboards tell a desperate story with their expired bottles of B12, Stamina Rx, Energy Plus and ginseng. Yet it remains a struggle to simply climb out of bed every day. The further along I am on a movie, the heavier the camera equipment becomes.

"Hurry, the actors will be here any minute." Damon jostles me aside and tries to look through the camera while I'm still struggling to set it up. "If you hadn't hung around the lab all morning, you'd have made it to set on time like the rest of us."

I raise two of the tripod legs while Damon adjusts the third. "I was just trying to get a copy of the wardrobe test. What did you think of it, by the way?"

"Ask Hank for more feedback. I don't have time for critiques—I have work to do."

Eternally optimistic, the rookie's tail wags on. "Can't you just tell me whether you liked it?"

Damon walks away without answering.

Fine. See if I ever waste my "day in the sun" singing his praises to Hank again. If this Morocco thing turns out to be a competition, may the best woman win.

The sweat I worked up earlier is chilling as I wait beside the camera. I won't make it through the afternoon without a warmer jacket. There is probably just enough time to run to the camera truck to—

"Don't go anywhere," Damon says. "Zara's en route."

Instead of getting my coat, I jump up and down on the spot until my cell phone starts vibrating in my back pocket. I snap open the phone to check the display and see that it's Miguel at his New York number. Two weeks have passed since he called me a fat pig and I feel less inclined to tell him to get lost than I did initially. Not because I don't want him to. Quite the contrary. I'm simply less inclined to *tell* him. Nor do I want to give him the satisfaction of leaving a click on my voice mail. Far better to make a statement by hanging up on him directly. So I hit the talk button and then the end button. The phone begins to vibrate again instantly. Again, I hit Talk and End.

When Damon looks up from the camera, I jam the phone back in my pocket and resume jumping on the spot. Though numb with cold, I won't whine.

"Stop," he says, "you're kicking sand onto my jeans."

Hank, however, is all concern when he joins us. "Roxanne, you look frozen. Don't you have a coat?"

"No time to go back for it," I reply.

"Of course there is, darling. Zara is running quite late."

Chiquita, it seems, has relieved himself on Zara's wig. She's blaming the hair department for leaving the wig on the counter where he could get at it—although no Chihuahua could achieve that feat without stilts.

At any rate, Hank is determined to recover lost time by simplifying the scene. He suggests dropping the exterior shots in favor of shooting inside the clubhouse on the Steadicam. I offer a silent cheer as I head to the camera truck.

Nonetheless, my intuition is telling me that the rookie's punishment is far from over.

F. C. Kugelman's laptop sits on a tiny wooden table in the shade. It's a gorgeous day in Santa Monica Beach and from his rooftop deck, F.C. can look over the neighbor's palm trees to the crowded boardwalk and the Pacific Ocean beyond. The sun warms his bald spot as he reviews his latest scene.

Interior Rowing Club, Day
Sergeant Trowbridge's point of view as the camera scans the empty building from the doorway. A dark shadow in the corner catches her eye. The camera moves in and we see the body of the slain rower. Detective Penny follows Sergeant Trowbridge into the room.

Lifting his eyes from the screen, F.C. watches the girls in bikinis spread colorful beach towels on the sand. After a moment's contemplation, he hits the delete key. What's the point in setting a scene in a rowing club if you can't even see the beach?

"Rox, grab your wellies," Gizmo tells Roxanne as he passes the camera truck. "We need to get closer to the water and the sand is pretty wet down there."

Roxanne grabs her boots and a Windbreaker and runs down the ramp after Gizmo. "Hank just told Damon that we're moving inside the club."

"Keep up, girlie. They've decided to shoot the entire scene from the beach."

Exterior Rowing Club, Day—Foreground water

Sergeant Trowbridge walks along the boardwalk beside the rowing club. A blue tarp poking out from behind one of the boats catches her eye. She pulls back the tarp and lurches away at the sight of the slain rower. She backs into Detective Penny, who has joined her.

Kugelman leans back and laces his fingers behind his head. The beach setting is working, but the scene's still not dynamic enough. Maybe if the camera captured the scene in a wide shot right from the water's edge…

"You've got to be kidding," Roxanne says. "It's winter!"

"Suck it up, Rox," Damon says, struggling into his hip waders. "We're only moving back a few yards. The water is six inches deep."

Roxanne rolls her jeans to the top of her rubber boots and wades into the lake, camera on her shoulder. Gizmo follows with the head and tripod.

F.C. stops tapping at the laptop. A couple of seagulls pass overhead, bawling lazily at each other. He tracks their path with his eyes until the birds land on the ocean. Smiling, Kugelman retypes the slug line.

Roxanne stands with hands on hips. "We can't go any deeper, Damon. There's no underwater housing for the camera."

"Why the hell didn't you order one?" Damon splashes to the shore, reaches for his script and reads the slug line aloud: "*Exterior Rowing Club, Day—Foreground water.* With the housing, we could have set the camera directly in the water just off shore. Without it, we'll need to carry the camera 100 yards into the lake to get enough water in the foreground." He steps out of his hip waders. "You can have these. Gizmo has his own."

Rox's face is a study in panic. "You mean you're not coming out with us?"

"I'll be watching the shot from the monitors with Hank."

"Great. Any advice on framing?"

"Yeah, get it right."

Roxanne pulls on the hip waders, the waist of which reaches her armpits. Gizmo uses a grip clamp to pin the excess rubber closer to her body to reduce the risk of flooding. Her feet slide around in the enormous boots as she clumps back to the shore.

Damon says, "This is your second upgrade opportunity in one week, Roxanne. Aren't you going to thank me?"

"This isn't an opportunity—it's me doing your dirty work."

Damon smirks. "Think of it as another shot for your reel."

Roxanne wades into the lake behind Gizmo, the icy water pressing against the thin rubber suit. The chill rises to her rib cage yards before she reaches the tripod. Just a few inches remain between the water and the gaping top of the hip waders. She sets the camera gingerly on the tripod, careful not to stir up any waves.

Kugelman brushes a ladybug off the screen, pondering. If the scene is taking place in the middle of the day, obviously the lake should be busier.

As Sergeant Trowbridge pulls back the tarp and discovers the body of

the slain rower, a police boat carrying Detective Penny breaks the
frame.

"Shit!" Roxanne exclaims. "That boat's coming in fast! Get on your walkie and tell them to slow down." Gizmo fumbles inside his hip waders for his walkie, but it's too late. The police boat whizzes across the frame, its wake surging toward them. Roxanne and Gizmo grab the camera and hoist it as high as they can to keep it dry. As the frosty waters of Lake Ontario slosh into Rox's hip waders, she whimpers quietly.

Twelve takes later, the sun has disappeared behind thick clouds. Roxanne plods out of the water. She fixates on several crew members sipping from steaming foam cups.

"I th-think there's soup!" she says through blue lips as she staggers toward the craft table. There is one cup left. Rox pauses to hand the camera to Christian as an electric, who has been sitting on his butt all afternoon, takes the solitary cup.

The electric lifts the lid of the cup and sniffs, his nose wrinkling in disgust. "Curried squash? No one likes this shit."

Roxanne's numb lips cannot shape the word *stop* in time. He tosses the cup neatly into the garbage can.

F. C. Kugelman powers down and moves to a teak deck chair. Reaching for a snifter of brandy, he squints blissfully into the setting sun.

I am brushing sand from the tripod outside the camera truck when Damon and Hank arrive. The sun is shining again and it's almost ten degrees, but I've traded my wet jeans for fleece-lined army pants that I found in the bottom of my foul-weather bag, topped by an expedition-weight parka.

"Good work today, luv," Hank says. "That may very well be the most interesting shot in the movie, particularly the take where you tilted the camera all the way over to one side. It contributed so well to the confusion of the scene."

"Th-thanks Hank." Stretching numb lips into a gracious smile, the rookie neglects to mention that the "interesting" shot arose when she almost toppled into the lake with the camera.

"Oh, you're freezing, poor thing!" Hank moves in to rub my arms briskly.

Conscious of Damon's gaze upon me, I step back and force my teeth to stop chattering long enough to assure Hank that I'm fine.

"Well, we're wrapped," Hank says, "so go home and soak in a hot bath. But don't stay up too late, because we're starting early with the car rigs."

Damon asks, "How can we be wrapped? We've got two more scenes to shoot at the studio."

"Dropped them. We've got a meeting in the production office tonight. Howard's plane landed an hour ago. It sounds like he's willing to consider a second unit."

I pull down the hood of my parka so that I can hear better. Did he just say the magic words—*second unit*?

A second unit shoots at the same time as the main unit and therefore has its own cinematographer. But there is far less pressure attached, because the second-unit footage has to match that of the main unit and there is no latitude for creativity. Hank is very likely to give me this opportunity to prove my worth. Even Damon would consider this a natural progression, under his watchful eye. If he has faith in me after the wardrobe test, that is.

"I don't see how Howard can refuse," Hank continues. "If we don't get a second crew to mop up the shots we've dropped on the main unit, we'll never finish this movie in time for a Labor Day release. So move it, Damon."

Damon disappears into the camera truck to collect his car keys.

The rookie's hand, still blue and clawlike, reaches for Hank's arm, but he is already turning to wave for his driver.

"Good night, darling," he says, getting into the car. "Nice job today. Your dedication hasn't gone unnoticed."

Libby's voice crackles above loud music. "Hell——?"

"Libby? It's Rox. Where are you?"

"Hi! I'm——Xacutti, with——ola."

Libby sounds a little tipsy, but the connection's so bad, it's hard to be sure.

"I'm wrapped early," I say, "can I join you?"

"Sure, we're in the Bird——ounge up——"

The connection dies but I've heard enough. I'm not far from Xacutti. Although there's no point in going home for a shower, Xacutti is one of those places where you're scanned by a cool-ometer at the door. I pull into a parking lot and rifle through my makeup bag. I can't do much about the clothes, but with enough mascara and blush, I might be able to pass off my look as "urban grunge."

The doorman holds up a massive hand: no reservation, no entry. At least, I think that's what he's saying, since only his lower lip moves. With his mirrored shades, it's hard to tell if he is even looking at me. Undaunted, I explain to my reflection that I'm meeting friends upstairs for a drink. Shades ignores me, waving a couple of girls in short skirts and high boots into the restaurant. Then he blocks my path with his monstrously huge pecs.

If he thinks he can intimidate me, he's got the wrong girl. Some of my colleagues in the grip and transport departments have criminal records as thick as this guy's neck and I'm not about to be scared off by a muscle-bound trifle like him. Still, it takes nearly ten minutes of nonstop talking to break him down. Finally, just to be rid of me, he opens the door and refers me to a smile-challenged blonde. When I repeat my request to join my friends in the lounge, she runs her heavily lined eyes over me from greasy roots to sandy work boots and declares that she "can't make it happen" for me tonight.

"Roxanne, you're here!" It's Libby's friend Lola, all shiny dark hair and flaming lips. In her white miniskirt and red fishnet stockings, Lola far out-hips the blonde. Whipping out her business card, Lola tells the woman, "I'm Lola Romano—'Night Out' editor at *Toronto Lives* magazine. I'm doing a review of the Bird Lounge for our 800,000 readers. I hope you've been taking good care of my friend."

Before the blonde can react, Lola yanks on my ratty parka and tows me upstairs.

"Thanks, Lola—although this place doesn't really deserve my business."

"Xacutti is the hottest place in town at the moment. Did you really think you'd get in dressed in army surplus castoffs?"

"I suppose I should be reading those day-to-night fashion stories in your magazine."

The walls of the staircase are lined with photographs of all the beautiful people who have visited. Second from last is a photo of the blonde downstairs, actually smiling, and a man in chef's whites. Between them, with an arm around each, is Miguel. In his sprawling script, he's written *Gracias mis amigos, for always making me feel welcome!*

"Let's go," Lola says, "or Libby will snag all the cute guys."

She leads me to the bar, where we await acknowledgement from the bartender. Raising her well-groomed eyebrows at me, Lola asks, "Why haven't I seen you in three years?"

"It's all work and no play for Roxy these days."

"And yet you're not directing. Or so Libby tells me."

Now I remember why I'm usually too tired to join Lola and Libby on their bar crawls. My secret nickname for Lola has long been Demolition Girl in honor of her remarkable ability to demolish my ego in under an hour. Her skills are sharper than ever.

I say, "Not yet."

"Well, it's great that Libby is helping you fix that with her script."

The bartender finally deigns to serve us and I drop a staggering fifty-five dollars on a round. Lola points the way to a long white couch at the back of the lounge, where Libby is entertaining a couple of strangers. Judging from her flushed face, I'd say she's four rounds ahead of me. And yet Lola, who has no doubt been matching her drink for drink, appears completely sober. Lola is known as much for her tolerance for alcohol as her sharp tongue.

I flop down beside Libby, pass her a bourbon and raise my wine. "Congratulate me, ladies."

Libby clinks her glass against mine too forcefully. "What for?"

"*Illegal Alien* is adding a second unit and I'm going to be the cinematographer."

As a rule I don't count my chickens until they're squawking in the yard, but Lola has me rattled.

"That's amazing," Libby says, hugging me with one arm.

"Well, it's not official," I hedge, "but Hank as good as told me the job's mine."

"Maybe he really will hire you for that Monaco thing."

"Morocco."

Libby giggles. "Whatever."

"Well, he'll be testing me, no question. So forget what I said the other day about hurrying with *The Counterfeit Wedding*. I've got a steep learning curve ahead and I might not have much energy for prepping another movie at the same time."

Libby's smile fades and Lola says, "I told you not to waste your time on that script, Lib. Roxanne's been threatening to make a movie for twelve years and nothing's come of it."

I don't know what Libby sees in Lola, but after a long day in a cold lake, I shouldn't have to put up with her. "As I recall, Lola, you were threatening to become a war correspondent for the *New York Times* twelve years ago. How's that working out?"

Lola opens her scarlet lips to reply but Libby intercedes, "Come on, you guys, I want my two best friends to get along. Lola, Roxanne is just trying to keep a lot of balls in the air and you're just annoyed because I've been spending time on the screenplay rather than starting a new book with you."

Lola huffily turns her attention to the guys at the end of the couch. Libby watches me in silence for a moment, drunkenly performing some mental calculations. Finally she says, "I'm nearly finished the script, Rox," she says. "You're not going to tell me that you don't need it, are you?"

"Of course not," I say, although that's exactly what I was going to tell her—before I realized that she has a four-bourbon advantage and Lola Take-No-Prisoners Romano for backup.

Better to wait until Libby is sober and alone to discuss this. Then she'll be able to see that with this second-unit gig under my belt, it won't be a big leap of faith for Hank to hire me for the Morocco picture, and subsequently let me direct *The Lobby*.

I don't see the point in running myself ragged to make a short calling card movie when I no longer need the experience. Better to put that money toward something else. Like a trip to Cannes to check out the competition.

Or another round of drinks at the Bird Lounge.

Chapter 12

Gizmo moves a little closer to me before shouting, "All aboard who's coming aboard!"

The sadist. As if I don't regret last night's visit to the Bird Lounge enough. What was I thinking? First I bragged to Libby and Lola about my ability to function on four hours' sleep and then I made good on my boast by leading the way to an all-night diner for fried egg sandwiches. I almost fainted in the shower this morning.

"Think fast!" Gizmo says, tossing a harness at me. He chortles as it hits me in the chest and falls to the floor. Damon, who still isn't really speaking to me, smiles, too.

Today we're shooting four scenes with Shawna and Burk, in human form. As Detective Penny and Federal Agent Potter, they'll be driving in Detective Penny's beat-up old Mustang. To make this look real, the Mustang is parked on a process trailer—basically a platform on wheels—and hauled around the city. The trailer is big enough to accommodate the car, several lengths of dolly track, multiple cameras and lights. Damon, Gizmo and I will be harnessed to the safety rails at the perimeter of the platform. Hank and a few others will ride in the truck towing the trailer, while the rest of the crew follows in a convoy of minivans.

Working on a process trailer can be an ordeal when it's raining or freezing outside, but on a bright, unseasonably warm morning such as this one, it's like getting paid to ride on a parade float. Because camera positions are so limited, we don't even work that hard. In fact, all we have to do is sit back and keep the actors in frame and in focus until the sun goes down. To this end, Damon and I have to wear headphones so that we can favor the right person at the right time.

Hank is growing impatient. Shawna is late and there's a limit to daylight hours in Toronto at this time of year. At last her Cadillac pulls up alongside the trailer. A minivan pulls up behind it spilling Shawna's two personal assistants, her publicist, her keeper, her dresser, her hairstylist and Genevieve into the parking lot. The young production assistant runs over and opens the door of the Cadillac. Shawna gives his butt a possessive squeeze as she emerges. He looks around anxiously to see if anyone noticed. To assure him I did, I tip my baseball cap and wink.

Martini climbs aboard the trailer and weaves toward us. "Okay, camera dude and dudette! We're off early tonight and I want to parrr-tay. Let's get this show on the road!"

She gives Damon a sloppy kiss on the lips and slaps my back so hard she knocks my headset awry. Singing a Courtney Love number off-key, she walks around the Mustang and slides into the driver's seat. The woman is obviously under the influence of something stronger than sunshine.

Finally the procession heads out of the parking lot and toward our first position on Bloor Street. Damon and I settle back on our dolly seats, soaking up the sunshine and waving at kids on a school bus. I'm hoping to find an opportunity to ask Damon again about the wardrobe test but at the moment we're too close to the microphones planted inside the car to have any privacy.

Shawna isn't burdened by such discretion. Over my headset, I hear her complaining to Burk about Genevieve. Damon's oblivious expression indicates that he's turned his headset off.

Shawna says, "If I don't watch what she's doing every second, I end up looking as old as Zara. She was fine when we started, but lately, she's been totally distracted."

"I don't find her that bad," Burk says.

"What would you know, you're a guy. A little foundation, a bit of powder, a spritz of GLH and you're done."

I stifle a giggle.

Hank's voice crackles over the walkie-talkie. "Okay, Shawna and Burk, we're in position. Are you good to go?"

They give the camera the thumbs-up, which Hank can see on the monitor.

"Let's turn over then," he says.

I switch on the camera and lean into the car to mark the scene. Shawna continues to rant as if there isn't a slate in front of her nose.

"I'm telling you, when things get complicated, Genevieve falls apart. Just look at the color of my nails." She spreads her fingers under Burk's nose. "Midnight-mauve to match my enchanted bra costume and here I am in a bright red coat."

Burk offers a tentative "That's bad?"

"Red and mauve? It's disastrous. The fashionistas will have a field day!"

While she pauses for breath, I quickly announce the scene number, clap the slate and pull out of the frame.

Completely unconcerned that this is all being captured on film, Shawna continues. "I told Genevieve to use the

Scarlet Sin and she has the nerve to say that no one will even notice."

Burk's eyes are glazing over. "But they will?"

"You bet they will! Plenty of people go to my movies just to see what I'm wearing, Burk. There's a reason I make every issue of *In Style*. And when I told Genevieve that, she had the audacity to say—"

Hank yells over the walkie: "ACTION!"

"The forensic team wasn't able to iden-tify the oily substance found under the nail," Shawna says, switching gears so fast that Burk is practically thrown into the windshield.

"Why would a forensic team be looking at your nails?" he asks, bewildered.

"CUT!" Hank's calls through the walkie. "Shawna, can we put this whole manicure crisis behind us and move on?"

Addressing the camera, Shawna says, "Don't patronize me Hank. You can thank these nails for your big budget."

"I'll do that—right after we wrap."

The procession pulls over at Bloor and Bay streets so that I can reload Gilda. Shawna springs out of the Mustang, climbs off the trailer and heads toward Holt Renfrew, Toronto's most exclusive department store, with her posse in hot pur-suit.

Hank leans out of the truck. "Shawna, where are you going? This reload won't take long."

"Won't be a sec!" she calls over her shoulder.

As the doorman opens the door, Martini pulls a flask from her back pocket and offers him a belt.

A runner soon returns from Holt's with the news that Shawna is in the spa getting a manicure.

Hank is incredulous. "We're barely going to make this day as it is. Drag her out by the hair if you have to."

The kid heads back into Holt Renfrew, a lamb to the slaughter, and returns a few minutes later.

"You're alone," Hank says, his voice eerily calm.

"Yes, sir," Lamb Chop says. "Martini—I mean, Shawna—asked me to tell you that she'll be ready to shoot after her manicure dries. She says if that's a problem, take it up with Genevieve."

"I am not getting involved in their petty squabbles," Hank sniffs. "If we fall another day behind, so be it. We've shot so much of this picture that Howard won't pull the plug now." He turns to the rest of us. "Does anybody know how long it takes for a manicure to dry?"

Being the only female in the immediate vicinity, all eyes turn to me. My own nails haven't seen polish in years, but I take my best guess. "About twenty minutes."

"Right, then," Hank says, "there's a Starbucks around the corner. Let's go."

Damon and Gizmo unhook each other and jump off the platform to follow Hank. I make a move to join them, but am yanked back by my harness. There isn't enough slack to allow me to unhook myself.

Hank turns around. "Roxanne, aren't you joining us?"

Damon answers for me. "Somebody needs to stay with the equipment."

There are two pay-duty police officers, three guys from locations, Burk Ryan has-been action star and literally dozens of crew members standing by to hold the fort, but I don't bother protesting. Instead I prop my feet on the safety rail and sit back to enjoy the sunshine.

I am dozing by the time Genevieve climbs onto the process trailer and slips into the Mustang to touch up Burk's makeup. I close my eyes again, only to hear Genevieve's indignant voice coming over the headphones.

"Can you believe that bitch?" she asks.

The soundman obviously forgot to shut down the mike inside the car. I reach for my headphones, knowing I should remove them, but my hand hovers. There's something intriguing about their familiarity.

"Rest assured I defended your honor, Kitten."

Kitten? I adjust the headphones for better sound.

"The odd thing is," Burk continues, "Shawna seems to think you've been distracted lately."

Genevieve giggles. "Tell her I was abducted by an alien."

"Care to be abducted again this weekend?"

Now they're both giggling. I pull off the headphones, having heard more than enough.

Gizmo climbs aboard the trailer, carrying a coffee for me.

"Thanks, Giz," I say, desperately grateful for the caffeine.

"Don't thank me," he says, "it was Damon's idea."

It may be my imagination, but Damon appears to be watching surreptitiously as I take a sip. I soon see why: the coffee is so thick with sugar that I nearly collapse in my harness in a diabetic coma.

Gizmo may not know how I like it, but Damon certainly does.

It's nice to see a grown man recapture his adolescence so effectively.

The smell of barbecue hits us as we pull into the studio parking lot.

Keisha comes running to greet us. "It's a crew appreciation party," she explains.

While we were riding the float, the rest of the crew had

a quiet day, which they put to good use by planning a tail-gate party. There are blender stations and a shooter bar outside the grip truck, barbecues and an oyster-shucking station by the electric truck and a table with shrimp and salad by the craft truck. The big garage doors to the studio are rolled up and inside a handful of part-time musicians are jamming on a makeshift stage.

I strip the camera gear off the process trailer in record time, put Gilda to bed and join the party. Dour-faced Damon is hanging around the margarita station, so I grab a beer and head for the food instead. No need to subject myself to his moods now that I'm off the clock.

Tucking my beer bottle under my arm, I hold a plate in my left hand and use my right to load it. Something tickles the back of my neck and I jump. It's Hank, swaying drunkenly.

"Let me help you, darling," he says, sliding the bottle out from under my arm with a suggestive smile. "Try the shrimp," he says. He sucks the cocktail sauce off one and dangles it in front of my mouth.

Damon appears behind Hank. Pleading with my eyes, I say, "Won't you join us?"

He hesitates for a moment and Hank slides a proprietary arm around my waist.

"I don't think so," Damon says, "I'm going to check out the band."

"Can't that wait? I need to talk to you."

"We can talk on Sunday. It's a short weekend, remember?"

I can tell from his expression that he knows I am begging to be rescued and is just being stubborn. So I try another tactic. "I had a problem with Gilda tonight and the camera rental house won't be too happy. Can you take a look at her?"

Damon rolls his eyes, but relents.

"I'll come along and offer my expertise," Hank says. "I do know my way around a camera, you know."

Damon says, "I can probably handle this one, Hank. Maybe you want to check on Shawna instead. I hear she's behind the wheel of the Mustang and threatening to take it home for the weekend."

"That's outrageous," Hank says, staggering off to investigate.

When he's out of earshot, I say, "Took you long enough, Dudley."

"Your damsel-in-distress act needs work, Nell," Damon says. "Seems like whenever I turn around these days you're talking to Snidely Whiplash. How am I to know when it's a legitimate emergency?"

"Your first clue was that he was all over me."

"He was all over you at the rowing club and you weren't complaining."

"He was just concerned about my health after spending the day in the water."

"Please. I got a black eye on *Seattle* when that actor kicked the camera and Hank never offered a rubdown."

"Hypothermia is life threatening. A black eye is hardly on the same scale."

"Don't go there, my friend. Until you've had your shoulder dislocated by a camera-shy grizzly, I hold the record for biggest sacrifice in the line of duty."

Damon smiles for the first time in two days and suggests we repair to the wine bar. I've already decided to take a cab home, so I trail after him happily.

Taking a perch on the tailgate of the grip truck, I bring up the wardrobe test again. "If you didn't like it, you should tell me," I say. "I want to improve, you know."

He hops up beside me. "I thought it was excellent."

This isn't the response I expected. "Really?"

"Yeah. Every detail of the costume was visible and you managed to turn something boring into something interesting."

"Why didn't you say so? You've barely spoken to me since the dailies."

"You didn't seem to care that much about my opinion. It was all about Snidely."

"Your opinion matters more than anyone's," I say. "I was worried that I'd let you down."

The slight quaver in my voice can surely be blamed on the combination of alcohol and fatigue. There is absolutely no need to get emotional over a wardrobe test.

"Don't worry, it was great. So was the footage from the lake yesterday." He grins mischievously. "But I'm disappointed you haven't thanked me for that opportunity."

"I sincerely thank you for the opportunity to freeze my ass off."

"You exaggerate. I saw your ass today, I'm sure of it."

"Was that before or after you spiked my coffee with sugar?"

He laughs. "What can I say? Hell hath no fury like a cameraman scorned."

"You know, I would never have thought of putting the camera so far into the lake. It was a great lesson in finding the best shot with the money, equipment and time available."

"You would have thought of something equally interesting. There's always more than one way to shoot a scene. You should have a chance to find that out for yourself soon."

I squeal. "The second unit?"

He shushes me with a hand over my mouth and looks around the parking lot for potential eavesdroppers. Everyone has gone into the studio to hear the band, so he says,

"Maybe. I've recommended you to shoot it." I mumble my excitement into his hand. "It's not definite. Hank will make the final decision, but I can't see why he wouldn't approve it when he practically nominated your wardrobe test for an Oscar."

When he moves his hand from my mouth to my shoulder, I lean over and give him a quick kiss on the cheek. "Thanks."

"You earned it." He's looking at me in a way that is strangely familiar. Then it hits me: the wrap party for *The Mauling*. His hand is still on my shoulder and unless the truck is tilting, he is pulling me toward him, ever so slightly.

ZOOM IN ON Roxanne's expression of resolve. She raises a warning hand.

ROXANNE

Damon, we can't. We went down that road before and decided not to mix business with pleasure. As long as you're my boss, we can only be good friends.

DAMON

"You're right, Rox. Thank God you have strength enough for both of us.

Damon lifts his hand from my shoulder to pluck something from my hair—a shrimp tail that Hank's groping hand deposited earlier.

"Were you saving this for later?" he asks.

"I was, actually, but if you want it, it's yours."

He drops it over the side of the tailgate, his face so close that I can see the flecks of brown in his hazel eyes. I find myself remembering what a good kisser he used to be. Chances are his skills have deteriorated during his time with Genevieve. I suppose there's no harm in checking—as a purely scientific exercise, of course. Sliding one arm around his neck, I go for it.

He doesn't put up a fight. In fact, it's not so much one kiss as a spell of what might best be described as necking, especially considering that we're dressed like teenagers and sitting on a tailgate. Happily, I find he hasn't lost his touch.

Finally I pull away and Damon hugs me close. We stay like that for a few minutes, my head resting on his shoulder.

When I open my eyes, Hank is watching from the studio door.

Chapter 13

I lean on the balcony railing and draw the cold, crisp air into my lungs. The early-morning light is washing the city in the golden pink glow of a Mark Rothko painting. Eight stories down, the headlights of morning commuters reflect off the icy road, as if the slick, dark asphalt had been sprinkled with red and white crystals. Shivering despite a thick terry bathrobe, I realize that I never fully appreciated the beauty of a December sunrise before.

Damon opens the sliding doors and wraps his arms around me from behind. His mouth close to my ear, he whispers the words I most long to hear: *"I made coffee."*

"You're a god," I say. The words blow away on the wind, so I turn and rest my head on his chest. "You can see Blow-fish from here. Let's have dinner there tonight."

"Sorry, we're ordering in." He leads me back into the apartment and slides the robe off my shoulders. "Restaurants don't serve naked people."

The sound of my own giggling awakens me. I am not in Damon's midtown loft, but my own bedroom. The dream's afterglow fades quickly, leaving in its wake the same uneasy disorientation that plagued my mornings for a long time after my mother died.

That was the year I learned about repression. By day, I'd manage to keep myself so busy that I couldn't think about what had happened. By night, I'd dream about her constantly. People told me the dreams would stop if I took the time to "process the loss," but I didn't even want them to stop. In the dreams, at least Mom was alive. The images were often drawn from memory: Mom wrapping me in a quilt as we waited in line overnight to buy Bruce Springsteen tickets; Mom crying through *The Way We Were* for the fifth time; Mom waiting outside my drawing classes at the Art Gallery of Ontario; Mom blasting opera on a portable stereo in her hospital room until the nurses begged for mercy; Mom, thin and pale, eyes still brightening when I walked into the room....

It was the waking that was hard. I'd have that moment of foreboding and then reality would come flooding back.

Today is like that. It's as if there is something I don't want to remember. Like the dream about Damon. There was a bathrobe, nudity, giggling... Odd, but it was just a dream. It's not as if we actually hooked up or anything.

Except that we did. Last night. On a tailgate. And Hank saw us.

So that's what the foreboding is about.

Okay, this is a problem. It's been well over three years since the last episode and we're still not in a position to indulge that kind of impulse. Damon is rebounding from Genevieve, I am rebounding from Miguel and he is still my boss. It was just a moment of foolishness stemming from our breakups.

It's not like I'm repressing romantic feelings for Damon.

If I were, I'd hate all his girlfriends, whereas I've only hated Genevieve, the praying mantis. If I were, I wouldn't be able to have a relationship with other men, whereas I've managed quite nicely with Miguel. If I were, I wouldn't feel as free to pursue independent career ambitions as I obviously do.

No, I am not repressing feelings for Damon, even though I am guilty of starting it last night. But who could blame me for finding the man attractive? Most women do. He's also talented and brilliant in the ways that matter to me. But what I feel for him is professional admiration. The thought of a fling is appealing and I could probably handle it if the stakes weren't so high. Besides, Damon is a challenging boss even when sex isn't factored into the equation.

The good news is that we didn't get carried away last night and if we were able to put that full-blown sexual encounter behind us years ago, sweeping this minor indiscretion under the camera truck shouldn't be that hard. It was just an innocent kiss between friends.

More like a dozen smoldering, knee-weakening kisses between friends. But no camera babies conceived or anything. Harmless enough overall.

Hank may not agree with my assessment. Although it was too dark to see his expression, I doubt that he was thrilled with his view from the door. By the time we went into the studio later, he'd already left.

So, the sooner Jack gets back in the box the better. I will call Damon today and talk it over. It's the adult thing to do. We're both under a lot of strain on *Illegal Alien* and there's no need to add to it. Better to deal with this up front. I'll ask him to meet for coffee in a romance-killing environment like Starbucks.

Only I sense that I'm repressing something else I have to do today.... I search my bedroom for clues until my eyes fall on the stack of cookbooks on the bedside table. That's it: I promised to make dinner for Dad, Gayle and Crusher.

There's no food in the house, the place is a mess and my head feels as if it's about to explode, yet I have precisely nine hours to transform myself into a passable hostess.

It's a good thing I enjoy a challenge.

I've always admired people who can throw a dinner party together on short notice and somehow make it both elegant and fun. Although I have certain natural gifts, the hostess gene is not among them. This knowledge has allowed me to rationalize the purchase of many kitchen gadgets to make up for the deficit. Unfortunately, a high-end lemon zester can't take you far if you lack the will to zest. In fact, entertaining is something I avoid at all costs. I haven't invited my father to dinner since my mother died—or anyone else for that matter. Libby, Crusher, Miguel and Keisha have occasionally had the pleasure of dining on takeout in front of my jumbotron, but that hardly counts.

The pressure to perform is really on today: it's my father's birthday and he is bringing his new girlfriend. Fortunately, I've read the magazines and I know that what I need to do is keep it simple. Simple and elegant and fun. I can do this. I take a deep breath and try to channel my inner hostess. I am a capable woman with a complex job. I can manage a dinner party for four. It's just a matter of planning.

I pluck a cookbook from the pile on my bedside table and turn to "Easy Celebration Menus."

Roasted red pepper and goat cheese phyllo pastry appetizers
Citrus grilled arctic char
Wild and brown rice salad with cranberries

Symphony of stir-fried vegetables
Chocolate toffee fudge cake

Perfect. Now for a schedule. If I clean my apartment by 10:00, I can take a cab to the studio to retrieve my Jeep, swing by Balzac's café for a latte and still finish the grocery shopping by noon. That gives me the entire afternoon to bake the cake, assemble the appetizers, marinate the fish, make the rice and prep the veggies. I'll wrap it up at 5:30, take a leisurely bath, blow out my hair, set the table and load the CD player. By the time my guests arrive at 7:30, I'll be lighting the candles serenely.

It's totally doable. Except for the fact that it's already 10:30 and my apartment resembles a crime scene. I jump out of bed and grab three green garbage bags from the hall closet. Mail and scrap paper goes into the first bag, clothing, clean and otherwise, into the second and miscellaneous crap into the third. I stuff the bags into my closet, fluff the duvet and pillows and chase a cloth around the bathroom. The kitchen, fortunately, looks clean enough, except for the pile of dirty dishes. I load these into a plastic storage bin and hide it in the bathtub. By eliminating vacuuming, I arrive at my Jeep by 11:15.

11:45   First glitch: megamart out of arctic char.
12:45   Three additional stores out of arctic char.
1:00   Race home with salmon steaks.
1:15   Drive to Balzac's to purchase cake; grab latte and croissant to go.
2:00   Tear phyllo pastry to smithereens.
2:15   Race back to megamart to buy frozen egg roll appetizer.
3:15   Assemble ingredients for fish marinade and discover marinade should have been prepared the night before.

3:45   Ditto wild rice.

4:00   Return to megamart for instant rice. Greet cashier by name.

4:10   Buy hotdog from vendor.

4:45   Pour first glass of wine.

5:00   Begin cleaning vegetables for symphony.

5:10   Peeling, seeding, chopping.

5:30   Peeling, seeding, chopping.

5:45   Peeling, seeding, chopping.

6:00   Dump pepper and zucchini back in refrigerator.

6:10   Lay out dress jeans and flowy black blouse on bed.

6:15   Start shower and step into plastic tub of dirty, wet dishes.

6:20   Wrap in skimpy kimono and deposit dishes on back deck.

6:35   Comb wet hair, apply mascara and lipstick.

6:45   Discover black bra is buried under wet towels in garbage bag. Locate navy embroidered designer bra, previously unworn because floral design is visible under most fabrics.

6:55   Discover floral design is visible through flowy black blouse.

7:00   Discover dress jeans are officially too tight.

7:01   Regret croissant and hotdog (but not wine).

7:02   Locate "fat" jeans.

7:05   Slip into high heels to make legs look slimmer in fat jeans.

7:10   Start setting table.

7:12   Open door to receive early guests.

Gayle's silvery blond bob has been combed back off her face and lacquered with half a can of spray. It almost slashes my cheek when she hugs me. I help her out of a floor-length fur coat while Dad doffs his jacket to reveal the loudest shirt I've ever seen.

"Hey, Dad, Magnum P.I. called from the eighties. He wants his shirt back."

My father's face turns pink. "It was a gift…"

"Tropical prints are in again, Roxanne," Gayle says, severely, revealing the source of the gift.

"Already?" I say. Silly me.

Gayle casts a surreptitious look at my too-visible bra. "With your job, I suppose you don't have time to keep up with fashion."

I offer a silent prayer to my mother for support and swallow my snarky reply unsaid. Gayle may have an edge, but at least she is closer to my father's age than anyone else in his string of girlfriends. He didn't choose her for her looks, either. Her eyes are small, her nose pointy and her chin missing in action. However, there's an enormous diamond on her right hand, a Versace *V* on the hem of her fuchsia blouse and a string of pearls the size of golf balls wrapped around her scrawny neck. She's not after Dad's cash.

I escort the happy couple into the living room, where Gayle stares at my jumbotron. "It's so interesting the way you've made your television the focal point of the room," she says.

"Thanks. My friends say I have a real flair for decorating."

I lead Gayle over to my Salvation Army sofa and offer her a drink. She inspects the orange corduroy fabric with trepidation before perching on the arm. Stretching her bright fuchsia lips into a smile, she says, "I'll have a dry gin martini."

My bar features only wine, beer and cooking sherry but I say, "You've got it. And red wine for Dad, of course."

In the kitchen, I pop the egg rolls into the oven before calling Crusher.

"I'm only three minutes late," he answers.

"I know, but hurry. Bring gin and vermouth. And ice—my freezer is on the fritz."

"I just bought that fridge. What have you done to it?"

"It's another relic, Slumlord. I suggested a new fridge, remember?"

A series of sneezes erupts in the living room.

Crusher asks, "What the hell is that?"

"I think Dad's new girlfriend is allergic to me."

"You know, I was thinking—"

"You're not bailing on me now, pal. Get up here."

I drink half of Dad's wine while waiting for Crusher. Poking my head into the living room on the way to the door, I find Dad plying Gayle with tissue.

"Allergic to dust," he says, shrugging apologetically. "She'll be fine once the antihistamines kick in."

"No vermouth," Crusher says, following me into the kitchen. "Whoa!" He's caught sight of Gayle's coat. "Somebody been shooting rats by the Dumpster?"

"Quiet," I hiss, "she'll hear you."

"Roxanne," Gayle calls between sneezes, "I think something is burning."

Smoke billows from the oven as I retrieve the egg rolls, now charred logs. Crusher opens the windows to clear the smoke while I concoct Gayle's martini: gin with a dash of cooking sherry.

"Everything okay in there?" Dad asks.

"Couldn't be better," I say, although my hands are shaking a little as I carry the tray into the living room. "Gayle, this is my friend Crusher."

Still snuffling, she stands on tiptoe to kiss Crusher on the cheek, leaving a pink lip print above the beard.

Grasping for a conversation starter, he says, "I was just admiring your coat."

"It's mink," she says, with another sneeze. "Rat is so showy."

Crusher blushes, something I would have thought impossible.

Stifling hysterical laughter, I propose a toast to Dad's health.

Gayle sniffs suspiciously at her martini. With her pointy nose and pink eyes, she looks a little ratlike herself. "Roxanne, do let me help in the kitchen."

"It's all under control, thanks." An outright lie, of course, but the last thing I want is help from the Rat Lady.

The doorbell rings. Grateful for a momentary escape, I run down the stairs and open the door. It's Damon, looking very serious. I suppose he's here for the "adult" discussion.

"Hi!" My voice is far too loud and my face is burning. All that rushing around is making my heart race.

"Hi, Rox." He peers past me up the stairs. "Can I come in? Or are you busy?"

"My father is here with his new girlfriend."

"Why don't I call you later, then?"

"No."

He looks down at my hand, which has, of its own accord, seized his sleeve in a vice grip. "No?"

"Stay for dinner."

"Are you sure?" he asks. He's already stepped inside and I'm not sure whether he did it voluntarily or I caught him in a tractor beam.

"Yes. Come in."

"I already did." His grin suggests that he's enjoying my discomfiture. "Nice top."

I cross my arms to cover the floral embroidery. "It's a blouse, actually."

"My mistake. No holes from Glenda, yet I can see right through it."

"It's *Gilda*. How many times do I have to introduce you two?"

A sneeze wafts toward us as Gayle pokes her head into the stairwell. "Please close the door, Roxanne, I'm getting a chill."

"The Rat Lady speaketh," I whisper. I lead Damon upstairs, conscious of my fat jeans every step of the way.

Dad rises to introduce Gayle, who stops sneezing long enough to plant a fuchsia lip print on Damon's cheek. Crusher dutifully reengages Gayle in conversation about a renowned Scandinavian sculptor while I fetch a glass of wine for Damon and refill my father's.

There is a distinct pink lip print on Dad's glass. A gracious hostess would offer Gayle a glass of merlot right about now. Instead, I ask, "How's the martini, Gayle? You've barely touched it."

She takes a sip, wincing slightly. "Lovely, dear, but I have to be careful after those antihistamines, you know."

Excusing myself, I put the instant rice into the microwave and prepare to set the table.

Gayle sneaks into the kitchen on silent paws. "Why, none of your china matches, Roxanne. How quaint. But if you're in the market for something more coordinated, I could help. I'm a table designer at Ashley's." She leans close and whispers conspiratorially, "Between you and me, Barney left me enough that I don't have to lift a finger for the rest of my life, but I love my work."

Ashley's is one of Toronto's most expensive dinnerware stores and brides from all over the country register there. My approach is more unique: I comb flea market stands for single pieces that I mix and match according to color scheme.

"What a quaint idea," she says, after I explain. "You young people are so brave today."

My blood pressure rises quite perceptibly. The timer is going on my fish, I haven't started the vegetables and half the cutlery I need is in a tub on the deck. Meanwhile, the Rat Lady prattles on about Royal Doulton patterns as if it's a common interest.

By the time Damon comes into the kitchen, I'm spinning in a futile orbit around the kitchen.

"Take a sip," he says, handing me my wine. He peeks into the oven. "The salmon will be perfect if you turn the oven off now and put some tinfoil over it." Pouring Gayle a glass of wine, he leads her back into the living room where Crusher presents another artist for discussion.

I am still paralyzed when Damon returns. "My symphony," I mumble, wringing my hands.

"Your what?"

"The menu calls for a symphony of vegetables…"

He takes a closer look at me. "Okay, Rox, time to sit down. You're losing it."

"I'm not losing it. It's just that…he can't be replacing my mother with *that*."

He leads me to a chair and presses on my shoulder until I collapse into it. "No one can replace your mother and your father knows that. Everything will look better after dinner."

In less time than it took me to burn the egg rolls, Damon tosses garlic, wine and an assortment of herbs into the wok and sautés the vegetables. Then he finishes the rice and concocts a sauce for the salmon.

Amazingly, he accomplishes all this without barking a single order at me. He's a totally different man with a spatula in his hand.

★ ★ ★

Winking at me, Damon holds out Gayle's chair, shakes out her napkin and places it in her lap. Like a temperamental actress, she quickly succumbs to his ministrations.

"Gord tells me you're a cinematographer, Damon," she says. "Did you know that my aunt, Lorna Lamont, is a legend of the silver screen?"

There's a collective gasp from Damon, Crusher and me. Lorna Lamont was one of MGM's 'it girls' in the 1940s. Her star burned out long ago, but I've seen many of the twenty or so movies she made.

Damon quizzes Gayle about her aunt, who has returned to Toronto since retiring. Thanks to his efforts, Gayle is soon giggling and looking less ratlike because of it. My father beams throughout, delighted that his ladylove is the center of attention. Even I am smiling, mainly over the matching pink lip prints on Damon's and Crusher's cheeks.

Damon helps me clear dishes between courses, leaving Crusher to moderate the conversation. In the kitchen, I collect dessert plates and mugs while Damon locates my coffee machine. Once the coffee is brewing, he carries the mugs into the dining room.

As soon as he is out of the room, I hurry over to the shiny chrome toaster to check my hair. As I feared, air-drying has left it with an odd warp on one side.

Crusher catches me trying to fluff it and asks, "So what's the deal with you and Damon?"

"What do you mean?"

"I mean you're out here tossing your hair and I'm guessing it's not for my benefit."

I scowl at him and resume fluffing. "Why didn't you tell me it was all warped on one side? What will Gayle think?"

"Like you care what Gayle thinks," Crusher snorts. "Anyway, the time I said your part looked like a lightning strike you got pissed."

"A crooked part adds volume."

"The warp adds volume to one side of your head."

Damon returns and piles the last of the dirty dishes by the sink. "What, no dishwasher?"

I jab a thumb in Crusher's direction. "Speak to the Slumlord."

Crusher hightails it out of the kitchen. "Better get out there—I'm the one keeping this conversation going."

I slide the cake out of its Balzac's box onto a platter.

Damon says, "You going to pass that off as your own?"

"You know I never take credit for other people's work."

"You don't have to—yours is better than most people's."

I find myself flushing again. Although he's only complimenting my camera work, that's a rare enough occurrence. "I assume you mean outside the kitchen."

"Well, your slicing could use work," he says, appraising my haphazard technique. "Allow me." Standing directly behind me, he takes the knife from my hand and cuts the cake into precise slices.

"Those are pretty big pieces," I say, just to say something.

"I'm trying to sweeten someone up."

I imagine he means the Rat Lady, but I don't ask. He's standing way too close to me and his words are buzzing in my ear.

Here's my chance to turn around and do the mature thing. I will say, *You're my boss, this can't happen. We spend too much time together as it is. I wish it could, but it can't.* That ought to do the trick.

Except that I don't say it. Instead, I stand transfixed as he slices the entire cake. Even when he starts lifting pieces onto platters, with one arm on either side of me, I remain silent.

The phone startles us both. Damon steps back, knife in hand, and I fumble for the receiver. "Hello?"

"So finally you decided to take my call."

It's Miguel and the timing could not possibly be any worse. "Oh. Hi."

Damon, arranging the cake, watches me.

Miguel says, "Is that the best you can do? I've been leaving messages for days. And you actually hung up on me. You can't still be angry, Roxanne."

"Can't I?" Damon is moving at half speed, obviously very much interested in this conversation. "Look, this isn't the best time. Let's talk tomorrow—"

"If I call back tomorrow you probably won't answer. Let's talk now."

"I really can't, I have guests."

"So I'll come by later."

"No! Don't come over. I'm exhausted and need to get to bed early. I'll call you tomorrow, I promise."

"Everything okay?" Damon asks as I hang up the phone.

"Sure. Just a friend in need."

The phone starts to ring again.

"Aren't you going to answer it? Your friend needs to talk."

"We can talk tomorrow. It's not that important." I look him directly in the eye and add, "Really." The phone stops ringing. "See? Let's just enjoy our dessert."

Before we're out of the kitchen, however, the phone starts ringing again. Damon's expression turns to annoyance.

Dad yells from the dining room, "Roxy, aren't you going to answer that?"

I hear Gayle mutter, "In my day, it wasn't considered polite to let a phone ring."

Damon sets the cake platter on the table and announces, "I must leave, folks."

"Already?" Gayle asks, saving me the trouble.

"I've got locations to survey before call tomorrow, so I'll be up very early. Good night everyone."

I trail after Damon, fully aware that something between us has taken a bad turn, but unsure how to fix it. "Do you really have to go?"

"Yeah, I'd better." He won't even look at me.

"Is everything all right?"

"It's fine, Roxanne. Go back to your guests. I'll see you tomorrow."

I reach out to take his arm again, but he's turning toward the door and doesn't notice.

Crusher stretches my blue rubber gloves over his big, hairy hands.

"Laugh if you must, Roxanne, but I happen to have very delicate skin," he says, starting to scrape at a waxy fuchsia ring on one of my wineglasses. "So, what happened tonight?"

"I didn't really take to Gayle and it ruined the mood, I guess."

"I'm talking about Damon and you know it."

"I told you already, there's nothing going on between us."

"You turned red when he arrived and stayed that way for three hours."

"That was the wine."

"One minute the kitchen is a disaster zone, the next you two are whipping up dinner like a well-oiled machine."

"Big surprise. We've been working as a team for years."

"Always professional?"

"That's right."

Crusher raises a wiry eyebrow. "Then why did things go south after the beret started ringing?"

"You think you know everything."

"I don't hear you denying it." Crusher moves from the sink to my refrigerator where he pulls out the leftovers and begins to transfer them to plastic containers.

"Use the vacuum sealer. It'll take up less room in your freezer."

"I'm storing your leftovers?" he asks, turning to my latest infomercial purchase.

"My freezer's broken, remember?"

"Speaking of freezing, you were about to tell me what happened between you and Damon."

"Can we please drop this subject?"

"No problem. So why did Damon stop by?"

I sigh. "He didn't say."

Crusher grunts in disbelief, but it's the truth. Whatever Damon came to say, he didn't say it. And I didn't say what I wanted to say either. So chances are we'll automatically revert to business as usual tomorrow.

I am going to work very hard at forgetting the tailgate party ever happened. And I'll very likely succeed. After all, I've been perfecting the repression thing for a long time now.

Chapter 14

"Sorry I'm late," I call into the camera truck. "There are so many trucks on the lot that I almost had to take a cab from my parking sp—"

The last word dies in my throat at the sight of Alana Speir rummaging through my workbench.

"FYI, sweetie, I'm a big fan of—" she raises her skinny arms and curls her manicured fingers into fake quotation marks "—punctuality. But enough said. I don't want to come across like a tyrant on my first day." She bends to yank open a drawer and her low-slung jeans creep even lower to reveal an aqua thong. "Now, where do you hide the batteries?"

I stare at her, dumbfounded.

"Rox? Are you *with me?*" Still hunched over, she does the quote thing again. "My light meter's dead and I need batteries."

Regaining control of my lips, I ask, "What are you doing on my truck, Alana?"

She straightens up and blinks her enormous pale green

eyes at me a few times. "Oh, sweetie, didn't Damon tell you? I'm the second unit cinematographer."

"What?" It comes out on a rush of air.

"Howard Weinstock wanted to get the second unit up and running ASAP. Hank thought of me right away and of course, I jumped at the chance—even though it means canceling my pre-Christmas *spa* vacation."

She throws some finger quotes around *spa* for emphasis.

Alana is still bragging about her recent dinner with "Hank and Daddy" when Damon arrives. She plants a breezy kiss on his cheek in approximately the same locale as Gayle laid on the fuchsia last night. "Morning, sweetie," she says. "Now, Rox, just run over to set with those batteries as soon as you get the camera built, okay? And clear a shelf for my foul weather gear when you get a chance." She points to an enormous designer duffel bag that takes up most of my bench before flitting off the truck.

I turn to Damon. "You knew about this?"

He nods. "I met with Howard and Hank yesterday afternoon."

In view of the "no crying in camera" rule, I promptly redirect my emotions toward anger. "Why the hell didn't you tell me?"

"That's why I came over, but when I got there it seemed like you were already stressed enough over your dad and Gayle. I didn't want to make the evening harder than it already was."

"How thoughtful of you to drop the bomb at work instead."

Damon starts rearranging the film stock. "I didn't have a lot of options, Rox."

"You could have stayed until everyone left."

"That was my plan," he says, banging the film canisters

around deliberately, "until your *friend in need* called. Didn't want to be in the way."

Damon manages to emphasize the words *friend in need* quite nicely without resorting to finger quotes. Alana could learn a thing or two from him.

He has some nerve being annoyed over that call, especially since he broke up with Genevieve so recently. If he has any interest in me beyond a tailgate snogging, he's had plenty of opportunity to say so. Instead, he waits until I'm reeling from the news of a lost career opportunity to raise his concerns about my late-night booty call.

Well, this just proves that he can't handle anything more than an occasional make-out session. Thank God I didn't let on last night that I was falling for his outrageous flirting.

At any rate, I don't intend to discuss any of this with him today. There are bigger fish to fry and one of them is wearing an aqua thong.

"After all the years we've worked together," I say, keeping my voice even, "I think you owed it to me to tell me yourself instead of letting me hear it from Alana."

Damon has the decency to look ashamed. "There's more," he says, "and you're not going to like it. Rick Meyer is coming in to pull focus for me on the main unit. You'll be joining the second unit under Alana."

I clutch the workbench for support. "That had better be a joke."

"It's not." He won't even look at me, the coward.

"That's so unfair. You're just punishing me."

He turns to meet my eye. "Punishing you? For what?"

For not falling for his halfhearted overtures? For not being his rebound girl? That'll do for starters.

I feel the whirring of mental gears as my repression machine kicks in.

"Never mind," I say. I add some finger quotes for good measure.

He shakes his head. "I don't know what you're talking about, Roxanne. At any rate, this was Hank's decision, not mine. I told him that Alana is a weak choice and he went ahead anyway. That's why I'm putting you on her unit. Her footage needs to cut with mine seamlessly and you know my style inside and out."

"Yeah, I know your style," I say, starting toward the door.

He blocks my path. "If you have something to say, say it."

"I'm saying that I am not babysitting Alana Speir for you. If Hank's decision affects the look of this picture, that's not my problem. Send Rick Meyer to safeguard your reputation."

"Roxanne, I'm not asking you, I'm telling you to get over to set and pull focus for Alana."

"I won't. I quit."

Damon turns away with a dismissive snort. "You won't quit."

I dodge around him and jump off the truck.

"Hey, where are you going?" he yells after me from the tailgate. "Call time was twenty minutes ago. You need to build the camera."

"Do it yourself, *sweetie*. Or wait until your new slave gets here."

Keisha cracks a sixth egg into a bowl of pancake batter. "You're not really going to quit, are you?"

"First I'm going to eat ten free pancakes and then I'm going to quit." I rummage around the shelves on the craft truck. "And I'm going to eat them with real maple syrup, Keisha. I know you have it, so don't lie to me."

There are secret stashes of many foods hidden on the craft trucks for the actors. While they feast on gourmet brands, the rest of us have to settle for cheap substitutes.

"If I give you the real stuff, will you promise not to quit?" she asks.

"No promises, but I'll think about it. For you."

Passing me the pancake flipper, she hops off the craft truck to collect the syrup from supplies.

While I'm manning the griddle, Hank climbs aboard. "Making a career change, Roxanne?" he asks.

"Why not? Flipping flapjacks might be more rewarding than camera work."

"Ah. You've run into Alana." There's a smug smile on his face as he watches me dump batter onto the griddle in one huge pancake. "Come now, Roxanne. Surely you're not going to sulk over one little setback? That worries me. Fledgling Films isn't looking for quitters."

"It's not looking to upgrade focus pullers either, apparently."

"I haven't reneged, darling. If you continue to prove your skills, I'll continue to keep you in mind for Morocco."

"Shooting the second unit would have been the ideal place to prove them."

Hank shrugs. "Martin Speir told me how much cinematography work Alana has been doing and convinced me she'd be right for the job."

Realizing that I won't have to go to the trouble of quitting if he fires me first, I say, "You mean he offered you something in return."

Ladling fruit salad into a foam bowl, he says, "You're skating on thin ice, little lady. But this business does thrive on reciprocity."

I struggle to flip the monster pancake. "You said you believed in taking chances on people."

"I do, and right now I'm taking a chance on Alana."

Daring him again to fire me, I say, "Are you ever."

He refuses to take the bait. "Your boyfriend agrees with you. He tried to convince me that you were the better choice. But then, he's hardly objective."

"If you're referring to Damon, he is not my boyfriend."

"No? It's so hard to read the signs these days. Now, could I get some pancakes?"

I break the pancake into three jagged chunks and pile them on a plate. They're still runny in the center, but I offer them with a flourish.

He inspects them dubiously. "Don't quit your day job."

"That's entirely up to you, sir. Now enjoy your order—and have a great day."

After he leaves, Keisha's walkie-talkie crackles. "Hello? Craft services?"

"Can you grab that, Rox?" Keisha reappears and hands me the maple syrup in exchange for the flipper.

I push the talk button: "Go for craft."

"This is Alana Speir, second unit cinematographer—Painter of Light, Illuminator of Stars." She giggles. "I'd like some ginger tea, an egg-white omelet, lightly browned, no bubbles, and a slice of low-carb toast with soy margarine."

"Copy that. One coffee, double double, a fried egg sandwich and a cinnamon Danish, extra butter for the on-set painter." I put the walkie down and empty the bottle of maple syrup onto my pancakes.

The walkie sputters again. "Roxanne? Is that you?"

Okay, I'm not quitting. A blot on my heretofore spotless record would punish only me, not Hank and Damon. No, it's better to take what Libby always calls the "moral high road." I'm sure it's around here somewhere, although probably not behind the grip truck, where I'm currently hiding with my pancakes.

I console myself that Hank may very well have given me the second unit job if it weren't for Martin Speir—or the fact that he saw me kissing Damon and misconstrued the signs. As for Damon, I hate him for making me work for Alana, but at least Hank confirmed he fought for me to shoot the second unit.

As it stands, Hank and Damon remain my best contacts for moving ahead in this industry. While there are no guarantees that they'll come through, I will certainly burn both bridges if I quit.

It looks like I will have to continue to play the game and proceed with my own plan on the side. That's what Libby did. When her bosses were making her life hell, she started writing a book with Lola on the side, saying "The best revenge is to succeed in spite of the bastards."

She's a goddamned inspiration, that Libby. I probably don't tell her that enough. I haul out my cell phone to do it now. My mouth is full of pancakes when her voice mail picks up, but that doesn't stop me from singing Chicago's "You're the Inspiration." The song has a special place in Libby's heart. Back in grade nine, she danced to it with Kevin Mallet. Then a full foot shorter than she was, Kevin rested his head on her chest with an expression of rapture. Libby's expression, by contrast, was one of utter mortification. Even now, the memory puts a smile on my face.

"Hey, Lib," I say, "You should invite Kevin Mallet to *The Counterfeit Wedding* premiere. Any idea when that will be? Oh right, you haven't finished writing the script yet. I really hate pressuring you, but get on it, will you?"

Knowing that my message will get a rise out of her gives me strength. There is life beyond *Illegal Alien*. I have friends. I have prospects. Assisting Alana will be my personal hell, but I'll be better able to endure it if I have my own project in the works—a project where I will finally be the one calling the shots.

On my set, no one will ever be denied a promotion for a drunken kiss.

Actually, on my set, there will be no kissing allowed. I will post signs prohibiting it: big fuchsia lips with a line through them. No one could misread that.

Christian helps me load Gilda onto a cart. Alana may be able to take me by force, but Gilda and Christian are coming with me. Rick Myers can manage with the daily equipment and crew.

As we're leaving, Alana's beige duffel bag slips from my bench onto the floor. An accidental kick from my dusty boot sends the camera cart careening over it, totally out of control. Christian wisely hops out of the way.

I feel so bad about the greasy tire marks running the length of the duffel bag that I take a moment to find a better location for it. Fortunately, nothing ever falls off the shelf where we store the muddy, mildewed tarps.

It will be quite safe there.

"Camera left," Alana calls from her chair by the monitor. "More…more…" she says. "Too far, Roxanne. Take it back a titch."

I slide 120 pounds of camera, head and tripod back to where they were two minutes ago. "Wouldn't it be easier to move the props?"

"No, I want the background to be the same. Just slide the

camera in a little more and you're there… Oops, now you've gone too far forward. Try that again, sweetie."

On my set, kissing may be off-limits, but punching will be encouraged. The sign will feature a fist with no line through it.

Alana sits protected from the downpour by a golf umbrella as I push the third and final cart of camera gear up the slippery incline.

She says, "Don't bother bringing up any more equipment, sweetie."

Puffing, I park the cart and tuck a string of wet hair behind my ear. "It's—all—here—anyway."

"Take it back to the studio. The shot's not going to match in this rain."

"I said that an hour ago—and you said you could light it—so the rain wouldn't show."

"It's raining harder now, *obviously*." (finger quotes) "We'll come back later when it lets up." Alana climbs into an idling minivan. "You'll need to move a little faster with the gear. We've got a lot to shoot today and I'm trying to make a good impression on my *first* day." (more finger quotes)

As the van pulls out, I shoot some of my own fingers into the air.

Alana is a pretty little moth attracted to Howard Weinstock's flame. Left to her own devices, I suspect she'd be singed in short order. But that probably won't happen because I have resurrected Super Focus Puller, my professional alter ego. Super Focus Puller must get the job done right. Not for Damon. Not for Hank. And most certainly not for Alana. Super Focus Puller does it for herself because she has integrity.

I set up a monitor and VCR so that we can review the main unit's footage to ensure that our work matches precisely. The shot they are missing is a tight close-up, or insert shot, of a business card. I examine the wide shot in which the card first appears, then place it on the desk in a similar position.

Alana, fluttering a few feet away from Howard, glances at the tape briefly before giving some vague lighting instructions to the second unit gaffer. Having discovered that the main light source she specifies won't match the master scene, the gaffer and I make the proper adjustments.

Returning to look through the viewfinder, she says, "A perfect match. I'm a genius, Howard." She appears to be genuinely oblivious to the fact that nothing is arranged as she instructed.

If she's so clever, I don't see why Hank is making us wait for his approval on each setup. These aren't major shots, but he's decreed that we aren't to roll a foot of film without his approval. Maybe Hank isn't as confident in his decision as he let on.

Alana pulls a sheet of paper out of her script bag and hands it to me. "Here's a list of everything you'll need to order for the rest of the week," she says.

I review the list and see that she's ordered the wrong film stock and overlooked several essential items. I try to lure her farther away from Howard to discuss this.

"Roxanne, the order is fine," she says. "Just phone it in."

As much as I'd like to stick it to Alana, embarrassing her in front of Howard won't make Super Focus Puller look good either. So I try once again to pull her aside. "Just a couple of things, Alana. It won't take a moment."

"What?" she asks, exasperated, suede boots firmly planted.

Okay, I'm willing to stick with the high road, but it would

help if she recognized that I'm on it. "It's just that Damon used daylight stock—"

"Roxanne, this is my call, so please order the stock I use." She rolls her eyes at Howard, as if I were a wayward child.

I take her by the arm and move her by force. "This isn't about preference, Alana," I whisper. "We're going to have to match the daylight footage Damon's already shot and at the moment we don't have any film to load."

The light finally dawns and she looks over at Howard anxiously before saying, "It's on the list, you must have missed it."

"What about the filters Damon used? Maybe I'm missing that, too."

"I've only had a few hours to come up to speed, Roxanne, so I can't know all the tiny details. That's why Damon assigned you to support me."

"Then I'll add some lenses to the list, because we'll need some."

She leans over and snatches the list from my hands. "Let me have another go at that. You're obviously having some trouble with my handwriting."

What this production really needs is another star and thank God we've found one.

Alana positively lights up when an entertainment reporter and videographer from a local television station arrive. They're ostensibly here to interview Shawna and Zara, but the cameraman takes an immediate shine to Alana's midriff-baring sweater. Once she points out that her belly stud is a tiny motion picture camera, he suggests getting some background shots of our team.

The only problem is that we're not actually doing anything worth documenting because Hank still hasn't approved our insert shot of a padlock. When the (female) reporter suggests finding someone busier to shoot, Alana springs out of her director's chair and rushes over to the camera to scrutinize the setup with the intensity of an astronomer who's spotted a meteorite rocketing toward Earth.

"Let's change this lens to a 150 mm, Rox."

I obediently replace the lens and step back to allow Alana to examine the frame again for the benefit of her personal videographer. "No, go back to the 100 mm."

While I change the lens, she poses fetchingly with her light meter. Then, when I attempt to adjust the lens, she brushes me aside.

"Do your fiddling later," she says. "Let me set up the shot first." She peers through the viewfinder again and frowns. "The image is awfully dark, Rox, what have you done?"

She pans the camera left and right, then up and down.

I let her struggle for a while longer before stepping into her fifteen-minute window of fame to remove the lens cap.

Alana is digging through our accessory bag when I return from the washroom.

"Rox, you really must organize this bag." She turns to let Video Dude's camera see that she is smiling as she chastises me. "I can't find the color chart."

"We already shot a color chart for this setup," I say.

"Well, I'd like to shoot another one." The videographer trains his lens on me as I retrieve the chart from the bag. To reclaim his attention, Alana tells him, "Roxanne used to be my boss and now I'm hers. Isn't it funny how things work out?"

He turns to catch my reaction to this before I can erase my sneer.

"Ooh, sweetie," Alana squeals, "your fly is open. That won't do for prime time, will it?"

Hank slings an arm around Alana. "How's it going over here, camera beauties?"

Alana turns so quickly to hug him that she whips me full in the face with her ponytail. "This is such fun, isn't it, Rox?"

"It sure is," I agree, wiping my streaming eye.

Hank says, "I hope you're taking good care of her, Roxanne."

Nodding, I pluck two mochaccino's from Keisha's tray and offer one to my new boss. "Have a mocha, Alana."

The bright light of the video camera shines down on us as Alana tilts her head coyly. "Now, Roxanne, caffeine is probably what's making you so crabby. Scoot to the craft truck to get us some ginger tea instead."

There's a gorgeous flower arrangement waiting when I get home and the phone is ringing.

"I hope you like them, *mi amor.*"

"They're beautiful."

"I asked the florist for those big gerbil daisies you like."

"Gerberas."

"You're correcting me, so there is hope for us yet. Why didn't you call me back last night?"

"My guests stayed late."

"Guests? Or guest? Is there someone new in your life?"

"Not yet. I'm auditioning next week."

"Then there is still time for me to apologize properly. Will you open the door if I come over?"

I suppose it's time to bury the hatchet. The truth is, I am Rubenesque right now and Miguel was only stating the obvious. "Maybe."

There's a knock at the door. I open it to find Miguel leaning against the wall opposite. Crusher must have let him in downstairs, so there will be hell to pay later. For the moment, however, I'm happy to see him—especially because he's gorgeously disheveled.

"Please forgive me," he says, wrapping his arms around me. "If I didn't adore your body, why would I keep coming back for more?"

Wine in hand, we stretch out on opposite ends of the sofa, our feet resting in each other's lap.

"I gather you took the Toronto job," I say.

"Yes. I'll be here for three months except for a couple of weekends in New York to pack."

"You're moving?" I ask. "To L.A.?"

He nods, shamefaced. "It will be cheaper and more convenient than flying there all the time for meetings with my agent and producers."

Miguel has always scoffed at directors who "sell out" by moving to L.A., maintaining that if he's good at his craft, the work will come to him. Although I'm tempted to tease him about his change of heart, the foot massage he's giving me is morphing into a very pleasant leg massage that I don't want to interrupt.

He shows his gratitude for my restraint by working his way up my thigh. "We still have some making up to do. And if you are a good girl, I promise to give you half the duvet tonight."

After a successful reconciliation, I reach for the remote control. Miguel is already dozing beside me on the couch, but I'm too wired from my day to relax.

I tune in to the local news just as it transitions to the entertainment feature on *Illegal Alien*. The jumbotron shows a very clear image of me handing a cup of tea to Alana.

Miguel mumbles sleepily. "Is that your show?"

"No. Go back to sleep."

The big-screen Alana tosses her light meter at me and I scamper away. In the next cut, she snaps her fingers and I pull out my cell phone and hand it to her. Anyone watching this footage will think I'm her personal assistant.

Now fully awake, Miguel props himself up. "Isn't that Alana Speir?"

"Who?" Maybe playing dumb will work.

"The blonde with the ponytail. The one you are fanning with palm leaves."

In fact, I am not fanning, but feeding Alana. On screen, I offer her a nice sandwich, which she dismisses, patting her flat stomach and pointing to mine.

I've had plenty of humiliating moments in my life, but this ranks right up there.

"What's she doing on your set?" Miguel asks.

I pull a blanket around my shoulders miserably. "Hank added a second unit and Alana's the cinematographer."

"I'm surprised he didn't give you the opportunity."

"Not as surprised as I was."

"If he's considering you for his Morocco movie, why wouldn't he let you try this first? It's a natural progression."

"He said Martin Speir convinced him to use Alana."

"Martin must be doing something for Hank," Miguel says. "But I still don't understand what you're doing on the second unit."

"Damon wants me to keep an eye on Alana."

"That doesn't seem fair."

"It isn't fair, but it is wise. Today, she gave incorrect lighting instructions for nearly every setup. The worst thing is that she didn't even notice I adjusted everything to match Damon's footage."

"You'll need to warn Howard Weinstock, Roxanne. That kind of incompetence could cost him thousands."

Miguel yawns and settles back to doze, leaving me to finish the wine. He may be right that I should blow the whistle on Alana, but it wouldn't be appropriate to run directly to Howard. The right thing to do would be to tell Damon, and ultimately Hank, about the problem, but given recent events, anything I say about Alana now will have the distinct flavor of sour grapes.

Chapter 15

Shawna exits the police precinct, climbs into the idling cruiser where Zara's screen double awaits and drives out of frame, exiting camera left.

"Cut!" Alana calls. It's the first time that Hank has let us roll without waiting for his approval and Alana is fizzing with excitement. "Let's hear it for one-take Shawna!"

Shawna climbs out of the cruiser. "Really? That's it?"

"It was perfect, sweetie," Alana says, throwing her arms around her new best friend.

Looking a little taken aback by the familiarity, Shawna nonetheless hugs her back. Anything that expedites a return to her vodka supply is okay by Martini.

I say, "Maybe we should do one more take."

Alana turns to me, frowning. "Why? What did you do?"

Super Focus Puller rises above the slight. "The shot won't match what Hank's already filmed. Here, you had Shawna exit camera left. In the next cut, the cruiser *enters* camera left."

Alana lets her fingers do the back talking with some air quotes. *"So?"*

"So—" I air quote back at her *"—*Shawna should drive out camera right. This is part of the same sequence, and the car needs to be heading in the same direction each time."

Alana's color rises and her fingers fall.

Shawna says, "Yeah, I did drive in from camera left when we shot the following scene. Hey," she adds, as if noticing me for the first time, "do you have a sister? You look a lot like the camera girl on the main unit."

"Same camera girl." Same rack, as a matter of fact.

"What happened? Are you here to keep an eye on things?"

Alana jumps in quickly. "When Hank hired me to shoot second unit, Damon decided he could spare Roxanne. It's great for me to have the support and great for her to have some downtime. Right, Rox?"

I muster a tight smile. Working for Alana is anything but a vacation. While we do have more downtime as a result of lengthy waits for Hank's approval, I pay for it with constant vigilance for SNAFUs—as in *Situation Normal Alana Fucked Up.*

In fact, today's SNAFU requires several additional takes and to make amends to Shawna for this, Alana graciously offers to shoot a big close-up inside the car. This time, a delighted Shawna initiates the hug.

Again, the spoilsport speaks: "Alana, I don't think that's going to work. A close-up inside the car would show that 'Zara' is just a photo double."

Both women glower at me and Martini exits camera right in a foul mood.

Hank passes her as he comes in. "What's wrong with Shawna?"

Alana explains, "She wanted a big close-up inside the cruiser and I had to put my foot down. Obviously, we couldn't risk seeing Zara's photo double."

"Good thinking, Alana."

Alana smiles beatifically and reaches for her vibrating cell phone. After checking the call display, she hands it to me. "Sweetie, I need a word with Hank. Could you ask my esthetician to book me a paraffin wax with next week's manicure?"

Since Hank is watching, I can't toss the phone into a trash can.

Instead, I book Alana for the full Brazilian.

The shot with Shawna was our first with a real cast member. Mostly, we've been photographing footprints, police reports, gun barrels and so forth. It's pretty basic stuff, yet not a day passes without a SNAFU. Alana continually dials her light meter to the wrong film stock, gives extras the wrong eye lines, neglects to add necessary color-corrective filters and ignores Gilda's technical limitations.

I knew even when Alana was my trainee years ago that she didn't have a natural aptitude for this type of work, but I figured that she'd make up for it by putting extra effort into learning the craft. The problem with Alana is that she never does her homework. Whereas I ask questions, tinker with Gilda, read manuals and visit the camera rental houses on my own time to learn all I can, Alana has chosen instead to put her energy into getting to know the right people. We have fundamentally different approaches to getting ahead in the film business.

Clearly, hers is more effective.

Her notion of the "right people" does not include those whom we're currently exploiting to fix her mistakes. Her oversights in planning, for example, mean that I frequently have to order specialty equipment on a moment's notice and beg the transport department to make our pickups a priority. I'm stretching the good relationships I've established over the years with other departments and the rental houses and have taken to buying bottles of "thank-you" scotch every week.

Not that Alana appreciates—or even notices—that I'm going above and beyond. She spends much of her time with the main unit to curry favor with Hank, leaving the gaffer and me to pre-light and set up the shots. Then she makes a couple of changes to show us who's boss, sometimes undermining hours of work.

Damon hasn't said a word to me about her. Mind you, Damon hasn't said an unnecessary word to me, period. Nor have I gone out of my way to speak to him since he off-loaded me onto second unit.

Today we are forced into each other's company when the entire crew breaks for lunch at the same time.

I cut in front of him in the food line and get straight to the point. "Alana is in over her head."

"Think so?" he asks, raising a skeptical eyebrow. "I've been watching the dailies and they've been pretty good. In fact, her lighting has been virtually identical to mine."

I resist the urge to hurl a stuffed pepper at him. Super Focus Puller has a much better chance of making her point if she keeps her cool. "That's because I'm working doubly hard to compensate for her mistakes." I reel off a list of recent blunders.

"Now, Rox, I can understand why you'd be trying to find fault, but results speak louder than words. Alana is doing a capable job."

This is exactly the attitude I was expecting, but it's infuriating nonetheless. Super Focus Puller deserves far better, she really does. "I'm just watching out for your interests, Damon, as you asked. But if you're fully confident in Alana now, I won't have to be quite as attentive. Maybe I can enjoy what she describes as my 'downtime.'"

He reconsiders. "I didn't say that."

Ha. Score one point for Super Focus Puller. "Fine, I'll stay on Alana patrol, but since I'm doing two jobs, how about doubling my salary?"

Having reached the huge roast of beef, Damon doesn't waste energy responding.

Even if he had given me permission to relax, I couldn't stop correcting the SNAFUs. I simply can't stand by and watch Alana wreak havoc on the set and possibly cost the production thousands of dollars. Instead, I've decided to view this as a learning opportunity. Hank and Damon may not recognize my contributions, but I know. Indeed, in covering Alana's butt, I am actually becoming more independent and resourceful. One day, this experience will come in handy.

Fortunately, Miguel has been in my corner lately. Or, more correctly, my bed. Since he is still on shorter prep hours, he's been at my place almost every night, either bringing dinner or cooking it himself. It's nice, but hard to get used to. Miguel has never been the typical boyfriend. He's the guy who orders ridiculously expensive champagne and insists that we drink it in the whirlpool tub of his luxury suite. He's not the guy who washes dishes, takes out the garbage or puts up shelves to store my videotapes, all of which he did last night. To my surprise, he's also been extremely supportive on *The Counterfeit Wedding* front. He willingly answers every question I pose, but also backs off when I want to figure things out on my own.

Miguel's transformation into a regular boyfriend would probably alarm me if I weren't so sure that his directorial alter ego would resurface on his first day of shooting.

★ ★ ★

It's all about the belly ring. Although it's mid-December, Alana wears a cropped top every day, all the better to reveal her seasonal jewelry. Today's red cashmere cardigan showcases the jingle bell in her navel. Yesterday, it was an adorable Christmas tree that flashed red and green. And the day before that, a tiny reindeer with a red crystal nose. I'm impressed by her efforts to bring the Christmas spirit onto set, particularly since she doesn't celebrate the holiday herself. Evidently Hanukkah-themed belly studs are in shorter supply.

Alana's arrogance has grown exponentially since Hank started loosening the reins and it's complicating our work even further. She's increasingly reluctant to ask anyone for advice. Since I am rarely privy to the discussions with Hank and Damon about the specifications for setups, I am left to piece the story together from Alana's fragmentary instructions combined with a lot of guesswork.

Generally I manage quite well, especially for simple insert shots. For something more complicated, however, like the cutaways we're doing today of the Creature's death, I'm groping in the dark. Guesswork only takes you so far when you're visualizing the demise of an alien.

Alana pushes up the sleeves of her cardigan and hooks her thumbs into the pockets of her jeans. After instructing me to set the camera up on a ladder, she rattles off some nonsensical directions that surely never passed Hank's lips. Eventually I tune her out, knowing that before long she'll get bored and wander off in search of powerful people to impress with her designer jeans—the precise jeans, in fact, that I recently had to retire.

F. C. Kugelman rests his soft hands on the keyboard and contemplates the death scene. It's the high point of the movie and it has to hit exactly the right note. Bringing down this seemingly indestructible being with a few bullets from standard police issue revolvers would be terribly anticlimactic. This has to be big. And gory. That's it, big and gory.

    The Creature flees the thundering
    tank through the deserted streets
    until he can run no more. He turns
    to face the tank with a show of
    bravado. The tank rolls over him,
    reverses and backs over him again.
    His otherworldly screams echo
    through the city.

Rubbish. If the Creature is flattened like a pancake, gore will be in very short supply. Maybe something more exotic....

    The force of the blow sends the
    Creature careening backward, arms
    spinning. The arrow pins him
    through the heart to the paneled
    wall of the museum.

Now for the gore... F.C. turns his attention to the salami-and-mustard sandwich on his lunch tray, pondering the eternal question: what's inside an alien?

    Mucus oozes slowly from the wound.

"Roxanne, damn it, I asked you guys to shoot *up* at the mucus," Hank says. "Get down here and put the camera on the ground."

Roxanne glances at Alana—who neglected to share this

pivotal piece of information with her worthy assistant—before pulling the camera off the ladder and setting it up on the filthy studio floor. Lying down beside it, she tilts the camera up at the huge plunger loaded with "mucus," or, more specifically, banana pudding.

F.C. feeds the last scrap of his sandwich to his golden retriever. Mucus is too predictable, he decides. Blood is better. No one will expect an alien to have blood.

```
The police officers stare in dis-
belief as blood flows from the
Alien's wound.
```

"I want the blood to stream down through the frame, Roxanne," Hank says. "You'll need to be on sticks."

Roxanne wrestles the camera onto the tripod while the head of the special effects department rigs several buckets of "blood" to a ten-foot ladder. Since it won't be necessary to adjust the focus during the shot, Rox attaches a remote power switch to the end of an extension cable. This way, she can switch the camera on and off from a distance, well out of the way of splattering blood.

"Stop fucking around, Rox," Hank says. "It's only a little movie blood and it will be pouring straight down." He wraps an arm around Alana's shoulders and leads her away. "Stand behind the tarps with me, sweet pea. That's a lovely top and I'd hate for you to get blood on your jingle bell."

F.C. is vexed. There's no "wow factor" here. The Creature needs to come to a spectacular, gory end.

The rocket explodes into the Alien's
chest, causing a geyser of murky blood
and entrails to spew from the gaping
hole.

"I want it blasting straight to camera," Hank tells the special-effects guy who is loading the canon with the secret
recipe for alien guts: movie blood, chocolate sauce, banana
pudding, coffee grounds, cooked spaghetti and broken-up
chunks of florist's foam.

Roxanne wraps Gilda in garbage bags and attaches a clear
protective filter to the front of the lens. Then she races to
the camera truck to grab her rain gear. Even with the remote power switch, she'll be in the line of fire.

"Hit the switch and run, Rox," the special-effects guy says.
"The canon is primed for maximum velocity. When those
chunks of foam hit, they're gonna hurt."

Rox extends the remote cable as far as it will go and
clears a path to bolt after hitting the switch. When the special-effects guys are ready, she turns on the camera and
sprints away.

"Action!"

The canon jams.

"Cut the camera," Hank says.

Rox dashes back to the switch.

"Cut it, cut it, cut it!" He emerges from behind the protective tarps. "Roxanne, why are you burning so much film?"

"It takes me a second to run back to the switch and turn
it off."

"You should be standing beside it, for Christ's sake."

"Special effects says the canon debris will hurt."

"It's liquid and a bit of florist's foam, Roxanne, how bad
can it be? At 120 frames per second we're wasting a lot of

film while you trot around. Stay beside the camera and cut immediately when I call it."

"Maybe I could just grab some protective gear."

"You're on my dollar, but if you're feeling fragile—"

"Never mind. Let's go."

F.C. knows that in an epic battle of good versus evil, there can never be enough blood. Blood is what puts butts in the seats.

`Blood spurts out of every orifice.`

Christian hands Rox another lens tissue soaked with cleaning solution and she scrubs the last of the sticky brown residue off the filter.

"That's quite a welt," he says, pointing to Rox's cheek.

"It's amazing how much a bit of florist's foam can sting when it hits you at forty miles an hour. At least it wasn't my eye."

"Roxanne," Hank says, "stop whining and go clean your boots. You're leaving bloody footprints all over the studio floor."

Hank plays back the main-unit footage of the Alien being chased down an office corridor. The scene is complete except for a few cutaway shots of security guards in pursuit. The carpenters have recreated the hallway in the studio so that second unit can do these shots.

For a change, I actually get to hear Hank's instructions directly. "I want several wide shots of the guards and then you can punch in for close-ups. It's got to look frantic, understand?" The second unit nods as one. "I'll be back in two hours and I expect to find you ready to shoot."

Alana looks nervous and for good reason. This is a much

bigger setup than anything our unit's done before and she's facing a real challenge. The hallway has to be lit to match Damon's shot of the Alien. Because Hank wants a wide shot, the entire hallway will be on camera, which means that lights have to be hidden in doorways or hung from above.

Recalling a movie of the Tour de France that Damon and I once worked on, I come up with an idea for capturing the frantic look Hank mentioned. "Hey, Alana, if we reduce the shutter angle we could get a strobelike effect on anything that moves in the shot."

Alana looks doubtful. "It sounds complicated."

"It's not," I say. "And I think Hank will love it."

Alana reluctantly gives me the green light to experiment, but when Hank returns, she has second thoughts.

"Roxanne, I want to talk to you about changing the shutter angle," she says.

"Excellant idea, Alana." Hank smiles as he approaches the camera. "Changing the shutter will give this scene the energy I'm looking for."

I glance at her, waiting for her to give credit where it's due, but she's silent, having conveniently forgotten that excellent idea was mine.

When we're ready to shoot, Hank hovers behind us to watch.

"What's the stop, Alana?" I ask. Normally, I'd know the aperture setting already, but I was so busy experimenting with the shutter that I didn't watch the lighting.

"Five six."

"Base or compensated?" If she's giving me a base stop, I'll have to adjust for the shutter change or we'll underexpose the film. If it's compensated, Alana's already done the math and made the adjustment.

She seems flustered. "Just set the stop at five six, Roxanne."

Alana probably doesn't understand that an adjustment is necessary here. Super Focus Puller is too classy to expose her boss's ignorance in front of the director, even though she dreams about such an opportunity each and every night. I look instead to the gaffer, who mouths the word *base*. While Alana is distracted, I quickly adjust the stop to the compensated setting.

Later, when Hank retreats to the large monitors, Alana examines the lens. "Rox, the stop is set at two eight. I told you five six."

"We need to open up and let more light in if we're reducing the shutter." I give her Gizmo's patented "duh" look.

Bristling, she says, "I don't believe you. You're just trying to ruin the footage because I wouldn't give you credit for the idea."

"Alana, I'm just trying to do my job."

She reaches over and sets the lens back to five six. "Who's the head of the second unit, Rox? Oh, right, me. So how about you stick to focus pulling and leave the lens where I set it?"

"How about you get over yourself?"

I leave the lens where she sets it, but by the time we finish the shot, Super Focus Puller has devised a solution. Removing the underexposed magazine of film from the camera, I tell Christian to rush it to the lab with a request to push the development. They'll be able to correct a lot of the damage by leaving it in the chemical bath longer than usual.

Heading back to the main unit, Hank says, "Obviously, you've got everything well under control, Alana. Go ahead and shoot those last close-ups without me. They need to be handheld to match Damon's work."

While I convert the camera to handheld mode, Alana puts on an enormous shoulder pad, a weight belt and a pair of driving gloves. I don't bother to point out that she's strapped the pad to the wrong shoulder and instead hoist the camera onto the unprotected one.

Alana grunts as the camera's pointy metal base digs into her flesh. Stripped down, Gilda still weighs about forty pounds and she's all sharp angles. Keeping a protective hand on the camera, I watch as Alana fights to keep her balance and look through the eyepiece at the same time. Her knees are shaking.

"It looks perfect," she gasps. "You can take it off now."

"Maybe you should switch that pad to your other shoulder," I suggest, noting with some satisfaction that Gilda has snagged Alana's cashmere sweater.

"No need," she says, handing the shoulder pad to me. "I've been having trouble with my rotator cuff since my last cinematographer gig. You can operate this shot, sweetie."

"Not after what you said earlier about being the head of this department, boss. I'd be overstepping."

She gives me a withering look. "As the head, it's my prerogative to *delegate*." She wraps her skinny fingers around the last word.

"I know, but it's a big responsibility for a mere focus puller. Maybe it would be better to ask Damon to do it after the main unit has wrapped. Given how much your shoulder hurts, I'm sure Hank won't mind if we go a few hours into triple time—and the crew certainly won't."

She injects some honey into her tone. "Okay, Roxanne, I'm asking you to operate this shot for me. Consider it a favor."

"I've been doing you a lot of favors lately and it's starting to get old."

"Favors? What favors?" She looks mystified.

What's the point in arguing, when she simply doesn't get it? But this she will definitely get. "You also took credit for my idea."

"Oh, don't be so possessive, we're a team here. And I would have thought of it eventually." Her green eyes narrow as she evaluates me. "If you agree to operate this shot for me, I'll tell Hank that changing the shutter was your idea."

"I want credit for the operating, too."

She pauses. "Okay, but I'll position it my way. I have an image to maintain."

"Who will pull focus if I operate? Christian is still in the darkroom."

"I will. I *was* a focus puller you know."

I roll my eyes but I'm already strapping on the shoulder pad. The truth is, I love operating and I don't get many opportunities.

Alana tries to hoist the camera onto my shoulder but she can't get it higher than her waist. A grip rushes to the rescue.

When I try to set the frame, something keeps yanking the camera down on the left.

"For God's sake, ease up on the focus knob," I tell Alana. "You're pulling the camera off my shoulder."

A few minutes later, I hook up a remote focus unit that allows her to keep the shot in focus from a distance. Our "team" works more efficiently if Alana doesn't get anywhere near Gilda or me.

Looking through Gilda's eyepiece, I try to keep the bouncing blob in frame.

"Come forward with the focus, he's closer than you think,"

I tell Alana. The camera is on my shoulder and I am running backward down the hall with the security guard in pursuit. At least, I think it's the security guard. Alana hasn't been able to keep the image in focus long enough to be sure. The blob spreads out even more. "Wrong way." The guard comes into focus, but goes out again just as quickly. "Too far, too far."

Suddenly, I'm shooting lights and flag stands: we've run out of set again.

A grip takes the camera off my shoulder and we walk back down the hallway to the first position for a tenth take.

Alana pulls out a tape measure and confirms the distance between the camera and the actor. "I've got the distance right, Roxanne. When's the last time you had your eyes checked?"

I sigh. "As the guy runs, he gains on us and you have to adjust accordingly. In fact, you have to adjust constantly to make sure he stays in focus."

There's a reason this job is called focus *pulling* rather than focus *setting*. Somehow Alana has spent six years in the camera department without grasping this fundamental concept.

Taking the camera from the grip, we try the shot again.

"Good, good." For the first few steps, I can actually see a glint in the security guard's eye. Then he slips out of focus and only the back wall is clear. "Cut. What happened this time?"

"I stumbled over a cable and dropped the focus unit. Let's go again."

"I'm only good for one more. I'm exhausted."

I figure we have enough sharp frames for an editor to cut this scene together. So, for the last take, I set the focus to six feet and attach a laser to Gilda. Then I ask the actor to keep his feet at the laser dot as he runs down the hall.

This will keep him around six feet away from the camera at all times.

It's an odd approach to filmmaking, but for today, it will have to do.

Miguel's message says he is working late. It's his first day of shooting and already my "boyfriend" is AWOL. Not that I'm disappointed to have a night alone. What I really need after a day of running with Gilda on my shoulder is a long, hot bath.

And for my reading pleasure, I have the script of *The Counterfeit Wedding,* hot off the presses. Libby needn't have bothered with the modest disclaimers that accompanied the draft. It's so funny in spots that I almost drop the script in the tub.

The central story is that the fortyish heroine, unable to find the groom of her dreams and unwilling to compromise, decides that she too deserves to be princess for a day. She will star in her own grand wedding production, collecting the glory—and more importantly, the gifts—that go with the role.

The concept is working, but the execution has become epic. The final reception scene is an elaborate celebration of materialism. For example, the Cinderella antibride arrives in a pumpkin coach with her father, who is dressed as an eighteenth-century nobleman. There's a fountain, a gazebo, orchids and a string quartet, featuring a harpist.

Obviously I will have to keep a tight rein on Libby's ambitious vision. But rather than risk waking her at midnight, I save the discussion of scaling back to another day.

I know I can make this work. If I can manage Alana Speir, chasing a faux bride around will be a breeze.

Chapter 16

I slip into the last row of the screening theater just as the second-unit dailies begin to roll. In the front row, a familiar ponytail is silhouetted beside Hank's baseball cap. Damon is sitting a row behind with several of the producers, who swarmed back to town when the second unit cranked up.

The footage with the reduced shutter angle looks amazing. The security guard's movements cause a slight streaking across the frame that contributes to the frantic mood Hank requested. Also, thanks to the push in processing, the exposure is right on the money. The result is a slightly grainier look than Damon's footage, which augments the shutter effect very well.

I am not in the clear yet; the handheld footage has yet to roll. I've never operated a handheld camera before, let alone raced down a corridor carrying one. I heave a sigh of relief. Despite the fact that the actor frequently goes in and out of focus, he is in a steady frame throughout. I clipped the top of his head only once. Not bad for a rookie!

The lights come up and I await the verdict.

"Fantastic!" Hank announces. "I am really impressed."

Damon echoes his approval. "Changing the shutter angle was a great idea."

My head is swelling to the point where the screening room can barely contain it.

Throwing an arm around Alana, Hank says, "I certainly made the right choice when I put *you* in charge."

"I'm so glad you like it, Hank," she says, with a giggle and toss of her ponytail. "It was an inspired moment, what can I say?"

The air leaks out of my inflated head with a high-pitch scream only I can hear. Alana is not going to keep her word about giving me credit.

"The handheld operating was pretty good, too," Hank says.

More giggling and ponytail tossing. "Especially considering my bad shoulder."

Hank solicitously massages her shoulder with one hand. "Poor baby."

This is too much. I clear my throat to signal my presence.

Damon turns in his seat. "Hi, Roxanne. Didn't realize you were here."

Alana's head spins so fast her ponytail knocks Hank's baseball cap askew. "Oh, hi, sweetie. Did you hear? Hank and Damon love the footage."

"I heard. You were about to explain how it all played out, no?"

Damon says, "Well, I hope one of you can explain why the focus on the handheld footage is so grim. It's the worst I've ever seen and that's saying something. Where were you when the camera was running, Rox?"

I repeat, "Alana can explain."

But Alana simply looks at me with a pained expression. Maybe her belly ring is screwed in too tight today.

Hank helps Alana to her feet and holds up her jacket. "I'm disappointed, too, Roxanne," he says. "If it weren't for that last take, we'd have to reshoot the whole thing and I can't afford that kind of a setback. You're lucky I know that you're capable of better or I'd be thinking about replacing a focus puller."

Alana leads Hank up the aisle, studiously avoiding my gaze. I reach out as she passes and give her ponytail a sharp yank. "Tell them what really happened."

Thus cornered, she finally speaks. "I guess I'm to blame for the soft focus."

"How so?" Hank asks.

"I was the one eyeballing the shot." She flicks imaginary quotations marks around *eyeballing*. "I should have noticed that we were out of focus, but I was tired from operating all day and Rox is usually dead on. I shouldn't have taken her for granted."

"Well, darling," Hank says, "I'm impressed that you're taking ultimate responsibility for what happens on your team. That's what leadership is all about."

Alana is feeling a little guilty. I know this because she is actually plugging a transmitter into the camera all on her own. Normally, her manicure is too fresh for that sort of manual labor.

I say, "Let me do that after I've finished bringing in the equipment, Alana."

"I don't mind," she says, flashing her even, white teeth. "You know I like to pitch in."

"Well, make sure you plug that into the right output or it could blow up the circuit board."

"Yes, yes." She dismisses me with a wave. "Don't worry."

Christian agrees to keep a wary eye on Alana, but he joins

me at the camera truck a while later. "She sent me back for another lens," he says. "What could I do?"

I race back to set, noticing immediately that Alana is a little flushed as she fumbles with the transmitter.

"Rox, there's something wrong with the camera," she says.

"What do you mean?"

"It's dead. I don't know what happened."

I rush to Gilda's side, noting that all of her display lights have gone dark. "What have you done? Oh, my God, Alana, you plugged a twenty-four-volt transmitter into a twelve-volt slot! Are you a complete idiot?"

She backs away a few steps. "I don't like your tone, Roxanne."

My heart is pounding as I advance on her. "Too bad. I'm fed up. You've been messing with me and I put up with it because it's the professional thing to do. But you've crossed the line by messing with Gilda."

She smirks. "You're so attached to the camera that you've named it? How adorable! At your age, I suppose baby cravings are inevitable, but wouldn't a cat be more comfort at night?"

The gloves are off. "If you were more attached to the camera, you might be able to touch it without wrecking it."

"Sounds like sour grapes, sweetie," she says, with a tinkling laugh. "Fortunately, my career path won't require much hands-on work. I already have quirky" (finger quotes) "experts like you to do it for me."

I suddenly see my future: I'll be a quirky—read pathetic—spinster holed up in a decrepit Victorian home with cats, cameras, DVDs and endless musty books on art and film. And Crusher downstairs, of course.

Sadder still, the vision has a certain appeal.

"Quirky but competent, Alana. Now, keep your hands off Gilda."

"That sounds like a threat, Roxanne."

"I guess you're not a complete idiot after all." I jerk my fingers into quotes around the word *complete* before heading off to change Gilda's circuit boards.

Christian leads me gently to a director's chair.

"What's wrong?" I ask, goose bumps prickling on my arms. "Have I been fired?"

"Rox, stay calm. It's Gilda."

I jump out of my seat and clutch his shirt. "WHAT DID SHE DO?"

"While you were eating lunch, Alana blew out the second set of circuit boards. She asked me to take care of it so I called the rental house to send a new set. We're going to be down for a few hours."

"Where is she?"

"She left set—said something about a doctor's appointment. I'm thinking she was afraid."

"I'm thinking she should be."

The skinny bitch must die.

Keisha adds a curvy summit to the mountain of cream that already floats on my hot chocolate. "Will Gilda survive?"

"Yeah. The guys at the shop were disgusted though, and I made sure they knew exactly where the blame belonged."

"Good, she deserves it. Especially after sticking it to you during dailies. I can't believe you keep covering for her."

"How can I stand by and let disasters happen when I can prevent them? Besides, I'm on second unit to watch Damon's back."

"Right, because he's been so great about watching yours lately. You should tell him what's going on."

"I tried. He thinks I'm exaggerating. I keep hoping he'll figure it out for himself."

"Don't hold your breath." But she smiles to let me know she understands. "So what are you going to do now?"

"I was looking forward to telling Hank the truth about why the camera is down, but he put us on standby anyway. The camera will be repaired by the time he's ready for us."

"So once again Alana has escaped justice."

"It'll catch up to her eventually, I have to believe that. In the meantime, I've got her scared. When she got back from her fake doctor's appointment, she actually dodged into the hair-and-makeup trailer to avoid me."

Keisha laughs. "Probably planning to go incognito."

"Don't worry, I can sniff out garbage in all its guises."

Gizmo comes to collect me from the craft truck. "You might want to skip the cinnamon bun, Rox."

I glare at him. "You could use a man-girdle yourself, pal. Maybe Burk can hook you up."

His eyebrows shoot up. "Wow, someone stuck her finger in the hormone socket today."

Keisha intervenes. "Zip it, Giz, she's having a bad day."

"Well, it's about to get worse. Hank wants second unit to work with Damon on the stunt sequence. You're going up on the crane later."

"No way." These days, it's rare to see a crane that requires crew to ride alongside the camera. Usually, we hook up a series of motors and cables that allows us to manipulate a floating camera while our feet remain firmly planted on the ground. "Were the remote heads booked?"

"No, we're on a tighter budget since establishing the second unit. It's cheaper to hoist a couple of people onto a crane than to book a remote-control unit."

"A couple of people? Who's going up with me?"

"Your best friend Alana. We've got a pool going on how long both of you will survive on a platform at thirty feet."

I assume a nonchalant expression. "What makes you think we're not getting along?"

"Heard about what happened to Gilda. Everyone knows she's your baby."

Jesus.

"Hey, Rox," he adds, "my money's on you. Toss her overboard at the twenty-minute mark, okay? I could really use the cash."

If I'd known I'd be airborne, I'd have started dieting weeks ago. The crane works on a counterweight system, similar to a seesaw. For every pound on the platform, the grips drop an equal amount into a bucket on the opposite end of the arm. This prevents riders from plunging to the ground or catapulting into the stratosphere. In short, it's like sitting on a giant scale in public. If that isn't a woman's worst nightmare, I don't know what is.

Gizmo drops a few weights into the bucket of the crane and slides Gilda onto the platform, along with the head and her accessories. Next, he tosses in some weights to balance Alana—*clunk, clunk*—and on she gets. Gizmo finesses briefly with some smaller weights—*clink, clink, clink*—to balance the arm perfectly.

"Okay, Rox," he says, "your turn."

Gizmo and team look me over to assess how many weights they'll need. *Clunk, clunk, clunk…clunk.* Acutely aware that they see me as two full clunks heavier than Alana, I climb aboard. Immediately, the weigh bucket jerks up. Alana squeals and clutches at her seat dramatically.

Gizmo and another grip struggle to keep their end of the arm down. "Run to the truck for more weights," Gizmo tells one of his guys.

The grip returns and—*clink, clink*—drops in the weights. They release the arm and once again, our end sinks.

"Christ, Rox, what have you been eating?" Gizmo asks.

I turn to sneer at Alana. "I've been swallowing a lot of anger, if you must know."

"You do seem frustrated," she says, feigning sympathy. "You need to get out more, Rox. You know, get away from your camera."

"Are you sure you want to bait me, Alana?"

"Sweetie, I'm just trying to help." *Clink, clink, clink.* "And in the same vein, I hear the South Beach Diet is genius."

"Pardon me if I don't trust your capacity to judge genius."

"Take it easy, ladies," Gizmo says. "You'll never last twenty minutes at this rate."

Clink, clink. This is worse than I thought. Although I typically gain weight when I'm on a film because of grazing all day, I've never ballooned this far out of control. Generally I can compensate at the end of the day and on weekends. The problem lately is that Miguel has been plying me with all manner of gourmet delights, often right before bedtime.

The crane is silent at last. Thank God that humiliation is—*clink*—over. Gizmo swings the arm toward the set and raises it slowly until we're suspended above the set.

And they say pigs can't fly.

"Listen, Alana," I say, "We're stuck with each other for a few hours. It will go a lot better if you don't speak to me."

"You know, I could complain to Hank and Damon about your disrespect for me."

"Go ahead. Then I'll complain about your disrespect for their budget and equipment."

"It will be my word against—"

"Mine. Plus the word of my witnesses, of course."

"Rox, I want you to know that I do realize it's been hard for you to go from being the boss to being my assistant."

"Alana, shut up."

Apart from the public weigh-in and the fact that I'm sharing a three-foot platform with the person I hate most in the world, I actually like the crane. It's nice to be removed from the madness that occurs on the ground during a stunt sequence. While others are scrambling to put out fires, I can relax. There's nothing I can do to help from up here. The other benefit is that I don't need to wear a face shield or ear protection for the gunfire.

Far below, the two crews are rushing to set up for the scene where Burk, in human form, engages several stunt "police" in gun battle before pulling one of them from the car. Since Burk isn't as fit as he used to be, Marty, the smallest and lightest of stuntmen, has volunteered for the assignment. Burk will have to rough Marty up a bit and pin him against the car door.

While they're rehearsing their moves, I buzz Christian on the walkie-talkie. "Hey, who's the guy in the bedspread?" A bald man in floor-length robes is standing about ten feet from Burk, his hands tucked into enormous sleeves.

Christian moves away from the guy so that he can reply. "It's a monk."

"I thought we'd finished with the monks."

"This one's the genuine article. Burk's flown in his spiritual advisor from L.A."

A props man approaches Burk and hands him a couple of

cigars. Burk lights them both and passes one to his robed companion.

"Since when do monks smoke stogies?" I ask.

Christian looks up and gives me an exaggerated shrug. I tuck the radio back into my pocket, pondering the notion of a monastery in Beverly Hills. There's a reality series in there somewhere.

Alana says, "Do you think this is a good frame?" I watch my monitor as she pans the camera slightly to the left and zooms in a little. "Or is this better?"

"It's entirely up to you."

Alana fiddles with her ponytail. "But which do you like better? I want to find the best frame possible before Hank and Damon look at the monitors below."

I shrug. "You've burned me once too often. You're on your own today."

"Alana," Damon's voice squawks on the walkie-talkie. I pull it out of my pocket and hold it to her ear. "Frame up for God's sake, we're ready to shoot here!"

"Better hurry," I say, watching my monitor as she moves the frame farther to the left, then back to the right. She zooms in a few millimeters, zooms out again and tilts the camera up and down. Finally she stops and looks at me again. I raise my fingers to signify quotation marks and say, "Unique."

Scowling, she zooms in again, pans farther to the right and yanks the walkie out of my hand. "Frame!"

She's composed the shot so that the actors just fill the frame with no air around them. It's poor composition, especially for a fight sequence. No matter what actors do in the rehearsals, they inevitably put more energy into their action when the camera is rolling. The way she's framed up, there's a very good chance that the actors will pop out of the picture once we're burning film.

Despite my intentions to let her sink or swim, I say, "Widen out. You're going to lose someone."

Damon's voice crackles on the radio. "That's crap, Alana. Widen out. The fight will get bigger when we roll."

It's my turn to smirk.

Finally, everything is set below. The AD grabs the megaphone and confirms that we're about to roll. But Burk, after conferring briefly with his monk, approaches the AD and gestures toward the crew, and then up at us.

The AD says, "Bring the crane down, please. Everyone gather around."

Once we're on the ground, Burk tosses his cigar aside, borrows the megaphone and stands on a crate. "As you know, there is an element of danger in shooting any stunt. Please take a moment and join me in forming a circle to pray for the safety of the actors and crew."

The crew looks at one another in disbelief. We've been shooting dangerous sequences for weeks and Burk has never shown an interest in the names of his co-workers, let alone their safety.

"Come on now," Burk encourages us. "Everyone join hands."

Genevieve herds everyone together and slowly but surely, grips and electrics, drivers and hairdressers, set dressers and stuntmen reluctantly join hands. Damon attempts to slink away, but the monk takes his hand and pulls him back to the circle. Since Alana and I can't get off the crane, the circle closes in around us. Hank takes Alana's hand on one side; Gizmo connects the circle to me on the other.

The ring of peace and love is broken in only one place: Alana reaches for my hand several times and I keep snatching it away. Eventually the monk catches my eye and I sheepishly allow her to hold the cuff of my jacket.

Damon, still holding the monk's hand, watches this little performance with evident amusement. I wonder how long he wagered we'd last on the platform.

Burk instructs us to bow our heads while he and the monk chant unintelligibly for what seems like a lifetime. Eventually Hank interrupts with a mighty "Amen!"

The crew scrambles back into position and the crane rises into the air. Leaning over the side of the crane, I see the monk reach into the folds of his robes and produce his own eye and ear protection.

Alana says, "I hope you'll be a little more forgiving after that, Roxanne."

"Nope. Buddha's on my side, sweetie."

We roll the cameras and Burk pulls Marty from the police car with much more force than he did in any of the rehearsals. As predicted, Alana would easily have missed the action had she not widened out. I don't say "I told you so," because that would require speaking to her. Instead, I concentrate on the focus.

The actors swing through their choreographed moves until Burk pushes Marty back against the car door with such force that his head goes straight through the driver's window.

I hold my breath. That wasn't in the rehearsal and unless I'm much mistaken, the car window is real, not "candy" glass. My suspicions are confirmed when the stunt co-coordinator runs onto the set screaming. I cut the camera and watch helplessly as paramedics race in, Hank close on their heels. They pull Marty's hand away from his head and even from thirty feet above, I can see blood on his open palm.

Gizmo lowers the crane and we join the rest of the crew in hovering a discreet distance from the paramedics. Hank helps Marty to his feet and escorts him to a director's chair, where Marty gives a thumbs-up to show that he's okay.

Everyone cheers. Burk retreats to his trailer with his monk, perhaps to pray for forgiveness.

"Is he going to be all right?" I ask the first AD, after the set nurse examines Marty's injury.

"He needs a couple of stitches and he wants the nurse to do it here, so that he can do another take."

While the nurse is fixing Marty up, Burk strides back onto set with his hairdresser and monk in tow.

"Look at what Troy found in my hair," Burk says, dropping two tiny pieces of glass into Hank's open palm.

"Looks like you dodged a bullet, Burk," Hank says.

Burk flushes. "This is an unsafe working environment!" he shouts, sending a shower of spittle over Marty's wound. "My scalp could have been cut open."

I can see the headline now: Alien Costar Saved By Protective Layer Of GLH!

The first assistant director makes the announcement: *Illegal Alien* will be on hiatus for two weeks to allow Burk to recover from an undisclosed injury.

Alana skips ahead of me to the camera truck. "Now I can take that spa vacation after all."

I make a face behind her and she turns just in time to see it.

"Rox, why don't you come with me?" she asks. "We can heal the rift over hot rock massages."

"No thanks, Alana. I've already got plans for the hiatus."

"What could you possibly have planned already?"

"I've been waiting for the right time to shoot my own movie and this is it."

She stops dead in her tracks. "What do you mean, 'shoot'?"

"I mean I'll be director, producer and cinematographer on my friend's original screenplay."

"You're kidding."

"Why is that so hard to believe?"

"It's just that you're more of a behind-the-scenes person, Roxanne." Cue the tinkling laugh.

"We'll see about that. I'm looking forward to the challenge during our break. But you enjoy your mud bath."

Once she's out of sight, I reach for my cell phone.

Crusher yells over a revving engine. "Speak."

"Don't make any plans for the next two weeks," I say.

The engine backfires a few times before sputtering into silence. "I haven't made any plans for the next two hours, woman. You know I don't make commitments."

"Well, I need you to commit to me now. I've decided to shoot *The Counterfeit Wedding* next week and I need your help."

"Did you quit?"

"Not yet. We've got a two-week hiatus and I want to take advantage of it. I've already talked a lot of the crew into helping me and I'm going to hit up the producers before I leave about using some of the equipment."

"Consider me your right-hand man. I'll start making calls about those locations this afternoon. But you do realize that this means I won't get around to replacing your refrigerator for a while."

I snort. "What's another few weeks?" I hang up the phone and dial Libby's work number to tell her about my unexpected downtime. "So we're good to go on *The Counterfeit Wedding,* Lib."

She screams so loud I have to pull the phone away from my ear. "Then the script is working?" she asks.

Writers are sensitive people, so one must tread carefully. "It's definitely working. There are just a few tiny changes I'd like to discuss."

There's a pause. "How tiny?"

Writers are suspicious people, so one must delude them. "Infinitesimal. Let's chat about it over brunch Saturday."

"Sure," she says, sounding convinced that I'm not out to butcher her masterpiece. "How else can I help? I've got vacation time coming and the boss has left early for Christmas break."

"I'm pretty much covered, Lib. I've rounded up the technical crew. Crusher is doing transportation and locations. And Keisha offered to be production co-coordinator and first assistant director. She wants to get some experience so that she can change departments in the union. The only thing missing is… But no, I couldn't ask."

"What? I want to help."

"I need someone to cover craft services."

"That's food, isn't it? I love food. I'm all over it."

Libby is the only one I know who's even more useless in the kitchen than I am. My volunteer crew might not survive the gig. "It's a bigger challenge than you'd think."

Indeed, craft services is a difficult, thankless job. Food becomes disproportionately important to a crew working long hours—even more so when they're working long hours for free. In fact, crew morale can fluctuate with the quality of the coffee. That's why I've budgeted generously for the craft department.

Libby says, "I used to be handmaid and jack-of-all-trades for the world's fussiest politician. How hard can it be to feed a small crew?"

I decide not to mention that I once saw a 250-pound electrician hurl a microwave oven across a parking lot after pronouncing the artichoke-frittata special "fag food."

Writers are anxious people, so one must be careful not to trigger their flight response.

Chapter 17

"Are you behind the wheel, Roxanne?" my father asks as an eighteen-wheeler thunders past the Jeep.

I raise my voice to yell above the noise. "Sort of."

"Pull over right this moment." To Dad's mind, a driver with a cell phone attached to the ear is as dangerous as a suicide bomber.

"Can't. I'm multitasking." Switching the phone to my left ear as I hit my exit, I gear down and yank my latest energy elixir out of the cup holder to take a sip. Replacing the drink, I flip open the glove compartment and root around for a pen. As I roll to a stop, I jot down a few items on my to-do list. Just as the driver behind me lays on his horn, I ease up on the clutch and rumble through the intersection.

"Roxanne, you've got to slow down," Dad says when he hears the horn.

"Actually, I've got to speed up. You have no idea how hard it is to pull together a film on a moment's notice."

How could he? Even I didn't realize. Bringing *The Counterfeit Wedding* shoot forward by a month has created an avalanche of administration. I've nearly worn out the treads on my tires and if Dad knew just how much time I've spent on my cell phone, he'd be booking me for a CAT scan immediately.

Fortunately, things are coming together. By forfeiting sleep, I've prepared a story board and lighting plan for each and every scene, ordered film stock and equipment, and secured permits for locations and parking from the City. I've recruited actors and convinced the business owners at our locations to play themselves. In short, I've pulled favors from nearly everyone I know professionally and personally. People have been incredibly supportive—especially the *Illegal Alien* crew members. Gizmo, who swore he'd never work for a woman, has not only agreed to grip this movie, he's been building sets for it as well. People are donating props, wardrobe and set decorating. And best of all, a local bridal boutique is lending me a satin-and-lace confection that is worthy of Cinderella herself, providing she is a size four.

Which brings me to my only hitch: shooting starts in two days, yet there is no Counterfeit Bride. She appears in every scene and none of the actors I know can afford to give up paid work for a full week. My cousin, a star in community theater, has offered to do it but she's no Charlize Theron. I am desperately hoping that Fate will send a better fit for the glass slipper.

"Rox? Are you there?"

I'd forgotten all about the cell phone. "Uh, sure, Dad."

"I insist that—"

"You're breaking up. I'll have to call you later."

I hang up and call the owner of a film lab, who has agreed to meet with me to discuss a deal on processing and post-production. Like so many people involved in the business, he is happy to support a creative endeavor.

I expected this to be a much harder sell and the positive response is healing my bruised and battered pride. The knowledge and contacts I've gained during my years in the trenches are paying off. Roxanne the focus puller may yet metamorphose into Roxanne the director.

With all the running around I'm doing, I may even fit into my cocoon.

Voula brings me a coffee and a bagel as I check my voice mail from the Metropolitan Diner. Five new messages have come in since I spoke to Dad. Three are from Keisha, who's been sifting through paperwork, coordinating the crew and putting out call sheets based on my scheduling. The fourth is from Crusher, locations manager and transport guy, who will be stopping by later with a progress report. And the last message is from Miguel, who is standing me up for dinner again tonight. Since he started shooting, I haven't seen him once. This would probably irritate me—especially after the faux-boyfriend stint—if I weren't so busy myself. Still, I do miss the steady supply of advice and information. Now it's just me, novice filmmaker, constantly groping in the dark.

Dropping my cell phone into my purse, I review the list I pulled off the Internet this morning in preparation for my script meeting with Libby: Top Ten Rules For Managing People Effectively. Libby is just one of many people I'll have to manage and I'm the first to admit that the subtleties of this art elude me. My natural inclination as a leader is to deliver my message as directly and concisely as possible, but that approach may not generate the best short film ever made. Many of the people involved will be creative types who require "handling."

With my scriptwriter, I have the added challenge of trying to turn a friendship into a professional relationship. Libby isn't going to accept the advice I frequently offer to the trainees and loaders who work for me: to wit, "suck it up." What I have going for me, however, is empathy. I understand that Libby's feelings about *The Counterfeit Wedding* script are similar to mine for Gilda—protective, possessive, somewhat irrational. Therefore, I must approach her as if she were barely stable.

If Gizmo were here, he'd start a pool to see how long we'd last in the ring without killing each other.

Waving to Voula, Libby slides into the seat opposite me and gets straight to the point: "So, what do you want to change in the script?"

Rule #1: Take control of the situation by creating a rapport.

"Hey," I ask, "whatever happened to 'How are you? What's new in your life? Are you still getting laid?'"

She takes a notebook and pencil out of her purse. "I thought this was a business meeting. I know that you've got a lot to do and I'm trying to respect your time."

"Well, we can still chat," I say, somewhat flustered. There are rules to follow; she's not supposed to have her own agenda.

"Sure. And you can tell me whether you're still getting laid right after we discuss the changes you want to the script."

"So, how's Tim doing? Did he bring you anything back from his trip to Europe?"

"A pair of ornamental clogs for my mantel. Should we start with page one and work through it?"

"And Cornelius? How's that cute kitty?"

"That cute kitty bit a courier last week. Rox, are you stalling? It's making me nervous. Is there something you're afraid to tell me about the script?"

Rule #2: Emphasize the positive.

"Don't be silly, I love the script, Lib. It's full of the mordant wit you're known for."

"Mordant?" Libby smiles for the first time. "I like that."

I start to relax.

Rule #3: Offer specific examples of a job well done and implement good ideas in a timely fashion.

"The whole Cinderella send-up is really working. I've already lined up a dress, along with the duke's costume you described for the father of the bride."

"That's terrific. But what did you want to change?"

Damn, she's persistent. Good management techniques are barely a match for her.

Rule #4: Show sincere appreciation.

"I can't tell you how much I appreciate your writing the script, Libby. This wouldn't be happening without your hard work."

"It was my pleasure. And I am eager to revise it for you as well."

She used to be so much easier to manipulate. The abuse she's suffered working for high-profile politicians has toughened her up.

Rule #5: Share ownership and encourage new ideas and initiative.

"As far as I'm concerned, *The Counterfeit Wedding* is a collaborative effort. This isn't *my* movie, it's our movie. If there are things that aren't working while we're shooting, I want you to tell me."

"No problem. You can count on me."

"And I'm sure you'd want me to do the same as far as the script is concerned."

Libby puts her coffee down and narrows her eyes. "There it is."

"There *what* is?"

"You're up to something."

"I don't know what you're talking about. You writers are paranoid."

"Voula," Libby calls, "better bring more coffee or there's going to be a fistfight."

Voula hurries over with the pot. "My money's on you, Libby."

Rule #6: *Provide specific feedback about performance.*

Okay, so Libby has the upper hand, but I can reclaim it. "As I said on the phone the other day, there are just a few things we'll have to revisit."

"Like what?"

She already sounds defensive and we've barely started. As the director, however, I have to remain firm. "For starters, the white stallion has to go."

"Why? It's the ideal way for the anti-bride to make her grand entrance. I already got rid of the pumpkin coach."

Rule #7: *Listen to people's concerns without judgment.*

"I hear what you're saying, Lib, but I'm not sure where I'd come up with a stallion on short notice, let alone a white one."

"There's a llama farm on Highway 12. A llama would be hilarious!"

"It sure would, but llamas are notoriously difficult to work with."

"I'm sorry, I forgot about your zoology degree."

"I've worked with a lot of animal wranglers over the years." Libby crosses her arms. "Then what do you suggest?"

"I'm thinking the bride should make her entrance with her father alone. The duke costume is funny enough."

"Fine. Are there other issues?"

I check my watch. I've got another meeting in an hour so I'm going to have to step up the pace.

Rule #8: Be sensitive when communicating change. Provide information gradually to empower people and help them feel secure.

"We're going to have to scrap the red carpet, the topiaries, the orchids, the rose petals, the harp and the gazebo."

Libby leans back a little farther with each hit. "Rox, the gazebo is important," she says. "It's basically the altar. Can't we shoot the scene in a park that already has one?"

"We're shooting that scene in Crusher's brother's backyard. There's no gazebo and we can't afford one."

"Is there a water feature, at least?"

"Only if you count the garden hose."

"I suppose you've nixed the thirty candelabras, too."

She's sulking. That probably wouldn't have happened if I'd stuck to the rules.

Rule #9: Address people's concerns directly.

"I'll get you thirty votives," I offer.

"What about the string quartet?"

"I've booked two fiddlers from Fionn McCool's pub who'll play 'Here Comes the Bride' in exchange for Guinness."

Libby slumps in her seat. "You've stripped the irony from the scene."

Rule #10: Acknowledge feelings and create a safe environment in which to express them.

"You're overreacting. The irony is still there, it's just more subtle. That's what happens with a tight budget."

"Okay then. I'll do some editing tomorrow."

"What's wrong with tonight?"

"Lola and I are going to that Drew Barrymore movie you wouldn't let me see."

"Oh." I look away and drum my fingers on the table.

Exasperated, Libby says, "Rox, can we have a talk about communication?"

"Of course." I'll share a copy of my rules.

"For our partnership to work effectively, I think you need to be more direct. Just say what you mean. I am not one of those flighty actors you work with and I'd prefer to deal straight up. In fact, let's institute a rule. *Always say what you mean as directly as possible.* Treat me like regular crew."

I heave a sigh of relief. "Great idea. I hate pussyfooting around, Lib, but I didn't want to offend you. So, in the interests of directness, I need you to cancel tonight to make the revisions. We go to camera in two days."

"In the interests of directness, I do have a life, you know. I'm not one of your slaves." She's only half joking.

"You told me to treat you like regular crew, so here goes—*suck it up.* This is a tough business. Get your ass home and revise."

She gasps. "Wait a second."

"You introduced the rule, I merely embraced it." I reach into my purse and pull out a list and a signed blank check. "Craft trucks don't stock themselves, Libby, so you'll need to find time to shop, too. Keisha's made some suggestions to get you going, but pick up whatever else you think we'll need."

Libby scans the list. "Ten pounds of coffee?"

"That's just for the first two days."

"Two babes in a booth," Crusher says, squeezing in beside me. "Libby, you look incredible, if you don't mind my saying." He leans back and hooks his elbows over the seat. "Love the script, by the way."

"Thanks, Crusher. I'm glad someone does."

"Do I smell a little tension?" Crusher scowls at me.

"Why look at me?"

"Obviously you've given the Lovely Libby the impression that you don't like her work, Roxanne."

"The Lovely Libby is too sensitive and I don't have time for kid gloves. I need her to scale back the set dressing for the ending. It's no big deal."

"No big deal?" Lovely says, her voice shrill. "How can we send up the whole fairy princess wedding if we don't go over the top?"

"Be creative. White stallions aren't going to work with our budget."

"I said I'd take care of that."

"You suggested a llama."

Crusher interrupts. "How about a hog?"

Libby says, "Rox hates animals."

I roll my eyes. "He means a motorcycle."

"Yeah," he says. "The bride and her father could roar up on the back of two Harleys."

Libby considers for a moment. "That could work."

"I love it!" I say. "I can visualize the scene already. The bike sends a strong anti-establishment message, but it's still very relevant. It's like the melding of two diametrically opposed art movements. Dadaism meets—"

"Ashcan!" Crusher slaps the table.

"Exactly." I give him a high five.

"Excuse me," Libby says, "I hate to interrupt this meeting of the Art Wankers Club, but could someone translate?"

"The protest against conservatism versus art for life's sake," Crusher explains.

Libby shakes her head. "That clears it up."

I grab her notebook and scrawl a few names. "Why don't you check these artists out on the Net? Lots of screenwriters use visual references. It might help with the rewrite." I turn to Crusher. "Can you get the bikers?"

"Four Cycle Demons have already offered to drive for us. And before you ask, they don't have criminal records."

Crusher tells us he's swung a deal on two cube trucks that we can use for grip and lighting equipment, and a panel van that can carry set decorations and props. Best of all, two of his buddies are lending us Winnebagos—one for cast changes, the other for craft services.

"I have to drive a camper van?" Libby sounds alarmed.

"Don't you worry," he says, "you'll be riding shotgun with me."

Libby doesn't look at all reassured to hear it.

There are two small, rusty Winnebagos parked in the driveway when we get back to the house. Crusher opens the door of the one covered in Cycle club bumper stickers and I walk up the steps. The walls are covered in a swirling red-and-black paisley pattern and two stained purple chairs dominate the small living area. The kitchenette comes complete with microwave, coffee machine, miniature fridge and stove. The appliances are well-used, but clean.

"Welcome to your new home," I tell Lib. I notice that she is trying to back down the steps, but Crusher is blocking her path.

"Hey, Rox," she says. "Remind me why Keisha isn't doing craft services?"

"She doesn't want to serve food forever, so I promised her production experience. You're not planning to skip out on me, are you Lib?"

"Wouldn't think of it. I already asked for my mother's famous chili recipe."

"First rule of craft, Libby—never serve beans to a crew working in close confines."

The second trailer is slightly larger and features a queen-sized water bed. There are mirrored tiles on the walls and ceiling.

"If we lose the water bed, this should do for the actors," I say. "At least we can put those mirrors to good use."

Crusher offers Libby a lift home because I'm already late for my next meeting. I hop into my Jeep, watching in amusement as Libby pulls the sparkly maroon "guest helmet" over her curls and clambers aboard Elvira.

I roll down my window as Crusher guns it up the street so that I can catch Libby's screech of terror.

There's a spring in my step when I leave Charlie Picton's office. Charlie runs the town's biggest film lab and he just agreed to process our film for cost, which is far better than the fifty percent discount I came looking for.

As I head for the door, Damon emerges from one of the editing suites.

"Fancy meeting you here on a Saturday night," he says,

falling into step with me. "Don't you have a hot date with the Mystery Caller?" Again, no need for finger quotes to add a spiteful emphasis.

I pick up my pace. "We had an early dinner, if you must know."

The loud rumble emanating from my empty stomach tells a different story, however.

He smiles. "Really? He's no big spender, from the sounds of it."

"I didn't eat much. We're still at that infatuation stage, you know."

"Then shouldn't you still be gazing into his eyes?"

"Damon, I don't want to spar with you. In fact, barring Alana, you're the last person I wanted to run into tonight."

"Ouch."

"Well, what do you expect?" I am suddenly furious. "You stick me with her to watch your back and then ignore the very legitimate concerns I raise." I turn and stalk away. "You're giving me an ulcer."

He follows me in silence out the front door and through the darkened parking lot to my car.

I shake my keys at him warningly, like a rattlesnake waiting to strike. "I don't need an escort. I am perfectly capable of taking care of myself."

"I'm just trying to think of a way to apologize before you get into your Jeep."

I let the keys drop to my side. "I'll wait while you find the words."

"Okay, I know that you operated the handheld shot and I realize that you've been covering for Alana."

"Rip Van Winkle awakens at last."

As it turns out, Damon spent the afternoon working with uncut takes of the corridor scene. Alana, with her usual efficiency, forgot to turn the camera off after a couple of takes and there was enough random footage for Damon to see me in the shoulder brace and Alana with the remote focus unit.

"I presume changing the shutter was your idea as well?"

"Correct again, Rip."

"Why didn't you say something?"

"I certainly hinted and you're awfully quick to pick up on subtleties when you feel like it."

"Why would I think you were operating? It's Alana's job and she led us to believe that she was doing it."

"She's led you to believe a lot of things that aren't true."

My stomach gives another noisy gurgle.

Damon points to a bistro across the street. "I'm going to grab dinner. Would you and your ulcer like to join me?"

"I think we're free."

"What about the Mystery Caller?"

"I'll put him on hold."

Damon slides the last piece of triple-cheese pizza onto my plate. "I really appreciate your looking out for me, Rox," he says, in a rare display of humility. "I should have listened to you."

I'd like to make him grovel a little longer, but I'm simply too tired after my eighty-hour week. "I hope you're going to share your discovery with Hank."

"I'll fill him in when he gets back from L.A."

"Do I still have to work with Alana?"

"After what you've told me, I'm afraid so. At least until he fires her."

"Fair warning—I'm going to kill her if she touches Gilda again."

"She complained that you're 'freakishly possessive' about the camera, by the way."

"Too bad." I hope he hasn't heard all the jokes about my displaced baby cravings. "That camera has never let me down. I can't say the same about many people I know."

"I said I'm sorry."

I sigh. "Yeah, I know. It's been a rough stretch."

"How's prep going for *The Counterfeit Wedding*?"

I nearly spit out my wine. "How did you know?"

"Half the *Alien* crew is working on it, Rox. Word travels."

I've been so focused on getting this project off the ground that I haven't even thought about Damon's reaction.

"Don't look so worried," he says. "I think it's great that you want to make your own movie."

"You do?" I've never had the courage to tell him that I want to direct and now it turns out that he's supportive.

"Why wouldn't I? You're creating your own opportunity to hone your cinematography skills. I admire that."

Ah.

He pours the rest of the wine into my glass. "Who's directing?"

It's a shame to ruin a perfectly good reconciliation with the truth, but facing adversity head-on builds character. "I am."

"You!" Batten the hatches, there's a shit storm approaching. "You can't direct."

"Why not?" Stand by to hold your ground at all costs.

"Because you've got to concentrate on the cinematography."

"Of course, but I'll have more control over the composition if I direct as well."

"Let me help, Rox. I can pick up the slack with the directing if you get too busy with the lighting."

"No, I can't ask you to volunteer your time during the

hiatus. You put in longer hours than any of us on *Illegal Alien*."

"At least let me support you in an advisory capacity."

I really want this to be my thing and if Damon comes on board, I'll end up in the passenger seat. But how do I tell him that? A small musical trio saves me the trouble by arriving at our table with instruments in hand. Although I shake my head to discourage them, they launch into a cheesy version of "The Lady in Red." Damon looks as alarmed as I feel, especially when the flautist hands him a rose and gestures to me.

Damon presents it to me with a sheepish smile. "For the lady in denim," he says.

"Tip the trio and maybe they'll go away."

This episode should have distracted Damon, but no.

"Let me help with your movie," he repeats.

"I've got it covered. Really, Damon."

"I promise I won't try to mow your grass."

"Unless you know a great actress who can fit into a size-four wedding dress, I'm all set."

"You don't have your cast yet? But you start shooting in two days."

Damon's shock makes me feel instantly out of control. "I have my cast but I'm not happy with the lead. I'm looking for someone more dynamic—and three sizes smaller."

A waiter presents a slab of tiramisu with a sparkler and two forks.

"We didn't order dessert," Damon tells him.

"The manager sent it over," the waiter says, grinning. "He said he sensed a proposal looming—and he's never wrong."

Damon flushes to the roots of his sandy hair. "He's wrong tonight."

"Damn it," I tell the waiter, "wore my best dress for nothing." The waiter checks out my worn jeans and torn sweater and laughs. I take one of the forks out of the tiramisu and hand it back to him. "All for me."

"What is wrong with these people?" Damon says, still flustered. "Can't two friends have dinner without causing a commotion?"

"Three friends. The dessert is for the ulcer you caused."

"Then I owe it to your ulcer to help with your movie. I'll just hang around and do what you tell me. And by the way, I know just the Cinderella to fit your dress."

"Who?"

"It's a surprise. Now stop worrying about casting and think about how you're going to light this picture. Trust me, I will find you the perfect bride."

Strangely enough, those words are music to my ears.

Chapter 18

It's still dark when Crusher pulls the craft service camper van into the Distillery parking lot. Libby is slumped over sound asleep in the passenger seat.

I open her door and carol, "Rise and shine, McIssac! The crew arrives in half an hour and they're going to be starving."

She staggers into the back of the camper and watches sleepily as I begin to crack three dozen eggs into a large plastic bowl. "I was going to make fruit and yogurt parfaits," she says.

"I'm going to share with you now the secret to a happy crew—egg burritos."

Too tired to argue, Libby yawns. "Remind me why my call time is in the middle of the night?"

"I need to take full advantage of the natural daylight since the windows in these buildings are huge." Although the sun won't rise for another three hours, the hair, makeup and wardrobe crew will arrive shortly to process the actors and the extras; the rest of the crew will arrive an hour before sunrise so that we're ready to shoot as daylight breaks.

"You never told me sleep deprivation would be in the

screenwriter's job description," she says, leaning weakly on the tiny counter.

I pass her the bowl and a whisk and reach for the bags of tortillas. "Don't talk to me about sleep deprivation. I've been up all night worrying about our leading lady."

Libby looks alarmed. "We have one, don't we?"

"Yeah, Damon left me a message confirming he's found our Stacey, but he wouldn't say who it is."

"Who's Stacey?"

Oops. "I forgot to tell you. I've changed the name of the bride."

"What was wrong with Jenna?"

"It brought on flashbacks of Jenna Kendricks from high school. She hijacked my locker because it was closer to Steve Hudd's, remember? I honestly believe it was locker proximity that made him ask her out instead of me."

Libby grins. "I hear he's doing jail time."

"I'm sure I could have kept him from going down the wrong path."

Whisking lethargically, she asks, "What's happening with Miguel, by the way?"

"Disappeared again. Only this time, he's disappeared within my own city, which adds a new layer of humiliation. Don't say 'I told you so.'"

"Would I do that?"

"If you were awake you would. At any rate, I'm too busy to worry about it."

"Back to business then." She takes several pages out of her purse and hands them to me. "I rewrote the final scene, as you so graciously requested. It took me forever to get a handle on the artists you mentioned, but I think I finally injected the right balance of Jackson Pollock and Edward Harper into the scene."

"You mean Edward Hopper."

"No, Edward *Harper*—the unsung talent who sculpts European landmarks out of Jell-O."

"As opposed to Edward *Hopper,* the celebrated artist who defined American realism?"

Libby stares at me for a moment before snatching the papers out of my hand. "I'll need a little more time with this."

The passenger door of the black Porsche opens and Genevieve hops out. She is one of the few crew members I didn't ask to volunteer on *The Counterfeit Wedding,* so I have no idea what she's doing here.

"Morning, Roxanne," she says, offensively chipper.

"Hi, Genevieve. What brings you to the Distillery at 4:30 a.m.?"

"Didn't Damon tell you?"

When these words spill from the lips of an attractive blonde, it's always bad news for me. "No, but let me guess. You're a size four."

"Of course not," she says, horrified, "but the wardrobe department can take the dress in."

My first scene shoots in two hours and it calls for a bride, but Genevieve is certainly not what I envisioned for Stacey. "I didn't know you were an actor."

"I used to be, but it's been a few years. I wasn't particularly interested in a comeback, either." She holds a conspiratorial finger to her lips and whispers, "I can never say no to Damon. One flash of that gorgeous smile… You know how it is."

Although I should be more interested in reviewing her credentials, I find myself asking, "Are you and Damon back together?"

"Sssshhh…" she hisses, walking around to the driver's side of the Porsche.

The tinted driver's window rolls down and Burk's head appears. He's wearing shades to ward off the harsh light of dawn. "Yo, Centerfold," he says, passing a garment bag out the window to Genevieve, "I gotta blow. My flight's in an hour."

"Hi, Burk," I say.

He pushes his sunglasses over his receding hairline and squints at me without a glimmer of recognition in his eyes. "Sorry, babe, I don't do autographs this early."

Burk revs the engine and Genevieve waves as he squeals into the road. "Don't say anything to Burk about Damon, okay, Roxanne? He gets so jealous."

I highly doubt I'll have the opportunity to discuss this with Burk. Damon, however, is another matter.

"So listen," she continues, "I've studied the script and I am totally into Stacey's headspace. It actually made me excited about acting again."

"That's nice to hear." I think this is our longest conversation in the five years we've known each other. "Why did you quit acting, Genevieve?"

"I couldn't take the pressure to be thin and pretty." She rests a hand on a protruding hip bone. "In the makeup department, I can just relax and let myself go."

"Well, I'm glad you could help with my film. How about we get you set up?"

She scans the parking lot and points to the cast Winnebago. "Tell the drivers to move that piece of shit so that they can park my trailer right here."

"That piece of shit *is* your trailer, Centerfold."

"Are you serious?"

"Not entirely. You have to share it with the rest of the cast and extras."

"This is a disaster," I tell Libby, pacing back and forth in the craft trailer and wringing my hands. "Genevieve is completely wrong for the part!"

Libby takes the news more calmly than I expected, perhaps because she is up to her armpits in burritos. "Well, she's here and she's willing to work for nothing."

"But she doesn't even get it. She's taking the script at face value. 'I can totally see what Stacey is doing,' she said. 'She's sending a message to the universe that she's ready to make room for love in her life.'"

"Oh, my. Did you explain that it's basically about the gift grab?"

"Yeah, but I don't think it penetrated." I grab a burrito and take a savage bite. "She's doing this as a favor to Damon. I think she wants to get back together."

"So? You're not interested in Damon." She looks up at me. "Are you?"

I inspect my burrito. "There are green flecks in the eggs."

"Don't change the subject."

"I'm just saying that movie crews are fussy. The closer you stick to boring and predictable, the greater your chances of survival. Just put some ketchup and hot sauce out on the table and let them fancy up their own eggs."

Genevieve knocks on the camper door. "Your star needs a little breakfast."

I introduce Genevieve to Libby, who watches covertly as the praying mantis scrupulously selects the smallest sections of grapefruit and a single slice of melba toast.

"Libby, your script is awesome," Genevieve says. "I love it!"

"I don't know why you're so worried," Libby says after Genevieve returns to the cast trailer with her feast. "I can definitely see her as Jenna."

"Stacey," I correct her.

"You've got thyme in your teeth."

★ ★ ★

Damon's gunmetal gray BMW sweeps into the parking lot. Before he even cuts the engine, I yank open the driver's door.

"Genevieve? What were you thinking?"

"I've seen her work," he says, collecting his things. "She's talented."

"With an eyebrow pencil, maybe. I need an experienced actress to play the lead."

"Now you're picky? Two days ago, you just wanted some-one to fit the dress."

"Well, why not one of your other ex-girlfriends?"

Damon smiles. "She's the only size four."

"You're wrong about that: the dress has to be taken in."

"Relax, Roxanne, she's going to be great."

"Well, she won't make a dent in my craft services budget, anyway."

The first setup in a stationery shop has already taken half an hour longer to light than I allotted. Although the scene is simple enough, Genevieve has changed her mind several times about how she wants to play it. Since I promised the crew that the days wouldn't run over twelve hours, I will need to recover thirty minutes from another scene later in the day.

Genevieve and I are still arguing when an electrician rushes in with a light and sets it behind the counter. He plugs it in and raises it a foot.

"I didn't ask for a backlight," I say.

"Damon did."

"Damon isn't shooting this picture. You can take the light away."

I step outside to find Damon giving instructions to another electric. "Ignore whatever he says," I tell the electric.

Damon waves the electric away. "I was only trying to help."

"You were mowing my grass."

"I checked your schedule and noticed you were falling behind."

I pretend to push an invisible lawn mower. "Vroom, vroom."

"Falling behind on your first setup won't inspire confidence in your crew."

"Thanks for the heads-up, Scorsese. I've got a plan to deal with the schedule, and I wouldn't be behind if your girlfriend would commit to how she wants to play the scene."

"My *ex*-girlfriend just needs time to get up to speed. Don't worry, I've never cast a dud before."

"Just promise me you'll park that mower."

"Already back in the shed."

"CUT," a voice that isn't mine shouts.

Christian shuts off the camera. I lift my head off the eyepiece and glare at Damon, who is already crossing the set to Genevieve.

"What?" he asks, sensing the evil eye upon him. "She got the line wrong. You don't want to waste film, do you?"

I pull Damon out of earshot of the crew and explain that I am fully aware of my film inventory. "I wanted the actors to play out the scene."

"But the scene obviously works as one shot. If they make a mistake, the shot's wasted."

"I'm not doing this in one shot. I'm doing close-ups so I can cut out of it."

"Rox, you've got three more scenes to get through today

and you're almost an hour behind. You have to prioritize and this scene isn't that important to the story. Save the coverage for the other scenes."

"There's a lawnmower idling hereabouts."

"Okay, okay. You're the boss."

Interior, Stationery Shop, Day:

> **STACEY**
>
> I need a hundred wedding invitations in yellow—the color of joy and idealism.

> **SHOPKEEPER**
>
> Uh, sure.

> **STACEY**
>
> Of course, yellow is also the color of deceit, jealously and cowardice. Maybe green would work better.

The shop owner stares at Genevieve in utter confusion. Behind me, Damon inhales but I beat him to the cut.

Reaching for her script, the owner of the stationery shop stammers, "I'm so sorry. Maybe I shouldn't have agreed to do this. I've never acted before and I'm confused." She points to the page open in front of her. "It says here that Stacey asks for a hundred invitations, and then I give my line about the groom."

"Genevieve," I say, drawing on my reserves of directorial

sarcasm, "she's absolutely right. The script—you know, that crazy stack of paper we follow—says you order a hundred wedding invitations. Period. There is no monologue about the color yellow."

Genevieve objects. "But the color of the invitations would be important to Stacey. She's planning the biggest day of her life."

"She's planning the biggest *joke* of her life. Stacey's mock wedding is all about retribution for the weddings she's attended, all the gifts she's bought. She's turning the tables."

"I think Stacey is a little deeper than that, Roxanne. After all, she's been a maid of honor many times and she takes the role very seriously. Stacey loves weddings."

"Where in the script does it say that?"

"It's not in the script. It's in the character background I invented for motivational purposes."

I take a few deep, cleansing breaths. "Genevieve, this movie is all about Stacey's contempt for weddings. She's sick of them and she's taking a stand on behalf of her single comrades everywhere."

Genevieve puts a slender hand on my arm. "Roxanne, I'm not sure you understand Stacey as I do."

"Action."

Genevieve's eyes fill and then overflow.

"I'd l-like to o-order a hundred wedding invitations."

"Cut!" Before I can say anything, Genevieve calls for a mascara touch-up. "Genevieve, Stacey is bitter, not sad."

"She's bitter because she can't find a man—and that's sad if you ask me."

It's tough to argue with this logic, but I try. "She's not bitter about being single, she's bitter that society places such value on weddings."

"Does she have a boyfriend?"

"That's not the point. The point is that she feels weddings are a crock."

"So you're saying she's okay with the fact that she doesn't have a groom."

"Correct." A breakthrough! I'll remember this pivotal moment when I'm delivering my first lecture at the New York Film School director's symposium.

Genevieve flips through the script for a moment. Then she says, "I don't get it."

Suddenly I'm less worried about the fact that Genevieve and Damon might be reuniting. If he fancies her, he deserves her.

"I'd like to order a hundred wedding invitations, please."

Genevieve leans over the counter and bats her eyelashes at the shop owner.

The owner manages to deliver her line for the first time. "Sure, what's the groom's name?"

"There is no groom," Genevieve purrs. "I don't need a man in my life—if you catch my drift." She slowly runs a finger up the shop owner's forearm.

"Cut," I call, before the woman demands danger pay. "Genevieve, Stacey is straight."

"But you said she doesn't have a man."

"Believe it or not, there are straight women walking this earth who simply do not need men in their lives."

"So you're not gay?"

We're struggling through the fifteenth take when Libby walks into the stationery store carrying an enormous tray of sandwiches. I'm practically crushed by the stampeding crew.

Keisha shrugs and says, "I guess that's a ten-minute break."

Libby sets the tray on a table and backs away. She calls, "I've got peanut butter and jelly pinwheels, cream cheese and pineapple triangles, salmon and watercress, egg salad with chopped pickle."

"These are shower sandwiches," I say. "The guys won't eat these. You need ham and cheese, or roast beef and mustard. Real food."

"Just trying to get into the spirit of the movie," she says. "Grab a pinwheel before they're gone."

To my surprise, the tray is nearly empty already. I take a couple and glower at Genevieve, who is sharing a plate with Damon in the corner of the shop.

"He's meddling again," I tell Libby. "He just can't keep his big nose out of it. I think I was finally starting to get through to her and now he's going to mess it up."

"Relax. They're probably just getting back together." I glance at her quickly and she's grinning. "Not that you'd care, of course."

"Not at all—as long as it doesn't affect her performance."

Finishing her single tiny sandwich, Genevieve rests her hand on Damon's knee and stares into his eyes.

"I'd say he's got her motivated," Libby offers.

"Don't you have dish duty?"

"She doesn't eat enough to push a mower, yet somehow she's mowing your grass."

"That sod doesn't belong to me."

Genevieve delivers a flawless performance on Take 16. I'm not sure whether I'm more relieved or annoyed that Damon somehow produced this transformation.

To give myself an opportunity to figure it out, I stop speaking to him.

★ ★ ★

I'm helping the crew push equipment to a new location up the street when I pass Libby and Crusher carrying trays of crudités to the craft table.

"I want to recast our leading lady," I say. "Is it too late?"

"What's the problem?" Crusher asks. "Genevieve makes a great Stacey."

Libby nods in agreement. "That scene you just shot in the flower shop was hilarious."

"But what about this morning? That was a disaster!"

"First day jitters? She's been doing great since the break."

"Since Damon 'motivated' her, you mean." I use some air quotes.

Having heard the Alana tales, Libby gets the joke. Crusher, however, takes me seriously. "Damon has more experience in talking to actors. Maybe you should let him help a little more."

"He'll take over."

Crusher says, "You're always saying that a filmmaker doesn't need to control every last aspect of the film to put out a good product."

Libby backs him up. "You whine about directors who don't trust the people around them."

"I do trust the people around me. I'm not a control freak."

"Then why are you rearranging the vegetables?"

I'm already more than two hours behind schedule and the only way I can keep my promise to the crew about wrapping on time is to cut most of the coverage from the last scene of the day. Unfortunately, it's the scene that requires it the most. As much as I hate to admit it, Damon was right: if I'd streamlined this morning's coverage, I'd have the time I need now to shoot the bakery scene as I planned it. Now, I have no choice but to brainstorm an alternative.

I take my script and step outside the shop, hoping inspiration will strike. In this situation, directors often turn to their cinematographers for help. Unfortunately, my cinematographer is fresh out of ideas. Ditto my producer.

The owner of the art gallery next door steps out of his shop and props the front door open, allowing strange whale noises to drift into the street. From where I stand I can see a disturbing self-mutilation video projecting onto the shop's wall.

"Who's in charge of this production?" he asks.

"I am. Is there a problem?"

"Your cables could trip my customers, your equipment carts are blocking the road and I'm tired of that woman—" he points to Keisha "—asking me to turn down the volume of my installation piece while you roll."

Normally, Crusher would deal with this but he's left to nail down tomorrow's location. Thankfully Snake, one of Crusher's biker pals, offers to speak to the gallery owner so that I can get back to work.

"Nice lighting," Damon says as I step back into the bakery. "It's not easy when the daylight starts to fade."

"I know I'm running late, don't rub it in."

"I didn't mean that. I really think it looks good." He pulls me aside by the sleeve. "Why are you so touchy with me today?"

I'm touchy because Genevieve seems to understand only the language that Damon speaks. Every time I issue a direction, she looks at me blankly for a moment before turning to Damon for a translation. He steps forward, whispers a few magic words in her ear and suddenly the light dawns on her perfect features. But I can't say that to him, because whatever he's doing, it's working. Frustrated though I may be, I can see that Genevieve is delivering a good performance. Instead I say, "This is supposed to be a learning opportunity for me but I feel like you already have all the answers."

"The best filmmakers learn from other filmmakers, Roxanne. Why do you think Hank sees a couple of movies every weekend? He's always looking for new ideas. Only hacks refuse help from others."

"At least Hank has the option of *asking* for advice." I regret the words the minute they're out of my mouth. Damon is the highest paid person currently donating his time for free. I am an ungrateful bitch.

Now he's annoyed, too. "If that's how you feel, I'll leave you to draw upon your vast experience to figure out how to shoot this last scene."

He heads toward the parking lot. I take a few steps after him, but the racket next store distracts me. Poking my head inside the gallery, I find the owner and Snake red-faced and screaming at each other.

I step between the combatants and tell the owner, "I'll move the carts and cables immediately and we'll be out of here in an hour. Would you mind corking the whales for one more hour?"

He gives me a belligerent stare. "Yeah I mind. You're disrespecting my art."

I stifle a snort. "I'm sorry, sir. It's been a long day. I'm a big fan of art—and whales, actually. How about if I offer your gallery some free publicity? I could feature the sign in an exterior shot and give you a credit at the end of the movie."

He extends his right arm and I extend mine in response, thinking we're going to shake on it. Instead, he grabs the remote control for the stereo and cranks the whale noises. "Fuck you," he says.

★ ★ ★

Miguel laughs when I tell him about the whales. "So loop the scene, it's no big deal."

Looping, which allows the actors to record dialogue over a scene that's already been filmed, is expensive. "It is when a big studio isn't footing the bill."

"Then leave it in. Your little movie is a comedy and whale sounds are funny." He sits on my couch and pats the cushion beside him. *"Venido aqui."*

I ignore the invitation. "I want *The Counterfeit Wedding* to be a professional product, not some lame home movie."

"I'm sure it will be fine," he says, more kindly.

I sigh. "The last scene is crap anyway."

"Would you come here please?"

I sit down beside him. I humbled myself by calling Miguel and asking him to come over. That's how desperate I am to unload about my first day of shooting.

"The thing is," I continue, "I only had an hour to shoot it and I panicked. I couldn't think of a way to make it interesting so I settled for a couple of boring wide shots."

Miguel kisses the back of my neck while I continue. "Genevieve's acting totally sucked because she completely misunderstood the purpose of the scene and I couldn't get through to her. She understands only Damon."

The kissing stops. "What was Damon doing there?"

"He was helping—just like Crusher and Libby and everyone else."

"I thought you were angry with him for assigning you to work with Alana."

"I was, but he apologized. He really liked the screenplay and he wanted to give me a hand. Anyway, what do you think I should have done with that scene?"

"How would I know if I haven't read the script?"

"I gave you a copy the last time I saw you."

"Do we need to discuss this now? I haven't seen you in weeks, *mi amor.*"

"Well, this is important to me."

He starts unbuttoning my shirt. "So we'll talk over breakfast."

I clap my hand over his to stop him. "You can't spend the night, Miguel."

"But I'm off tomorrow."

"I'm not. I need a good night's sleep so that I can concentrate tomorrow. You always insist on five hours when you're shooting."

"I *have* to be clearheaded. Empire Pictures has $20 million riding on that."

"I see. Whereas it would be okay for me to sleep through my 'little' movie."

"Must you always overreact, Roxanne? You never used to be such a drama queen."

"Wow, you used that term in context." I stand and cross to the front door. Opening it with a flourish, I say, "Good night."

"Roxanne." He reaches for me and I push him into the hall.

"*Buenas noches,* Miguel." I slam the door behind him and lean on it.

He puts his mouth to the crack. "Does this mean you're not coming to New York to help me pack?"

Chapter 19

In my fantasies of directing, other people take care of the details while I keep my eye on the big picture. Reality, of course, is nothing like that. Even on a movie with a huge budget, the director doesn't sit around sipping champagne while the minions make it all happen. Hank Sanford, for example, solves dozens of problems every day on the *Illegal Alien* set. He's like a general fighting alongside his troops in the trenches. Yet somehow he manages to keep the big picture in mind at the same time.

Although I am far from naive where filmmaking is concerned, I've clearly been ignoring the small print in the director's job description that specifies "You will be on the hook for fixing every single thing that goes wrong." Nor did I fully appreciate how many things *can* go wrong on a small movie with only twenty-five cast and crew.

Today, for example, has been fraught with enough setbacks to destroy the confidence of any novice filmmaker. We're shooting at Chez Bouche, a catering company located in a warehouse in one of the most congested parts of the city.

Delivery trucks blocked the parking spaces allotted to us through special permits, so it took nearly two hours to park our unit. By that time, a storm set in, dumping sleet on us as we loaded equipment into the warehouse. And then, long before we'd finished bringing the gear to the third floor, the building's only freight elevator died—with Genevieve in it.

While the repairman worked to free our star, I helped to haul the rest of the equipment up three flights of stairs. Just as we delivered the last load, the freight elevator lurched to life and disgorged a near-hysterical Genevieve, who promptly locked herself in the only washroom. I talked and I wheedled and I even bribed her but she greeted my performance with ominous silence. Finally I resorted to begging her not to quit. Genevieve may be hard to manage, but I simply cannot afford to reshoot yesterday's work with a new Stacey.

There is only one thing to do and having already abandoned the last of my pride, I don't hesitate to dial Damon's number and plead with his voice mail:

"Hi, it's Roxanne, calling with beret in hand. Damon, I am *so* sorry for overreacting yesterday. What's a little lawn mowing between friends? Please come back and trim my hedges today. We're at Chez Bouche and there's a little problem that only you can resolve— Genevieve won't come out of the bathroom. I've tried begging but she apparently can't understand a word I am saying, even though I've translated everything into grovel-ese. Please come as fast as you can. I need you."

It doesn't hurt as much as I expected. Sure, I would have preferred showing up on the *Illegal Alien* set next week all smug about my successful shoot, but a director can't afford to let her ego stand in the way of the big picture—especially when said director has a ferocious headache gnawing at her brain lobes. Humbling myself to Damon is the least of my worries.

Once again, we're behind schedule and we haven't even rolled yet. If Genevieve ever emerges, the hair, makeup and wardrobe assistants will need to start over again. In the meantime, there is a lot of lighting to do. When we scouted this location, the enormous ten-by-ten windows running the length of one wall let so much sunlight into the kitchen that it practically lit itself. Even though it's the same time of day, there is nothing but gray cloud outside. Therefore, it's up to me to re-create late-afternoon sunshine. Roxanne the producer may be anxious about the time it will take to do that, but Roxanne the cinematographer is actually excited by the challenge.

The kitchen is beautiful, with its exposed beams, russet brick walls and gleaming stainless steel, and I want to show as much of it as possible in the first scene. Woody Allen often composes a wide shot of a room and simply lets the actors play the space. If the actors walk out of the frame, the camera doesn't follow. Instead, the viewer listens to off-screen dialogue until the actor returns. That type of shot would work perfectly here and if Hank can borrow from other directors, so can Roxanne Hastings. I could do worse than imitate Woody.

The hour it takes to illuminate the set passes in a flash and when I'm done, the kitchen is bathed in a warm, late-afternoon glow. Genevieve still hasn't emerged, but my headache has vanished and I'm filled with new optimism. In retrospect, this morning's glitches were minor irritations, like so many mosquito bites.

Hopefully my manufactured sunshine will keep the bugs at bay for the rest of the day.

★ ★ ★

"Hastings, we have a problem." Keisha is waving her script around as if to fend off imaginary mosquitoes.

The bliss of a few moments ago quickly starts to wane. "What is it this time?"

The actress scheduled to appear as the chef in two of today's three scenes has canceled. When she read her script last night, she was offended by its tone.

Keisha says, "She's engaged to be married and doesn't want to have any part of mocking a sacred institution."

"Marriage may be a sacred institution, but weddings are fair game," I say. "Did you tell her that?"

Keisha nods. "She's got the whole bridezilla thing going on so she would have sucked anyway. But it leaves us with a big hole. Got any ideas?"

I ponder for a moment. "Actually, I do. There's someone who already knows the part."

Fortunately, Rox the Director/Producer/Cinematographer hasn't entirely subsumed Rox the Best Friend.

"Forget it. I absolutely refuse."

I ignore Libby's protests and reach up to cram the tall chef's hat over her bushy hair.

"Did you hear me?" she asks, swatting at me as if I have become one of the mosquitoes on set. "I will make your bloody egg burritos, but I am not acting the part."

"You're used to the camera. I used to shoot you all the time."

"And I used to complain all the time. I still haven't recovered from *Gross Me Out*."

"That was twenty years ago. And you said you'd do anything to help, remember? Mostly you just have to offer up the food, which you've been doing anyway."

"And who would continue to do it while I'm in front of the camera?"

"Crusher would be glad to take over—simply for the pleasure of seeing you on the big screen." I take a small leap and get the hat over her surprisingly large cranium. Her hair mushrooms below it and I choke back a guffaw.

She catches sight of her reflection in the stainless-steel refrigerator. "Oh, Jesus."

"It's coquettish."

"It's lame. Nigella Lawson doesn't wear a hat."

Crusher appears and I ask him to take over craft services for a few hours.

"Not if it means wearing that hat," he says.

Libby tears the hat off and fluffs her mane. "I'll say the lines, but the curls go free."

Before she can change her mind, Keisha signals the hair and makeup people and Libby disappears behind a cloud of hair spray and powder.

No sooner is this annoying mosquito squashed than another is whining in my ear, this time in the shape of a bearded biker.

"Rox, we lost the location for tomorrow's gift registration scene," Crusher says. "Got any ideas?"

And to think I used to complain that no one ever wanted to hear my ideas. I never realized how easy it is to take direction until I had to start giving it.

"How sorry are you?" Damon asks, his hazel eyes twinkling.

I'm so relieved to see him that I forget the mosquitoes for a moment and give him my very best smile. "How sorry do I have to be?"

"Dinner-on-you-at-Blowfish sorry."

The dream I had after the tailgate party comes rushing back to me and my face starts to burn. "Blowfish is more like insulted-your-manhood sorry, isn't it? I've been meaner to you a hundred times and made amends with a three-dollar latte."

"Yeah, but this time I was giving you advice and labor free of charge and you totally dissed me."

"You don't look wounded," I say. He actually looks quite happy to be here—not to mention quite sexy in his faded jeans and *Seattle* T-shirt. Maybe I should humble myself more often.

Crusher clears his throat behind us and I jump. How long has he been eavesdropping, the bastard?

"Just bringing a snack around," he says, offering cookies.

I help myself to a couple. "Yeah, well keep your beard off the tray, will you?"

"You should get out from under the lights, Rox, you're all flushed."

Damon waits until Crusher leaves and raises his eyebrows. "So? Is it Blowfish?"

Crusher stops and cocks his ear our way.

"I'm a starving director," I say. "I can't afford Blowfish. But if you can get Genevieve on set in less than ten minutes, I'll pick up your Starbucks tab for a week."

"I'll take it," Damon says, apparently not too disappointed.

Crusher continues on, shaking his head.

I watch through the viewfinder as Libby offers a sampling of canapés to Genevieve. Examining them carefully, Genevieve backs away from the tray. Libby proffers it more insistently and again Genevieve declines.

"Cut!" I hop off the camera. "Genevieve, Stacey is here to taste the appetizers she might order for the wedding. In fact she was counting on this as a free lunch. You have to eat something."

She wrinkles her nose. "I can't. These are full of trans fats."

"You don't know that."

"I don't need to see them to know they're there. Are you trying to kill me?"

A girl can dream. "Just take one small bite. Chez Bouche has generously provided the food for this scene and I can't ask them to make something else."

Genevieve pouts. "I won't eat that artery sludge."

Libby says, "Let me grab the other tray from the fridge. It was Atkins friendly, Genevieve—heavy on the protein."

Genevieve gives Libby an angelic smile.

Raising a canapé to her rosebud mouth, Genevieve pretends to take a bite and chews vigorously.

I cut the camera. "Genevieve, it's obvious that you're faking it. The canapé is still intact, for God's sake. You have to take a real bite."

"All right, but I am not swallowing."

I dispatch the props department for a spit bucket.

Who knew it was possible to be a mosquito and a praying mantis at the same time?

Genevieve takes a bite out of a canapé, chews for a nanosecond and reaches hastily for the spit bucket. She expels the food with surprising force for such a frail thing.

I switch off the camera. "Genevieve, wait until I call cut before you spit that out. Libby has a line after you sample the food."

On the next take, Genevieve allows Libby to speak, but her expression suggests that she's fighting nausea.

"Try to look like you're enjoying this, Genevieve. Stacey is excited to be here."

"I hate smoked salmon," she whines.

The last of my patience expires. "I've got a radical idea. Why not *act* as if you like it?"

Genevieve's pretty face collapses and she bursts into tears. "I never would have agreed to do this if I thought I'd gain twenty pounds."

"A molecule of smoked salmon won't make you fat," I say, struggling unsuccessfully to regain my cool.

"Oh, what do you know? Look at you!" With that, she storms off set.

If the entire crew weren't staring at me right now, I might burst into tears myself. Instead I shout, "Damon!"

He emerges from the shadows off set. "Did someone call for a lawn mower?"

I manage a weak smile. "Now what do I do?"

"When the going gets tough, the tough call a break," he says.

I give the crew ten minutes and Damon leads me to a window. He collects two cups of coffee and sits down on the sill beside me.

"The small things are joining forces to take me down," I say.

He nods understandingly. "You're falling into the same trap I did when I shot my first film. I was determined to make every decision myself. Since then I've realized that filmmaking is about collaboration—that people are your greatest asset."

I watch as Genevieve returns to set and flops dramatically into her director's chair. "Even when they deserve a spanking?"

Damon smiles. "You know you have to coddle the talent."

"That woman is impossible. I don't know how you lasted a year with her."

"Six months. But she's not so bad." He gives me a significant look and adds, "I like impossible women."

I'm still trying to think of a snappy comeback to this when Crusher clears his throat beside me. I jump. Again. It's astounding that his custom-made size-fourteen biker boots don't make a sound on the tiles.

"Have some coffee, Rox," he says.

He sees the full cup in my hand. "Thanks, but I'm cutting back to one cup at a time." I gesture reluctantly toward Genevieve and tell Damon, "I guess I'd better start coddling."

"Why don't you delegate?" Damon asks. "Let me manage her while you figure out how you want to shoot the other scenes."

Once Damon is out of earshot, Crusher says, "Why don't you two have it off on the marble counter and be done with it?"

My jaw drops. "You just lost your credit on this film, buddy." I collect the remaining shreds of my dignity and retreat to the relative safety of the camera.

Libby is welded to my side as I light the second scene.

"Why the hell did I give the chef so many lines?" she laments.

"There are only three lines."

"That's three opportunities to screw up."

"You won't screw up."

"But if I do, there's always another take, right?"

"You know we're way behind today, Lib. We need to get this fast."

"So no pressure, then."

"Don't worry, you'll nail it."

"Couldn't Keisha do it?"

"She's busy fighting fires. Besides, a tall chef is more convincing."

Libby rolls her eyes. "That's ridiculous."

"Not at all. Who else here could reach those top cupboards?" I tie an apron around her waist. "Now get out there. I have complete confidence in you."

"Cut! Stacey is a potential client, Libby. Smile when you offer her the tray."

"Cut! The bride has just explained that there's no groom. Let's see a little reaction, please."

"Cut! You're surprised, Lib, not appalled."

"Cut! Are you in pain? Is your apron too tight?"

"Cut! Now you're anticipating. You looked surprised before Genevieve said her line."

"Cut! Watch your mark. You're drifting further away each take."

"Cut! Raise the tray a little higher, Libby, it's not getting into frame."

"Cut! I said raise it a *little*. Don't block your face with it."

"Cut! Now you're hiding behind your hair."

"Cut! I need to see your face, Libby."

"Cut! If you don't come out from under that mop, I'm putting the chef's hat back on."

"Cut! Hey, where are you going? We're not done here!"

I rest my forehead against Gilda's cool metal housing; my headache is back with a vengeance. We've finally moved on to the last scene of the day, but only because Damon offered to coax a performance out of Libby. He used the video playback to demonstrate how her words and actions translate onto film and she did fine after that.

I lift my head long enough to ask Damon, "Why didn't I think to show her the monitor?"

"Because you know it's risky," he says. "Some actors become so self-conscious after watching the playback that they're paralyzed."

"What made you think it would work with Libby?"

"She's new to the business. She needed to see something concrete."

I drop my head back with a small clunk. "I'm useless."

He rubs my shoulders reassuringly. "You're tired and overwhelmed, that's all. By the way, you did a great job on the lighting—better than I would have done."

"You're just trying to cheer me up."

"Am I known for false flattery?"

"Uh, no, come to think of it."

"Then believe me, the lighting in this kitchen is as good as any I've seen. And it isn't easy for me to admit that my assistant has better ideas than I do."

I lift my head again. "I'm not your assistant today, I'm your director."

"Now you're going to accuse me of sucking up to the boss, aren't you?"

This time I anticipate Crusher's silent approach. Turning, I find him pointing silently at the counter.

It's amazing how such a simple gesture can be obscene.

Damon is managing the actors so that I can attend to lighting. Maybe if everything else had gone without a hitch today, I'd have the patience and tact to deal with their insecurities, but I'm not so sure. When Genevieve sulks, my hand tingles to slap her.

Something about Damon's proficiency on *The Counterfeit Wedding* is making me look at him with new eyes. It has nothing whatsoever to do with wanting to toss him onto the counter. Although there is no denying that hours spent under hot lights are making the prospect of cold marble under my bare back very appealing.

"I could give you a hand," Crusher offers, appearing as usual out of nowhere.

"With what?"

"Throwing Damon onto the counter. You're worrying about lifting him that high, am I right?"

"Would you stop?" I hiss. "I am not thinking about Damon."

"I see. You were just studying the counter for inspiration."

"Damon is my boss and my friend. Why are you trying to demean it?"

"I'm trying to expedite it. If you got this out of your system, maybe you could concentrate and get us wrapped on time."

Our discussion is aborted by the arrival of some unlikely VIPs. For the second time in less than a month, my father has appeared on set and this time he is accompanied by Gayle, whose Day-Glo orange lipstick is visible across the warehouse. I notice that the tropical trend shows no signs of waning. Dad's turquoise sweater is surpassed in brightness only by Gayle's orange blouse, peach trousers and tangerine pumps.

"Aren't they gorgeous?" she asks, catching me staring. "And a steal, too."

"Tangerine is so underrated," I say.

Gayle's eyes narrow and my father swiftly intervenes. "Good news, Roxanne. We bumped into Libby on the way up and she told us about your location problem. Gayle called Ashley's and they've agreed to let you shoot there tomorrow."

"That's amazing!" I exclaim, immediately regretting my opening salvo. "Ashley's is *the* place to register for the up-scale bride. Thanks so much, Gayle."

She beckons me into a tangerine embrace and pecks me on the cheek. "Naturally, the store wants me to supervise," she says. "I'll take the role of merchandise representative." By this, I assume she means salesclerk. "Our registration tool is quite sophisticated so you'll need a pro on hand. And there is one small catch." She pinches thumb and index finger together.

Riveted by the daisies painted onto her orange claws, I ask, "What's that?"

"You have to be out by eleven when we open."

"But the shoot will take at least six hours. That means we'd have to load in at 4:30 a.m."

"The store is fine with that."

I'm not so sure the crew will be. But an early wrap and a bottle of scotch for each department will probably help ease their pain.

Libby, clearly much happier with her craft service duties now that she's tried life on the other side of the camera, approaches us smiling. "Hey, Rox, you've got Hi-Liter on your face." She holds a tray of quesadillas with one hand and points to my cheek where Gayle kissed me.

"I'll get that," Gayle says. She licks a napkin and scrapes at my cheek with it.

Crusher turns away to prevent an explosion of laughter.

"Cinnamon-chicken quesadilla, anyone?" Libby asks, her voice suspiciously strangled. She presses one on Gayle, who immediately offloads it onto my father. Libby helpfully extends another. "It's Moroccan."

Gayle recoils. "Such an imaginative combination."

"Grilled cheese might have been a better option," I whisper.

"I was inspired by my role as a chef. I'm still 'in the moment,' as Damon would say."

"The moment has passed. You said you were going to focus on simpler food."

"And you said you were going to conquer your control issues."

As Libby marches off to present her latest concoction to the crew, we toss our quesadillas into a nearby garbage can. All except Crusher that is, who pronounces it delicious.

Gayle says, "We have more news, Roxanne. Your father met my aunt today."

"Lorna Lamont, star of the silver screen? I hope you got me her autograph."

"I did better than that. When I mentioned that you were making a movie, she offered to do a cameo."

"Are you kidding? What an honor!"

Swelling with pride, Gayle explains that Lorna has had a difficult year. She's lost several good friends and become reclusive. "When your father mentioned the movie, you should have seen her light up," she says. "You'll have to keep it simple though. Lorna isn't young anymore and she may have some trouble with her lines."

I instantly create a role for Miss Lamont as mother of the bride and race off to tell Libby to revise the script to accommodate our celebrated guest star.

Damon manages to cajole a funny bit of improv out of Genevieve—on the very first take. I'm able to call an early wrap, which puts me in the crew's good books despite tomorrow's brutally early call time.

Genevieve is so happy with her performance that she actually hugs me. I hug her back, even though it gives me the creeps to feel the bones of her tiny rib cage. It reminds me of the shock I felt as a child to discover that there were real bones under the soft blue fur of my lucky rabbit's foot.

Damon doesn't seem nearly as put off, because he lets Genevieve hug him for much longer. Crusher looks over at me meaningfully and tips his head toward the counter, mouthing, "Last chance."

My father comes over after he puts on his coat. "I never realized how much work is involved in making a film," he says.

"That means he's proud of you," Gayle supplies.

My father doesn't have an opportunity to confirm this before the biggest mosquito of the day homes in on me, thirsty for blood.

Shutting his cell phone, Crusher says, "My brother just bailed on us, Rox. His old lady flipped when she found out he was going to let us shoot in their backyard."

I close my eyes. "That means we have nowhere to shoot the wedding reception—the most important scene of the movie."

"Got any ideas?" Crusher asks.

"Stop asking me that." Why can't this ever be simple? As soon as one thing falls into place, another immediately falls apart.

Dad says, "You can shoot it at our house."

I wonder who the "our" refers to. "Thanks, Dad, but I can't do that to you. We need to drive motorcycles across the lawn."

My father's lawn is his pride and joy. Long ago, I was so angry that he spent what little spare time he had working on the lawn that I spray-painted it orange—about the color of Gayle's lipstick, in fact. The lawn violation garnered a punishment far more severe than the one I received the same year for serving "space juice" to my friends at my E. T.-themed birthday party—a blend I concocted from crème de menthe borrowed from his bar.

"It's December, honey. I'll reseed next spring." Surreal.

Crusher says, "We'll need a new father of the bride, Mr.

Hastings, if you're interested. My brother pulled out of that, too."

My father squares his shoulders. "Well, I suppose if Libby and Gayle can do it, I should pitch in, too."

I give him a hug. "Dad, you're the best."

"Watch your back with Lorna," he whispers in my ear. "She isn't quite the helpless old lady Gayle makes her out to be."

As he's pulling away, he adds something so faint I can't quite hear, but it sounds like "bird of prey." It doesn't make any sense, but with Gayle hovering nearby, I don't ask for clarification.

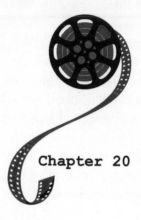

Chapter 20

As with so many things in this business, Lorna Lamont doesn't quite measure up to expectations. In fact, when she arrives in the doorway of Ashley's, she looks less like a Hollywood legend than a refugee from *Dynasty* circa 1981. Tiny and wizened, she's wearing a yellow velour track suit with enormous shoulder pads, a lime-green scarf secured with a daisy broach and an auburn wig backcombed to add several inches to her height. I can see where Gayle gets her fashion sense.

Clopping toward me on apple-green mules, Lorna extends bejeweled fingers, as if expecting me to kiss her hand. *"Adsum,"* she says in a gravelly voice.

I grip her fingertips and shake them awkwardly. "Pardon me?"

"Adsum," she repeats.

I turn to look quizzically at Gizmo and Damon, who have hurried over to join us.

"She said, *I'm here,*" Gizmo offers.

"In Klingon?" I whisper.

"Latin," he whispers back.

Turning back, I say, "Welcome to *The Counterfeit Wedding* set, Lorna."

She examines me with watery, red-rimmed eyes. "That's Miss Lamont."

"Of course. Miss Lamont. These are my colleagues, Damon Laporte and—" I pause, briefly "—Gizmo." Like Kramer on *Seinfeld,* Gizmo goes by one name only.

Damon steps forward. "It's such an honor to meet you, Miss Lamont. You are even lovelier in person."

She exposes a blinding expanse of denture and extends her fingers again. "You must be the director, Mr. Laporte."

He bends to kiss her liver-spotted hand. "I am a director, but not of this picture."

"Really?" She turns to Gizmo. "Then you must be at the helm, Mr. Gizmo."

Mr. Gizmo lurches back a few steps to avoid kissing her hand. "Uh, no, that would be Roxanne." He points to me.

"I don't understand," she says. "Where is Gordon's son?"

"I'm Roxanne Hastings, Gordon's daughter."

"His daughter? I distinctly heard him say 'Rocco.'"

I give her a warm smile that's been known to melt the heart of the crustiest senior citizen. "I'm the one at the helm, ma'am."

"Women can't direct." She turns to Damon and adds, "Whatever is the world coming to? Next thing I'll be hearing that women are cinematographers, too."

He says, "Roxanne also has that role here."

"This is too much," she squawks. "Get me a chair." Happy to do something useful, Gizmo quickly positions a chair behind her. Damon attempts to ease her into it but she shakes him off. "You do realize, Roxanne, that it's unnatural for women to be cinematographers?"

"Unnatural? Why?" I am taken aback. In all my years of

working in this sexist industry, I never imagined the most blatant discrimination I'd experience would come from another woman.

"A man looks at the world through different eyes. A man knows how to make love to a woman through the lens. A woman couldn't possibly understand."

I toy with the idea of assuring her that I do understand how to make love to a woman, but decide instead to comport myself with the poise of an old-school director. After all, she is of a different era. More important, she's working for nothing. "Ms. Lamont—"

"*Miss* Lamont."

"Miss Lamont, I am sure that my camera work will be up to your standards."

She sighs. "I'm just so used to working for the big studios." By my recollection, she hasn't worked for anyone since the 70s, but no doubt it's a comedown. "Now that I am here, I suppose I must do it—for Gayle's sake. She likes your father and she hasn't had a suitor since her husband died, poor thing. I'm afraid she wasn't blessed with the Lamont charm." Rising from the chair, she passes me her boxy white purse and says, "Now, you may get me a coffee. Black and strong."

I lead her to the craft table, where Mr. Gizmo is carefully constructing a thick peanut butter and potato chip sandwich.

Lorna scrutinizes my army pants and black T-shirt as I pour her coffee. "In my day, directors and cinematographers dressed smartly, not like storm troopers," she says. Catching Gizmo's delighted grin, she adds, "Unless you're playing a tramp in this movie, you're in no position to smirk."

Not a moment too soon, Keisha descends on Lorna and starts to lead her away.

"*Per angusta in augusta,* Roxanne," Lorna says, over her shoulder.

"You're quite welcome," I reply, assuming she's thanking me for the coffee.

Gizmo waits until she's out of sight before translating, "She said, *Through difficulties to great things.*"

"How do you know so much Latin, anyway?"

"Any refined gentleman does," he says, spewing a fine mist of potato chip crumbs.

"Who's the old bag in the cast trailer?" Genevieve asks, hooking her arm chummily through mine.

The spirit of Hollywood possesses me and I sling an arm around my new pal. "That's Lorna Lamont, one of MGM's golden girls."

"Who?"

I reel off the titles of Lorna's movies until Genevieve recognizes one. She's unimpressed. "What's she doing here?"

"She's come out of retirement to do a cameo as mother of the bride."

Genevieve is aghast. "That's impossible. She's prehistoric."

"She's eighty-one, actually."

"I can't have a fossil for a mother. What will people think?"

Genevieve isn't far off forty. "I know it's a stretch, Genevieve, but it isn't impossible. Anyway, no one is going to do the math."

Pressing a tissue to her nose, she flees the set.

Genevieve's whine drifts over the display of crystal champagne flutes.

"This Lorna person can't play Stacey's mother, Damon. You must speak to Roxanne—you're the only one she'll listen to."

"It's her movie and her decision, Genevieve," he says.

"But people will think I'm middle-aged!" Her voice is shrill.

"That's ridiculous. You're ageless. Why, you could play twenty-five if you wanted to."

"Do you think?" [hopefully]

"Of course, the camera loves you."

"It does?"

"Absolutely."

"You know, Damey, *you* should be directing this picture," Genevieve says. "I've been *so* impressed by your work this week."

I send Keisha to haul Genevieve back to set before I succumb to the urge to throw china.

"More powder," Lorna barks at the makeup assistant. Then she turns on the hairdresser who is furiously combing back her wig and snaps, "Higher, man, higher! Ouch! *Cura ut valeas!*" The hairdresser stops teasing to stare at her. "It means *take care,* you fool." She slaps his hands away in disgust. "Gayle, pull your stomach in. You look pregnant in that top."

Gayle's eyes widen in shock and she pelts over to the wardrobe assistant to request a costume change. I feel for Gayle, but I'm also relieved to see that Lorna treats everyone with equal disrespect.

Everyone, that is, except Damon. "I'm ready for my close-up, Mr. Laporte," she coos joining him at the camera.

"Over to you, Rox," he says.

I indicate the bright blue *T* marked on the floor with tape. "You can take the mark behind Genevieve, Miss Lamont."

"Oh, no, I'm always red," she protests, pointing to the red *T.*

Typically, we mark the lead actor in red. "Red is Genevieve's color, I'm afraid."

"But I am the legend of the silver screen," Lorna says.

"But I am the lead actress in *this* production," Genevieve parries.

Damon steps forward to run interference.

"It's okay," I say, "I'll handle it." I'll never grow as a director if I always let Damon solve my problems. What I need to do is channel Hank Sanford. I won't go ballistic as he usually does, but I won't be a pushover, either. "We don't have time for turf wars today, ladies. Miss Lamont, unless you prefer to be written out of this scene, I suggest you stand on the blue mark now."

Silence descends over the set. Although I desperately want to cave and beg her to cooperate, I meet her eyes calmly. Hank would never cave. Lorna stares at me for what feels like an eternity before finally relenting. She steps over to the blue mark. Before I have a chance to bask in my victory, her lips are flapping again.

"Move the camera along a bit more," she says, "my right side is my good side."

I tell Gizmo to push the dolly an inch to the right.

"There had better be some diffusion in front of that lens," she adds. "I may be sixty-eight years old, but I prefer not to look it."

Somebody's tales are as tall as her wigs. "I give you my word that you will not look sixty-eight in this movie," I say. Gizmo and Damon smother grins, but Lorna hears what she wants to hear.

"Mitchell B filters are the most flattering to my complexion," she continues, "And I'm warning you now, I'd better not see that lens dip below eye level. Ever."

I say, "I know how to flatter a lady on screen."

"Then you'll want to move that fill light over. Nose shadows are flattering to no one." She turns and snaps her fingers at her niece. "Gayle, for pity's sake, don't tilt your head down so much. You have a hundred chins."

I study Lorna through the camera and discover that she

knows her stuff: there is a tiny shadow beside her nose. I signal the gaffer to move the light a little more and the shadow disappears.

Damon watches me curiously and I wink at him. "Only hacks refuse help from others, right?"

Genevieve steps forward to pull Damon away from the camera. "Do I look okay in this light?"

"Radiant," he assures her.

Somebody bring me a spit bucket.

Using my director's viewfinder, I scan Ashley's until I find the best angle for Genevieve's entrance.

The novice filmmaker rehearses with her thespians.

CLOSE-UP, FASHIONABLE STORE ENTRANCE:

    Stacey enters with her elderly mother
    and—

"Stop!" Lorna shouts, flapping her arms. I'm getting a sense of what Dad meant by the "bird of prey" reference.

"What's the problem?"

She points to her script. "It says here, that Stacey's mother is *elderly*. She is sixty-eight years old—hardly ancient."

    Stacey enters with her senile mother
    and leads her to the H_2O bar, where
    they help themselves to complimen-
    tary bottles of mineral water.

                STACEY
    [sweeping her arm across the glass bar]

    I told you this was a classy joint.

Genevieve strides into Ashley's with Lorna and the maid of honor close on her heels. She stops at Gayle's sales desk and sweeps her arm across the computer.

    I told you this was a classy joint.

I put down the viewfinder and tap my script. "Genevieve, you deliver that line at the H_2O bar."

"Yeah, I saw that," she acknowledges, "but I think Stacey would follow her instincts and go straight to the salesclerk."

"But *I* think Stacey would follow the script and head straight to the H_2O bar where she enjoys an imported mineral water. Otherwise the line doesn't make sense."

"So I'll drop the line. Stacey had lunch in the last scene. She wouldn't be thirsty already."

"There are no calories in mineral water, Genevieve."

"I know that. I just don't see why Stacey would need a drink of water right after lunch. I think she'd get straight to business."

The novice filmmaker counts to ten.

"The H_2O bar establishes what a lavish place Ashley's is. Besides, Stacey loves to take full advantage of freebies, remember?"

Genevieve digs in her heels. "But she wouldn't be thirsty!"

The novice filmmaker questions her life's ambition and turns to a veteran for help.

Damon walks to the water bar; Genevieve follows like a teacup poodle adrift on the end of a leash.

"Stacey has been running around all day and she's dehydrated," he tells her. "She knows the water will help her maintain her energy for a long shop. More importantly, she knows that water keeps a bride's skin glowing for the big day."

Genevieve pauses to consider for a moment. "That makes perfect sense, Damey." She flips the cap off one of the cobalt bottles and tips it in my direction. "Why didn't she say so?"

The novice filmmaker considers a career as a greeter at Wal-Mart.

Damon hoists the camera onto my shoulder. "Are you sure about this?"

"My mind is made up," I say. "For this scene, you direct, I shoot. It's the least I can do now that you've offered to handle Lorna."

"My pleasure," he says. "I like her."

"You need to get out more."

He's designed the shot and it's only fair that he direct it. Besides, I can only handle one challenge right now and if I relinquish the camera to him, it will validate Lorna's view that women belong on the craft truck.

Craft services would be a welcome refuge. Directing, as I'm discovering, is a never-ending struggle. We have only one hour left at the store and with this deadline pressure, I simply could not come up with a solution. Damon quietly offered a fabulous idea and stepped aside. I, in turn, insisted that he take over directing and turned my attention to the lighting instead.

If we can pull it off, the shot will play against Ashley's upscale, stodgy image. Here, couples normally work with a table designer who methodically selects and scans items into the computerized registry database. Since our counterfeit bride values quantity over design, Damon suggested shooting the scene as a relay. To pump up the energy even further, he's adding music playback in the form of the theme from *Rocky*.

"Action!"

The music starts and with the camera on my shoulder, I pursue the actors.

> Stacey snatches the inventory gun out of the salesclerk's hand and races down the china aisle. With the clerk hot on her heels, Stacey scans several settings with the gun before sprinting to the next aisle to scan half a dozen serving platters and bowls. The clerk is closing in but the maid of honor blocks her while Stacey passes the gun to her mother. Mom dodges into the appliance aisle scanning the most expensive gadgets before passing the gun off to the maid of honor, who blasts through the cocktail section and over to the crystal tableware. The maid of honor tosses the gun back to Stacey, who does a final sweep through the pots and pans. She crashes into the salesclerk, who seizes the gun and locks it in a nearby drawer.

Damon calls cut and the crew bursts into cheers and applause. "That was terrific," he says. "We've got the scene." He slaps my back as Christian takes the camera. "Great operating, Roxanne."

In an instant, we're surrounded by the actors.

"Was I fast enough, Damon?" Genevieve asks.

"I scanned the toaster twice," Lorna announces. "Did you notice?"

Even Gayle, still panting from the exertion, seeks The Great One's approval. "Did you see the way I timed my grab of the scanner?"

Genevieve wraps her arm around Damon's waist in a proprietary fashion and tows him away from us. "I need to discuss the next scene with you."

Damon looks happier than he has in months, if not years. I hope that has more to do with directing than it does with Genevieve. It hasn't escaped my notice that his notorious temper has gone into remission over the past few days. He is probably relieved to be out from behind the camera working his magic on the cast. I sense that he likes leaving the technical details to me and I, in turn, like taking care of them more when he isn't micromanaging me. There's an odd sense of things falling into place.

He looks hotter, too. There must be some truth to the line Hank used to give me: *Directors and rock stars always get laid.*

I am kneeling beside Gilda's case when Damon resurfaces. "Well, aren't you just the belle of the ball?" I say.

"What are you talking about?" His expression is deliberately obtuse.

"They're on you like maggots on compost. Genevieve practically proposed."

He squats beside me. "Jealous?"

It's my turn to be deliberately obtuse. "Nah. I prefer my girls with some beef on them."

"Wait," he says, with a far-off look. "Let me visualize that for a moment..."

"There won't be any girl-on-girl action in *my* film, pal."

"Give it some thought. Sex sells."

"You're a pig."

He smiles a tailgate party sort of smile. "You say the nicest things to me."

I return the smile. "Wouldn't want your head to get too big for your beret."

Crusher, who has kept a low profile all morning, materializes beside us. "Hey, Rox," he says, "Did you check out that sales counter? It's faux marble. Almost as good as the real thing."

Damon looks up at him, puzzled. "What's he on about?" he asks me.

For Crusher's benefit, I snap the clasps on a lens case with unnecessary force. "Don't ask."

When our unit breaks for lunch, I forgo the food in favor of a short nap on the couch in the back office of the jewelry store we've commandeered for the afternoon.

I've barely closed my eyes when a whiff of strong perfume assails my nostrils. Jerking upright to sneeze, I knock my head against Lorna's and drop back onto the couch. She is leaning over me, dangling a chain with a black rock.

"What is that?"

Lorna adjusts the wig I've knocked askew. "Obsession."

"Not the perfume—*that*." I point to the rock she is slowly passing over my body. This must be a satanic ritual to vanquish me so that Damon can make love to her with the camera.

"Black onyx. I'm assessing your chakras—your spiritual centers."

I cross my arms behind my head and prepare to be entertained. How many people get the voodoo treatment from a legend of the silver screen? "Cool. Did you study in India?"

She peers down her beak at me. "Don't be silly. I learned it in yoga class at the senior's center."

"You take yoga?"

"Doesn't everyone?"

She moves the rock over my forehead and it spins wildly.

"Your third eye is open. Excellent."

"What does that mean?"

"It means you can see beyond what is visible. You have insight, intuition."

I am pleased to hear this, but before I have time to become complacent, the onyx slows considerably in the region of my throat.

"Uh-oh," she says. "Trouble in paradise. You're a poor communicator, are you? Your emotions are stuck in your throat."

"It's for the best, believe me."

"It's never best for your health—believe *me*. I never swallow what I feel."

That I do believe.

She repositions the rock over my chest where it stops dead. "My goodness, I've never seen such a sluggish fourth chakra. Your heart is like a backed-up sink, young lady. I'm guessing that grief is at the root of the problem."

"Think so?" Obviously Gayle's been talking about my mother.

"I do. You must work on balance, compassion, self-acceptance and positive relationships to unplug it. A little spontaneity wouldn't hurt either."

"I'll swallow some Drano for good measure."

The stone picks up speed again midway down my torso. "Ah, plenty of determination, I see." She gives me a wry smile and for a moment, I can almost imagine liking her—at least, off my set.

Nearing my navel, the stone begins to spin frantically. "Whoo-hoo, look at it go!" Lorna cackles wildly. "Your second chakra is popping! Nothing wrong with your libido."

I sit up quickly, pushing the onyx aside. I can endure only so much, even for the sake of a good story to tell my colleagues. "Thanks for the reading, but I'd better start lighting the set."

She assumes an air of wounded dignity. "I'd advise clearing out those blocks in your fourth and fifth chakras. Otherwise, there will be an explosion one of these days. And an explosion, my dear girl, is never pretty."

"Yeah, yeah," I say, leading the way out of the back room.

"Damnant quod non intellegunt," she says.

"Did you get that?" I ask Gizmo.

"Yup. They condemn what they do not understand."

Lorna gives me an arch look.

"Whatever."

Damon and I are sitting on the tailgate of the grip truck. It's a cold night, but the skies are clear and studded with tiny diamond chips.

"This isn't half bad," he says, raising his foam cup.

"I wasn't going to buy bargain scotch for my hardworking crew."

He looks at me thoughtfully. "All these years and I never realized you wanted to direct."

I look down, embarrassed. "I thought you'd be mad that I wasn't putting my heart into cinematography."

"I can't give you a hard time for having the same ambitions I have."

"Well, I'll never be a threat to you," I tell him ruefully. "I'm not much good at directing."

"It's a little early to throw in the towel. You can't expect to be an accomplished director overnight."

I swallow the rest of my scotch in one gulp. "That's exactly what I expected," I say. "I've always believed that directing is a calling—that if I were meant to do it, it would come naturally."

"Well, if that's your measuring stick, you should invest in a better light meter."

I pour another shot into each cup and we drink it in companionable silence. I am sensing a disturbing energy in my second chakra. Before Damon can pick up on it, I hop off the tailgate and zip my parka up to my chin. We've got a few days left in the shoot and I don't want things to become awkward between us again. Especially when my lead actress has a busy second chakra herself, not to mention explosive tendencies.

"Leaving already?" he says. I may be flattering myself, but he seems disappointed.

"Yeah, I'd better."

"Mystery Caller?"

I'd like to set him straight about that, but there's no penetrating the clog in my fifth chakra tonight. So I settle for offering an enigmatic smile.

Chapter 21

With Gilda on my shoulder, I make my way through the narrow back alleys that run between the garment district and Chinatown. Shivering kitchen staff in greasy aprons sit on the stoop of a nearby restaurant and drag on cigarettes, their tired eyes following me as I step over a partially frozen stream of garbage juice that's seeping from a row of overflowing Dumpsters. There's a fish head beside the back door of the Enzo Zappa's Bridal Emporium, one eye fixing me with a blank stare.

"Yorkville it ain't," I tell Crusher, who's waiting for me in the dark hallway. "You're sure we can't get into Vera Wang?"

"Without approval on the parking permits, you'd be humping Gilda at least a mile. You know what Yorkville is like. They welcome the celebs, but they don't want to see any greasy film crews doing the actual work. Enzo's is the best I could do on short notice."

I pull off my parka and flip through a rack of pastel bridesmaid dresses, each individually cocooned in rigid plastic. The store doesn't have the elegance I'd envisioned.

"It'll look great, don't worry," Crusher reassures me. "Wait until you see the front room. It's quaint."

"*Quaint* is code for *shabby,* right?"

"Nope. The place has atmosphere. Go take a look while I give Libby a hand with the breakfast table. I don't want her doing any lifting on her own."

I heave Gilda onto my shoulder again. "Right, those muffin baskets are killer on the back."

Inside the store's tiny office, Lorna is reclining on a worn leather desk chair with a black-and-white photograph in her lap. Her hot-pink mules are propped on Mr. Zappa's antique oak desk, proving that yoga works wonders at any age.

She is so intent on autographing the photo that she doesn't notice me in the doorway.

"To Enzo," a man dictates in a shaky voice. *"Fondest regards, your good friend Lorna Lamont."*

Lorna lifts the marker off the photo and looks toward someone I can't see. "Good friend?"

"Please? Everyone I know will be jealous. The star of *The Secretary Pool* is sitting here in my office! I saw that movie five times when it came out in 1941. That was in the Old Country."

"Enzo, in *this* country, it isn't considered polite to mention numbers to a lady." Her tone is positively melodious.

Enzo chuckles. "You are still a beautiful lady. No wonder directors are calling."

"You flatter an old woman," she says, feigning modesty. "I do get a lot of offers, but I have to turn most of them down, I'm afraid. I'm only doing this as a favor to my niece. Her beau's daughter is directing and shooting. Let me tell you, the kid doesn't have a clue. I'm the only thing holding this movie together."

I clear my throat. "Morning, Miss Lamont."

She isn't the least embarrassed. "Good morning, Roxanne. This is my good friend Enzo."

I poke my head into the cluttered room and the old man rises stiffly from the sofa to extend his hand.

Lorna gives him the photo, which appears to be about thirty years old. He accepts it with a courtly bow.

After I excuse myself, I hear Lorna tell Enzo, "Blocked chakras."

Damon warned me that he would be late this morning, but I already miss him. When he's around, I don't have to make all the tough decisions on my own. Nor do I have to deal with Genevieve.

Still, I've managed to design a visually satisfying scene. Now I see how lucky I am to shoot in this shop, where diffused shafts of light shine through the old windows and soften its shabbiness. The place is quietly comfortable.

At least it was, until the poodle pranced in and sent my self-esteem plummeting. One moment I feel like an accomplished filmmaker, the next like a fraud whose reach exceeds her grasp. The performance I want is so clear in my mind, yet I continue to convey it in a way that Genevieve can't—or won't—comprehend. As much as I'd like to place the blame squarely on her shoulders, I haven't fared much better with Lorna. Or Libby for that matter.

If only actors were more like cameras. With Gilda, I know exactly what I'm going to get. For every action, there is a corresponding and reliable reaction. And if she's ailing, there are concrete steps I can take to coax a good performance out of her.

Genevieve, on the other hand, is a constant conundrum.

She watches me now with furrowed brow and says, "I don't get it."

Did I mention that Gilda never talks back?

"It's straightforward, Genevieve. The manager tells you that you should have ordered your dress months ago and you're angry. You've finally found the perfect dress and you want it now. Your reception is in two weeks."

"I'm having trouble getting in touch with my anger here, Roxanne. Stacey wouldn't get mad about this because everyone knows it takes four months to order a wedding dress."

My voice rises as I get in touch with my anger. "I don't think that's common knowledge, Genevieve."

If Damon were here, he'd devise some clever bit of back story to help her put herself in the situation. Maybe something about shopping… Say she was shopping for a dress for a wrap party… That's it!

Before I can share this idea, however, Genevieve asks, "Couldn't Stacey just postpone her wedding? I mean, I'd postpone my wedding for the right dress."

I shake my head. "No, Stacey cannot postpone the Counterfeit Wedding." Now I'm so frustrated that I've forgotten my analogy. "Okay, just pretend that you're frustrated over this obstacle. And…rolling."

A buzzing noise immediately disrupts the scene.

"Cut!" I turn to the crew, my exasperation peaking. "Okay, guys. Page one of *Filmmaking for Dummies*—turn off your cell phones when we're rolling. Putting them on Vibrate only works if you're actually wearing them."

We roll another take and the buzzing resumes.

"Keisha, find that phone and break it, please."

Keisha walks straight over to the camera cart and

reaches into my accessory bag. Brandishing my cell phone, she asks, "And how would you like that broken, ma'am?"

Genevieve is flitting around the set, getting in everyone's way.

"We're shooting with Lorna next," I say. "You can leave for an hour if you'd like."

"I'll hang around," she says. "I'm waiting for Damon."

"He's scouting locations for *Illegal Alien*."

"I know. He called me."

Why is Damon still calling her to report on his whereabouts? "Hey, how's Burk doing, Genevieve? What a great guy—so talented."

"We broke up." She pulls a compact out of her purse and checks her lipstick impassively.

"That's too bad. Maybe you could visit him in L.A. and try to patch things up."

"I don't think so." She looks over the mirror at me. "He's not that bright, you know. And I really need a bright man to challenge me."

"I hear you."

Since we're bonding, she offers, "I was only trying to make Damon jealous anyway."

I busy myself with Gilda. "Did it work?"

She snaps the compact closed and slides it into her purse. "It's a time-honored strategy, Rox. It always works."

I turn on my cell phone and it rings immediately. Hoping it's Damon, I answer without checking the call display.

"She speaks to me at last," Miguel says.

"It was an accident, not a decision," I reply.

"How many times do I have to apologize to you?"

"Depends how many times you offend me."

"Why don't you tell me how your movie's going instead of picking a fight?"

"Because you're not interested."

"Excuse me? Who helped you with the prep?" he asks.

"You did," I concede, "but it's not like it ended there. This has been an ordeal, Miguel. Genevieve needs a full-time wrangler, and Lorna, well she's just—"

"*What?*"

We must have a bad connection. I step out the back door into the alley and continue. "I was saying that Lorna is a piece of work. For one thing, she likes to throw Latin phrases around."

"Who the fuck told her to do that?"

"Who knows? It's an affectation." I jump up and down on the spot to stay warm.

"I did not tell the set dresser to paint these walls purple."

It finally dawns that he isn't talking to me at all. Here I am wasting precious moments of my shooting time listening to him snap at his own crew. Worse, he doesn't even see how rude he is.

"I must go, *mi amor*," he says. "I'll come over tonight and you can tell me all about this Lynette."

I look down to see that I've been jumping on the fish head. "You know what? Erase my number from your speed dial instead."

Sounding completely bewildered, he says, "What have I done now?"

"Nothing. Forget it." Keisha pokes her head out the door and taps on her watch. "Please don't call me again. I mean it."

★ ★ ★

Lorna was a handful yesterday, but at least she actually performed. Now I realize that this was because she didn't have to memorize any dialogue. Today, she can't deliver her lines to save her life and there are only three.

"Take 15?" Lorna asks when Christian prepares to snap the slate. "That's impossible. The boy counted wrong."

Sensing that she's flustered, I call a break and ask Libby to simplify Lorna's lines. Then, when we resume filming, I give the scene a new number so that we can start slating at take one again. The psychological trick fails and Lorna continues to stumble, blaming everyone but herself.

"Hello?" she says sarcastically when I cut the camera yet again. *"Aliquisne domum est?"*

I turn to Gizmo who whispers, *"Is anyone home?"*

She continues her rant. "How can I perform when I'm surrounded by amateurs? Someone is waving around in my eye line and throwing me off."

"We've cleared your eye line, Miss Lamont," I say. "No one is waving."

"I'm telling you, there's movement and it's disrupting my concentration."

"The only thing moving is the camera."

"Then it will have to stop."

"We can't stop moving. This is a dolly shot. The camera tracks with you throughout the entire scene."

"So stop tracking with me. I can't focus."

"Miss Lamont, the scene works beautifully as it is. I'm not going to change the design of the shot. Would you like a moment to study your lines?"

"No I would not! I am a professional. I was acting before you were born, young lady."

★ ★ ★

I change the design of the shot. Lorna continues to blow her lines. She's running out of excuses, I'm running out of ideas, and if I don't get the scene soon, I'm going to run out of film. Where's Damon when I need him?

"Damon was supposed to be here by now," I complain to Keisha.

"He got here an hour ago," she says. "He's in the office with Genevieve."

"But he said he'd handle Lorna. What are they doing back there?"

"I don't know. They've been there awhile. Want me to get him?"

I shake my head. I'm damned if I'm going to interrupt their tête-à-tête with a plea for help.

Christian comes over. "We've only got enough stock left for five takes, Rox. I've ordered more, but we won't have it until later this afternoon."

I sigh. "Keisha, break the crew so that I can go outside for a smoke."

"You don't smoke," they chime in unison.

"Then I'll spend the time trying to remember why I ever wanted to be a director."

On my way to the back door, I pause outside Enzo's office. I could pop my head in for a moment and ask for Damon's advice. It might look like I'm trying to break up their little liaison, but I shouldn't let my pride stand in the way of getting my scene. Maybe they aren't reconciling anyway. It's equally possible that he's telling her to take a hike. That would explain why it's taking so long: he's letting her down gently. Mind you, if they only went out six months, an hour is probably overkill. Especially when I am sinking on set and there's a life jacket in this office.

Just as I raise my hand to knock, Genevieve lets out a volley of giggles. She's taking the bad news awfully well.

I continue on my way to the back door. I'll come up with my own solution—or drown.

Inspiration arrives while I'm eating chocolate, as is so often the case. I jump off the craft truck and run back to set to ask the soundman to find an earwig—a tiny speaker that's inserted into the actor's ear to receive the voice of a prompter. I've only seen the device used once, when it allowed a child on a cereal commercial to reel off a complicated list of ingredients.

Lorna submits to the earwig with less resistance than I anticipated. She only wallops the soundman once as he sticks the device in her ear.

"You do know that earwigs spell the death of acting?" the soundman cautions me while setting Keisha up with a mic and a script. "The actor stops living the part and starts parroting the prompter."

"I know, but I have no choice. It's a foolproof way of getting the lines right."

Unless of course, you're working with a fool.

Even with the earwig, Lorna continues to struggle, blaming the substandard quality of the prompters. Keisha didn't enunciate clearly enough. The next reader spoke too quickly. Ditto three, four and five. Number six was too *sotto voce,* and number seven, *declamito* (too loud). Number eight had a "strong Canadian accent." Number nine "gabbled." Numbers ten and eleven "mumbled." And Number twelve suffered *spiritus asper* (rough breathing). Every crew member who doesn't have a job to do while the camera is rolling has been voted off the mic.

As a last resort, I recruit Enzo Zappa. Despite his quavering voice, when he takes his place at the microphone, a miracle occurs: Lorna delivers her first two lines flawlessly. She is opening her mouth to deliver the third when the power blows and the store is plunged into darkness. Flashlights flicker on almost instantly as the electrics examine the power cables to locate the source of the problem.

Lorna snorts in disgust. "Amateurs!" She throws her script across the set, hitting Enzo in the chest and sending him reeling. "I am so sorry," she says, sounding quite sincere. "I didn't see you." She shuffles over to whisper something in his ear and then announces, "I'll be rehearsing with Enzo in the trailer. Don't interrupt until you get this sorted out."

As my eyes adjust to the dim, I notice something moving under the craft table. Seizing a flashlight, I creep over, aim the beam and switch it on. There in the circle of light is Libby on her hands and knees.

"Hi," she says, with a big smile. Make that a big, guilty smile.

"What are you doing under there?"

"I'm checking out this power cable," she says. I direct the flashlight's beam to the cable and see a streak of black on it stretching to the junction box.

"Is there something you want to tell me, Libby?"

She tries to sit upright and bangs her head on the table. "I plugged in the microwave," she says, rubbing her crown.

"Ah."

"I thought the crew might like some hot popcorn on a cold day."

"Did you clear it with the electrics?" She shakes her head. "Lib, I warned you about that on day one."

"I forgot. I'm sorry."

The apology isn't enough to stem the rising fury. "You forgot. Well, that's great. I've been killing myself all morning to get a performance out of Lorna and when she finally spits out two correct lines, you ignore the rules and blow up the generator."

"I was just trying to do something nice for the crew. I said I'm sorry."

"You ruined the only usable take I've got. You have to focus, Libby." I know that I'm overreacting but it's like I've been possessed by the spirit of Hank.

Libby may be surprised, but she isn't cowed. "I could focus better if you stopped demanding last-minute rewrites."

"I asked you to tweak three lousy lines this morning. Big deal."

"If it's no big deal, why didn't you tweak them yourself?"

"I had a few other things on my plate, like producing, lighting and directing this film. I'm amazed you didn't ask me to pop the corn, too."

"You might as well do it all yourself, you're such a control freak. It's just like the time you hijacked our grade-nine science project."

Libby drags out this example every time we disagree. She wanted to measure pH levels in the mouths of different animals and I wanted to make a pinhole camera. I say, "You really need to let that go."

"And you really need to let other people have an opinion. Whatever happened to 'I welcome your input, Libby' and 'This is a team effort, Libby'? You won't even let me decide what food to serve, let alone change something critical in the script."

"When have I stopped you from making a critical change?"

"I've asked you twice to move the reception scene inside. I wrote it as an exterior when I thought you'd shoot in spring. They're forecasting snow."

I manage to shake off the spirit of Hank and try to lighten my tone. "Snow would be interesting."

"Snow would be disastrous. Stacey wants lots of guests to come bearing lots of gifts. Who the hell would come to an outdoor wedding in a blizzard?"

"The guests can wear fun fur. It'll be cute."

"You're not using your head."

"And you're not using your imagination."

"You know what, Roxanne? You've become the asshole director I've listened to you complain about for a decade."

Before I can deliver a stinging retort, the power comes back on. Libby crawls out from the table and stalks away.

I'll have to let Lorna know that I've blown out the blockage in my fifth chakra. And she's right, it wasn't pretty at all.

Damon arrives at the camera in time to see Lorna deliver her three lines flawlessly—and without the earwig. The rehearsal with Enzo has done the trick.

"Hey, that was great," Damon tells me. "You've worked wonders with her."

I give him a baleful glance.

"What?" he asks.

"I almost threw myself under the wheels of a garbage truck an hour ago, I'm so upset. That woman has cost me a ton of film—and maybe my best friend. And you promised you'd handle her."

"Sorry, Rox, but I told you I had to scout locations for *Illegal Alien* this morning."

"Keisha said you got here 800 feet of film ago."

"I was rehearsing Genevieve in the back office."

"In the dark? Is her script in Braille?" I can't seem to stop myself. It's as if I've flicked my own auto-destruct sequence.

He ignores my implication. "She was having trouble with tomorrow's scenes. Since it's the climax of your movie, I thought you'd be happy I was coaching her."

I roll my eyes. "I'm totally thrilled that you were coaching her on the climax."

"It's a good thing you said you weren't jealous, or I'd be wondering about now."

"I don't have time to be jealous, egomaniac. I have a movie to ruin."

Crusher is standing in front of me, arms crossed. "Apologize to Libby," says her knight in leather armor. "You hurt her feelings."

"She blew up the set, Crusher. And then she called me an asshole."

"She's upgraded that to 'psychopath.' And she's packing up her measuring cups to go home."

"Another diva, just what I need. This whole production is cursed." I rub my forehead wearily.

Crusher eases up. "I guess there have been more setbacks than successes."

"That's for sure." My eyes sting with tears and I turn to walk away before anyone sees me cry. Following me into Enzo's office, Crusher gives me a bear hug.

"I never thought it would be this hard," I mumble into his vest, embarrassed by my tears. "Hank doesn't cry when the going gets tough."

"From what you've told me, he fires people instead. Now you know why so many directors are tyrants."

"Libby's right, I am an asshole."

"You're just tired and frazzled."

"I'm frazzled because I suck at this. Here I've been dreaming about making movies my entire life and I wreck everything I touch."

"That's not true. And one short film is not a deal breaker. Even if you decide you hate directing, there's still cinematography. I've noticed you really enjoy the lighting."

"That spells *Failure* with a capital *F.*" I cry harder at this thought. A tear trickles down the black leather to glisten on Crusher's Harley belt buckle.

"That spells *Pragmatic* with a capital *P.* If your calling is cinematography, you might as well find out sooner than later. You always say it's a well-respected career."

I stand up straight and wipe my nose on my sleeve. "Well, I guess I don't have to decide today."

"Right. Get the movie done and sort out the career decisions after you've had some rest. In the meantime, why not hand over the reins to Damon and focus on lighting?"

"He's got his hands full 'coaching' Genevieve with her 'climax.'" Alana is really onto something with these air quotes: you can take a sentence from pithy to bitchy in two easy flicks.

"Man, you are stressed. Damon didn't give up a hiatus to work twelve hours *gratis* just to run lines with Genevieve."

"He's trying to impress her with his directing skills."

"If he wanted to get back together, all he had to do was pick up the phone."

Pondering this, I push my hair out of my face and tuck my shirt back in. "I didn't think of it that way."

"That's why I'm here," he says, handing me a tissue from

the box on Enzo's desk. "But you owe me for dry cleaning the mascara off my vest."

"I'll buy you a bottle of Windex."

I find Libby throwing things into a box in the craft truck.

"Hi, Lib," I say, "I'm looking for a slice of humble pie."

She throws muffin tins into the box with a clatter. "You'll need more than a slice."

"I don't know about that. You did call me an asshole—and apparently a psychopath as well."

She turns her head slightly to allow a fleeting glimpse of smirk. "I'm wasting good vacation time on you, Roxanne. I'd rather be at work than be abused here."

"I'm sorry, Lib, I really am. I'm under a lot of pressure, but I know that's no excuse. Will you please stay?"

She turns and takes in my puffy eyes. "Meltdown?"

"Big-time. How bad is it?"

"You've looked better." She opens the fridge, pulls out a cucumber and cuts two thin slices. "Put these on your eyes for a few minutes."

I obediently hold them to my eyes. "I'm sorry about the pinhole camera, too."

"That's okay. We did get an A plus."

"You know what I'd really like, Lib? Some more of those cinnamon quesadillas."

She laughs. "The crew hated them. But I've been thinking about a frittata…"

"The crew never—" I pause "—gets to try new things. Bring on the frittata."

"Hey," Damon says, stepping onto the trailer, "nice eyewear, Rox."

I snatch the cucumber slices away and clutch his arm. "Listen, Damon, I really want you to direct the rest of the movie."

He studies my puffy eyes. "Everything okay?"

"Yeah, I just want you to finish it out. You're so much better at it and I want this movie to be as good as it can be." I glance at Libby. "Partly to do the scriptwriter justice."

"Okay," he says, peeling a cucumber slice from his sleeve. "You got it."

I stand on the pedestal in the dressing room and stare at my reflection. I have never looked worse: my eyes are bloodshot, my face splotchy and my hair is squashed and riddled with static from the toque I wore earlier. I thought the mirrors in these shops were bewitched to make every woman look beautiful but the magic must apply only to brides. My butt—as every angle in the 180-degree mirror confirms—is gargantuan.

A sudden movement in the curtains startles me as Damon steps into the room.

"I thought everyone had gone for lunch," I say.

"We're the only ones left in the shop." He steps up onto the pedestal beside me and addresses my reflection, "I'll bet I know what you're thinking."

"I'm thinking my butt is gargantuan, if you must know."

"You're wondering how you're going to hide a camera and lights to shoot in a small space dominated by mirrors."

"That, too."

"It's not, by the way."

"Not what?"

"Gargantuan. And you're wearing my favorite jeans."

"They're ripped and stained," I protest, secretly thrilled that he has a favorite.

"And tight," he adds, with a lascivious grin.

"Perv!" I give him a little shove that knocks him off balance. He topples backward off the podium and when I grab for him he pulls me down, too. We lie on the carpeted floor, laughing.

FADE UP FROM BLACK:
Two fuzzy objects move within the frame. As they come into focus, we recognize a man and a woman making out on the change room floor.

WOMAN

This is so unprofessional.

The man ignores her and the camera zooms in until only body parts fill the frame.

WOMAN

We really shouldn't. We have to work together.

His hand caresses her face. Hers travels down his back.

WOMAN

Someone might see us.

His leg rubs against hers. She kicks off a grubby sneaker and runs a foot along his calf.

WOMAN

It's all because of that chakra business.

The camera pans up her body and follows her T-shirt as he hooks a finger through the hole in the front and pulls it up over her head.

WOMAN

There's a "no kissing" rule on my set.

MAN

It's my set now, and I'm all for it.

EXTREME CLOSE-UP:
A zipper is yanked down. A pair of jeans is thrown at the camera, momentarily blocking the lens. The fabric slides off camera and we cut to a medium shot of our naked couple as the woman catches sight of her bare butt reflected again and again and again in the surrounding mirrors.

SNAP ZOOM INTO THE WOMAN'S HORRIFIED FACE.

QUICK CUT TO THE OUTSIDE OF THE CHANGE ROOM as the woman's scream echoes in the empty store.

PAN AROUND THE STORE TO REVEAL a pair of pink mules shuffling away in the opposite direction.

"Did you hear something?" I ask Damon, groping for my jeans.

"Just you screaming at your own reflection." He dangles my minimizer in front of me and pulls it away when I reach for it.

"It wasn't my best angle," I explain, snatching the bra out of his hands. "But I swear I heard something else—a slapping noise."

Damon slides my T-shirt over my head and pulls me close. "Don't be so paranoid. The entire crew is in the church across the street. We have the place to ourselves."

I check my watch. "Not for long. We've got ten minutes to figure out how to shoot this scene, so put your pants on, Mr. Director."

"Operator 6429. How may I help you?"

I reach for the remote control to turn down the volume on the jumbotron. "I'd like to order the Butt Blaster. Could you ship it express?"

Chapter 22

I stand in the stillness of my father's dark backyard and shiver. The mercury has plunged and a light snow is beginning to fall. Winter's frosty breath on my neck reminds me that Christmas is just around the corner.

I hate Christmas. Correction: I hate Christmas *now*. I enjoyed it when Mom was alive, even though I used to complain about how she'd never update a single tradition. Every year, it was the same pine boughs and plaid ribbon, the same berry wreaths, the same gilt angels and the same type of tree in the same corner of the living room, decorated as the same Christmas CD played. Everything went up on December 14 and I had to be there to help, no matter how late I shot. One year, she waited for me until three in the morning and we were still drinking eggnog when Dad left for work. Everything came down again on January 1 and I had to be there for that, too.

It drove me crazy that nothing ever changed—until everything changed. Since Mom died, we don't really "do" Christmas. Dad introduced a new tradition of sharing a meaningless dinner at the Park Hyatt Hotel in the company of similarly displaced strangers. This year, things are changing again. Dad has offered to cook a turkey for Gayle and me, although I'm reasonably sure he won't know which end to stuff. Hopefully Gayle has more skill in the kitchen. With all signs pointing to a Very Gayle Christmas, the gifts will be under a palm tree.

Brushing the snow off a stone bench, I sit down among the bunnies. The stone bunnies, that is. My mother had a thing for rabbits and gave it free rein in the garden. Big ones, small ones, skinny ones, fat ones, they're all staring sightlessly into the night. For the second time in two days, tears sting my eyes. I quickly look up to the indigo sky, where a handful of stars are already visible. Filling my lungs with the cold air, I shake off old memories. The crew will be arriving in less than an hour and I can't afford to be sniffling down memory lane.

I turn my attention back to the yard. Despite the ominous weather reports and Libby's pleading, I've stuck with my plan to shoot the reception scene outside. The electricians and I spent many hours preparing with our set dresser this afternoon. Finally, I hit the switch on the power cable and see that I made the right decision: hundreds of twinkle lights glitter in the bushes and trees around me. The floodlit gazebo in the center of the yard holds dozens of brightly wrapped packages. Chinese lanterns in two even rows illuminate the aisle leading to the gazebo.

There's a familiar rumble in the distance. I race around the yard with a propane lighter and make the final touches before heading around the house. Crusher has pulled the craft camper into my father's long driveway.

Libby hops out. "You're here early," she says.

"I'm making sure the set is as the writer imagined it," I say.

She snorts. "Nothing has been as this writer imagined it."

"Hold the cynicism," I say. I lead her along the path beside my father's house. Our boots crunch on the fresh snow.

"Please tell me you're moving the reception scene into your father's rec room," Libby says. "Anything would be better than shooting outside on a night like this. It's sheer—" She stops dead as the backyard comes into view, shining like a miniature wonderland.

"Madness?" I finish her sentence.

"Magic." Libby turns and gives me a hug. "It's beautiful, Roxanne."

"We still have a lot of lighting to do, but I'm glad you like it."

She turns back and starts counting. "There are thirty candelabras. And a gift gazebo. It's just as I envisioned—only a hell of a lot colder."

"Consider it an apology for acting like a jerk yesterday."

"I'm sorry, too," she says. "You're not a psychopath."

"Or...?"

"Or an asshole. At least not most of the time." She grins at me, her nose already reddening in the chilly breeze. "Hey, where's my llama?"

"There's no magic in llama dung, Lib."

"And you think *I'm* cynical?"

Damon gives me a casual hug by way of greeting, but he holds me tighter and longer than a friend would. Relief and happiness surge over me as I hug him back. I was afraid that one or both of us would pretend that yesterday never happened, especially in front of a yard full of cast and crew. My repression machine appears to have malfunctioned.

He gestures around the yard. "Impressive. I can work with that."

"I like the way it's turning out," I say, alluding to more than the setting.

He squeezes my arm through my parka to let me know he gets the point. "When you release this movie, brides everywhere will be clamoring for a backyard winter wedding."

"I doubt that," I say.

"I'm telling you, an intuitive designer is already channeling Dr. Zhivago."

"I'm on the forefront of a trend—at last."

Damon is silent for a moment, staring around the yard. "I owe you an apology."

"Yeah?" I'm in the mood to forgive anything. "For what?"

"For thinking that shooting Hank's Morocco project might be a stretch for you. You're definitely ready for it and whether he hires me to direct or not, I'm going to recommend you as cinematographer."

At the mention of Hank's project, Wonderland transforms instantly back into my father's cold backyard. I've been so busy lately that I'd conveniently forgotten going over Damon's head to try to land that job. I keep meaning to tell him, but it never seems like the right moment. With our last scene looming, this isn't it either. Better to do it at wrap. What's another few hours?

"You said you were going to shoot it yourself if you didn't get to direct," I say.

"I'm not so sure I want that anymore, and you need the break."

Oh, great, now he's being selfless. That means he'll be even more upset when he hears what I've done. Maybe it would be better to tell him right now after all. "Damon, there's something I've been meaning to say—"

"Hey, Rox," Keisha interrupts. "Our wedding guests are dressed and ready. We're just waiting on Genevieve."

"Okay, thanks," I say, grateful for the temporary reprieve. "You can seat everyone in the folding chairs."

I pull a light meter out of my pocket and walk over to the idling motorcycles. Lorna is standing beside Elvira in an ancient fur coat. Crusher sees me gawking at it and mouths "weasel." I cover my mouth with a mitten to conceal my laughter but Lorna's huge glasses apparently allow her to see through wool.

"What's so funny, young lady?"

"Nothing. I'm just enjoying the evening."

"I don't believe you," she harrumphs. "But I do notice that your fourth and fifth chakras are clearer today."

"Wow, you can do that without your voodoo rock?"

The wardrobe assistant is trying to push a helmet onto Lorna's head, but our venerable star fights her off valiantly. "You're giving off a lot of energy, Roxanne," Lorna says. "In fact, you're glowing."

"Clever lighting," I say. "A female cinematographer lit the scene you know."

She gives the wardrobe assistant a savage pinch. "It's more than that."

"Okay, I used the Drano."

The assistant circles Lorna quickly and jams the helmet over the old girl's wig from the rear. Lorna lands a punch, which is cushioned by parka.

"Joke all you like," Lorna says, her voice muffled by the helmet's visor, "but I know your little secret."

"What little secret?" I ask, signaling the wardrobe assistant to run while she can.

Lorna lifts the visor and there's a gleam in her rheumy eyes. "You've made *room* in your heart for a change."

"What are you talking about?" I stall for time, giving my

mind a chance to put two and two together. Finally it hits me: the slapping noise I heard outside the change room yesterday was the sound of mules hitting calloused heels.

Fortunately, my father's arrival in his nobleman costume prevents me from having to confirm or deny. Gayle snaps a few photos of him as he swings his leg over the third motorcycle.

"Dad," I say, "I want Crusher to give you a few more pointers on handling that thing."

"It's not like I haven't driven a chopper before, dear," my father says.

Who is this man masquerading as my father? "You have?"

"There's more to Gordie that meets the eye," Gayle says, giggling. "Crusher is letting us take Elvira for a spin later."

I try to visualize "Gordie" and Gayle flying through stodgy Rosedale on a Harley and fail utterly.

"Yoo-hoo, Prince Charming," Genevieve calls, waving a gloved hand at Damon. She's standing in the center of the yard in her bridal gown, a long white cape trailing in the even whiter snow. The many layers of satin and lace over a hoop skirt have turned her into one of those crocheted dolls the church ladies used to make to cover a roll of toilet tissue. "Come help me with my tiara."

"Sorry—outside my area of expertise," Damon says. "I'll get someone from wardrobe."

"I want *you* to help," she says, gliding toward him on invisible legs.

"It looks fine to me." When her hoops stop swaying, he makes a minor adjustment to the tiara. "What do you think, Rox?"

"You look perfect, Genevieve," I say.

My words must be carried off before reaching her ears, because she doesn't acknowledge me. Instead, she stares into

Damon's eyes so intently that he squirms uncomfortably. "I need to ask you something," she says.

Realizing that I should excuse myself, I immediately take a step closer.

Genevieve rests a gloved hand on Damon's arm and parts her rosebud lips, "Do I get off the motorcycle in this take or not?"

Damon extricates himself from her grip and glances at me questioningly.

I shrug. "You're the director. I've got my hands full with the lighting."

Pretending to slip on the snow, Genevieve wraps her arms around Damon's waist. He helps her regain her balance and steps out of reach before saying, "Stay on the bike. We'll overlap the action on the next setup."

"Fine," she says. "It's easy working with a director like you. You always make things clear." That shot is directed at me, of course, and to make sure I know it, she looks at me sideways and adds, "Roxanne, it was so brave of you to recognize that you were overwhelmed and take a back seat to Damon."

Keisha hands me a bagel with cream cheese and lox. "Libby is laying out a great spread on the craft table," she says.

I fall on the bagel as if I haven't eaten in hours, although I had a cookie mere moments ago. "Did she remember the champagne?"

"Already chilling in the snow," Keisha confirms. "And I've told everyone to join us inside your dad's house for the wrap party later. Congratulations, Rox. You did it."

"It's not quite over yet. Don't jinx me."

"It couldn't get any worse than Lorna screaming her freakin' head off behind Crusher on the motorcycle. He's probably deaf."

"If he is, it's his own fault," I say. "He deliberately hit that stone rabbit. It was my mother's favorite, too." Mind you, it was well worth the sacrifice to hear the note of hysteria in the old hag's voice.

Aside from that, shooting has gone like clockwork. I was sure that Genevieve would overact when she had to play drunk but her performance was spot on.

As if reading my thoughts, Keisha says, "Genevieve is pretty good."

"She is," I concede. "That's mostly Damon's doing. He brings out the best in actors."

"And you make them look good. You and Damon are a great team."

Keisha probably doesn't mean anything by that. Aside from Libby and Crusher—and now Lorna—I don't think anyone has picked up on what's going on between Damon and me. I'd like to keep it that way through the last weeks of shooting *Illegal Alien*. By that time, it should be clear whether we've got a real relationship brewing here.

Whatever happens on that front, I feel good about making *The Counterfeit Wedding*. It's been hard but still an amazing experience. Maybe I'm stoned on fresh air, but I can't help feeling that everything is unfolding as it should. Tonight, I am confident that I'll make it in this business, even if it isn't in the role I'd always imagined. Hank may never hire me as cinematographer, but I believe other directors will.

Damon would, I suppose, but I don't think I want to work that closely with him anymore, at least not until we get our relationship on surer footing. I've never been one to put romance ahead of work, but there's always a first time. Being here in Mom's beloved garden must be inspiring me to lay down some roots of my own. When she died, it was easier to put my life on ice for a while than think too much. Dad's getting serious about Gayle seems to have given me the impetus to dig my way out of the snowbank. As I check out the landscape, I can't help but notice that Miguel is nowhere in sight. The new Roxanne, fresh from the deep freeze, wants more from a relationship than fancy dinners and occasional sleepovers.

"What do you make of those two?" Keisha asks, jarring me out of my reverie. She's pointing toward the gazebo, where Enzo is running lines with Lorna.

"Whatever he's done, I'm grateful. She's been nailing her dialogue."

"Yeah, and did you notice? No more Latin."

"Praise the Lordicus."

After the last foot of film rolls through Gilda's gate, I thank everyone for their hard work and call a wrap on *The Counterfeit Wedding*. I'm sorry that it's over—and not just because it means returning to *Illegal Alien* and Alana. My crew members apparently feel the same way, because they migrate into a massive group hug. Finally, I get everyone moving toward the trucks by pointing out that the sooner we break down the equipment, the sooner we pop the corks on the champagne.

I am packing my light meters into my Jeep in the driveway, when I hear Crusher and Damon chatting on the other side of the dense cedar hedge.

"So, Roxanne pulled it off," Crusher says.

"She did," Damon agrees. "This may be the most beautifully lit mockumentary ever made." Smiling, I click the trunk closed and lean against it. Damon continues, "I'm going to encourage her to make a print so that we can enter it into a short-film festival."

"Great idea," Crusher says. "I'm glad it turned out so well. Now she'll see she doesn't need that sleaze Hank to make a go of it in this business."

Damon pauses. "No, she doesn't."

Crusher misses the significance of the pause. "I mean, big whoop if he reneged on their deal. She doesn't need to shoot that Morocco flick. Better to make it on her own terms, like I always said."

Shit. I stand paralyzed as Crusher unwittingly reveals what I should have told Damon long ago myself.

"Hank was going to hire Rox as his cinematographer?" Damon asks, sounding confused.

I hold my breath in the brief silence that follows, silently chanting, *Shut up, Crusher. Please shut up.*

"Well yeah," Crusher says, sounding equally puzzled, because I never admitted that I didn't tell Damon about our deal. "Or at least he said he would as long as she passed his so-called test. If it had worked out, he was going to take on *The Lobby.*"

Well, there's no point rushing back there now. This train wreck is already underway. Better to hold my position and see what's left standing when it's over.

"The Lobby?" Damon sounds more confused than ever.

"Yeah." I can tell by the way Crusher drags out the word that he's noticed he's already knee-deep in quicksand, but can't see a way out. "You know, the screenplay she commissioned. Hank said he'd consider letting her direct it for Fudgling."

"Fledgling," Damon says.

"I said that Hank was only trying to get into her pants, but she didn't believe me." Crusher is speaking faster and faster, clearly self-conscious now. "Then he showed his stripes by hiring that useless bitch on second unit."

"Alana," Damon supplies.

"That's the one," Crusher says, before babbling, "Rox was so set on directing *The Lobby* she'd have made a deal with the devil himself if he agreed to produce."

"Of course," Damon says. His voice is a little stronger, proving he's determined to get all he can out of Crusher before hammering the gavel down on my case.

Crusher is encouraged. "Not that I'm criticizing, understand. I admire her tenacity. If there's one thing I've learned from Rox, it's that it takes balls and persistence to make it in this business."

"It does," Damon agrees. After a moment he adds, "But you don't have to forget who your friends are."

"She wouldn't!" Crusher exclaims, alarmed to find that the quicksand has reached beard level so quickly. "That's not Rox's way." His voice is louder and I realize that he's calling after Damon, who is leaving the backyard.

I dodge around the Jeep and chase Damon down the driveway to his car.

"Damon, wait!"

EXTERIOR, NIGHT, AN URBAN STREET: Roxanne scans the driveway and street as she runs, worried that someone might be watching. The only thing she hates more than taking part in a drama is knowing there's an audience.

ACTION ON THE DRAMA:

Damon ignores me and unlocks his car door. I grab his arm.

He shrugs me off. "Let go, Roxanne."

"Let me explain. It's not like it sounds."

After opening the door, he turns and says, "No? Then Crusher's a liar?"

"Okay, it's sort of like it sounds—but not as bad."

CUE THE CORNY MUSIC.

Damon shakes his head and slides behind the wheel. "You didn't respect me enough to mention going behind my back to make career plans with Hank."

"I tried to tell you about Hank and *The Lobby* earlier tonight, but Keisha interrupted."

"*Earlier tonight?* This started weeks ago."

Make that months. There isn't much I can say without digging myself in deeper, so I settle for stepping in front of the car door to prevent his closing it.

He continues, "I might not have been happy about it, but I wouldn't have stopped you. Did you think I was trying to hold you back?"

"I don't know." I look down and scuff my boot on the snowy asphalt. "Maybe."

"Why would I do that?"

"To keep me as your assistant?" Even as I'm saying it, I realize how feeble it sounds.

THE CORNY MUSIC SWELLS.

Damon says, "Do you really think so little of me?"

Roxanne launches into an unrehearsed reconciliation script, explaining all the ins and outs of her convoluted logic. While Damon impatiently drums his fin-

*gers on the wheel, she emphasizes how
each and every plan she made backfired
in her face until she finally saw the
light.*

"Crusher must have been right about Hank's intentions," I conclude, "because he made Alana the second-unit cinematographer right after he caught us kissing at the tailgate party. Meanwhile, I don't even want to direct anymore."

Damon ignores the last comment. "You didn't tell me Hank saw us kissing. Or wait, maybe you were kissing someone else?"

*Roxanne deviates from the reconciliation
script.*

"Yeah, I had a man on every tailgate. It's not like you're the king of full disclosure."

Damon walks right into the trap.

"What have I kept from you?"

"Imagine how I felt upon learning from Alana herself that she was shooting the second unit."

"I came to your house to tell you that."

"But you didn't do it."

Damon tries to close the car door. "It's not the same thing anyway."

"Of course not. If *you're* the one sidestepping the truth, it's far different."

ZOOM IN ON DAMON'S SCOWL.

Pushing me out of the way, he says, "I am not going to have this ridiculous argument." He yanks the car door closed and turns the key in the ignition.

Roxanne forgets all about the neighbors.

Banging on his window, I bellow, "Oh, yes, you are."
Damon says, "Can't hear you."
Reaching for the rear door before he can lock it, I jump into the back seat.
"Get out of the car, Rox." He refuses to look at me.
"No."
"I mean it. I am not arguing with you."
I lean forward between the seats. "Where has *not* arguing gotten us before?"
He continues to look straight ahead. "The same place we're going now—nowhere."

ZOOM IN ON ROXANNE'S STRICKEN FACE.

"So you're giving up already?"
"That's the plan."

CUT TO THE RIVAL, STANDING BESIDE THE CAR: She taps on the window.

"Damon, I've been waiting for you inside with a glass of champagne."
He rolls down the window. "Thanks, Genevieve, I don't think so."
She leans in and notices me. "Oh, hi, Roxanne. I didn't mean that back seat comment literally, you know."

Roxanne waits until Genevieve is gazing at Damon again before flipping her the bird. Damon's eyebrows rise as he catches the gesture in the rearview mirror.

"Damon," Genevieve entreats, "the director never leaves without saying thanks."

Damon acknowledges his professional duty with a slight nod. He opens the door and steps out without so much as looking at me. Linking her arm through his, Genevieve escorts him across the street and up the walk to the house.

"Don't worry about me," I say to no one in particular. "I'll just sit here until I freeze to death. Then he'll be sorry."

I notice my father at the front door welcoming Damon and Genevieve. It won't be long before he sends out a search party. Sighing, I pick up a small cosmetic mirror from the well between the seats—Genevieve's, no doubt—and smile at my reflection. There's a row of poppy seeds wedged between my front teeth.

SAD MUSIC SWELLS. Roxanne climbs out of the car and the camera rises up, up, up, until she is just a tiny dot standing alone on the side of the empty road.

END SCENE.

I have a great view of the party from the top stair in my father's front hall. Lorna and Enzo are teaching Dad and Gayle the Macarena on the makeshift dance floor in the dining room. Gizmo and Christian are dancing with the hair and makeup assistants. Snake is sharing a joint with a couple of the drivers beside the patio doors. And Damon is chatting to some cast members while Genevieve clings to his arm.

"You were invited to the ball, Cinderella," Libby says, climbing the stairs with a bottle of champagne and two flutes in her hands. "In fact, I'm pretty sure it's your ball." She settles beside me on the top stair and fills the glasses. She clinks her flute against mine and takes a sip. "Congrats on a job well done."

"Thanks." I gulp half the glass and hold it out for a refill.

"Hey," she says, pointing to Genevieve, who is feeding a chocolate-dipped strawberry to Damon, "she's not allowed to do that."

"It's all right," I say, guzzling more champagne, "I poisoned the fruit."

"Uh-oh, trouble in paradise already."

I nod ruefully. "Crusher told Damon about my deal with Hank and he flipped."

"Did you grovel?"

I think about it for a moment. "Yeah, I groveled."

She smiles. "If you have to think about it, you didn't grovel enough."

"Well, I *explained* and he wouldn't listen. Maybe he was distracted by the poppy seeds in my teeth."

"In that state, they're only capable of hearing begging. So get your sorry ass down there and do it up right."

"Let me raise my blood alcohol level first. It adds feeling to a grovel."

"That it does," she agrees, "but there's no time to lose." Below us, Damon is walking toward the front door with the Genevieve barnacle attached to his side.

I rise unsteadily to my feet and Libby holds on to my belt buckle to make sure I don't take a header. Before I can make it to the landing, Damon and Genevieve slip out the door. I turn and walk back up past Libby and into my old bedroom to watch them from the window. Damon opens the passenger door of his BMW for her and closes it gently once she's settled. Genevieve gets the front-seat treatment all the way.

Libby joins me at the window. "Too late," I say, offering my glass for a refill.

My old bedroom looks virtually the same as it did when I moved out thirteen years ago. Mom had an open-door policy. There was no telling when her only fledgling—make that fudgling—might come home to roost.

Libby and I are sitting on the floor beside my bed, just as we did for hours when we were teenagers. I tune in to the same radio station we always liked, only to find it's become "easy listening."

"Give a swish," Libby says, pouring more champagne into our glasses. "The poppy seeds are still in your teeth."

"See, that's why girls are better than boys," I say. "Damon never mentioned it. He was too busy pulverizing my heart."

"And you're never going to smile again."

"Correct." But I smile anyway.

She clambers over to my bookshelf on her knees and retrieves my Ouija board. "Remember Bernie?"

I lean back comfortably against the bed. "How could I forget?"

Bernie was our main man in the spiritual realm. Whenever we had a teen-sized problem requiring more insight that we possessed, Bernie was there to offer cryptic observations on our world and his.

"Shall we?" she asks, laying out the board on the floor between us. "Bernie probably has something to say about Damon."

"I don't know that he'll be much help," I say. "Remember Derek Sykes?"

Libby laughs so hard she has to lie down on her side. I move her champagne off my cream shag carpet onto the bedside table.

The year I turned fourteen, Bernie directed me to ask Derek to the school's "Sadie Hawkins" dance. Although I was hardly brimming with confidence, I knew that I was out of Derek's league. He was in the school's UFO Club, for God's sake. When I protested Bernie's edict, however, he responded with several impatient jerks of the pointer: "Eat it." Who knew spirits could be so crude? Libby urged me to obey, fearing that Bernie would blight our already floundering love lives. So I asked Derek to the dance and he accepted, with much blushing and stammering.

"You totally pushed the pointer," I tell Libby. "That was your idea, not Bernie's."

"Was not," she says, grinning up at me. "You're still burned because your Trekkie boyfriend copped a feel during 'We've Got Tonight.'"

"I was surprised Derek had it in him," I say. "I lost a little faith in Bernie that day."

"I know, but think about it. He's on the 'other side' with unfettered access to the romantic greats like the Brontë sisters."

Sighing, I throw myself down on the floor and rest a finger lightly on the pointer. "Hi, Bernie, it's Roxanne. Are you there?"

The pointer moves to "yes." I look at Libby, now lying on her stomach. I can almost see that uncontrollable afro she used to have.

"Okay then, Bernie, what should I do about Damon? Check in with the Brontës before you answer, okay?"

The pointer spells out "call him" and then, after a short pause, "grovel."

"Libby! Pushing!"

"I'm not. Can I help it if the spirits agree with me?"

The pointer starts moving again before I can ask another question. Slowly it spells out "nothing ventured nothing gained."

"See?" Libby says. "That has the feeling of Charlotte Brontë about it."

Actually, it has the feeling of my mother about it. That's what she always used to say when she was trying to talk me into trying something I was afraid to do. Libby might know this, but she would never consciously play the "mom" card, particularly when she knows I'm drunk enough to veer quickly into maudlin territory.

Before I can say anything, there's a knock on the bedroom door and my father opens it tentatively. "I should have known I'd find you girls here," he says. "I see you've been talking to Bernie."

Libby and I ask in unison: "How'd you know?"

"About Bernie? Your mother told me," he says. "She got quite a kick out of your exploration into 'another realm.'" He throws up some finger quotes.

"Dad," I say, as severely as a slur will allow, "absolutely no finger quotes. It's so lame."

He shrugs at Libby. "She's thirty-four and I'm still embarrassing her."

"Going on thirty-five, Mr. Hastings," Libby says.

"Well, say good-night to Bernie and I'll call you two a cab."

Libby and I weave down the stairs and out the front door. My father follows with our coats.

"Honey, you did a fantastic job with this movie," he says, helping us into the cab. "I'm really proud of you."

"Thanks, Dad," I say. Somehow you're never too old or too drunk to enjoy hearing those words. "I really appreciate your help. And Gayle's."

The lady herself is waving from the front door, her neon lipstick aglow under the porch light. "I'll tell her," Dad says. "Now, go straight home, girls."

"We will," we chime again.

As we pull up in front of Libby's apartment, she says, "Listen to your father. Go straight home and don't do anything stupid."

I try to pat her arm and miss it completely. "Don't worry, I've got it all under control."

"I can see that," she says. "Or I could if you hadn't just spit in my eye."

We're both still giggling as she closes the door.

After we pull away from the curb, I take out my cell phone and, with difficulty, press the tiny buttons.

"Hello?" the voice answers.

As Bernie would say, nothing ventured, nothing gained. "I know it's late, but can I come over?"

"Of course, *mi amor.* I'll be waiting."

Chapter 23

I follow Dad and Gayle into the dim lobby of the Windsor Arms Hotel.

"Nice to see you again," the doorman says, tipping his fur hat.

"Does he know you?" Gayle whispers.

"He probably says that to everyone."

"He didn't say it to me," she says, still suspicious.

"I'm a moviemaker now," I joke. "He can tell I'm important."

When my father invited me to breakfast, I had no idea it would be at the scene of a recent crime. After the party at Dad's a few nights ago, I briefly visited Miguel here. And I do mean briefly. I climbed into his warm, rumpled bed, had second thoughts and climbed back out again. Then I did what any silly young thing would do: faked a headache and bolted. Miguel was furious and rightly so. I've left an apology on his voice mail, but I'd prefer to avoid a direct encounter today.

At the table, my father taps my arm as I scan for a glimpse

of beret. "Roxanne, if you need to be on set in an hour, you'd better look at your menu."

"It's okay, I know what I want." I don't need Voula to confirm that I have my French toast face on.

"Is everything all right?" Dad asks. "You seem distracted."

"Sorry. Just tired. Rough reentry onto *Illegal Alien*."

That's true enough. Going back to focus pulling after shooting *The Counterfeit Wedding* hasn't been easy and kowtowing to Alana has become almost unbearable. Super Focus Puller seems to have fallen overboard during the hiatus.

Dad and Gayle are clearly delighted to see me and we have a pleasant meal together. I don't even get upset (at least, not very) when Dad tells me that he and Gayle are spending New Year's Eve in Savannah, yet another place my mother always wanted to go but my father wouldn't take her. It occurs to me for the first time that Mom's death may have served as a wake-up call for Dad. Perhaps he is rethinking his priorities.

After we finish eating, Gayle excuses herself to freshen her lipstick and Dad says, "I have something for you." He reaches into his jacket for an envelope.

I open it to find a blank check made out to me. "Wow, Santa isn't usually this generous," I say.

"It's not a Christmas present. It's for *The Counterfeit Wedding*."

"I don't need money, Dad."

"Damon wants you to screen your movie at a festival and you'll need a print."

"How do you know that?" I asked, bemused. Dad's never shown an interest in the details of filmmaking before.

"Crusher told me. We chat now and then."

"Since when?"

"Since I decided to get a Harley. Crusher is giving me some advice."

I'm all for resetting priorities, but this is taking it a bit too far. "Dad, please don't tell me you're joining the Cycle Demons."

He laughs. "I'm not much of a joiner, dear. Anyway, I want you to get your print made."

"That's really nice of you, Dad, but I still have some savings."

"I don't want you touching your nest egg," he says, sounding more the dad I know.

I accept the check as a loan and try to act excited for Dad's sake, but all I can think about is how demoralizing it will be to edit this picture without Damon.

I'm in the last seat of a twelve-passenger minivan en route to one of the city's seediest street corners. The second unit will be shooting several points of view, or POVs, for the Creature in which a couple of dozen people will be running away. It seems straightforward, but since Kugelman has submitted last-minute revisions, I'm prepared for the worst.

Thirty-plus pounds of Gilda dig into my thighs every time the driver hits a pothole. At the front of the van, Alana is talking to Hank on her cell phone. I can't hear what she's saying, but there's enough giggling to make me suspicious. Finally, she hangs up and cranes around in her seat.

"Rox, I forgot to mention that Hank wants us to do some ramping in this scene."

By this, she's referring to the process of varying the film speed during a take to create a slow-motion, or quick-motion effect.

"When did he say that?" I ask, as the driver pulls into our location.

"Oh, I don't know…. Before the hiatus, I guess. Why?"

I shake my head. "Because we've paid four cops to close down a busy intersection and assembled forty crew and extras for nothing, that's why."

"What do you mean?"

"This camera doesn't ramp without a special attachment and you didn't tell me to order one."

Silence descends on the van as everyone awaits Alana's response. Her fingers rise, but there's nothing to punctuate. "I thought all cameras ramped," she says.

"They don't. You should know that."

The doors on both sides of the van slide open instantly and ten crew members bail out. With Super Focus Puller currently on the lam, there is nothing to stop me from lambasting my boss. It's a lousy career move, but I don't care.

"You can't speak to me like that, Roxanne. I could fire you."

"Great idea," I say. "I could use a break from covering your ass, so consider me fired." I clamber to the front of the van and set Gilda on her lap. "Over to you."

I've seen my future, and it's looking pretty good, even if I burn a bridge with Hank. Besides, it's better to be fired for mouthing off to Alana than to get the boot from Hank when she blames me for one of her blunders.

Taking out a purple marker, I scrawl a phone number into her palm and say, "If I were you, I'd call the rental house for a ramping unit on the double. It will take at least an hour to get it here and there's not much daylight left to get these shots."

I jump out of the van and stand with the rest of the crew.

Pinned to the seat by Gilda, Alana calls out the window, "What kind of ramping unit do I ask for? What kind of camera is this?"

"You did your time as an assistant," I say. "It will come back to you."

The crew titters.

There's a new urgency to her tone as she says, "You can't quit, Roxanne."

"I didn't quit, you fired me."

"I didn't fire you, I just said that I *could.*" She frees one hand from Gilda to offer a finger quote. "But I won't if you stay and call the rental house."

"Nah. Make it official and fire me." That way I'll get severance pay.

"If you stay, I promise I'll tell Hank how much you've helped me."

"I've heard that one before. Why should I believe you now?"

"Because I mean it, now."

"That's what Lucy tells Charlie Brown every time she pulls the football away. And unlike Charlie, there's a limit to my gullibility."

"I promise," she says, with a distinct quaver in her voice. "I need you. Please?"

Damn her. Now if I say no, I'll look like a bitch instead of the worm that's finally turned. Worse, I'll feel horrible about abandoning Christian with this mess.

Disappointed to learn that there's no limit to my gullibility after all, I pick up my cell phone and call the rental house.

"They'll have one here around five," I tell Alana, who has managed to get herself out of the van and is staggering toward me under Gilda's weight.

"That's too late," she says. "It gets dark at six. And if we don't break the crew for lunch at five, the production will have to pay overtime."

"If we're organized, we can get the shots in an hour. And we can keep the crew out of penalties by breaking for lunch early."

That's when I notice her sweater is torn in two places and there's dirt on both knees.

"Did you fall?" I ask.

"Yes," she says, sounding tearful again. "But don't worry, I'm all right."

"I'm only worried about the camera."

"Oh, your precious baby is fine," she snaps. "That's all you care about."

Which means that Super Focus Puller has returned. As hard as I try, I can never shake her for long.

F. C. Kugelman hoists his laptop onto the white linen table-cloth at one of Santa Monica's most exclusive restaurants. As he sets up, waiters parade by carrying menus, wine lists and a silver water jug.

Roxanne Hastings hoists her camera onto the tripod at one of Toronto's most run-down intersections. As she sets up, winos parade by, carrying bottles in brown paper bags.

F.C. bends over his keyboard. The staff fill his water glass, deliver a basket of exotic breads and ask how everything is.

Roxanne bends over her camera battery. The men check out her butt, try to cop a feel and ask how much.

Kugelman is alone because his dinner date, a legendary busi-nessman, had a last-minute deal to close. Dining alone in a restaurant can be uncomfortable but tonight it is for the best, because F.C. wants to make last-minute revisions to the Crea-ture POVs.

Roxanne is alone because her colleague, a legendary fool, has joined the crew for lunch at a nearby restaurant. Standing alone on a dodgy street corner can be uncomfortable, but tonight it is for the best because Roxanne can think about where to place all the extras without interruption from the fool.

F.C.'s mouth waters as waiters set plates of Southern California's tastiest fare before him.

Roxanne's stomach growls as one of the loitering men pulls a squashed bag of chips out of his pocket and tosses it at her.

F.C. turns his attention to his computer screen. Sipping his wine, he re-reads his last entry.

Exterior, Inner City Street, Day, Alien POV:
Standing in the middle of the street, the Creature watches as dozens of panicked citizens run for their lives.

Roxanne pours the last of the stale chip crumbs into her mouth and turns to the ramping unit. Sipping a cold coffee that a crew member delivered, she checks her watch. There's just over an hour to get this scene before sunset. Thankfully, the camera set-up is simple enough.

F.C. beckons the head waiter. "Excuse me. Do you think it's possible for an alien to be all places at once?"

"I do, sir," the waiter replies, unfazed by the question. Having worked in California for ten years, he's pretty much heard it all.

Exterior, Inner City Street, Day, Alien POV:
From a second-story ledge, the Creature watches as panicked citizens run for their lives.

Alana points toward the apartment above the variety store. "We don't have time to rig a tripod up there, Rox. You'll have to put the camera on your shoulder and lean out. The grip will hold you."

"It doesn't say 'cinematographer' on my paycheck. He should be holding you."

"But I have to be down here to direct the extras."

The grip's expression conveys that he'd rather work with Roxanne. It's flattering, considering there's a hell of a lot less of Alana to hold. Setting Gilda onto her shoulder, Rox follows the grip into the building.

"What's with the blanket?" Rox asks, as they start up the stairs to the second floor. "Wait, I get it," she adds, as a foul smell assails her nostrils. "It's to cover the body."

The locations manager ushers them into a tiny apartment. "Tuck your jeans into your boots," he says. "I got half a dozen fleabites when I scouted the place."

A stained mattress sits in the center of the living room floor. Beside it is a small pile of animal feces. Cockroaches scurry across the counter in the galley kitchen to hide behind a coffeemaker, in which a cloud of mold floats. Roxanne holds her breath. The grip lays the blanket over the windowsill and Rox leans out to shoot.

Kugelman contemplates the complimentary platter of French cheeses. "I need a more dynamic shot," he tells the waiters when they gather beside his table. As unemployed actors, they immediately grasp his concern.

The bartender hands him a port and says, "How about a POV where the camera is moving?"

Kugelman pops a piece of pungent Fourme d'Ambert into his mouth. "Genius!"

```
HANDHELD CAMERA: The Creature chases
several victims through the revolv-
ing doors of a run-down hotel.
```

"We're going to have to clean these glass doors," Rox says, after rehearsing the shot once with the camera.

"No time," Alana objects, "we lose the sun in twenty minutes."

"The doors are so covered in fingerprints that the shot will be useless anyway if we don't clean them. It'll take two minutes. There'll be enough ambient light to get the last shot even after the sun sets."

"Fine, clean the glass. But don't tell me how much light I have left, Roxanne. That's my call."

Roxanne is so dizzy after several takes that she has to sit down.

"Get up," Alana says. "No time to waste."

The head waiter reads the scene over Kugelman's shoulder before asking, "What about a really high angle?"

"We have the second story window," Kugelman says, smearing a cracker with a thick layer of Buchette. "But maybe something much *higher…"*

```
Once they realize that they are no
longer being pursued by the Crea-
ture, the citizens slow down and peer
around anxiously. An eerie calm de-
scends over the street from our
rooftop POV. The Alien is still
watching.
```

Roxanne trots after the locations manager through a maze of catwalks to the tiny, winding staircase. The tower is so narrow that she must carry Gilda in front, arms outstretched.

Alana is already on the roof when they emerge. "Forget it," she says. "We're out of light. That's a wrap."

"No way," Roxanne says. "We hauled the gear up here and we're getting a shot."

"It's supposed to be daytime."

"The next scene is night so a twilight shot is fine," Rox argues. "The extras are all in position below so let's roll."

Alana finally yields when her blond head is held to the viewfinder by force. It's a spectacular shot and even Alana can see that.

Kugelman reads aloud to the wait staff.

```
The sky has turned a deep midnight
blue. The setting sun tints the
clouds the color of pink grapefruit
flesh. The citizens gather in the
```

```
fading daylight to face the horrors
of the coming night.
```

"Brilliant," the busboy enthuses as Kugelman hits Save and closes the file.

"The perfect way to end the scene," the bartender agrees.

The headwaiter nods and pours F.C. another glass of port. "Do you think you could get me an audition?"

Alana, in her wisdom, has decided not to send the rooftop footage to the lab. She insists that it will be too dark, although I explained that I had removed a filter to give us a better exposure.

"I didn't tell you to remove that filter," she says, leading me into the camera truck. "Now you've ruined the color balance."

"They can correct that in postproduction."

"Roxanne," she explains patronizingly, "you can't add to production costs by developing film that's no good. Hank already flipped when I told him you ordered that ramping whojamaflopsy."

"He was probably overwhelmed by your technical terminology."

"I'm serious, Roxanne."

"Let me send in the rooftop footage and I'll let you take credit for it. It will be one of the prettiest shots in the movie and you'll score big points with Damon."

"I don't care what Damon thinks."

"You should. His name is going on our work."

"You've become so *argumentative* since the hiatus, Roxanne," she says, flicking her fingers into the air with renewed verve. If it weren't for the broken nail on one hand, I'd al-most believe this morning's breakdown never happened. "Maybe you think that shooting your own movie makes you an *expert,* but it doesn't. Especially when you caved and begged Damon to direct."

Super Focus Puller wills herself not to take the bait. "Alana, we're talking about *Illegal Alien.* This was a good shot and Hank should have a chance to see it."

She puts her hands on her hips. "That footage is not going to the lab, Roxanne. And just to be sure of that, I want you to give it to me right now."

Damn. The dimwit is getting brighter.

Fortunately, I'm still ahead of her. "It's in the mag. I'll have to download it."

"I'll wait."

I step into the darkroom. Ignoring the rooftop footage, which is already canned and waiting to be shipped to the lab, I stuff a short end of unused stock into a second can. For Alana's benefit, I click the latches on the empty maga-zine case before stepping out and presenting her with the bogus can.

She accepts it triumphantly and asks, "What's that horri-ble smell?"

"I have no idea," I reply, although I'm reasonably sure it's the stench of that hellhole apartment clinging to my clothes.

Nose wrinkling, she backs away and hops off the camera truck with the film can.

Damon pokes his head out of the lounge area at the far end of the truck. "Nice move."

I jump. "Were you eavesdropping?"

"Sure. If it works for you, why not me?" He doesn't wait for an answer. "I assume you gave her the wrong film and are shipping the rooftop shot to the lab?"

"That's the plan." I start to pack Gilda away, just to look busy.

"I admire your professionalism, Roxanne."

"Thanks." I try not to read too much into this. Complimenting my professionalism isn't a declaration of undying love. Better to wait him out. There's a reason he was lurking in the lounge and he'll likely share it soon enough.

"Look," he says, "I came to apologize."

I look up from Gilda, a smile igniting and spreading like wildfire across my face. "There's no need. I should have told you about the Morocco thing sooner."

"Not about *that*," he says, frowning. "I'm apologizing because I haven't had a chance to tell Hank that you've been covering for Alana."

My smile flickers out. "Oh. Well, no problem. Whenever you get a chance."

"He's been so busy since he got back from L.A.," Damon continues. "But I've booked an appointment with him for later today."

"Okay." He doesn't say anything more, but he doesn't leave either. So after a few awkward moments, I say, "If you're interested in seeing *The Counterfeit Wedding* dailies, I'm going tonight."

He waits an eternity before responding. "Since we're both professionals, I guess I could come."

This dancing around the real issue is wearing me down. "You'd better check in with Genevieve first."

"We're not back together if that's what you're implying."

"No? You looked pretty cozy at my dad's place."

"I don't owe you any explanations," he says, his voice rising.

"Shh. Keep your voice down."

"You're going to believe whatever you want, anyway," he says, in a fierce whisper.

"Says the man whose mind is sealed tighter than a jar of plutonium."

"A jar of plutonium? I'm 'overwhelmed by your technical terminology.'" He walks to the door of the truck. "See you at the lab, Stinky."

Damon enters the screening theater long enough after me that I'm convinced he won't show. Eventually, however, he takes the seat beside mine. Thank God I had enough time to run home for a quick shower and change.

As the lights dim, I experience the usual flutter of excitement jacked up tenfold. I've never had so much invested in the footage before. I'm glad Damon is with me, even if it's only in a "professional" capacity. It would be anticlimactic to see it alone.

To my delight the images are exposed exactly as I had calculated and it's much funnier than I recall. Obviously, I was too frazzled during shooting to appreciate the performances fully. Despite her tiny stature, Lorna has a commanding presence on screen—at least, when she gets her lines right. Her insistence on using her own wardrobe actually adds considerably to the visual humor, although she wouldn't thank me for saying so. The shop owners also did well, especially Gayle, who obviously inherited more from her aunt than a fondness for bright colors. Even Libby was convincing, once Damon took over directing her.

The biggest surprise, however, is Genevieve. She was such a pain in the butt throughout shooting that I am stunned to see how good she is as the counterfeit bride. So good, in fact, that I can't imagine anyone else in the role.

"It looks great," Damon says as the lights come up. "You should be proud."

"I couldn't have done it without you. Thank you."

He finally cracks a smile. "You're welcome."

"I hope you're going to help me edit this," I say. "In your capacity as director, I mean."

"In my capacity as director, I wouldn't trust you to edit it alone."

The projectionist enters the theater to see if I want to make a print. I'm still not happy about using Dad's money, so I've decided to transfer the film to DVD while I think about it. That's a much cheaper process, but it will at least allow me to use the film as a calling card.

Damon has other ideas. "Transfer it to print," he tells the projectionist.

"But—" I begin.

He waves the projectionist away. "I'm paying for post-production."

"No you're not."

"Excuse me. As director of this movie, it's only fair that I share the costs. Maybe I want a print so that we can enter it into festivals."

"Festivals? Plural?"

"Let's keep our options open."

I'm thrilled that he's so enthusiastic, but I'd prefer to pay my share. And thanks to Dad's generosity, that is now possible. "I'm paying for half the cost of the print."

"Save your money for the dialogue looping in the stationery shop scene. What the hell was that, anyway?"

"Whale calls. You'd know that if you hadn't left in a snit."

"As I recall, you dismissed me."

That sounds like something I'd do. "Okay, maybe I was a handful that day."

"That day and every day," he says. But he's actually grinning.

This from the man Hank describes as a hothead. "Look who's talking." Since he's loosening up, however, I add, "Damon, I hope we can move forward. I really am sorry about the Morocco thing. I got myself into a state about it for some reason and I was afraid to tell you."

He stares at the darkened screen for a moment. "I've been thinking about what you said about holding you back. Maybe you were right."

I turn in my seat to get a good look at him. "Really?"

"Maybe I was trying to keep you as part of my team—at least unconsciously."

I settle back in my seat and stare at the screen myself. "Maybe I didn't want to go, either."

"Let me buy you a drink so that we can discuss this further," he says, turning to meet my eyes.

I nod, pushing my 5:00 a.m. call time right out of my mind. As Mom would say, nothing ventured, nothing gained.

Damon pulls me to my feet and leads me through the labyrinth of hallways toward the lab's entrance. He continues to hold my hand and I swing on it like a mischievous four-year-old until a voice startles me:

"¡Querida!" Miguel is standing at the door of an editing suite.

I greet him as coolly as if he were a mere acquaintance, hoping desperately that Damon never studied Spanish.

Miguel walks over and extends his hand to Damon, forcing the latter to release mine. "Hello, Damon. What brings you here?"

Damon shakes Miguel's hand. "Just looking at some rushes."

"Roxanne mentioned that you were helping out on her little project," Miguel says, his eyes jumping quickly from Damon to me and back. "You are over your fight, I see."

"What do you mean?" Damon asks, surprised that Miguel and I are on such intimate terms.

"He doesn't mean anything," I say, taking Damon's arm and hauling him toward the door. "Good night, Miguel."

Miguel follows. "When she came to my hotel the other night, she was upset about fighting with you. But I see she is over it already. With me, she never forgives."

Damon pulls back and stops. He stares at me for a moment before saying, "The Mystery Caller." It's a statement, not a question. And before I can respond, he shrugs off my hand and walks out of the building.

I start after him, but Miguel stops me. "Where are you going, *querida?* You can't be serious about him."

I turn back. "Listen, you know I'm sorry about the other night. I shouldn't have come over. But all I owe you is an apology. It's always been that way with us."

He wraps his arms around me. "Perhaps it should be another way. We could make a commitment—have a real relationship."

I push him away. "You'd last about a month and you know it. Imagine having to consider someone else every time you got an offer to film in some exotic location. And believe me, I'd have a lot more to say about your disappearances if we had a commitment. If you think I'm difficult now, you should see me in a 'real' relationship."

Miguel doesn't argue the point. There's a reason the man has two ex-wives. But he says, "We've been doing this for years and we've both been happy."

"That wasn't a relationship. And we weren't happy enough."

He studies me with his dark eyes for a moment or two. "So this is adios, *amor?*"

"I guess it is."

We hug as if we mean it. It's been over between us for a long time but there's still a strong undercurrent of friendship.

To prove it, Miguel says, "I am sorry if I didn't support your project enough, Roxanne. I am proud of you for making the film and hope you'll send me a copy when it is done. I know it will be wonderful."

Some guys are their sweetest when you're saying good-bye. I'm glad Miguel is one of them.

Chapter 24

Stubborn: *Unreasonably, even perversely unyielding; bullheaded.*
Damon: *See above.*
Indignation: *Righteous anger over injustice.*
Roxanne: *See above. See also,* **guilt, anger** *and* **frustration.**
Miguel: *Not worth fighting about. See* **history.**

Our current set spans one city block but it isn't anywhere near big enough for Damon and me right now. He's angry with me about Miguel; I'm angry at him for refusing to hear me out. Not that I deny that I'm more at fault, mind you. Hiding a professional arrangement from Damon was one thing. Hiding a personal relationship with a man he can't stand is quite another. The "it wasn't serious" defense rarely holds up in the court of romance.

As if things weren't awkward enough, I still need Damon's help to cut together *The Counterfeit Wedding* and I'm not sure how "professional" he'll be about that. Without his expertise, I'll have to spend a lot more time and money fumbling my way through the process. Yet it's hard to imagine that a small editing suite can contain all this tension.

Otherwise, life on *Illegal Alien* continues to annoy in the usual ways. As predicted, Hank loved the rooftop shot. When Alana recovered from her surprise at seeing it in the dailies, she was quite pleased to accept his accolades. So pleased, in fact, that her promise to disclose the truth to Hank immediately vaporized. Like Charlie Brown, I am stretched out flat again.

Damon's promise to enlighten Hank also seems to have vaporized. Summoning my nerve yesterday, I tried to broach the subject with him. In as few words as possible, Damon said that Hank has been too busy for "that sort of conversation." In as many words as possible, I then accused him of lying to me. It wasn't a wise move in view of my recent history, but it did provoke Damon to say far more, using words such as *duplicity* and *hypocrisy*. I resorted to huffy non sequiturs and retreated in a sulk.

I have decided to focus my righteous indignation instead on Genevieve, who still hasn't given up the fight to win Damon back. Judging by her increasingly obvious attempts to attract his attention, he hasn't completely fallen for it. Tonight I will have plenty of opportunity to study her behavior because the second unit is working with the main unit on a massive stunt sequence.

Welcome to Wild Kingdom, Hollywood North Edition. *Today our esteemed anthropologist, Roxanne Hastings, will be sharing her insights into the cross-species mating rituals observed on an average Canadian film set.*

CLOSE-UP on a photograph of Roxanne Hastings in a safari jacket and a pith helmet, handheld camera on her shoulder. Recorder music swells as we cut to video footage. The voiceover continues…

Professor Hastings will be observing in particular the mating rituals of the Lesser Striped Makeup Artist. Indigenous to many North American film trailers, the Lesser Striped is a cousin of the cougar and has remarkably little need of sustenance.

Genevieve makes her entrance wearing skintight jeans and four-inch heels, her jacket hanging open to reveal a striped tank top. She positions herself favorably in relation to Damon.

The camera follows the female Lesser Striped as she strolls onto the film set. It is a very cold night indeed, but the creature is hardier than she looks. Her obliviousness to the conditions can be explained very simply: she is in estrous. In this condition, the Lesser Striped is prepared to endure much discomfort to attract a mate.

The Lesser Striped identifies her target across the set, specifically the Curmudgeonly Cinematographer, known on film sets worldwide for its difficult temperament.

CLOSE-UP on the dark eyes of the Lesser Striped as she initiates The Gaze, Phase 1 in a series of flirtatious ploys. The Lesser Striped stares intently at the object of her desire, pupils dilating.

Observe how the Lesser Striped angles her chin down and glances away briefly before looking back at her target. This maneuver is repeated several times before the female proceeds to Phase 2, which features more serious courtship displays, including smiling, strutting, hair tossing, preening—anything to signal, "I'm here and I'm in heat."

The Curmudgeonly Cinematographer initially appears to be insensible to the female's charms. The Lesser Striped steps up her efforts, lacing her fingers behind her back and bending into an elaborate stretch, her meager chest thrust forward. She bats her painted eyelids and traces a lazy pattern on her own paw, er, forearm, with one digit. (The last is often more effective without the parka.)

Pulling a strand of highlighted hair across her face, the Lesser Striped pouts briefly at the Curmudgeonly Cinematographer before blatantly licking her unnaturally rosy lips.

At this point in the ritual, an interested male generally approaches in some haste, sensing imminent coitus. Today, however, Professor Hastings observes that the Curmudgeonly Cinematographer is regarding the female with apparent indifference. In fact, he turns away and busies himself with mundane tasks—a move that may be perceived by the female as a rejection.

Watching the male through narrowed eyes, the female Lesser Striped retreats to the shelter of the craft truck to regroup. Some moments later, she emerges carrying steaming fluid in two foam vessels. The female is ready to launch another strike—with props. Displays of domesticity and feeding are quite common during courtship rituals.

"Hey, Sharp Shooter," Genevieve calls across the set. "I made you a cappuccino—extra sweet, just the way you like it."

Each female has its own distinctive call and a particular gait. Both are exaggerated during estrous. The voice, for example, may take on a yodeling quality. The gait, in turn, may develop a peculiar sway, as if the earth were shifting underfoot.

Genevieve struts toward Damon. If she had hips, they'd be swinging.

"Hey, Puss 'n' Boots," Gizmo calls after her. "I see non-regulation footwear. Put something sensible on before I find myself filling out a Workers' Compensation form."

Immune to feedback from any male other than her target, the female Lesser Striped continues on her mission to hydrate the Curmudgeonly Cinematographer. He looks up from his work to see the preening female and accepts the drink, thereby granting tacit permission for her to advance to Phase 3: physical contact. Social grooming is an essential part of communicating willingness to copulate.

Genevieve touches Damon's hand briefly as he takes the cappuccino. While he drinks, she zips his jacket up higher and adjusts his scarf.

The mimicking of physical postures is one of the more intriguing components of the mating ritual. The female Lesser Striped, thus encouraged by the Curmudgeonly Cinematographer, pivots until her shoulders are aligned with his.

Damon sips his cappuccino; Genevieve sips hers. Damon adjusts his hat; Genevieve adjusts hers.

The female moves in perfect synchronicity with the male, trying to maintain eye contact all the while. The male, however, appears distracted—a common ploy with the Curmudgeonly Cinematographer, who tends to be overcautious.

Fidgeting with his cup, Damon fixates on a point above Genevieve's shoulder and offers monosyllabic responses to her babbling. Sensing his distraction, she reaches out and takes his hand.

If the female Lesser Striped misconstrues the signs and crowds the Curmudgeonly Cinematographer, she risks a more pronounced rejection.

Damon interrupts Genevieve midsentence to thank her again for the cappuccino and walks away.

As Professor Hastings correctly concludes, beauty and technique are not necessarily sufficient to satisfy the needs of a female in estrous. This Lesser Striped would do well to select a less challenging target than the Curmudgeonly Cinematographer, whose argumentative nature makes him resistant to feminine wiles and often to reason itself.

Join us next time for Wild Kingdom: Hollywood North, *when Professor Hastings introduces us to the mating habits of the Garrulous Grip, a species that routinely solicits the attention of female extras, usually to disastrous effect.*

★ ★ ★

Damon's ears might be closed, but his eyes are still open. Therefore, I've made an effort with my appearance. The effect will be lost quickly on a winter exterior, due to high winds, precipitation and foul weather gear. I blew out my static-challenged hair today in full knowledge that a toque will flatten it shortly. To ensure that Damon at least sees it first, I risk frostbitten ears to parade around in his sight line. I've concealed my December pallor with layers of foundation, bronzer and blush. And, recognizing that I resemble a charred marshmallow in my black, puffy down coat, I've elected to wear instead a streamlined and flattering powder-blue ski jacket that says "chalet" more than "slope." What it lacks in functionality, however, it makes up in style.

In short, I'm no better than Genevieve.

We're shooting on an unused stretch of road by the docklands. The wind off the lake has sent the temperature spiraling into the single digits. It's going to be a long night. Fortunately, I need only look fetching for the two hours the second unit overlaps with the main unit. Damon and his crew are lighting the underpass and grabbing a couple of establishing shots with Zara and Burk, after which they'll head back to the studio, leaving us to film with stuntmen. Later, I will pile on expedition-weight clothing and try to salvage what's left of my core body heat.

Normally, I would find a stunt sequence like this one extremely arduous. Night exteriors require huge lighting setups and competent cinematographers. Today, however, I have it pretty good because Damon has taken care of the lighting himself, thereby relieving me of the pressure to babysit Alana. He issued his instructions to Alana alone, either to avoid me or to hold her more accountable. Either way, the result is less stress for me.

While setting up the camera for a close-up of Zara, I feel a tugging at my pant cuff: Chiquita. Pleased that he remembers me, I bend down to scratch his ears.

"Don't touch that thing," Alana says.

I scoop Chiquita into my arms. "Why not?"

"It's a sewer rat," she declares.

"It's a chihuahua."

"I heard about this lady who bought one in Mexico. When she got home, a veterinarian confirmed that it was an oversized rat. You can't be too careful, Roxanne."

I roll my eyes. "That's an urban myth, Alana."

"Well, don't come crying to me when you get rabies." She tosses up some finger quotes to highlight the danger.

Zara appears beside her. "My purebred dog does not have rabies," she says, raising her talons in retaliatory punctuation.

Alana blanches. "Er, excuse me, Ms. Duncan."

While Alana backpedals, I stare at Zara. Although it's only been two weeks since I last saw her, she seems to have aged ten years. Then I realize that her face hasn't yet been taped for the scene.

Zara turns away from Alana. "You're looking well, Roxanne," she says.

"Thank you," I say, taking a second to enjoy Alana's shock that our headliner knows my name. I set the dog on the ground. He makes a beeline for Genevieve's makeup bag, which is sitting on the floor near Zara's director's chair.

Alana steps directly in front of me and extends her hand to Zara. "It's wonderful to finally meet you," she trills. "I've been so disappointed not to have you on my set."

Zara ignores Alana's outstretched hand. "And you are…?"

"Alana Speir, second-unit cinematographer."

Zara continues to stare at her impassively.

"Martin Speir's daughter," Alana adds, weakly.

Before Zara can decide whether to respond, Burk arrives in full alien costume and commands our attention. "Zara," he mumbles through the mask, "who is your lovely friend?"

Alana turns the full wattage of her smile on Burk and says, "I'm Alana Speir, second-unit cinematographer."

"Not you," he says, gesturing with a slimy tentacle. "Her."

Alana's jaw drops as she realizes that he's pointing at me. It's almost worth the affront of Burk's not recognizing me again.

"You look familiar," he tells me, smearing his spray-on hair as he removes his rubber head. "I remember. You're the one who wanted my autograph when I dropped Genevieve off at the Distillery."

"Actually, I was the director of the short film Genevieve starred in."

"You mean the cinematographer," Alana corrects me.

"At that point, I was still director."

Zara says, "I didn't realize that you were a filmmaker, Roxanne."

"I did a short film on the hiatus, that's all. I ended up asking Damon to direct. He did a great job, too."

"Well, I admire your ambition," she says. "Why don't you send me a copy when it's done?"

"I will, thanks."

Chiquita lifts his leg on Genevieve's makeup bag. Unfortunately, Genevieve notices this and teeters toward him on her heels. One foot catches on an electrical cable and she plows face-first into the director's chairs. Damon steps in to steady her and Genevieve collapses theatrically into his arms.

Burk sees me watching and says, "Relax, babe, I'm not with Genevieve anymore."

"Oh, for Christ's sake, Burk," Zara snaps, "this is Roxanne, she used to be our focus puller."

"The one who got canned?" he asks.

"I did not get canned! I moved to second unit."

Burk raises a tentacle to his chin for a puzzled scratch. "Did you lose weight on the hiatus or something?"

Alana scoffs, "Not the way she packs it away."

Burk ignores her. "BOTOX?"

"Definitely not," I say. Although his backhanded compliments aren't doing much for me, I prolong the exchange to irritate Alana.

Meanwhile, my avenger Chiquita sprinkles Alana's weather bag.

"Well, whatever you've done, it's working," Burk says. "You look hot."

"Why, thank you," I say, summoning a giggle for Alana's benefit. "The hiatus agreed with you, too. I've never seen an alien with a better tan."

Damon disengages himself from Genevieve and says, "No point flirting, Roxanne, Burk isn't a director." He smiles, but he isn't kidding.

"Maybe not," Burk says, "but I could take you places, baby."

Turning to walk away, Damon says, "Bon voyage."

The main unit has left us to shoot the stunt sequence, in which the Creature commandeers a pickup truck and flees several police cruisers. During the chase, two cruisers flip, one explodes and a driver escapes, on fire.

Over the years, I've learned to dread stunts in general and car stunts in particular. Despite careful choreography, car stunts are unpredictable. When the adrenaline's pumping, a little extra gas or pressure on the wheel can send four thousand pounds of airborne glass and metal careening into film equipment—or crew members. Needless to say, it isn't easy on the stunt people, either. I've attended the funeral of one and visited several others in the hospital. The pay may be good, but this job is about the thrill.

Given the safety and cost implications, productions want to shoot a stunt like this once and once only. That's why it takes us more than three hours to set up, even with two extra camera crews to help. I check, double check and triple check the cameras, especially if Alana has touched them. When she trots off to fetch a sweater, I adjust her frame, knowing that we'd miss the flipping cars if they landed even a foot from their marks.

Since Damon took care of the lighting and Hank assigned the camera positions, Alana has nothing to do except plug the eyepiece when we roll. Nevertheless, she's been marching around issuing orders at top decibel for the simple reason that *Entertainment Now* has a video crew on set.

"Let's make sure everyone has eye and ear protection," she yells as the props department distributes this equipment to the crew. "We don't want anyone getting hurt."

"Get a wide lens on that camera," she tells a daily focus puller, who took care of that an hour ago.

"Have the paramedics and firefighters standing by," she hollers, interrupting the assistant director's review of emergency procedures with these very people.

Eventually she is distracted by a real emergency.

"Roxanne," she shrieks, brandishing a handful of chewed black wool. "Look what that sewer rat did. This is a $500 cashmere sweater."

"*Was,*" I say.

"I can't believe you left my wardrobe bag on the ground."

"I am not your valet, Alana." She opens her mouth to continue but I cut her off: "If you're really upset, take it up with Zara. Mention that he peed on it, too."

★ ★ ★

Alana has assigned herself the critical role of cuing the action on the stunt. The cue has to be visual because a walkie talkie could prematurely ignite the rigged pyrotechnics. Therefore, Alana will wave a red baseball cap in the air.

Five cameras are ready to roll at her signal, three with operators and focus pullers and two in crash boxes, unmanned because they are too close to the site of impact. Gilda is on the ground about twenty feet from the impact point, which makes us the closest manned camera. Alana and I will work beneath a Plexiglas shield and fire-retardant blankets with a grip standing by to haul us out of harm's way if anything goes wrong.

A few minutes before we're ready to roll, I give final instructions to the camera assistants, keeping a constant eye on Alana at the same time. I notice that a young trainee assistant director has approached her for a rundown of the shot. Eager as always to show off, Alana describes the shot with elaborate gestures. When she looks down at the red baseball cap on the ground, I have a sudden premonition.

I bellow, "ALANA, DON'T!" She doesn't hear me and sweeps the red hat off the ground with one hand to demonstrate the cue for the trainee—a cue that the stunt drivers in their idling cars will consider genuine. I sprint toward her, calling to Christian over my shoulder, "Turn on as many cameras as you can."

When the cap soars above her shoulder, the cars rev their engines. Alana looks around stunned as the cars race toward the air ramps.

"Wait a second," she says. "I didn't—"

"You did," I say. Shoving the trainee out of the way, I pull the blanket over Alana and me and switch on the camera just as the cars hit the ramp.

The first car goes airborne, lands on its roof and scrapes along the pavement. The second car hits a moment later and bursts into flames. One door flies open and the driver emerges, clothing ablaze. He runs several paces from the car—beyond what Alana's original frame would have captured—and falls to the ground. The paramedics rush in with fire retardant blankets and it's all over. There's a moment of silence while we wait to see if the stuntmen are okay. The paramedics give the thumbs-up.

Then the screaming begins.

Damon's unit is in the lunchroom by the time our unit arrives at Lakeside Studios. While waiting in the cafeteria line, I examine the black-and-white photos mounted on the walls. The first is a fifteen-year-old shot of Gizmo, still sporting a full head of hair. The next shows Alana during her trainee days, smiling in the foreground as my fuzzy form behind her buckles under the weight of two camera cases. The next picture features Alana standing beside her father and Russell Crowe at the film festival. There she is again at the Film Institute, belly ring on display as she cuts the ribbon on the Martin Speir screening theater. And finally, one more smile as she perches on a dolly, pretending to pull focus on *The Mauling.*

Martin must have shares in Lakeside Studios.

"Hey, Rox," says Christian, a few feet ahead. "Here's a picture of you."

Actually, it's a picture of Damon and Hank on the *Seattle* set, but I can be seen in the background cramming a slice of pizza into my gaping maw. Appetite waning, I head for the salad bar to make a modest selection before taking the only seat available, which happens to be beside Damon. If I could eat salad standing up, I would.

"I heard what happened with the stunt," Damon says. "Four of the cameras rolled in time, so the producers think there's enough footage."

Although I am happy to hear this, I ignore him and focus on my salad.

"Roxanne," he says, "I'm speaking to you."

"Since when?"

"This is business, Roxanne."

"Ah yes, it's Professional Damon, once again allowing Hank to be misled. He's over there now congratulating Alana for a stunt she fucked up."

His brow furrows. "What do you mean? It wasn't her fault that the drivers took their cue too early. In fact, it was her quick thinking that got the cameras rolling."

I pause with my fork in the air. "Is that the story she's telling?"

Hank's hand on my shoulder saves him from answering. "Good work out there, darling," Hank says. "Thanks to your hustle, we got most of the stunt and won't need a costly reshoot."

I drop my fork in shock. "Alana told you that I—?"

"—reacted quickly to her instructions? Yes, of course she shared the credit with her team. I certainly made the right choice in putting that little spitfire in charge. Which reminds me, I have something to tell you two."

In the matter-of-fact tone he might use to request a lens change, Hank says that he's decided to let Miguel direct the film in Morocco. Alana will be the cinematographer.

I wander shell-shocked through the empty studio. Hank has blown me off, just as everyone predicted. Although I'm no longer interested in directing *The Lobby,* I still wanted to shoot the Morocco film. Further, I wanted Fledgling to buy *The Lobby* and let me be the cinematographer for that, too. *The Counterfeit Wedding* was supposed to prove I'm up to the job.

I follow the sound of raised voices to a deserted set. When I'm closer, I realize they belong to Damon and Hank. I should give them their privacy and get back to the camera truck, but my feet stop moving of their own accord.

"You've made a mistake in hiring Alana, Hank," Damon says. "I just heard from the camera team that it's Roxanne who saved the stunt today after Alana prematurely signaled the action."

"That's ridiculous," Hank says. "Alana would have told me so herself."

"You're kidding, right?" Damon asks, incredulously.

"I don't believe it," Hank says.

"The *Entertainment Now* video footage will likely prove it and you'll see who the real cinematographer is on that crew. Roxanne has been carrying Alana all along."

"If that's the case, why are you only telling me now?"

There's a silence as Damon ponders how to answer a very good question. Finally he says, "I should have. You kept canceling my meetings, but I should have cornered you. It didn't seem that urgent because Rox was shadowing her every step of the way. I guess Alana got ahead of her today. It's my fault."

"If there's any truth to this, it is your fault for not managing your team better. But I think you're just trying to talk up your girlfriend, as she did you a few weeks ago."

"Roxanne and I are just colleagues, nothing more. As her boss, I owe it to her to explain what's been going on. This hasn't been easy on her. When you gave the second-unit cinematography job to Alana, Rox didn't quit—as I would have in her shoes, incidentally. She stuck it out for the good of your picture, like a pro."

"She stuck it out for you, Prince Charming. Look, we both know that what you're really angry about is my choosing Miguel for Morocco."

Before Damon can share his thoughts on that subject, I hear Christian calling my name in the distance. I check my watch and see that I'm nearly fifteen minutes late returning from lunch.

On the camera truck at day's end, we tell and retell the stunt story, safe in the knowledge that Alana is celebrating the Morocco assignment over dinner with Hank. Each of us takes a turn playing Alana as she notices the red baseball cap on the ground and decides to signal the action. With each telling, the gesture becomes more flamboyant, until Christian—as Alana—does a triple axel and knocks over a stack of empty film cans.

"Do it again," I chortle, practically prostrate with hilarity and beer.

Eventually a driver arrives to collect the day's film for the lab. I go over to the loader's bench. "Hey, where's the rest of the film?" I ask. "We're a few rolls short here."

"That's all of it," the film loader assures me. "I sent this morning's work into the lab right after lunch."

"Why?" I ask, alarm bells starting to clang.

"Alana told me to," he says. "She wanted to see how the pushing will look."

I turn to Christian in horror. Alana learned about pushing from me last month. It's a great technique for producing a grainy image, but it requires adjusting the exposure at the time of shooting. Otherwise, the image will become overexposed and bleached out when the negative is left in the developing solution longer than usual. We did not adjust the exposure on any one of the four cameras that

rolled during today's stunt. And when I left Alana unat-
tended after lunch, she obviously took it into her head to
atone for her screwup by doing something creative.

I fumble for my cell phone, hoping against hope that our
film has not been processed yet, but the lab confirms that it
has just gone through the developer.

The entire morning's work is ruined.

Chapter 25

Crusher is wrestling with a tangled string of Christmas lights when I emerge from my apartment.

"Jesus, Rox, you look like shit. Up all night watching infomercials?"

"When the Fishin' Magician arrives, can you sign for it?"

"You don't fish."

"No, but the guy on TV said it's the ideal Christmas gift for a landlord."

"That's what I get for sending you upstairs drunk, I guess."

"Consider it a thank-you for finally forking out for a brand-new fridge."

"The ideal gift for a tenant, I hear. So, did you get any sleep?"

I groan. "I dreamt that I flashed exposed film and ruined an entire day's work."

Crusher throws the twinkle light spaghetti into a shopping bag and selects another equally tangled string. "Alana ruined that film, not you."

"It might as well have been me. If I'd been back from lunch on time, it wouldn't have happened."

"Where were you, by the way?"

I start to untangle one end of the light string as an excuse not to look at him. "Wandering around the studio looking at old sets."

He gives me an evil grin. "Mooning over Damon, am I right?"

"More like reeling over Hank's decision about Morocco. He's asked Alana to shoot his movie."

Crusher gives a low whistle. "Well, that didn't come out in the Budweiser last night."

"I wasn't quite ready to hear 'I told you so.'"

"You said Damon told him about Alana."

"Not until after Hank made his decision. Naturally, Hank didn't believe him."

"He'll have to when he sees the ruined stunt footage."

"I'm sure she'll charm her way out of it somehow."

"Well, anyhow, it's not your fault."

It is though, at least partly, because Super Focus Puller was asleep at the switch. "I left Alana unsupervised on the camera truck."

Crusher sticks a plastic poinsettia behind my ear. "You can't be everywhere at once, Rox. Only big-screen aliens can do that."

I manage a smile. Crusher relishes my stories about F. C. Kugelman's constant script revisions.

I just wish I could pay someone to rewrite *my* story line right now so that everything in my life would play out as it should. The evil blonde would be uncovered as a fraud before being flattened under the wheels of a camera truck. The slimy director would apologize to the hapless heroine on bended knee and beg her to shoot his movie in Morocco. The flirtatious makeup artist would be force-fed ice cream until she gained twenty pounds and split the seams of her jeans. And finally, the Curmudgeonly Cinematographer would come to his senses and choose the right girl.

We'd all live happily ever after.

Except Alana.

One thing that kept me tossing and turning last night is the fact that I didn't speak to Damon about what happened. Instead I called Alana directly and told her she'd ruined the stunt footage—the footage we very nearly lost because of her screwup in the first place. I advised her to come clean with Hank before he discovered the truth for himself. Then, to cover my own butt, I added that there were witnesses who'd enlighten Hank if she wasn't up to confessing.

"Oh, sweetie, you worry too much," she said, already half in the bag during dinner with Hank. "It's going to be perfect, you'll see. Go home and relax. I'd chat longer, but Hank's eating more than his share of our foie gras." I hear the awful sound of a grown man giggling.

Afterward, I dialed Damon's number—and hung up before he answered. What good would telling him do when the film was already ruined? There will be time enough to tell him if he shows up at the lab today.

His BMW is already in the parking lot when I arrive and he's leaning against it with his arms crossed. I can't tell from his expression whether he's come to help me with the edit or to fire me because Alana has already managed to pin her latest SNAFU on me.

Before he can speak, I say, "There's something I have to tell you."

"No need. I already talked to Miguel."

Miguel? What does Miguel have to do with it? Did Alana somehow drag him into this sorry affair?

"What do you mean?" I ask.

"He was on set last night for a meeting with Hank and he came over to explain."

I am so not getting this. "Explain about what?"

"For starters, he said you didn't know anything about his negotiations with Hank about Morocco. I thought you'd kept that from me, too."

With all my other worries, that one never occurred to me. For once, a bullet inadvertently dodged.

Damon continues, "He also wanted me to know that it's been over between you two for a while."

Somewhere beneath my bewilderment, anger stirs. Damon and Miguel shouldn't have been discussing me so casually. Since I can only manage one crisis at a time, however, I stick to the matter at hand. "The stunt footage is ruined."

It's Damon's turn to look confused. "How do you know that?"

"Alana pushed the film two stops but she didn't compensate. I was late getting back from lunch and she sent it to the lab on her own. By the time I found out, it had been processed."

Damon digests this for several moments. Finally he sighs,

a white wisp of breath escaping from his lips to swirl in the cold air between us. "Okay," he says, "let's get inside. We've got a movie to cut."

"That's it?"

"There's nothing we can do about it now, Rox."

"Aren't you going to call Hank?"

"The editor will give him the news soon enough."

I take his wrist to feel for a pulse. "What have you done with the real Damon? He'd never be so calm in this situation. It'll cost a hundred grand to reshoot that stunt."

"Probably more. But it's time Hank learned the truth about Alana and it won't have the same impact coming from me."

I follow Damon across the parking lot, still shaking my head. He stops at the door and says, "I shouldn't have made you cover for Alana. It wasn't fair. And I should have spoken to Hank about her weeks ago. I haven't been thinking clearly lately and this whole mess is my fault."

"I should have watched her. I knew better."

He waves my protest away. "Your only mistake was in covering for her in the first place. If you hadn't, she'd have shown her stripes before something so major went wrong."

But if I hadn't covered for her, I wouldn't be the "professional" he respects. My story line really is in bad shape. The hapless heroine gets bitten in the ass even when her intentions are noble.

Our cars are covered in several inches of snow when we leave the lab later. While I warm up the Jeep, Damon takes the brush from my back seat and clears the snow off my windows and headlights. He takes so long about it that I eventually roll down the window to complain about the service. "Want a toothbrush? It'd be faster."

He makes a snowball and tosses it so that it misses my face by inches. "Ingrate," he says. "And after I held your hand all day in the editing suite."

"Did not. I'd have noticed that for sure."

He comes over the window and grabs my hand, mitten and all. "I'll do it for the rest of the night if you like."

"I could let you have it for a while, I suppose."

We smile at each other long enough to melt the snow on the side mirror.

"Hungry?" he asks at last.

"Always." I confirm.

"I make a wicked mushroom risotto."

"I don't know," I say, doubtfully. "It sounds like you'd need two hands for that."

"Good point," he says. "But I'll need both of them later anyway."

Damon pours me a glass of wine and assigns me the task of slicing mushrooms.

"You didn't say anything about my having to be your sous-chef," I say.

Damon examines the bowl of mushrooms. "I said thinly sliced—those are chopped."

I set the knife down with the pout I learned from Genevieve. "You're not the boss of me tonight."

"So you're good with a camera, lousy with a knife—it's nothing to be ashamed about." He pulls me off the bar stool and leads me to a small sofa. He sits down beside me and adds, "You should take a time-out and let your wrist recover."

"I think I just got fired from a job I never asked for," I say. "As if I haven't endured enough ego-battering lately."

"We'll have to do something about that," he says.

"Some compliments wouldn't go amiss about now."

He leans in to kiss me but jerks away before he makes contact. "Garlic."

I cover my mouth in horror. "That's impossible. I had fruit salad for lunch. I'm suing that catering company."

He jumps and rushes back to the stove. "My garlic is burning."

I call after him, "So you're good with a camera, lousy with a stove—it's nothing to be ashamed about."

"For that, you forfeit one compliment."

"Please. I wouldn't know one if I heard it coming from you anyway."

He sits down again and pulls me onto his lap. "What do you mean, I call you a pro all the time."

"That one definitely won't work in this context," I say. "Better stick with the standards."

"Did I ever mention that you have the most beautiful eyes?"

"Now you're cooking."

I'm luxuriating in a profusion of bubbles. Our shadows flicker on the bathroom wall in the light of several candles. Damon is scrubbing my back.

"Are you this nice to all your 'colleagues'?" I lift my hands out of the soapy water and curl my fingers into foamy quotation marks.

"What do you mean?" he asks.

"You told Hank yesterday that we're 'just colleagues.' If

that's true, it stands to reason that you might be equally nice to Hank."

Damon stops scrubbing. "Were you eavesdropping on my private conversation?"

"Sure. It's the only way I ever learn anything."

"It's unethical."

"You've done it yourself."

"That's true. Well, we have been 'just colleagues,' although it's been tough to keep it that way lately. I didn't care to discuss it with Hank at that point."

"Better to break it to him during a nice, hot bath."

Shuddering at the thought, Damon gathers a handful of foam. "Don't make me wash your mouth out, Roxanne."

"Did I ever mention that you have the most beautiful eyes?"

He wraps his arms around me from behind. "Actually no. Tell me more."

"So you're not mad about the eavesdropping?"

"You're naked in my bathtub—nothing you say would make me angry right now."

Damon reaches for the pizza box at the foot of the bed. "Another slice?"

"Sure." I wrap the sheet under my arms and lean back against the headboard. "Good decision to hold off on the risotto."

"My ability to make good decisions has gotten me where I am today."

"Which is?"

"Not Morocco, obviously." His phone on the nightstand rings and he reaches over to check call display. "Speak of the devil." Hitting the talk button, he says, "Hi, Hank, how are you?" He listens for a moment. "The stunt footage is ruined?" He manages to sound surprised. "What happened?"

Holding a finger to his lips, Damon presses Speaker.

"It's overexposed and unusable," Hank says. "Apparently the film arrived at the lab with instructions to push two stops. Why the hell was that?"

"I have no idea," Damon says, calmly. "That's a question for Alana. I lit the set myself and told her to process the film as usual."

"Then how did it happen?"

"Like I told you, she's in over her head. Maybe she was trying to do something interesting after fucking up the stunt."

"Christ." There's a long pause, during which Hank sucks loudly on what I hope is a cigar. "This is going to cost at least 120 grand and insurance won't cover us because it's technically our error."

"I know."

"Tell me this, are you a hundred percent sure it's Alana's fault? If you're not, speak now, because firing her could screw me with Martin forever."

"One hundred percent."

"Then I want a replacement on set by Monday."

"Roxanne can do the job."

I clutch Damon's arm and shake my head no.

Hank says, "We need someone with experience. I can't afford any more fuckups."

"Rox has been doing it all along anyway. Alana just gave her the slip yesterday."

"Okay, Roxanne it is. But it's your ass on the line. I won't have another black mark beside my name."

I'm still shaking my head. Although I believe I'm up to the job, the reshoot will be extremely high pressure.

"I'll take full responsibility," Damon says.

"You bet you will," Hank says. "One more thing, Damon."

"Yes?"

"No kissing on my set—on tailgates or anyplace else."

To give Hank the most bang for his buck during the reshoot, I've requested two additional cameras and set them to capture the action in slow motion. That brings us to a total of seven camera angles. With cameras pointing in all directions, I'm grateful I had the opportunity to watch Damon light the set last week. Keeping lights and cameras out of each shot is a real challenge.

```
Veering to avoid an oncoming motor-
cycle, the police car swerves into
a parked car and launches into the
air. The car flips over and lands on
its roof. A second police car takes
air and bursts into flames upon im-
pact. The driver runs out of the car,
his clothing ablaze.
```

Kugelman's new assistant looks up from his computer screen. "How many cameras would a stunt like that take?"

"I don't know. Five, maybe six," F.C. replies.

"It must take hours to set that up."

"That set had better be lit when I get there, Roxanne," Hank barks into the phone.

"Ready and waiting for your blessing."

"Don't hold your breath, darling."

Kugelman leans over the assistant's shoulder and hits the delete key.

"What are you doing?" the assistant asks, alarmed. "I've got to fax these pages to production in an hour."

"I was never happy with the first part of this sequence," F.C. explains. "The re-shoot gives me an opportunity to write something more visually dynamic."

```
Veering to avoid an oncoming motor-
cycle, the police car swerves into
a parked car and launches into the
air. From an angle on the ground, we
watch the car flip above us. CUT AWAY
TO: a wide shot of the second col-
lision. CUT BACK TO: a low angle
where the roof of the car gradually
fills the screen like an ominous
shadow.
```

"Isn't that going to be tricky to shoot?" asks the assistant. "How can you land an airborne car on top of a camera?"

F.C. shrugs. "I win awards for my action scenes, kid. Filming them isn't my problem."

Christian waves the pages in front of Roxanne. "Did you see these script revisions? How the hell are we supposed to get that low angle without destroying a camera? The guy that writes this shit doesn't have a clue about how a movie is actually made."

"Funny, I've often thought the same thing. But he's not bringing me down today, Christian. I know how to get that shot."

The locations department has already obtained permission from the City to cut away a one-by-four-foot section of pavement. The grips will then dig a hole big enough to set a crash box inside to hold a camera.

"Our crash boxes are wider than a foot," Christian points out.

"That's why I ordered a small one. And before you say it, I ordered a smaller camera body, too."

"You're a genius," Christian says.

Rox flatters herself that she is.

```
CUT AWAY TO: a wide shot of the sec-
ond collision. CUT BACK TO: a low
angle where the roof of the car grad-
ually fills the screen like an omi-
nous shadow. Just before impact, the
image slows right down. Two seconds
stretch into ten as we watch the car
descend in slow motion.
```

Christian says, "We're in trouble, Rox. We need a ramping unit."

"Not to worry, I ordered one just in case. It's on the truck."

Christian returns with the ramping unit. "The rental house forgot to send a transmitter and no one can man this camera. How will we start the ramp?"

"With this." Roxanne produces a fifty-foot piece of cable from the bottom of the case. "We can't use a transmitter with live pyrotechnics away. If we run the remote cable from the camera, someone can activate the slow motion from a safe distance."

```
ALIEN POV: Returning to the scene of
the automotive carnage, the Creature
winds   through   the   crushed   cars,
eventually moving up and over them
until  we  are  looking  down  on  the
wreckage from above.
```

Kugelman's assistant asks, "How would they get a shot like that?"

F.C. shoots him an impatient look.

"I'm just trying to learn, sir," the kid says.

Kugelman relents. "There's a crane with an arm that extends up to fifty feet. The camera attaches to the end of the arm so that it can move along between the cars at ground level and then rise into the air."

"But that only works if the Alien takes a straight path. You've got him 'winding through the carnage,'" the assistant says.

"So they'll do it in two shots and sew them together in postproduction."

"Isn't that expensive?"

Kugelman glares at his eager helper. "And...?"

"And that wouldn't be your problem, sir," the kid squeaks.

"Now you're getting it."

Gizmo rigs a large circular platform in the place where the camera is normally mounted. Mimicking the Creature's POV, the Steadicam operator winds his way through the wreckage before stepping onto the crane platform. Gizmo clips his harness to a safety post and the crane immediately rises. The operator tilts the camera down to look at the wreckage from above.

Christian raises his beer to mine: "To Roxanne Hastings, winner of the Innovative Lens Award for resourcefulness on the field of duty. It's high time you traded your focus knob for a light meter."

"Hear! Hear!" Gizmo clinks bottles with the other crew members who have crowded into the camera truck to congratulate me. "That crane shot was fucking brilliant."

High praise indeed, coming from Gizmo.

Keisha says, "I can't wait for the book, *Outfoxing the Hollywood Scriptwriter.*"

I raise my beer bottle high. "And now a toast to F. C. Kugelman, to whom I say, bring it on."

What a night. The endless, last-minute revisions kept me on my toes, but I don't think I've ever had a better time on a film set—and that includes *The Counterfeit Wedding.* I loved using my ingenuity to resolve problems as they arose and I sure didn't miss crawling around in the muck with the equipment. By the end, I was actually having fun. I must be on to something here.

My cell phone vibrates. When I see Damon's number, I step outside to answer it.

He says, "You're going to make me look bad if you keep wrapping before the main unit."

"Is it my fault if you can't keep up?"

"I heard from the producers that you guys rocked today. Apparently you saved Hank some major cash on postproduction with that crane shot. Great idea."

"I had no choice but to do well—your ass was on the line. I have a special interest in that ass now."

"Hold that thought," Damon says. "Incoming director."

There's shuffling and then Hank says, "Way to go, darling. I was impressed with the way you ran that set tonight. If the dailies are good, I might even let you keep your new job."

"Thanks, Hank. I appreciate the opportunity—"

"You can stop sucking up," Damon says. "He's gone."

"To run a bath, no doubt."

"There was a day that you respected me," he says.

"Not really. I'm just more honest about how I feel now."

"A mixed blessing, evidently. Want me to come over when I'm wrapped?"

"Sure, but I'll need my beauty sleep. Moving up in the ranks means I need to be fresh in the morning."

"Don't worry, I'll see that you're in bed early."

Chapter 26

"Are you ready yet?" It's Crusher calling for the fourth time.

"I'll never be ready if you keep calling to ask if I'm ready." The phone is wedged between my ear and shoulder as I hop around on one foot, trying to jam the other into panty hose.

"Wait, don't tell me—you're trying on fifty outfits and doing the whole mirror-mirror thing."

"I chose my outfit days ago." And thank God I did, because the panty hose are trouble enough. I'm already on the second pair. "When did dressing like a girl become so damned hard?"

"If I knew the answer to that, I'd have to kill myself. Look, the cab will be here in three minutes. Don't make me come up there and dress you."

"The new fridge was enough, really." I carefully work the hose up over the knee and immediately rip them. Another twenty bucks down the drain. "Shit, shit, shit."

"What now?" Crusher sounds alarmed. "Can I call someone? Libby?"

"Better the Queer Eye guys." I pull off the hose and reach for my last pair. "You've got to relax, pal. You'd think this was your first screening."

"It is my first screening—and my first credit, too. I don't want to miss it. The film is only twenty minutes long you know."

"Crusher, it's my movie. They are not going to roll until I get there. Now, go wait for the cab and chill. I'll be down in a few minutes."

I sit on the edge of the bed and ease on the hose ever so gently until I run out of leg at midthigh. The crotch is eight inches below where it needs to be and the waistband only covers half my butt, but it will have to do. Slipping into my skirt, I hobble toward the closet to find my boots. During those eight steps, the crotch of the pantyhose slides down until it appears under the hem of the skirt. I can't go like this: Damon will dump me.

The phone rings again and I ignore it, knowing that Crusher will be as close to hysteria as a biker gets. Tearing off the stockings, I pull on the boots, grab a bottle of nail polish off the dresser and rush down stairs.

"Are you nuts?" Crusher says, noticing the four-inch expanse of bare leg. "It's below freezing. Don't you own pants?"

"Trust me, switching to pants would have taken even longer."

Hose issues aside, I've chosen the perfect outfit. It's dressy, but not overdone; hip, yet elegant; sexy, not slutty. Throwing dress pants into the mix now would be disastrous. The only pants that fit me at the moment are brown, which would mean changing my top, shoes and purse.

Not that there's any use explaining this to someone who wears the same maroon leather pants to every event, paired with one of three black shirts.

I give the taxi driver the address of the film lab and settle into my seat. "Could you take Dundas, please?"

"Queen Street is more direct," Crusher argues.

"I need a smooth ride." I hold up the bottle of nail polish. "There are no streetcar tracks on Dundas."

Crusher lapses into a disgusted silence, which is just as well, because I want to be alone with my nerves. I am not worried about the quality of *The Counterfeit Wedding:* Damon has edited it largely on his own and I have full confidence in his judgment. But it's still my baby and I want everyone to love it. Somewhere in a cab nearby, Libby is thinking exactly the same thing.

I am also worried that Hank will accept his invitation. He's become quite a fan of my work lately. After he saw the stunt footage, our modest second unit morphed into a full-fledged main unit overnight. He doubled our shooting schedule so that *Illegal Alien* can wrap on time. We've been doing entire scenes on our own, often with principal actors. For me, this has meant production meetings and location surveys on top of fourteen-hour shooting days.

It's been grueling, yet exhilarating. Thanks to Alana's incompetence, I seem to have found my calling. Second guessing her every move has prepared me for cinematography in a way that working with Damon never could. In a perverse way, I owe her one.

My only regret is that I've been so busy that I've missed out on the experience of editing *The Counterfeit Wedding.*

Tonight I'll be seeing the finished product for the first time alongside friends, family, colleagues, cast and crew.

Hopefully all eyes will be on the screen and no one will notice the nail polish on my knuckles.

I turn to Crusher. "Did you bring nail polish remover?"

He rolls down the window to release the fumes and says, "Check my purse."

I sneak out of the theater before the credits roll so that I can catch candid reactions to the film as people exit.

Crusher is the first one out and his expression is deliberately blank.

"Well, what do you think?" I ask.

He strokes his beard meditatively. "The skirt's okay but the legs are a little pale."

I bend over in mock hilarity. "Oh, you slay me, Wendell."

Crusher gasps, truly shocked. "How did you know about that?"

"I saw your driver's license two years ago and I've been saving this gem until I really needed it. Now tell me you loved the film or I'm making a surprise announcement."

Crusher hastily assures me that he did love it and I can tell that he means it. To rebalance the power in our relationship, he adds, "How could you lose with a script like Libby's?"

The screenwriter herself soon emerges, surrounded by admirers, including, to Crusher's dismay, her handsome and talented boyfriend, Tim Kennedy.

"What did she have to bring him for?" Crusher asks.

"Well, it would have looked odd if she hadn't—at least to Tim. But she's not the only woman in the room, Crusher. Time to spread your charm around."

Genevieve pretends not to see me when she steps out of the theater with Gizmo, Keisha and some of the other *Illegal Alien* crew members. Damon recently broke the news to her about us and she's still sulking. I imagine she'll come around faster now that she's seen *The Counterfeit Wedding*.

"I looked luminous in the final scene, didn't I?" she tells her posse. "I'd forgotten how much the camera loves me."

"Too bad Roxanne couldn't light you all the time," Gizmo says, slyly.

Genevieve pouts. "You can't enhance beauty that isn't already there."

My father and Gayle descend on me, wearing sleek black outfits.

"Is the tropical trend out already?" I ask Gayle.

As usual, she takes me seriously. "It's a film party, Roxanne. Everyone knows you have to wear black."

"No wonder they're talking about my pink skirt."

"They're actually talking about your white legs," Gayle says, pursing thin lips.

"If I didn't already know how much you like each other, I'd be worried," Dad says, wrapping an arm around each of us.

I don't *dis*like Gayle anymore, but I still need periodic reminders of that. "What did you two think of the film?"

"It's terrific," Dad says. "Your mother would have been very proud."

"I know."

"As for my little sweetie, she has never looked better."

Gayle squeezes his arm and titters. "Now stop, Gordo."

I'd be indulging in another smart remark here if it weren't

for the fact that Gayle organized a post-screening party at the bistro across the street and Dad paid for it.

"Why don't you two go ahead to the party and do the host and hostess thing," I say. "I want to make sure everyone is out of here."

Just before I leave the lab, Lorna steps out of the theater. Her huge eyeglasses are askew and her gold jumpsuit partially unzipped. She pauses to zip it and pat down her Alexis Carrington wig. Then she whips a compact out of her purse and reapplies crimson lipstick. The theater door swings open again to spit out Enzo, who looks equally disheveled. There's a ring of crimson lipstick around his mouth. Grinning like a mischievous teenager, he gives Lorna's backside a squeeze.

I track Lorna down at the bar, where she's puffing on a stogie and sipping a martini.

"You can't smoke in restaurants anymore, Miss Lamont."

"I'm well aware of the bylaws, Roxanne," she says. "The only good thing about aging is that no one has the balls to tell an old lady to butt out."

"What does Enzo say?" I ask.

"He keeps his mouth shut. The man knows better than to ruin a good thing."

"He does seem keen," I say.

"Of course he is. But there's never been a dearth of men in my life." She jabs the cigar in Damon's direction. "You, on the other hand, had better get while the getting is good."

"I'm *getting,*" I protest. "You'd know that if you'd brought your onyx along."

"You've cleared your chakras and I take full credit for that. But if you continue to dress like a man and pursue a man's career, you won't have endless opportunities. Damon is a catch, so I am going to give you a valuable piece of advice."

"Yes?"

"Don't fuck it up."

"Truly words to live by."

"And get your behind to an image consultant, Roxanne. You cannot be so misguided as to think bare legs work in Toronto at Christmastime." Before I can explain, she gives me a brisk karate chop between the shoulder blades. "For heaven's sake, straighten up. Your bosom will be sharing real estate with your navel soon enough. Make use of it while you can."

"Another pearl to be treasured."

"Don't sulk, young lady. You'll thank me when you're accepting your Academy Award."

"My what?"

"You heard me." She signals the bartender for another martini. "You're a good cinematographer and I should know, I've worked with the greats. But do us all a favor and leave the directing to those with the temperament for it. If you stay behind the camera, I think you'll go far."

I am so overwhelmed that I set my glass on the bar and lean forward to give her a hug. "Thank you, Lorna, I—"

She raises a bejeweled hand. "Don't get carried away. Sentimentality is the crutch of the weak and this is a tough business, Roxanne. If I were you, I'd start working the room." Shuffling toward Enzo on golden mules, she calls over her shoulder, "And it's still Miss Lamont to you."

★ ★ ★

"How's the screenwriter?" I ask, sitting down beside Libby, who has dispatched Tim to the sweets table.

"Loved the movie, loving the party," she says, gazing around the room. "I'm just trying to soak it all in." She gestures to Crusher, who is at the bar sketching Genevieve on a napkin. "He's quite an artist, isn't he?"

I nod. "Some of his work is stunning. There's this sketch he did of a pair of hands—"

"Yes, his mother's," Libby interrupts. "She died shortly after he did it."

"He never told me that." How could Libby know more about my friend than I do?

"We spent an awful lot of time together in a small camper van, remember."

My jealousy evaporates when I notice that Gizmo has cornered a tall man at the sushi bar and is regaling him with a "gripping" tale of life on set.

"Oh, my God, that's Martin Speir," I say. "What's he doing here?"

Libby shrugs. "Let's go talk to him."

"Are you crazy? Alana probably has a hit out on me."

"Come on, Ms. Paranoid, we could make a good contact."

"Look at you, all about the networking now."

"Well, don't you want to make another movie?"

"I haven't recovered from the last one yet. But that doesn't mean you can't write another screenplay. I do have other contacts I'm not embarrassed to approach."

"Would one of them be Oliver O'Brien's agent?"

I point to Hank, who is coming toward us swinging some mistletoe. "He could probably hook you up."

Libby blanches. "Maybe I'll aim a little lower to start."

★ ★ ★

Hank offers to buy me a drink from the complimentary bar. "I enjoyed your film," he says. "It showcased your talents very well."

"I'm so glad you liked it," I say.

"Really, I think you have the touch, Roxanne," he says, putting his hand on my butt. He is still holding the mistletoe.

"Thanks," I say, moving his hand and stepping away before he gets any strange ideas.

He slings an arm around my shoulder and pulls me back. "I want you to shoot my Morocco picture."

The offer doesn't come as a complete surprise. With Alana out of the picture, I knew that Hank would be considering other prospects. I've given it a lot of thought and made my decision. "I'm grateful for the offer, but I'm afraid I have to decline."

Hank is so stunned that he withdraws his arm from my shoulder voluntarily. "You can't be serious," he says. "Surely you're not holding a grudge over my giving second unit to that incompetent little wretch. What was her name?"

"Alana Speir. Your friend Martin's daughter, remember? And no, I'm not holding a grudge."

I am, of course, but that's not why I'm turning him down. In an industry where no one can be completely trusted, Hank's character is bottom of the barrel. With my cinematography career just beginning, I'd rather not tie my balloon to his float. Better to find something on my own.

"You must do it, darling," he says. "You'll have a jolly good time with your boyfriend directing."

How did he learn about my relationship with Miguel? "He's not my boyfriend."

"Oh, come now. Damon confessed ten minutes ago when he accepted the job. I assumed you'd come as a package deal."

I recover my composure quickly. "What happened to Miguel?"

"He pulled out and recommended Damon."

"He did?" That doesn't sound like the Miguel I know. Something is fishy here.

"He's usually wild for foreign shoots, but he's been pussy-whipped by his girlfriend, I'm afraid. She's insisting that he be in L.A. when the baby comes."

I struggle to keep my expression neutral. "I didn't know Miguel was 'expecting.'"

"Knocked up some actress," Hank says, adding, "the fool."

I'm doing the mental math. If Miguel's girlfriend is far enough along to deliver during the Morocco shoot, he was definitely seeing both of us at the same time. And yet he had the nerve to talk to me a few weeks ago about making a commitment. The man is incorrigible.

Fortunately, he's no longer *my* man. While I may feel a little foolish at the moment, I'm not hurt. I was never in love with Miguel and that's become increasingly apparent since I started seeing Damon. I am so glad I got out when I did.

Hank gives me a little shake. "You must take the job, Roxanne. Don't shoot yourself in the foot simply because another blonde was my first choice. You won't have many chances like this so soon after upgrading."

For a moment I hesitate. With Damon directing, the offer is far more appealing, especially when I've just been re-minded of the perils of long-distance romance. But I hon-estly believe it would be better for us to let our relationship stabilize before putting it into the pressure cooker of a reporting relationship. After all, there was a rocky stretch on *Illegal Alien* where neither of us focused fully on the job.

Finally I say, "I don't think so, Hank, but please keep me in mind down the road."

And then, since there's nothing to lose, I ask him what happened with *The Lobby*.

"I showed it to my partners," he says, "but it doesn't suit our needs at this time."

"The form letter rejection," I say. "Looks like Fudgling strung me along."

"Don't piss me off, darling. Remember, *Fledgling* has a lot of clout."

And one day I may need it. So I say, "Sorry about the sour grapes."

"You should be. Because I gave your screenplay to someone who might be better suited to the project." He beckons Martin Speir. "Let's ask him what he thinks."

"No," I say. "Not now, Hank. This isn't the right—"

A familiar voice behind me says, *"Carpe diem."* I turn to find Lorna Lamont blatantly eavesdropping. She taps her throat chakra warningly.

I say, "I'd love to talk to Martin about *The Lobby*."

"Come on, Rox," Damon says when we finally have a moment alone together. "We've been a team for years. We can do this."

"I told you, I'm not mixing business with pleasure. Besides, I've accepted another offer." I explain that Martin Speir wants to produce and direct *The Lobby*.

He hugs me so long that Gayle clears her throat disapprovingly somewhere behind us. "Debuting as Martin Speir's cinematographer…" he says. "I do believe I've caught myself a rising star. But aren't you worried Alana will executive produce?"

"Martin told me that her career is taking a 'different direction.' She's going to work on her mother's magazine in L.A. as an entertainment photographer."

Damon laughs. "Sounds like Martin is worried about his own reputation. So when does this project of yours get rolling?"

"We don't go to camera until next summer, which is perfect, because I've decided to winter in Morocco this year."

"Excellent idea," he says, "I've got a lead on a place you can share, cheap."

As Damon and I walk back to the bar, it occurs to me that the kinks in my personal story line have worked themselves out rather nicely in recent weeks: Alana's incompetence was exposed; Damon chose the right girl; and Hank saw the error of his ways and offered me his film. I'd pretty much given up on *The Lobby,* so Martin's offer comes as a major bonus.

I suppose it wouldn't be right to complain that Genevieve is still skinny and Alana is still standing.

A girl can't have everything.

Damon and I are parked on the couch in front of my jumbotron watching Zara Duncan and Burk Ryan tub-thumping *Illegal Alien* on a late-night talk show.

"What's happened to Zara's face?" I ask.

"Looks like she's given up the tape for a more permanent solution," he says.

Clearly, rumors of Zara's recent appendectomy were just

that. Her tight, shiny face is still raw from surgery. Even Chiquita, perched on her lap, looks drawn.

Burk's appearance is an even bigger shock. His tight T-shirt and trendy jeans show off every ripple of a newly trim body. The spray-on hair is gone and what's left of his own is cropped close to the scalp.

The host runs a clip of *Illegal Alien* before interviewing our stars. "People all over the country are talking about that sex scene," he says. "Give us the scoop."

Though unable to smile per se, Zara manages a chuckle. "It was my first time with an alien and it was quite…memorable."

Burk says, "I had a hell of a time getting this girl into bed."

Zara laughs again. "Well, that was before your transformation, honey."

I look at Damon incredulously. "Those two hate each other. Box-office whores."

"Zara had to be sedated for that sex scene," Damon says. "Hank called in Dr. Feelgood."

Burk rests a hand on Zara's thigh and Chiquita rouses himself long enough to snap at it. Restraining the dog, Zara leans over and kisses Burk's cheek.

"I cannot believe this business," I say. "Totally fake."

"It makes me sick," Damon says.

"Me, too," I agree. "Pass the remote—*Entertainment Now* is on…"

"*Illegal Alien* was number one at the box office again for the third week in a row. Ticket sales soared even higher on the weekend after Burk Ryan held a press conference to confirm his romance with up-and-coming actor Todd Russell. Ryan is confident that his fans will support him in this new phase of his life and credits his coming out to an L.A.-based monk.

"Due to the overwhelming success of *Illegal Alien,* World Studios has given the green light to a sequel, once again penned by screenwriting mastermind F. C. Kugelman.

"*Illegal Alien II: The Resurrection* goes into production next month, after Shawna Glass is released from rehab. The original cast will star, along with newcomer Alana Speir, a former entertainment photographer discovered by a top Hollywood agent during a photo shoot last year. Her boyfriend, Spanish playboy Miguel Rivera, is on board to direct."

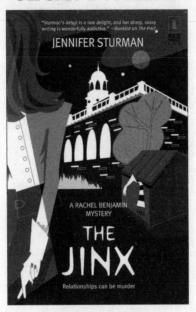

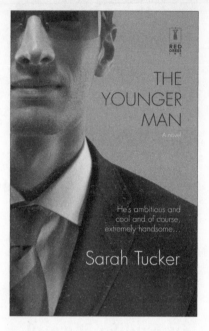

Speechless

From authors
Yvonne Collins & Sandy Rideout

Libby McIssac, known for having a way with
words, has landed a job as a political speechwriter.
But Libby has to be careful not to find herself at a
loss for words when a media leak of a big-time
scandal sends everyone into a tailspin, and
Libby fears she may get caught in the cross fire.
Cue the fake alliances, the secrets, the sex,
the hidden friendships: It's politics after all.

RED DRESS INK
TM

Are you getting it at least twice a month?

Here's how: Try RED DRESS INK books
on for size & receive two FREE gifts!

Bombshell
by Lynda Curnyn

As Seen on TV
by Sarah Mlynowski

YES! Send my two FREE books.
There's no risk and no purchase required—ever!

Please send me my two FREE books and bill me just 99¢ for shipping and handling. I may keep the books and return the shipping statement marked "cancel." If I do not cancel, about a month later I will receive 2 additional books at the low price of just $11.00 each in the U.S. or $13.56 each in Canada, a savings of over 15% off the cover price (plus 50¢ shipping and handling per book*). I understand that accepting the two free books places me under no obligation ever to buy any books. I can always return a shipment and cancel at any time. Even if I never buy another book from Red Dress Ink, the free books are mine to keep forever.

160 HDN D34M   360 HDN D34N

Name (PLEASE PRINT)

Address   Apt. #

City   State/Prov.   Zip/Postal Code

*Want to try another series? Call 1-800-873-8635
or order online at www.TryRDI.com/free.*

In the U.S. mail to: 3010 Walden Ave., P.O. Box 1867, Buffalo, NY 14240-1867
In Canada mail to: P.O. Box 609, Fort Erie, ON L2A 5X3

*Terms and prices subject to change without notice. Sales tax applicable in N.Y.
**Canadian residents will be charged applicable provincial taxes and GST.
All orders subject to approval. Offer limited to one per household.
® and ™ are trademarks owned and used by the trademark owner and/or its licensee.

© 2004 Harlequin Enterprises Ltd.

RED DRESS INK

RDI04-TR